SPRING'S CONTEST

Don't miss the other books

in the Rise of Fall Series

DECHARLATHAN
PUBLISHING

Spring's Contest

Contest

Rise of Fall – Book 3

WRITTEN BY

Jeremy Graves

Spring's Contest

ISBN: 978-1-954298-06-4

Cover design by Chiara N. Monaco

Special thanks to:

Teresa Wheeler – Lead Editor

Charlotte Graves – Alpha Reading & Development

Nicole Young – Developmental Editing

Catherine Graves – Line Editing

Lacey C – Beta reading & Development

Jess Loftus – Beta Reading

First Printing Edition, 2021

Join us on the web site to browse upcoming volumes and enjoy full color maps at:

www.decharlathan.com

For Cathy,
The accumulated aspect of air
beneath my surfboard-like construct.

CHAPTER 1

The young elf pushed himself past endurance. Spring's cherry blossoms were the height of nature's beauty in the light of day. Now the forest seemed to trip and slow him with every step. Words flowed through his mind over and over as tired legs ran through familiar trees.

The cutters don't belong here!

The taunts and jeers of the cutters echoed from both sides of the path he ran. Behind him, he could hear the thumping footsteps of booted feet.

He had been careless; he knew that now. The cutters were here to harvest the living wood of the dryads of these woods. Twelve springs was much too young to run the poachers from the forest, at least not directly. Instead, he had harried them for weeks. Using his control of the flora of this place, he had ruined supplies and broken tools. His efforts generally slowed any progress to a crawl.

Once he had tried to petition the queen, traveling all the way to the Spring Capital of Amaya. He was refused an audience. Then he noticed how many in court were using the very things he was trying to protect.

A woman with a cane that sought sure ground to steady her stride. A young man with a dagger, its handle able to mold to his hand for a perfect grip. A wealthy child with a carved wooden dragon that could move about on its own. They knew the living forest was being harvested! They didn't care, not as long as they had these cursed trinkets.

He tried to do, as a boy of twelve springs, what the kingdom would not. He tried to fight back. But he forgot to adequately scout the camp, intent to begin his night's work of breaking ax handles and tearing open packs of supplies. He was spotted and they were ready. Now he was surrounded.

Running through a clearing, he could see they were almost on him. The boy broke for the thick brush on his left. He was smaller, and if he could get through, there was a copse of tall trees where he could hide until morning. His pursuers seemed to sense his plan because the second he made his move, they rushed to stop him.

He dove into the thick brush and just avoided the swing of the bronze ax blade. He rolled and hopped nimbly to his feet again. They had gained more ground, but he was fast among his beloved forest.

As soon as he reached the tree line, he leaped as a small sapling moved to vault him high into the branches of a tall cherry blossom. The slender limbs seemed to embrace him as he landed and moved to the other side of the trunk. Then he froze.

Only seconds passed before the cutters walked underneath his hiding spot. He slowed his breathing and made himself one with the forest. He would have been fine; he could have escaped that night. It was not what fate had in store for him.

The frustrated cutter slammed the ax into the trunk of the tree. The very one he was holding on to. The boy felt the tremor of anguish through the thick bark, then the slow spread of damage to the mighty trunk and the pain of the dryad inside. He felt that pain and gasped.

He regretted it instantly when the cutter looked up. A cruel smile widened as the man spotted his dark silhouette among the lighter shades of the blossoms. A cry of triumph escaped the curled lips.

Elves and men, eight in total, joined the cutter at the base of the tree. The words held contempt as they rose from the forest floor.

"Come on down, lad. We need to teach you a bit of a lesson."

The boy stayed still, hoping they would decide he was not a young elf in a tree but a shadow among the flowers. A dull thud rang out, then another. His heart sundered with the pulp of the wood. He could feel the mind inside the tree crying out, the pain and helplessness.

Many of the trees were filled with a spirit of renewal, the tree spirits known as dryads. This one was old and powerful, but it moved slowly, and the spirit was spread out through the massive tree. It could not focus its power fast enough to stop the cutters.

The living wood could be shaped by certain earth spirit users with a type of maker magic called Wood Weaving. The trinkets drew a high price. Every last copper talon was blood money.

One more chop and he could not hold still any longer. He pushed the branches away and leaped to the ground, vines lashing out and slowing his fall. He hit the hard soil with a roll and pulled the same vines around one of the cutters.

He clenched a fist. A sapling leaned over and grabbed another enemy. The flexing trunk swung back and released him to fly through the air. He turned to attack a third.

An ax handle slammed into his head. The world seemed to be shifting and wavy. Through the stupor, he could see a cutter holding his arm. Another lifted an ax.

The flash of pain almost made him black out, the first swing stopping on the bone of his upper arm. The second broke that bone with a snap. The third severed the limb from his body with a wet slap.

He could still feel the sensation of touch on his fingertips and the cold night air on his naked forearm. Yet these sensations were phantoms in a young mind fogged with pain and stress.

They left him on the forest floor. The boy would bleed out or be eaten by a roaming predator. The wretch who made killing the spirits of the forest slightly more difficult had been dealt with.

He did black out then. Crimson lifeblood leaked out onto the forest floor.

He did not know how long it was before she saved him. It could have been seconds or hours. Surely, it was not too long. The wound would have bled him out within minutes.

She stood over him, her skin slightly textured like the bark of the tree he had clung to. Her leafy hair was streaked in the white and pink of the cherry blossoms that had covered him. She was still connected to the tree through a tendril of spirit energy. That connection was invisible to most.

Not to him. His power allowed him to see the flow of life in the plants of Fairie. Her tree would not live. The ax had been swung too many times, and he had failed.

She spoke in his mind, touching his forehead with a long willowy finger.

"You failed to save me; they were too many. I was unable to help you; I was too slow."

The strange head tilted slightly as if considering another option.

"Perhaps we could still save each other. The others have offered to sustain us if we agree to fight for them."

The heart of the tree was revealed in the dim light of the forest. The wood slowly flowed out of the safety of the trunk. The pulsing life of the plant was already beginning to fade. The tree it called home had lost its grip on the spirit energy of the earth below.

The woman reached over, took the heart, and pulled it toward his mangled stump of an arm. The raw flesh throbbed as his blood oozed onto the ground. His head swam from the loss.

Then the wood touched his raw, broken stump. A pain like liquid fire poured through his shoulder. He could feel roots working into his flesh, fusing into the shattered bone. She hummed a slow tune as she worked. It was the tranquil melody of a quiet breeze through the leaves of her tree.

It was her tree no more; her home was in him now. The boy did not know how he stayed awake through the pain of the attachment. He felt every nerve and sinew tie together.

Then it was finished. The woman was still there. Now her tendril of spirit was unmoored from the tree. Its wooden corpse stood tall, a towering effigy of his failure.

She was linked to him, to his left arm. Now he really could feel with the fingertips. The chill air really did tell him his arm was bare. It was different, though, foreign and strange in its control and power.

He slowly sat up and put the new hand in front of his face. Wooden fingers moved as he began testing the dexterity of the limb. There was the smooth grain of the wood where his own brown skin had been.

He looked to the woman; she did not appear much older than him. In his core, he could feel that she had lived over a century in that tree. The tree he had failed to save. He spoke the only words he felt worthy of.

"I... I'm sorry I failed you."

Her eyes turned to meet his. Those grief-filled orbs were neither elven nor human. She was a spirit of the forest. The alien face showed her grief, but her wooden cheeks did not glisten with tears.

She didn't need to touch him to speak now. She would never be away from contact with him. Her words came faster; her pace increased as their bond grew.

"We speak among our kind, you know. Our words would seem terribly slow to you, but we talk to one another. Word of the boy who tries has made it through the whole of the forest. You have not saved all, but you have saved some. We are grateful."

He fought back the tears now. His would flow freely; he was not made of wood. Not completely.

"I couldn't save you. Even now, the cutters are at their work again. Others pay for my failure."

"You do not understand the gift we have offered. It was my spirit that fused the heartwood to your flesh, but all gave the power. We will do together what you could not do alone."

He thought about this for a moment, then nodded. All his life, the plants had served him; he had spent that life trying to be worthy. In his mind, this was not so different. He looked once more into those strange eyes.

"My name is Naoki. If we are going to work together, you should know me."

He felt her smile, even though her wooden face did not move. It was as firm as the tree she once inhabited. He only felt her emotion of happiness.

"My name would take too long to say in your tongue. Please call me Sakura. It is time we got ready; we have had our last failure this night."

Suddenly his arm moved on its own, the control hers in this moment. Strong fingers struck deep into the earth. He felt the power flow into him from every living plant within a day's walk of his spot on the forest floor.

No single life gave enough to matter. The sum of all combined filled him with a bounty of power woven into his very core. His eyes glowed a pale green, and Sakura flowed back into the arm they shared.

This was the night the Green Man was born: the ghost of the forests and protector of the eastern kingdom's flora. Only cutters were nearby when he joined with the plants of Spring.

None of those men lived to tell the tale.

***

Claire was taking a much-needed break from her duties in the throne room. The tea was hot, and Norim's biscuits from that morning were perfect. Never one to completely relax, the queen had a stack of parchment in front of her.

She tapped a quill to her lips as she considered the best way to word her letter. Joobel was sitting across from her, her own quill darting rapidly across the large sheet of drafting parchment. Her adopted sister was hard at work, making arrangements and designing a dress for the upcoming wedding.

Joobel called it 'a walk through the pumpkins,' but it was essentially the same thing. The gnome had a way of sticking her pink tongue out to one side when concentrating. If Claire mentioned it, her friend would deny having done so.

The queen was grateful to have such a gifted tailor and seamstress at hand. Her own wardrobe was overflowing with lovely, well-made garments. Today she wore a dark gold dress, the thick belt tying the skirt in place around her waist.

As was usual for her, she wore fitted leggings under the skirt and boots to her knees made of soft leather. She'd gotten in the habit of wearing something that wouldn't be uncomfortable or immodest should she have to hop aboard a dragon. Also, she tended to get cold, and the layers helped keep her comfortable in the chill of the Blood Keep.

Joobel was also wearing one of the fine dresses, but hers was a light green skirt and blouse combination. She had long sleeves made of a sheer lighter green, and her skirt flowed just past her knees. The golden-brown of her skin was contrasted by bracelets of various colors on her ankles and wrists. Many were infused with magic to serve a purpose.

Claire had made a few of them herself, as her lessons with Issabol were starting to pay off. Her own wrists had bands as well, though fewer. All were powerful magical items.

Norim returned from the kitchen in a dress of her own making, more straightforward than those made by Joobel. Still, the tall woman was no less beautiful for wearing something so simple.

Claire was now over nineteen autumns, and Norim looked about the same age as her now. She would seem only slightly older when Claire was an old woman.

The water naiad had not even had a chance to sit down when there was a knock at the door. It was against the queen's orders to disturb her rest unless it was urgent. Three concerned faces turned to the sound.

Norim opened the door to let in a guard. He was holding a large envelope with a royal seal on it. The package had not come from Winter, which was quite common after the treaty, but from the kingdom of Spring.

The packet was large and thick enough that the guard had to carry it under his arm to not risk it slipping from his grip. He gave a formal bow and apologized for the interruption, then handed the package to Norim before taking his leave.

Norim finally got to sit, her graceful form resting on a comfortable couch on the opposite side of the low table. She set the envelope down for Claire and then took a long sip of the hot tea before looking to her queen.

"Well, it isn't addressed to me."

Claire gave a wry smile and then slipped out her slim dagger. She carefully cut around the wax seal, imprinted with the emblem of Spring. The queen slid out a stack of parchment. The top paper was a letter; the rest were forms. Claire squinted at the complicated script, small and flawlessly written.

To the Ruler of Autumn,

It has been too long since the kingdoms have come together to partake in the Contest of Champions. Spring is hosting a tournament to give a chance for those who have been newly appointed to rule a kingdom of Fairie to prove their strength of arms and wit against those more seasoned.

Enclosed, you will find the registration forms for the competitions. There will even be a junior division for that talented prince I have heard so much about. All royals can bring two guards, two advisors, and two dragons to the proceedings. I realize for some of us that is all you have, so we restricted it down. If you can muster the talent to compete, please have your forms in by the next new moon.

Alder King Zankoku

Claire had no sooner finished reading than Joobel glanced up from her work. "What an ass."

Norim scrunched her nose and chided, "Language, dear." She turned to Claire and continued. "What do you intend to do, child?"

Claire tapped her lip once more. Only Norim could get away with calling her that. Queen or not, when someone has changed your nappy, you have trouble getting past it.

The letter was an obvious taunt, but there was some truth to the fact that Autumn was playing catch up. The treaty with Winter was all that held Summer back from a full-blown attack on the southern border. There was talk of Spring taking the existence of Bloom as a national insult.

Having any dragons at all was a victory. Only a few years ago, they were thought to have died out in Autumn. Yet what her kingdom lacked in numbers, they made up for in raw power. Harvest alone was a match for any two other dragons save Depth or Puddle.

Joobel huffed as she set her work down and stood. She flitted her stiff wings twice before stretching and padding over to take the letter. Her face went to a frown as she looked it over, not seeming to like the whole idea. Her words confirmed the hunch.

"It's an obvious trap. The King of Spring is a pompous fool. We show up and either fail to show any power, in which case he can try and gain influence over our own people or Winter's. Or we show a good deal of power and give away our most potent secrets right before we get attacked. I say just stay home and send him word that we aren't interested in silly games."

The gnome set the letter down and walked over to the teapot. She topped off all three cups before sitting down. Claire waited for her to settle, her mind flipping through the possibilities.

"Well... I have a pretty clear picture from one advisor. What wisdom is offered by the other?"

Norim set down her cup and seemed to look wistful, then she brought up an issue Claire had not thought of.

"The last time the games were held, do you know who won the grand prize?"

Claire did. The man was an insanely powerful fire spirit who could melt a fortress into bubbling magma. That same man used to read her stories and have tea parties with her. Jack didn't even remember their father's face. Norim took another sip, then gave her council.

"Jack loves you and supports your rule. His faith in you goes a long way toward keeping the people behind you. Your changes have been hard on some, and he is the only man I know of who could actually serve as a true king. His power lets him access the great spirit."

Claire knew that; so did a handful of other people. To most, Jack was a versatile and potent user of a basic fire spirit. But he was much more than that.

His power of Transition allowed him to draw on any aspect of energy. He could gift it to another or weave the power through either his heart-fire or heart-dew. His control over ice was nearly as strong as his fire now.

If Jack ever did decide to take away his support, or worse, if he challenged her for the throne....

Claire shook her head and cast such thoughts aside. Her brother would never work against her, and she loved him. Norim could see the dark musings on the queen's face.

"Jack would never try to be king or openly defy your wishes. He loves you. One word from Joobel and the prince would fall in line. He only has a few things he really cares about. One of them is proving himself to a father he does not remember. Because of this, if the Contest happens and you say he cannot compete, he might go against your wishes and fight anyway."

Joobel's eyes widened; her voice quivered. "If he went without support, without Harvest and Gray, without people to watch his back...."

Norim interrupted the gnome, "I have no doubt Spring would see him captured or killed if Summer did not beat them to it."

"If they killed Jack, Maeve would tear down all of Spring," Claire countered.

Joobel shook her head before correcting her queen.

"They don't know what Maeve can do. They might pay the price, but my Jack would already be dead."

Claire nodded; the prince wasn't her only concern. There was a third option. She could play this game and have Autumn come out ahead. She just needed to put all the pieces in place. The queen looked up at her advisors.

"We could show up and appear weak. We could show up and go all out."

She tapped her lip furiously, the picture forming in her mind.

"What if we show some of our power but hold enough back to have a fallback in case Summer gets overconfident. We have a whole batch of new students who have been hard at work. Jack can go as a fire spirit and still likely beat most anyone. We have the portals and can get out of there if need be. And Raine would be there with no small amount of support should we need her."

Norim nodded with a wry smile. Claire decided this was what the naiad had intended from the start. Joobel still seemed skeptical, her perfect face pulled into a childish pout. The gnome looked at the other women.

"Do you think he would stay if I asked him to?"

Claire nodded. "I think he would change who he was if you asked him to. The question is, would you want him to be someone else?"

The gnome's bright blue eyes narrowed. "It isn't fair to put it like that."

Claire shrugged. "You know, most of my time is spent trying to make things fair. It seems I have a long way to go."

Joobel seemed to be fighting her tendency to walk on the ceiling. Finally, she huffed before letting out a long sigh.

"I give up.... I knew what I was getting into. If we are going to go, let's make sure to make it count."

A mischievous grin formed on the young queen's scarred face.

"Oh, I intend to."

***

The flash of blades whipped through the air as the Winter Queen sparred with her new guard. Many soldiers and guards were retired after the night of the Bitter Challenge. Trust was a precious thing in Winter, and Raine had made both allies and enemies on her way to the throne.

The swords she held were practice blades, their dull edges coated in a red paint that would mark flesh without seriously harming an opponent. The young man darted and blocked, matching her blow for blow.

Cruor was in the running for the title of Winter's Champion. His swordplay was excellent, and he moved like a viper. Some were his match in a duel of blades, but few could fight him if he was using his spirit.

The young man was from the great Mira family to the north. His father had taken a seat on the council when an older man died from the Black March's influence. The family had been keeping this young man a secret. It seemed they were afraid he would be called away to the Citadel if the queen knew what he was.

When Raine found out what Cruor was, she immediately called him to the Citadel. He was just over nineteen winters, still lean with youth, yet he fought with remarkable skill and stamina. Few could ever hope to match a Leech.

There was no mistaking one with his power. Bright red eyes tend to stand out most anywhere. The only hope a person could have in combat against someone who could take power from blood was to keep him at a distance. That was not easy.

Raine herself had been honing her skills with a blade. She still preferred a short sword in her right and a long dagger in her left. Her usual weapons were a reforged version of the long sword Frostbite, altered by Issabol and Claire into the two blades the queen typically wore on her belt.

She only needed a scratch to win. The blades' magic would freeze the blood pumping through an opponent. The queen would lose this fight even with those enchanted weapons.

Her new bodyguard never showed emotion while fighting. The duel went on for several minutes before a long red line ran across the queen's arm and neck. He had pulled the killing blow so as not to bruise his queen, but he never let her win.

Most would throw a match against her and then flatter her skill. Raine never bothered with people like that. False words were a luxury she could not afford.

She touched the paint on her arm and cursed. "By the spirits... I thought I might get you that time."

The young man who fought with no emotion smiled widely and handed the woman a cloth to wipe off the paint.

"Much longer and you might have. I tend to rely too much on my powers. I was growing tired."

Raine knew he meant his words, at least the part about her getting better. Someday she wanted a rematch with her cousin; Jack needed some humility.

A man stood hesitantly at the edge of the practice field. Though she and Cruor were wearing training robes consisting of loose-fitting pants and a sleeveless shirt, the messenger could identify the queen by her long white hair pulled back and tied with a black ribbon. He held out a large envelope.

Raine ended training early. She had the package brought to her council chambers. Soon she was changed and sitting in a room with her advisor Hurley and General Kenn.

Cruor leaned against the wall wearing a black long-sleeved shirt and leather pants. His dark hair was worn short on the sides and back but long in front. It tended to cover his red eyes and helped give him some element of surprise in a fight. He was unarmed now; in a real battle, he would create his own weapons.

Hurley shook his head, brow furrowed. "This is an obvious trap for our ally to the southwest. Autumn has to either expose themselves to an attack or bow out and be called a coward. Summer is expecting us to send some fighters to represent the kingdom but avoid any exposure to danger for our queen."

Raine pushed her white hair behind an ear and reread the letter. Her eyes narrowed just as much as they had the previous three times. She slammed a pale fist to the table.

"Who does this pompous jerk think he is? I am tempted to just have him and his palace frozen solid. Then we can hurl rocks till it shatters."

Hurley nodded, acting for all the world as if she were serious.

"A fine plan, my queen. Shall we ready the drakes or wait for the cover of night?"

Cruor laughed noisily, gaining a stern look from the general. The Leech answered directly to his queen, not caring what the general, or anyone else, thought of him. The white of his broad toothy smile contrasted with the black of his hair. Raine thought he might stick his tongue out. She sighed at the odd people in her life.

"*Grr....* You two stop. I'm trying to overreact here."

Hurley nodded. "A fine job you are doing, my queen. No one overreacts quite like you."

Cruor rarely spoke with anything other than childish banter, but now he sighed and took a serious tone.

"You know we have to go, right?"

Raine seemed more shocked at this than at the man's impudent comments.

"Why is that? I have nothing to prove to Spring."

The young man pushed his hair aside to make eye contact with her. He said one word. She instantly understood.

"Jack."

Raine put her head in her hands and leaned down to the table. She screamed into them and looked up at her personal guard. Her fists were clenched tight enough that the pale skin of her knuckles was even whiter.

"The fool will never back down! He'll go no matter what Claire says."

Hurley nodded, genuinely having forgotten how the Prince of Autumn would react to this.

"His father won the last tournament in Winter many years ago. He won't likely turn down a chance to compete. Spring might either kidnap him or kill him."

Cruor smiled, the sharp teeth showing more than needed.

"They would try. I still haven't beat him, and I cheat."

Everyone else replied at the same time. "We know."

Cruor shrugged and went back to leaning against the wall, hair falling once more to cover his crimson eyes. Raine looked thoughtful for a moment, then her own eyes widened. Hurley spoke her thought out loud.

"Yes, if Spring did something... there is a good chance that unusual hound thing of Jack's might very well destroy the capital city of Amaya."

Raine once again put her hands over her face and leaned down to the table. This time she only took a long deep breath. After a moment, she stood and made her decision.

"General, get Hurley a list of fighters who would excel at the various events. Choose a trusted member of the military to serve as an advisor. Hurley will serve as the other, and Cruor will be one of my guards. I'll still try to speak with Claire, but I doubt I will prevail."

Cruor grinned. "Who will be the other guard?"

"I don't know yet. I think perhaps one of the yeti. I trust them more than most."

Hurley began sifting through the papers, not looking up as he planned his evening.

"I assume there will be a meeting tonight through the special door in the royal chambers?"

Raine looked out the window, voice absent as her mind raced at the possibilities.

"I have little doubt."

***

Issabol was ready to pull her long blonde hair right out of her head. The ancient girl had long avoided getting too deeply involved with the matters of the outside world. Sure, she would help a queen from time to time, but now she had invested too deeply. Not only had she grown attached to her many greats niece and nephew, but her home was now crowded with children.

She stood in the middle of her workshop as a young Battle Shaper drew sigils of power on parchment. The little girl was quite odd and often got lost in her own mind. They had to make sure she ate and slept, or Laris would spend hours looking at the patterns in the wood of the floor and lose all sense of time.

In the corner where Joobel often worked her sewing sat another girl named Toma. She also had a form of maker magic, a spirit known as Mimic. The child could copy complex constructs as long as identical raw materials were available. The girl with brown skin, long brown hair, and eyes like almonds was currently pulling carved figurines out of a large chunk of oak wood. Each was exactly like the original, down to the grain of the lumber.

Then there was Varam. The presence of the boy made her brain hurt. She had spent over three thousand years thinking that she was the only Portal Master to ever exist. Yet here he was, thrilled to be called something other than a screwup. Issabol knew what it was like to have a power with no real offensive aspect.

Previously thought to only be found in royal families and great houses, the new school revealed rare magics to be more common than once believed. Only the training and nurturing of such skill was so unique.

Now that people recognized these abilities and had access to mentorship, life would be better. These students would never have to live out lives of obscurity thinking they had only a weak spirit.

Now, with one crop of pupils, Issabol had become the flustered older sister to three extraordinary and dangerous children. Any one of them could change the future of Autumn, making it better or so much worse.

There were several reasons for the three little change spirits to stay with her. Top among them was the need for security. Only a handful of people knew where Issabol's home was, and any of these children would be a target for Autumn's enemies.

Also, each needed training that few could offer. Only Issabol currently had long experience in the maker magics of change, though Claire was learning quickly.

Finally, each of these young ones were both fragile and dangerous. Some of their creations could change the course of history, yet none of the three had stable homes before. Even with her own age and experience, Issabol was at a loss to help them adjust. Now they had been here for several weeks, and she found she loved them all.

Varam was currently stirring a small amount of the purplish liquid that was used for many magical constructs. The boy had made it from scratch. While it was weaker than what she could create, it was an exceptional attempt for one so young. Already he was weaving the strands of spirit through the liquid, giving it a specific purpose before allowing it to harden into a more permanent shape.

He was just over twelve autumns and seemed to be a great help in her shop. His hair was a dark brown, and he was already taller than her. She would have to be careful of how much he did while so young. He was already beginning to show signs of slower aging, though he spent more time in the workshops and was growing older rapidly. She didn't wish her eternal youth on anyone.

On top of the time she now spent training and babysitting, Claire had commissioned several other projects. Gray had given her two more. Typically, Issabol could work for half a day and then rest her child's body. Now she was stretched thin. Areena had left some time ago on one of her expeditions. If it were not for the fourth new resident of her home, she would have gone mad.

Bilney walked into the room with a tray of refreshments and smiled widely at her. She was short and graceful. Her slender build was honed by hard training; she was quite pretty in an athletic sort of way. Once, the woman had been the only female palace guard.

Like Claire, she possessed a potent form of change spirit called Entropy. While Claire inherited her Entropy from her mother, Bilney was born with hers.

Neither the fact that she was a woman nor her ability with magic were the reason she had been given the most important post of any guard. Bilney was good with people and had the queen's trust.

When Claire was only the Autumn maiden, Bilney had gone out of her way to give the girl a sense of self-worth and confidence. As queen, Claire now ruled quite decisively but never forgot the guard's kind words when she was feeling low.

Issabol watched the guard enter the room, making her rounds with the children. Bilney leaned down and picked up one of Toma's figurines.

"Wow! This is perfect, Toma! Do you think I could take it to put on my dresser? It is so lovely!"

The young girl beamed with pride, her eyes squinting as she looked up at the older woman.

"Sure, Biwney! You can take as many as you want."

Bilney set a snack and some weak tea before the Mimic, then moved over to Varam. The boy was stirring a thick liquid with a copper rod while infusing it with a form of energy storage he learned from Issabol.

Bilney spoke softly, having him explain each step of the process as she laid out his food. He was methodical in his efforts and confident for one so young.

Next, she set out a plate and cup for Issabol, saving Laris for last. Bilney gave her a smile and nod before moving to approach the youngest girl slowly.

She set the food just close enough that it could be pushed closer once she was comfortable. She sat next to Laris, peering intently at the sigils drawn in soft charcoal. Her words were sweet and kind.

"That's pretty, Laris. What does it do?"

The young girl seemed to either have trauma or some side effect of her power. She struggled to connect with others and hardly spoke to anyone, Issabol included. Over the past couple of weeks, she slowly began to open up to Bilney. Laris answered the question, saying each word in a singsong tone.

"The maaaaark will gather pooooower. Then will allooooow one to release it all at ooooonce. *Boooooom!*"

The sound of the described explosion was betrayed by the soft voice she used in saying it. Her tiny hands cupped into a ball and then expanded.

Bilney smiled as if this was a wonderful gift she could share and not a death curse.

"Who would be able to use this gift? Who could you give it to?"

Laris sang her answer to no particular tune.

"The little ones carry the seeeaaaal... The pixies carry the pooooweeeer."

Issabol shuddered and walked back to her desk. The Battle Shaper gave her the creeps. Of all the students, Laris was the one she was most unsure how to train.

Issabol had studied Transmutation and tutored Claire in its application. A Mimic like Toma was rare, but there were books in the study at the Blood Keep with some direction on how to train and what techniques were most effective. Varam was of the same spirit as Issabol and would be able to learn anything she knew.

But Battle Shapers were dangerous. So much so that some queens would kill them rather than risk them going rogue. Others kept the secret closely guarded and never shared what little information they had.

The only references Issabol had found were of a Shaper she once met over a thousand years prior. He had been a bit odd as well, though the kingdom prized his skills and carried his creations into battle.

Laris was dangerous. Issabol would see that she wasn't turned into a tool of greed and war. She didn't fear that from Claire, but rulers change with time.

No one understood that better than the ancient child. Queens passed to the ageless girl like grains of sand through an hourglass.

CHAPTER 2

G ray stepped through the portal to a mountain peak at the gateway into the realm of Dawn. The large room had an open wall that looked out over the Mountain Wyld far below. His last visit had found his host reading a large book. Now his group was expected.

He had wanted to take on this challenge much sooner. Yet Shirdos made it quite clear that no one had succeeded in his time as a second trial champion. Shirdos was a griffin, created with powerful maker magic long ago.

In exchange for Claire's reconstruction of his wing, the chimera had given Gray as much information as he could without breaking his oaths to the realm of Dawn. With all the information available to him, Gray had worked with Claire and others on the tactics they would use today. He had waited long months for this chance.

Failure was not an option. Gray knew the key to defeating the Black March was in getting help to find the ooze's weakness. He needed to visit his home, and this was the only way.

His choices for the other trials exited the portal behind him. He had once thought to choose Maeve and Harvest, but the griffin had implied it would be seen as cheating. Maeve wouldn't be one of his warriors in the trial, but she accompanied her master anyway.

The prince was slightly taller now. He was eighteen autumns, and his lean features were more defined with a few days of light stubble. He wore a pair of short trousers. The cut was stylish and matched his sleeveless tunic that was also tailored in the latest fashion.

Gray knew well that the quiet man would wear a pillowcase without a care. The gnome who was betrothed to the prince made sure he always looked well dressed. She never could get shoes on him, though.

Jack stepped onto the open balcony that was the checkpoint on the journey into the realm of Dawn. He unconsciously scanned for threats as he breathed in the crisp, thin air of the mountain top. Gray knew Jack was tasting the magic around him, a habit he'd picked up some time ago.

The prince had gotten quite good at determining other spirit users' abilities from the aura of energy that emanated out their cores. Jack, seeming to not find anything of interest, leaned against a wall to wait.

The small brown hound moved to stand beside him, leaning against his leg and wagging her tail so hard it moved her and, in turn, her master. Jack seemed not to notice.

Then Gray's other ally arrived as well. The first time he met the woman, he had to carry her to be healed by the dragon Bloom. Myrin was stabbed through the chest by her own sister in the Bitter Challenge. Gray's anger at the woman had faded some as he got to know her.

He wasn't a psychologist, but he was pretty sure she was a sociopath. Once she was out of the Winter Court, where her worst tendencies were admired, she seemed to become more like Jack. She spoke only when needed and liked to choose the most destructive solution to any problem. He wasn't sure he would call her a friend but was glad she was an ally.

Myrin once wielded a powerful water spirit known as Frost Fire. She had pushed that power into her younger sister to solidify Raine's claim to the throne. That selfless act was what gave her a chance at redemption in Gray's eyes. It would have killed her if not for Jack's quick thinking.

The prince gave her the earth spirit he'd fed to Maeve years earlier. Though she'd only held this power for a few months, she honed her skills to a razor's edge.

The woman wore fitted leathers of deep red trimmed in golden browns. She had several silver bracelets on her left wrist and one bronze bracer with tiny green gems on her right. A coiled whip sat on her hip. The tip was barbed with small pieces of stone she could influence with her power over earth.

Once, her long white hair had framed a pale face with high cheekbones. While she kept her name, her appearance was changed to leave her former life in Winter behind. Now her hair was a deep red, the face rounder, while her skin had gained a light brown tone. She had a sprinkle of freckles on her nose.

Myrin strode past Gray like a jungle cat, fearless and looking for something to pounce on. In the center of the room stood the griffin Shirdos. His once mangled wing was folded to his side, a mirror image of the other.

The chimera stepped forward, the front talons acting like lion's paws but clacking a loud beat on the shaped stone floor. His beak clicked twice before he began to speak.

"You have made your preparations. *Click*. Have you chosen your allies? *Click*."

Gray stepped before Shirdos and nodded.

"I have prepared and am ready to face the trials. I must have an audience with the sage. In the first trial, I have asked Myrin to stand for me in the battle with Lampago the manticore."

The griffin looked the woman up and down, his gaze one of appraisal. He seemed indifferent to the shapely form of her tight clothing. He nodded and spoke to the woman before him.

"Do you accept the challenge? *Click*. And the risk that comes with it? *Click*."

Myrin gave a slight, coy grin. Then she performed a perfect curtsy, her sarcasm flowing through the gesture.

"I look forward to the fight, good griffin. I only hope it will be as entertaining as promised."

Shirdos either did not catch her impudent tone or did not care. He nodded his sizeable beak as Gray gestured toward the prince.

"In the second trial, I have asked Jack to stand for me in the battle with Shirdos the griffin."

Gray left out the many titles his friend held. Jack preferred to leave them at home, and the griffin wouldn't be impressed anyhow. Shirdos clacked over to the prince, who was still leaning against the stone wall.

The cold of the mountain top was enough to force Gray into a warm coat; Jack just let steam roll off him. The chill did not bother the man who caught fire when angry.

The griffin again looked the contestant up and down.

"Do you accept the challenge? *Click*. And the risk that comes with it? *Click*."

Jack gave a single nod. "Yup."

Gray smiled; Jack was always quite the wordsmith. Never use two words when one could be wedged in.

The griffin nodded as if Jack was an acceptable choice; Shirdos would fight him after all. Now the chimera eyed the hound, his head turning hard to one side to focus on Maeve's narrow face.

***

Maeve saw the attention she was getting and moved to stand right before the strange creature who smelled of bird, cat, and somehow rabbit. It hadn't offered a threat to Her Boy. Or Her Boy's first girl's bigger man.

Maeve didn't care what happened to the whip girl. She wasn't her boy's first girl who smelled of apples and dry leaves. Or Her Boy's Good Girl, who smelled like strawberries and rain. Good Girl was important to Her Boy and rubbed Maeve's belly.

Whip girl smelled like bitter metal, like the bad maker. Maeve was sure the maker had been eaten by the black dragon who smelled of cabbage and fear. Maker's smell was on this girl, so she must be bad.

Maeve didn't hurt Whip Girl. She seemed to be family. It was all complicated. Maeve didn't like complicated.

Now, this creature was looking at her. Maeve thought the animal might be afraid. She walked over to him and sat close. Then Maeve reached out one paw and set it on his front limb.

She gave him her '*don't worry it will all be ok cause Maeve is here*' look. The bird-cat-rabbit seemed confused. Maeve hoped Her Boy would explain it for her. Then Maeve would sit on him.

Also get treats.

***

Gray watched as the griffin stared at Maeve. The hound put a paw on Shirdos and stared back. He cocked an eyebrow as the stalemate went on and on... and on. Finally, Shirdos seemed to realize the hound was never going to stop. He shifted his head twice and then spoke to Gray with a click.

"This is no normal animal. *Click*. It must not interfere in the trial. *Click*."

Gray gave a muffled chuckle. "That hound is called Maeve, and she was almost my choice to battle Lampago. I decided against it because it wouldn't be a fair fight. The manticore would have no chance."

Shirdos could sense Maeve wasn't what she appeared but seemed to think the idea of a little brown hound defeating a powerful chimera silly.

"Surely, *Click*, the animal is not that strong. *Click*."

Gray cast a glance to Jack, who nodded, then turned and explained further.

"Maeve is the only thing Autumn's Named death drake is afraid of. He will tell you so openly. She has run through hordes of powerful enemies, killed a dragon, and helped hold off an army with Jack here. I'm not bragging; we don't even know what all she can do. The last time Jack tried finding out, she knocked over a mountain. We just assume she's enough for whatever is needed."

Gray sighed, locking his eyes on the griffin.

"The hound is here because I intend to win today. If the sphinx decides he isn't willing to concede an honorable defeat... Maeve will end him."

Shirdos hesitated before nodding the large beaked head and clacked over to the balcony.

"I think you are ready. *Click*. It is time we meet the sage. *Click*. Part of your test, *Click*, is that you must carry your allies, *Click*, if they cannot carry themselves."

With that, the griffin spread golden wings wide and leaped into the open sky. Gray hesitated for only a moment before he pulled the thin air into a large platform. He'd been working on carrying passengers, usually Joobel, as he didn't have to worry about her falling. The gnome was her own parachute.

Now he looked at his party. Jack was already beside him with Maeve against his leg. Myrin had to make a point of slowly walking over, shifting her hips in such a way to make him blush. He just knew she did it on purpose.

This could be tricky. There would be four of them, and Maeve weighed several times more than what she appeared. He pulled the edges of his platform to curve up, keeping everyone inside a bowl of dense air. Then he pulled the currents behind and below him, making them airborne.

Gray had learned to add wings, taking advantage of natural currents. He could also harness the lift of warmer air from below. He would have significantly struggled if a hand hadn't set against the back of his neck and poured energy into his core. Jack was handy that way, and Maeve had enough stored power to keep them all topped off until the trials began. For all he knew, the hound could power Autumn for days.

The griffin was truly fast but stayed close enough to allow the group to see his gold and white form in the sky ahead. Grey knew that it had been some time since an outsider had seen the more significant part of the realm of Dawn. Today he would be going home in a sense.

The tall, dark man was no longer the only known spirit of air in Autumn. There were several others. Many were still children, but some of those would most likely end up much stronger than he was. Someday he wanted to bring them to this place.

It was almost an hour of swift flight before they reached their destination. Gray was now truly skeptical about whether he could have carried so much so far without the flow of energy gifted to him.

The griffin made no mention of the fact that Gray landed with about the same amount of power he'd left with. Whether he couldn't tell or didn't care was hard to read on a face with no expression.

As the construct was released, he looked around to see they were on land. Hardy grass-covered solid earth was dominated by trees in the distance. He could see small, winged figures flitting around. A few steps away was a path of yellow stone, leading through a sparse forest. Gray was confused; they had flown at a steady climb the entire trip.

Moments ago, he had to pull a bubble of denser air around himself and his allies so they could breathe comfortably. Now the air was thick enough to move about without growing winded. He was warmer now than when he had left Autumn.

Gray and his allies stretched from so much time motionless. Except for Maeve. She was frozen and staring at a large bird. Slowly one front leg came up to point at the feathery beast.

Shirdos flapped once before shifting his wings to allow them to fold at his sides. He cocked his head and looked at his guests.

"Welcome to the sky islands. *Click*. It is tradition to walk from here to the temple. *Click*."

Gray smiled as he fell into step behind the chimera, the others moving to follow.

***

The Beryl Gardens were home to the royal family of Spring. A main domed building made of white quartz was trimmed with green marble that housed the various trees and flowers of the royal family. Birds and pretty insects flew around the fragrant air and several animals were part of the menagerie.

Four towers surrounded the crystal peak of the domed garden, each rising high into the clear sky. Walkways connected the higher levels and the space inside each held the royal apartments, servants' quarters, and guest suites. Currently, servants bustled to arrange the accommodations for visiting kingdoms.

There was an assumption that Autumn might not show up and Winter might only send a group of fighters and emissaries. As it happened, all three of the invited kingdoms were to be present. The registration forms had not been received, but letters of acceptance were already delivered, weeks earlier than expected.

Despite all the stress and bustle, Yoshiko Cerelia decided to take some time to feed the animals and tend to the garden. She sang a sweet melody as she worked, her hands rough from her labor despite the admonishments of her mother and step-sister.

Yoshiko just turned fifteen less than a moon ago and was eligible for the tournament. She'd been honing her skills for some time, determined to reclaim her family's honor. Despite the less than favorable image her powers conjured and the commonness of her spirit, she was quite strong.

The Cerelia family had always been powerful; Yoshiko was sure that was why the Alder King had chosen her mother after the death of the previous queen. Her mother was a Thorn Weaver and quite powerful.

While her mother dealt in the sharp and poisonous thorns of her magic, Yoshiko was a Shiro. Of all the powers for a royal daughter to have, mushroom manipulation wasn't one most would have chosen.

The princess knew better. Despite the fact that her power wasn't flashy or terrifying, she knew just how powerful it could be. A spore cloud could put an enemy to sleep, and a toxin could paralyze or kill an opponent. She could push such toxins through her skill or mist them into the air.

Only fools would think her weak. Most of the royals thought her just that.

She brushed the dirt from her hands on the loose-fitting work clothes. More often than not, the people walking through the garden thought her a servant.

Yoshiko liked working with the soil and plants. She adored the animals and most would come to sit with her. She was careful not to harm the insects or worms when she worked in the soil.

Under about a foot of rich earth was her other reason for spending so much time in the garden. She didn't plant the massive mushroom that sat below the surface. It had been there long before she was born. It was old, probably thousands of years or more. Its tendrilled roots reached deep into the earth, attached to the very bedrock of her realm.

It wasn't just under the garden, only closer to the surface here. As far as she could tell, over half of the kingdom of Spring was sitting on the mushroom. She had named it Honey, though it hadn't answered to that just yet.

Yoshiko couldn't explain how she communed with the fungus, only that she could sense what it felt and it didn't like her new family members. She'd been a visitor to the garden long before she was a princess, and Honey seemed to worry about the events to come.

The princess held her hand down in the deep hole she dug, her skin just brushing the mushroom. Then she set the small sapling in the hole and pushed the dark soil around it. She was beginning to stand when she heard a voice.

"Playing in the mud again, little sister?"

Harumi Legerdemain was the daughter of the Alder King. She was famed to be the loveliest woman in all the land. Most in the land had never met Harumi on a personal level. Her power was responsible for as much of the praise as was her appearance. The spirit of Enchantment allowed her to influence any man she was able stretch her aura around. With direct contact, her control became near-absolute.

Her appearance was admittedly the other half of her reputation. The elf maid was tall and slender, her skin never touched by the sun. Her long black hair hung down to the small of her back and she wore a shimmering dress of emerald silks.

Long pointed ears were dotted with lines of sparkling emeralds. She was adorned with similar gems around her slender neck and wrists while her long fingers held several rings, some connected with silver chains. All the stones were carefully selected to match her bright green eyes.

Yoshiko was shorter, curvier, and had curly chestnut hair that would have reached just past her shoulders if she ever wore it down. Her work clothes were a far cry from a dress and the only jewelry she liked to wear was a pendant her real father had given her when she was very young.

Despite the contrast, Yoshiko spent little time feeling inferior. There just weren't enough hours in the day.

She looked up at the woman with eyes a shade of brown that was common among the peasantry. The princess had long given up on making friends with the stepsister who was over thirty springs older than her. At almost fifty, Harumi was still considered a child to the long-lived elves.

Yoshiko seasoned her response with her own barb. "I like to spend some time keeping our kingdom beautiful. It seems a shame to spend it all on myself."

Harumi scrunched a cute button nose and chuckled. Her tone was sweet, the words pointed.

"Oh, I understand. If I started where you are, I would give up quickly, too."

Yoshiko never got the chance to reply. Harumi was already walking up the path. The princess breathed out slowly, refusing to let the vapid woman get to her.

She finished her work and then headed to bathe and change. The princess still needed to travel to the markets for seeds. The plants on her balcony needed some color and she liked to tend to them herself. The mushroom thrummed with power beneath her as she walked to her quarters.

At least Honey was on her side.

***

Gray had expected to at least see the sage of Dawn before the trials began. He arrived to find the temple empty save for the other two chimeras. The manticore named Lampago was an honorable sort from Shirdos' description.

As described, he had a lean dark-brown lion's body with matching eagles' wings. His human head seemed to struggle to keep a comfortable angle atop the lion's neck. Gray noted the long serpentine tail, tipped with several long barbs, all coated with a poisonous white goo.

The sphinx sat watching from the edge of the large circular arena. Several others had arrived to see the show, though it looked as if most seats were empty. Lampago approached and made a bow that stretched his sinewy cat body. His words were clear and spoken with a human's tongue.

"I have heard much about you, Gray of the lower world. I have looked forward to today's trial since I first saw my old friend fly home on a newly mended wing."

Gray bowed in turn. He gave a wide smile and used the diplomatic tone he had learned from Claire and Joobel.

"I have heard much about you as well, honored Lampago. Have no doubt I have brought you a challenging opponent for this event."

The manticore nodded and smiled back. He looked sincere despite the fact that the fight could bring death to either contestant. The chimera glanced over at the sphinx.

"I must apologize for the lack of manners of our brother. He seems to think that since few ever make it to him, he need not introduce himself."

Gray knew much of Hawlabu the sphinx. He'd worked hard to make sure he wouldn't end up like those who came before him. The slight mattered little to the tall dark man. He tended to lean toward Jack's policy on politics: they can think as they like until they decide to act on it.

He smiled at Lampago. "Your honor cannot be tarnished by those who show none. It's nice to meet you."

The manticore returned the smile. "Shall we begin? Who will be facing me?"

Before Gray could speak, a woman with dark-red hair sauntered forward. Myrin only spoke one word.

"Me."

***

Myrin never would have imagined being a part of this quest. Once, she was the clear choice for Winter Maiden, future queen of a powerful kingdom. Now she spent her time training a borrowed spirit and working for a kingdom she once thought pitiful. Also generally trying to make Gray blush.

Once Myrin found out Raine had proposed to the man, she'd made it her life's mission to make him miserable. It really didn't seem to be working. That only made her try harder.

All games aside, she was honored when he asked her to stand with him for this event. She worked even harder to make sure she didn't fail.

Relationships were hard for Myrin, as she didn't feel anything when others experienced emotions. Without highs or lows, she mostly just found ways to keep from being bored.

When she woke up in a dragon stable months earlier, smelling like a drunk who got lost in a pigpen, it was the first time someone had told her that she was a terrible person. Gray had been that someone. Since then she'd worked to be better. Aside from keeping Gray in check and beating up bad people, she'd turned over a new leaf. Or at least attempted to.

Now she needed to beat up this perfectly agreeable guy named Lampago. What a stupid name. Also, who chose the parts to make this guy? Why a human's head? That was the worst choice for biting things. Whatever. She was already bored.

Lampago moved to the other side of the circle and Myrin moved to stand opposite of him. She loosened the whip on her hip and adjusted the bracelets on her left wrist.

She often wore her hair brushed and down her shoulders. It made Gray blush more when she did. Today it was tied back in a long braid. Her boots were flat on the bottom, though heels made her backside sway more. She intended to win this fight. Only a fool battles in heels.

The manticore bowed once and she did the same. The sound hit her ears at the same time the barb hit right where she'd been standing. The rush of wings told her the enemy was on the move. She crouched down and put her left hand against the earthen floor of the arena.

There was a loud '*WOMP*' sound and a cloud of dust rose into the air, covering the whole of the circle in a haze that hovered a dozen feet in the air. Lampago's human head meant a lousy sense of smell and hearing. She could see with her spirit any time he touched the dust in the air.

Myrin rolled to one side as Lampago slammed down and whipped his tail toward her head, the barbed spikes slashing lines in the hard soil. He swung again but this time she sidestepped. As the tail slammed the ground, the soil opened up to catch it.

Then the earth closed tight, trapping the appendage and grounding the chimera. She lashed out and the sound of the cracking whip echoed all around the arena. A cry of pain echoing back confirmed she struck true.

The ground shook as he pulled up with a strength that was far beyond human. He tore open the ground to free his tail. In one motion three barbs shot toward Myrin while she was pulling the whip around.

Now she dropped to the ground and rolled as two of the barbs harmlessly stabbed deep into the earth. The third pinned her wrist to the hard surface. In only seconds the dust began to settle, and Lampago was shaking his head in shame. He turned to Gray.

"She was a strong opponent. My poison was the only way I could hold out. I'm sworn to fight with all my abili—"

The earth erupted underneath him. The whip that caught his side was much larger now. It wrapped around his lean body and was much thicker than his neck. The end had a large ball of hard rock that finished the coiling motion with a sickening thud against his ribs.

Myrin stood with the barb still in her wrist. She leaned forward and pulled it out with her teeth, spitting it on the ground in disgust. Her skin had taken on a color closer to that of her hair.

"Never!" Her eyes rolled with fury. "Never turn your back on me!"

She stomped the hard dirt and rounded spears of earth rose up to slam into the chimera. She continued her assault over and over, the impacts tossing him about. The sound of the thunderous blows was accompanied by several snapping bones and a weak cry of pain.

A blast of air swept in and pushed her back. Myrin sank her boots into the ground for purchase and continued her assault. Now Jack was in front of her, his hand on her arm. He spoke only two words.

"You won."

Then the prince pulled away enough of her power to save the manticore from certain death.

***

Gray hadn't seen Myrin lose her temper in some time. It was the barb that pushed her over the edge. It was a kill shot. Had she not been wearing the purifying bracelet from Raine, the woman would've been dead already. Lampago tried to kill her, and she tried to do the same.

Only his power over air had allowed Gray to hear the whispered words, 'I yield.' He couldn't fault Myrin for doing her best to stay alive while she was fighting for him. The guilt hit Gray hard, but he had to win this day.

There was so much at stake.

***

The young prince stretched and moved around to loosen his muscles for the trial with the griffin. He was impressed by Myrin's show of power but disappointed in her loss of control. She needed to learn to channel that anger. Then again, not everyone could vent by setting their own face on fire.

Jack was glad Lampago would survive and now focused on doing the same. Preferably in a way that wouldn't require healers and lengthy recovery times. He'd experienced enough of that to last a while.

The prince was careful to give Maeve a stay command. She was insurance for this event and while there was little doubt that the griffin would do his best, the creature would go no further than needed to win. Jack was in no real danger; it was Gray he was worried about.

Three times Jack asked to be the one to fight the sphinx and every time his big friend refused to give in. Now the griffin had walked out into the circle, standing in the center. The prince went out to meet with him.

"I cannot hold back. *Click.* Please know I consider you a friend. *Click.* Whatever happens, *Click,* it is my hope we can remain so. *Click.*"

Jack went into his own speech, professing his hope for continued friendship as well.

"Yup."

Shirdos nodded and moved to his side of the field while the lean young man did the same. As the gong was getting ready to sound, Jack began to form a giant ball of ice. He held it and waited. At first, he was going to hold back and only use his fire, but Gray made it clear that failure here could cost lives in the fight against the Black March.

He simply wouldn't lose. The gong sounded and the griffin charged. The chimera hit an exploding ball of steam and rolled out of the sky onto the ground. Shirdos was back up in an instant, trying to look around through tear-filled eyes.

Jack stood three feet from where he started, only moving to the side to let the griffin roll past. In his hand was a ball of orange fire the size of a pumpkin. Shirdos shot to the sky, flying to put the sun at his back. Jack changed the form of the ball and tossed it up.

It came to its apex, missing the griffin by a narrow margin. Then it exploded. The sound echoed like thunder, while the wave of scorching heat rolled across the air. The blast singed and damaged the feathers of the chimera.

Jack knew that the griffin would fight fair and it never occurred to him he might lose. He hated the politics of rule and he dreaded the histories his tutors would hammer into him. Torg's lessons about tactics, though. Those were interesting.

He was now performing for an audience of one. Jack couldn't fight the sphinx, but he knew that the one called Hawlabu would think the weaker fighters would go against the griffin and manticore and the strongest would face him.

Myrin had done her part, even if it was just going into a rage and crushing everything. Now he wanted to give the last chimera something to think about.

The griffin was slowed by the heat damage to its feathers but was still quite fast. Shirdos charged at him, thick beak snapping. Jack rolled and slammed a ball of ice into the lion ribs hard enough to crack bone.

Then the prince channeled his anger. He wasn't really angry at the griffin but he found he could focus on other things. The strange race of slime creatures that wanted to eat everyone he loved was enough on its own. He threw in his feelings on bards who wrote annoying songs just to be sure.

Eyes glowed a bright yellow as liquid orange fire ran down his light brown cheeks. The molten fire ignited at the chin and soon Jack was a ball of orange flames from the neck up. A staff of conjured flame grew in his hands. He spun the weapon around, slammed the end on the ground, and took a deep breath.

Shirdos had started to swing around to attack once more. Jack blew out a gout of flame, like a dragon. The heat from the blast singed the feathers enough that the chimera could no longer maintain flight.

The hit to the ribs was showing and the griffin limped as it ran toward him. He spun and connected the staff to the side of the beak, only hard enough to push the griffin to one side.

Jack's hand slapped down against the top of the feathered head and he pulled most of the remaining energy from his opponent. The griffin slowed and fell, all but dead. Jack leaned over the fallen Shirdos. He raised his voice to make sure the creature could hear him.

"Yield?"

The beak snapped as it forced out the words. "I yield. *Click*."

Jack nodded and set his hand on the creature, giving back all the energy he had taken and then some. Then he looked hard at the sphinx before releasing the visage of flame and reabsorbing the staff.

He helped the griffin limp to the edge of the arena, where healers began to do their work. As the prince walked back to where his friends were waiting, Gray smiled.

"That was... dramatic. Any wisdom for me before I go out there?"

Jack went into his detailed explanation of recommended battle tactics.

"Win."

Gray rolled his eyes and removed his coat.

***

It had taken Bilney several days to begin to understand the little girl named Laris. As a guard, she often saw what the evils of this world could do to a person, to their mind and body.

At first, she thought the girl had been a victim of some sort of abuse. She'd seen others react similarly to that kind of trauma. It could shatter a person's self-worth, even to the point where they would think they deserved it. It wasn't true, of course, but healing those wounds took time and kindness.

With Laris, she wasn't sure, but time and kindness were in short enough supply that if she was wrong, it would still do some good.

Now she thought she indeed had been wrong. Not about the kindness but about the girl. The guard watched the tiny Battle Shaper drawing again, another strange symbol. If she had to guess, she would say the girl was maybe five or six autumns old.

Laris was now dressed in an outfit that had once been Joobel's when she was growing far faster than anyone should. The clothes had stayed with Issabol after Joobel left for the Keep, and now they were a perfect fit for this girl.

Bilney had brushed the long dark hair that almost seemed black against dark-brown skin that was clear and free of scars... and those eyes. Bilney couldn't say what drew her to them, but she could lose time staring.

In time she understood. Laris had trouble talking with people because she didn't see people. Her power was, as least in part, in her eyes. She didn't see faces and expressions. She saw people like machines to be improved and fixed. Her ability clouded her perception.

Tears began to form in the guard's own eyes. Laris wasn't broken; this was how she was born. How she was meant to be. The idea of this sweet girl spending a lifetime without making friends or finding love broke her heart. The other children were kind to her, though Toma seemed cautious and Varam was usually busy at work on something.

Bilney spent most of the time she wasn't patrolling or caring for the children with the little girl who was always so distant. She wanted Laris to understand how precious she was. Not for her unique power but for who she was. There had to be a way to communicate with her! It would take time. Here in the workshop, time was one thing she had plenty of.

She held on to hope.

CHAPTER 3

Joobel was running late. She hated losing track of time, but she was still so excited about Jack's proposal that she had lost herself in the preparations. Even worse, if she was late at all in Fairie, it would seem like hours in the war room, where time moved so much faster.

The quickest way to get around was to fly at breakneck speeds through the halls of the Blood Keep to the portal room. Of course, that would be insane. The gnome only did so in emergencies, or if she really had to pee.

She weaved through the portal to Issabol's and then turned to zip right into the war room. Her arrival was so abrupt and loud that Cruor had produced a sword of dark-red and was ready to strike.

The gnome pulled in her speed and landed softly on the floor to the room, took two steps, and sat in her chair next to Claire. The Autumn Queen rolled her eyes and leaned over.

"The dress?"

Joobel bit her lower lip and sighed. "The dress."

Hurley had the floor and continued speaking. "To answer your question, Claire, the whole thing is almost certainly a trap of some sort. Over 94% certainty based on the available information. Not something we would want to walk into."

Claire shrugged. "The funny thing about traps is that when you know they are there, they lose much of their advantage."

Raine looked ready to throw her shoe at someone, her tone exasperated.

"Knowing that two other kingdoms have set a trap for you halfway across the world isn't a good reason to go jump into it headfirst!"

Joobel could see this wasn't going smoothly. Winter had Raine coming to counsel with Hurley and the scary guy Cruor. Without Jack and Gray around, Claire had been here alone. Not only was that unsafe in principle, but the gnome felt like she let her friend down by not being on time. She took a deep breath and stood.

"Raine, you are of course, correct. This whole thing is dangerous and certainly designed to hurt Autumn in some way. Yet not going would be an even bigger risk. We already rely too much on the strength of Winter to deter attacks from the south."

Joobel's wings flitted as she paused to meet the eyes of the Winter Queen.

"This trap is also an opportunity for us to show the might of Autumn. That we aren't just a haven for escaped slaves and refugees. We need to bring the people of Spring and Summer to our way of thinking. We need to win them over and gain their support."

The room had grown quiet. Claire was tapping her quill against her lips while Hurley seemed to be calculating. Cruor just leaned back in his chair, a sharp smile on his lips.

Raine let out a long sigh. "Is there no way to talk you out of this?"

Claire looked tired; her eyes seemed to hold back her weariness as she spoke.

"This is an attack on our future. We only have so much time before we face our real enemy. I don't think it wise to turn the other cheek."

"Not when we can take 'em off at the neck."

All eyes turned to Cruor. The young man flicked his head to move his hair away from his face so he could look back.

"Let's set aside all the talk of danger and such. We all know we're going to go. Let's spend our time talking about how we are going to put on a show. Half the soldiers in Winter still tell the story of the evil queen from the west who defeated an army with some ghosts and a zombie dragon."

He turned his red eyes to Raine.

"Our queen has her own legend of riding the lake monster into Winter and taking the throne with two strange dragons, a white demon warg, and the man of frost. If we are going to Spring, you ladies are going to make some noise. Let's talk about that and stop pretending we might stay home."

Joobel almost laughed. Raine's guard was like Jack but with words. She found that she liked the man, even if he did look frightening. For the first time all day, Joobel saw Claire smile.

"Well... this is what I had in mind."

***

In the Ornella School of Autumn, everyone has a place. Regardless of race or type of spirit, children are taught how to work for the benefit of all. The concept of everyone having a chance to train both the mind and the various types of spirit magic was still a new one.

Granted, some had a natural advantage, but almost all of the young people present would have never had the chance to shine only a few short years ago. There was not a person present that didn't realize they owed this opportunity to the queen and her insistence on them getting the best Autumn had to offer.

It was the nature of spirits that they always give an edge to those who carry mature spirits in their core. Some were formidable without such advantages, but only elves and humans could weave to cast or enhance at the highest levels.

Even among mature spirits, some held more powers than others. Some of the most powerful of those were chosen to train with the prince. Bayu was one of the strongest students in this group.

This particular session met only once a week in place of spirit training and worked as a type of test for student rankings. Both humans who had a bonded spirit and the races that had inherent magic were allowed to attend.

Few non-humans could keep up with this type of exercise, but there were some. Circle matches were a common way to test your abilities against other forms of spirit magic. As a Tempest, the young man had the potential to be the most potent air user in Autumn.

Though, there was another who also shared his brand of power. Zephyrina was in his combat class and was also in spirit training. Zef, as she preferred to be called, was still a bit stronger than him in raw power. But she seemed to have a good deal of trouble using her abilities against people.

Bayu wasn't sure if the fact that he had no trouble at all was a bad sign. Either way, when they went head-to-head, she tended to win in strength and endurance, while he would win any combat exercise. Bayu also thought that she was a pretty awesome person. The fact that he'd been able to give her the bracelet on her wrist was a point of pride for him.

Tempests were driven by emotion. Like most air users, they could put up shields, use air as an extension of their body, or even make constructs like spears or orbs. The thing that made

Zef and Bayu special was the ability to use emotional control to form a literal thunderstorm and control the chaotic power inside.

Bayu became well known for accidentally blowing the roof off the East Wing on the first day of school. Queen Claire ended up forgiving him. He was, after all, trying to help. The bracelet helped him calm himself when he was getting wound up.

As the queen knew he wasn't the only Tempest, she made him two and let him 'choose' to give the other to Zef. Shortly after, they'd become quite close. Bayu just celebrated his fifteenth autumn and was eligible for the tournament that was announced earlier in the day.

There would be a test and some of his classmates would be eliminated. He was confident he would get to go, while also quite sure Zef wouldn't. This thought tempered his excitement. Despite this and the bracelet, he was ready to bounce off the walls.

The tournament was something he'd only heard stories about. The last one had been before he was born and was held in the arena of Winter. The grand champion was from Autumn, the current queen's father and a master of flame.

Bayu was lost in thought when his turn came up. He was up against an earth spirit user who had a good deal of talent with tunneling. Bayu formed the shield under his feet to stop the inevitable attack from below and hit the boy with blasts of air from three different directions.

His opponent blocked two of the hits, while the third flung him out of the circle. The Tempest bowed and walked out to await the next contest. It would be several hours yet before he would face someone that required his full attention.

***

Naoki lay in a sunny clearing of chestnut trees. He often moved around to check on the various forests of the kingdom. He was stretched out on a thick carpet of grass and bare from the waist up, soaking up the sunshine. The elf had never quite figured out why he needed sunlight when he had no leaves.

Sakura, his symbiotic dryad, seemed to weaken if he did not spend a portion of each day directly in the warm glow. He had chosen a spot just downwind of some honeysuckle bushes. The sweet fragrance was now drifting over him as he felt the day's warmth.

There was a time when he would have fallen asleep. Now he seldom needed to. From time to time, he would let his arboreal passenger take control of his left arm. She would pull roots from the heartwood of his wooden limb, and they would both absorb a great deal of energy. The heartwood had demonstrated many abilities.

Even after four years, he was still learning just how powerful the gifted arm was. He was almost sixteen springs now. He'd grown a great deal since he had been attacked in the grove of cherry blossoms. The arm grew as he did, his body now so accustomed to it that he often forgot the nature of the thing if he wasn't focused on it.

His passenger dryad resided in the very wood of the strange limb. The heartwood of a tree could house a spirit, and if it was harvested and shaped by skilled Wood Weavers, it could be made into magical objects. Spring was currently experiencing a shortage of this precious wood.

Those who collected it had a tendency to have short careers with unknown retirements. Most kingdoms had lost the dryads of their forests. Only Summer and Spring still had any to speak of. It was his mission to maintain that presence.

During his brief times in the sun, he could allow his left hand to contact the soil and learn about his realm. The kingdom he'd stopped caring about long ago, but the realm was of the great spirit of renewal and the plants and animals it sustained.

He loved and served his realm, but had no love for the royal family. The Alder King allowed nature's balance to shift in a bad way. The realm was controlled by those who didn't value the life that lived upon it.

That was a concern for others; it was all he could do to simply defend the dryads.

It was on this day, in the soft grass among a grove of chestnut trees, breathing in the rich scent of the honeysuckles, that Naoki learned of the strange bustling in the capital. The news flowed through the royal gardens, through the trees of the city streets, and into the grasses of the plains.

Now he felt words through his power. He still didn't understand them; only the oldest of dryads could speak with the common tongue. Sakura explained what was happening so far away.

"They are saying that there is to be another Contest of Champions. It's to be held in Spring this time."

Naoki may as well have kept listening to the grass. He rolled his eyes.

"Oh, is that what is going on? Mind telling me what that is?"

"The Contest of Champions takes place every few seasons. The last one was about twenty springs ago in Winter. This one is going to be here, in Amaya."

Naoki thought about this for a moment.

"Why would anyone risk death or injury in a silly fight?"

Sakura closed her eyes and turned to let the sun flow through her spirit form. She only manifested physically if she needed to speak to someone other than him. He could naturally see such things. As she basked in the bright light, her words took on a whimsical tone.

"Those who do well may get an audience with the queen. The winner is given much more."

The young elf thought about this for a moment.

"What did the last winner get?"

She turned, the white and pink hair swaying lightly. "If the rumors were true, he received wealth and prestige. Also, the Queen of Autumn's hand in marriage."

The elf scoffed at the thought of winning a bride. What a silly notion. Wealth and prestige were of some use to him. If he could afford to hire help caring for the forests of Spring, that would help him with his mission. He considered for a few moments, then asked one more question.

"Sakura, is there any urgent business we need to deal with in the forests?"

The dryad closed her eyes and concentrated. "Right now, things seem quiet. The rumors of your deeds have deterred many who would harm my sisters."

The elf stood and pulled his tunic on, stretching and leaning over to draw power from the soil. The dryad tilted her still face, seemingly confused. "What are you doing?"

Naoki grinned as he stretched his long limbs. "We're going to Amaya."

Then the elf used the gifted power to fuel his sprint through the forests, his lean legs pushing well past normal speeds. His long black hair flowed behind him as he began to devour the distance with long graceful strides. So far from the capital, it should take nearly a week to travel to the city of Amaya.

Naoki would cover the distance in under two days.

***

The sphinx was quite a bit bigger than the other chimeras. Gray watched as the lion paws padded to the opposite side of the ring, great wings flapping slightly to give the bulk some balance.

His human face was wreathed in coarse brown fur and as he yawned, Gray caught a glimpse of teeth that seemed to lean toward the lion side of his nature. Hawlabu made no effort to pay respect or speak before the match. He only sat on his haunches and stared across the field.

Gray focused his mind, having only been a little worried about Myrin and unconcerned for Jack. He chose the most challenging opponent himself. For one thing, if someone else was hurt, he'd never have forgiven himself. He also wanted no doubt as to his victory here today.

Seeing the sphinx up close made him wonder if that was wise. His bulky form rippled with muscle and long claws ripped up the ground as he walked.

Gray required an edge against this opponent and from Shirdos' description, he believed he was prepared. So many times, Jack had grown annoyed with Gray's jokes and references. Now it was time to weaponize them.

As the gong sounded, Gray made no move to attack, only stood with his arms behind his back and a smile on his face. Hawlabu seemed confused and slowly stalked forward.

Before the sphinx could speak, Gray began to examine his fingernails, ignoring the looming presence. Hawlabu spoke with a deep rasping growl.

"Do you take me as weak, not even preparing yourself for battle?"

Gray made no move, intent on a fleck of dirt under one fingernail. The sphinx growled in annoyance.

"What fool takes his eyes off his opponent in a duel?"

Gray began looking at the other hand. Hawlabu eyes began to bulge as he roared.

"Have you not heard a single word I have spoken?"

Gray looked up and seemed startled, as if seeing the chimera for the first time. He put on an offended tone.

"What a strange way to start a conversation."

Now the creature seemed confused again but settled into what Gray had been expecting. The sphinx lowered his voice to a somewhat normal tone.

"A trial of combat is well and good, but true power is in one's intelligence. Perhaps you would like to have a battle of wit instead of violence."

Gray leaned his head back and rubbed the short stubble on his chin. Then he nodded.

"I suppose that will suffice. I concede the weaker mind to ask the first riddle."

"Which creature has one voice and yet becomes four-footed and two-footed and three *grr*..."

Hawlabu's voice trailed into a growl as he realized the meaning of the sentence and the insult that came with it. Gray interrupted him.

"A woman, or a man, I suppose. Is that really the level we are playing at? Let me ask an equally difficult question. How does a one-armed swordsman win a fight?"

The sphinx was starting to dig his claws into the ground, anger burning red on his human face. Then he paused. Gray waited patiently. Finally, Hawlabu began to growl his reply.

"The question has no definitive answ—"

Gray interrupted the verbal dodge with the answer, his volume rising just a touch.

"He wins *single-handedly*. I thought that was obvious. I suppose it's your turn again. How many times do I need to win to claim my prize?"

Now the sphinx was furious, but he was also aware of his audience. His brothers were watching and if he attacked now, he would be thought a fool forever. His pride meant he had no choice but to proceed.

"There are two sisters: one gives birth to the other, and she, in turn, gives birth to the first. Who are the two sisters?"

Gray tapped his lips with his finger, much like Claire would have done. Then he spoke as if thinking hard, his words dripping with sarcasm.

"The first one is obviously day, but the second seems to escape me. Oh, I wonder if it's... *night?* You really need better material. Perhaps I should give you one even you can get right."

It didn't hurt that the griffin had given Gray both the questions and answers ahead of time. The riddles weren't part of the trial and so Shirdos was able to share them without breaking his oath. Gray made a show of searching his mind for a simple question for the chimera. Then he held up a finger while leaning forward.

"Why... can no one hear... a sphinx go to the bathroom?"

Hawlabu was on the verge of breaking. He seemed to have some trouble staying upright. His words were slurred as he growled, "That question has no answer!"

Gray rolled his eyes and raised his voice, slightly adjusting his pitch.

"Does that mean I win? I thought you would've at least some smarts in that ugly human head."

The creature snarled and tensed as if he would pounce, his words now a sneer.

"Your question is stupid and makes no sense!"

Gray smiled widely and leaned toward his opponent.

"Of course, it does. The '*P*' is silent." He grinned. "Get it?"

The sphinx roared. Well, he tried to. Hawlabu stumbled and tried to charge, but only then did it become clear what was happening. Controlling air well enough to make constructs is complicated, but most users get quite good at it with practice.

The telltale cloudy nature of air constructs can sometimes give away what you are trying to do. Gray had slowly woven a shield completely around the sphinx, channeling his own power through the bracelet Raine had given him.

The pure air and intricate weave of the sphere were nearly invisible. The sound would have been a bit off, but Gray had changed his tone and volume repeatedly to make that harder to detect.

Once the creature was entirely inside his makeshift hamster ball, Gray started taking the air away from inside. Even a beast of the skies needs to breathe. By the time Hawlabu realized what was happening, he was nearly unconscious.

Now Gray stood over him, slowly shaking his head as he repeated in a slow, profound tone.

"The '*P*'... is... silent."

Then he looked to the griffin, who still looked worse for wear. Gray shrugged and yelled at him.

"He's mostly unconscious; I need a judgment call. I either have to kill him or let him breathe."

The sphinx started tapping an unsteady paw on the ground, working his toothy mouth like a fish on the shoreline. Gray looked at him and then to the griffin.

"It is a clear victory. *Click*. You may choose to spare his life or end it. *Click*. You know what he would do. *Click*."

Gray kneeled and spoke, his voice now stern and severe.

"I choose to let you live; this fight is over. If you try anything, you won't get mercy twice."

Gray unwove the sphere around the sphinx. There was a slight '*woosh*' as the air rushed in. Hawlabu gasped loudly and coughed as he struggled to pull air into his empty lungs. In seconds he was breathing slow and deep. Gray was already walking toward Jack and Myrin.

He never looked back when he heard the roar of fury and rage.

***

Never had anyone so humiliated him! Hawlabu was first among the chimeras. By far the strongest and most cunning. The man cheated! His questions had no real answers. He deserved to die for his insolence!

The sphinx took two long strides and leaped at Gray's back. Hawlabu was faintly curious why no one made a move to stop him. Only the boy of ice and flame reacted. All he did was hold up a hand and make a strange sign. Then the huge lion's body was torn from the air.

The impact crushed one wing and paws even more massive than his own pinned him to the ground as they landed. He could hear his ribs cracking as he fell hard. Then a vast maw closed on his neck. For the second time, he was unable to breathe.

This time he never would again.

***

The large body of the sphinx lay on the torn surface of the arena. In the throes of death, its lions' claws had ripped and scratched both the ground and the huge earthen form of Maeve. She'd shrugged off such attacks in her more substantial form and the chimera died in short order.

Lampago and Shirdos both approached and let out a long mournful keeling, an otherworldly sound of mourning. At first, Gray expected them to try and fight once again. He sincerely hoped the sphinx would accept defeat and not die in such a way. He'd known enough to bring a contingency and the hound had done her job well.

It was Lampago who spoke first. He was limping badly and the healers on hand were a far cry from Bloom. This would explain the once shattered wing of the griffin.

"He never could be gracious; you beat him fairly. Even used his own tricks against him. I would have loved to have lost without having half my bones broken."

The manticore eyed Myrin warily but she was looking down at the broken body of Hawlabu.

Gray sighed with regret. "I would have rather not had it play out like this."

"You showed mercy. *Click*. He was the one who refused it. *Click*."

"I have waited long for this day."

The voice seemed to come from everywhere at once. As one, the griffin and manticore both turned and bowed. Gray spun to see what they were looking at. Only a few paces away stood an old man.

He was a bit large around the middle and was much shorter than Gray's own towering height. He wore a robe of yellow with clouds along the hem. His white beard was long, and his feet were in leather sandals. He was mostly bald on top with a few stubborn hairs poking off in random directions.

Despite the mundane appearance and the serene demeanor, the power radiating off the man was intense. Far beyond that of anyone Gray had ever met, including Jack. The old man shuffled over and looked up to him.

"Only one of you holds the spirit of air, so that would mean it is you who has passed my tests."

Gray nodded once and then bowed at the waist. He tried to sound like he thought Claire would have.

"I did my best to meet your standards in the trials. You honor me with your presence."

The little man waved his hand as if to brush away the words of praise. He turned and gave a slight bow to both Jack and Myrin, then spoke to them both.

"You have served your friend well. In doing so, you have brought me my disciple. What boon would you have me grant?"

Jack shrugged his usual indifference, but Myrin stepped forward. Her eyes darted to the manticore.

"I'd ask for another fight with him." She pointed to Lampago and bared her teeth.

The old man laughed and then seemed to pause. He looked over to the body of the sphinx as a sad sigh left him.

"I have asked enough of the chimeras. They have served me well and long; our bargain is complete and I have no authority over them. Perhaps another boon would satisfy you?"

Myrin walked away to sit on a bench on the edge of the arena. The ground rumbled as she moved. Jack stepped forward.

"I require nothing, but I'm the Prince of Autumn. If you agreed to meet with my sister, the queen, at a later date, I'd consider it a fair boon."

The old man seemed surprised but agreed to the terms. He looked to Gray. "Did I offend your other friend somehow? I cannot grant what isn't mine to give."

Gray was still thinking about so many words passing Jack's lips. He looked over to Myrin, who was still fuming. Maybe he should have let her kill the sphinx. He looked to the sage of Dawn and shook his head.

"She's quick to anger and slow to forgive. Give her time. Perhaps you can hold her boon for later when she has cooled down."

The sage nodded and waved a hand, causing the broken body of Hawlabu to drift away. Gray couldn't tell where it was going, but the old man seemed confident it would arrive where he intended.

The amount of concentration it took to levitate such a tremendous burden would have taken much of Gray's attention. To send it somewhere else seemed unthinkable. Perhaps disciple was a proper term for spending any time with this fellow.

The old man shuffled away, his words trailing behind him.

"Well, come along. We have much to discuss."

Gray began to follow, then remembered his friends. A nod from Jack explained that he would keep Myrin from killing anyone or destroying anything. Maeve seemed content to dig a hole through a large rock. After the incident with the sphinx, Gray doubted anyone would tell her she couldn't. The other chimeras were gone, no doubt back with the healers.

It was no trouble keeping up with the sage. Despite his impressive power and control, he walked quite slowly. They moved in silence until they came to the edge of the floating isle.

He walked right off the side and Gray almost gasped. Curiously, the short round figure seemed to float effortlessly in the air. It took only a few seconds for Gray to put together the constructs he used for flying, but he had to push himself to catch up.

Once away from the island's sphere of influence, the air was again quite thin and cold. This time he didn't have Jack's gifted power to work with. Luckily, he was only carrying himself at the moment and kept up well enough.

Instead of hours, the flight was only a few swift minutes. The sage landed on a dirt path just outside a little hut sitting on a smaller island. The home was rustic and simple, but the surrounding garden was beautiful and well cared for. The little man walked inside and left the door open, a clear invitation.

The large frame of Gray required him to duck through the low opening. There on the table was a modest meal, seemingly set out for the two of them. The man began steeping tea leaves and moved to sit on one side of the table, gesturing a wrinkled hand at the other. Once both men were seated, the sage spoke his first words since leaving the temple arena.

"You first came to my attention when you made a rather amusing attempt to fly out of Summer. Nasty business taking people like they do. You made it out though, and I decided to move you a little farther than you intended. There was someone I wanted you to meet, you see."

Gray was surprised, angry, and impressed in what seemed equal measure. He almost died that night. The brownie Korul, a friend who aided in the escape, came closer still. This man could have helped, so why had he left them to perish?

He clenched his fist as his jaw tightened. The words came to his lips; sage or not, he had no right!

"You could have helped—"

The sage seemed to read his fury and held up a hand.

"Do not think I see all. The currents carry whispers to me. I help those who I can, when I can. You needed to develop your skills. You needed allies among the kingdoms. Most of all, *she* needed you."

Gray was speechless now. Claire? This man had sent him to the Autumn Maiden. It made sense in a way. He was new with his power then and never should have made it out of Summer. Yet they landed far past the border he was aiming for. He asked the only question he couldn't figure out on his own.

"Why? You sent me off to meet a stranger when you could have brought me here. You could have been teaching me long ago. Why send me to a field of grass on the edge of a failed kingdom?"

The old man sipped his tea and pushed some sort of honey rolls toward his guest. He smiled as if he just thought of a joke from earlier in the day. Then he leaned forward.

"*Is* Autumn a failed kingdom?"

Gray snorted. "It was pretty close when you blew me off course."

Now the old man laughed, his joke complete. His chuckle was hearty and infectious, though the anger Gray was feeling kept him from sharing in the old man's fun. Again, the sage responded with a question.

"How many have you saved, has she saved? I hear the whispered cries of those hurting from my garden. I can help a few, but there are so many. Long ago I learned to watch for the right people. When I find them, I try to put them in the place they can do the most good. You had potential, as did the Autumn Maiden. I hoped you might help lift each other up."

Gray sighed. "What of her brother, the prince?"

"You mean the one they call Demon? Or Jack O'Lantern? The Man of Frost, perhaps? He's powerful, but has more fear than you can see. He blames himself for his absent father and for the death of his mother. He's driven by anger and is single-minded. I believe he will help shape the future, but hope he won't be the one to make the mold."

Gray thought for a long moment. The revelation of the sage's interference in his life had distracted him from his purpose in coming here. He took a deep breath and chose his words. He asked the question he waited so long to have answered.

"Normally, I wouldn't be able to visit my home world. Only those of renewal can survive there for any amount of time. There is a way to craft a connection to my great realm spirit so I could visit for a time. There's something I need to be able—"

The sage shook his head. "Dawn has no bedrock."

The old man's words were abrupt and hurt Gray more than he feared. There would be no aid from his home in the fight against the Black March. He failed and would never see his family again. The old man held up a hand and gave a wry smile.

"Earth and water are drawn to the ground. Fire cannot live where there is no fuel. Renewal and change are bound to the plants and animals, and they mostly live below. Air is different; it is the essence of no realm and a part of them all."

The sage made a motion to encompass the islands, the realm of Dawn.

"This place isn't a realm as you know it. It's a name we give to those below so they can try to understand. You have traveled many realms; what happens to your power when you do so?"

Gray often pondered this. He had used his spirit in all of the other realms, except for Spring. Starting in Summer, there was no shortage of power, if not the skill to use it well. Years living in Autumn allowed him ample energy. He fought at the Bitter Challenge alongside Raine in Winter. He traveled the Mountain Wyld on more than one occasion and fought here in this place.

"I'm not stronger here... or anywhere."

The sage nodded but added a correction.

"You are also not weaker anywhere. From the moment a spirit of air bonded to you that night in Summer, you have never left your realm. Where there is air in this world, you have power."

Gray nodded, starting to understand. This explained a good deal. It still didn't help his quest. He decided to just ask again.

"Is there a way for me to visit home?"

The sage smiled and his beady eyes twinkled. He was enjoying this way too much.

"The only way to link to the power of air would be to have a piece of the avatar in its physical manifestation."

"What is the avatar of air?"

The old man gave a wide smile, clapping both hands to his round belly.

"Have you ever heard of something called the Thunderbird?"

CHAPTER 4

The sun was just beginning to move toward the distant mountains to the west. The air was still warm and Yoshiko felt alive as she moved through the streets toward the markets. She sought vendors who had more varieties of the seeds she wanted. They would be past the districts a princess would normally travel.

Yoshiko loved to leave the confines of the Beryl Gardens and walk the streets of Amaya. She didn't need much of a disguise to hide her identity; she usually just wore her regular clothes and would walk out to enjoy the city.

Sure, if Harumi tried to move around town, she would be plagued by admirers. Still, she was more of a princess, whereas Yoshiko just loved watching the people go about their day.

Most of the people of Amaya were elves like her. The distinctive ears and cheekbones were seen on all but a few of those walking through the capital. Those of the other races were mostly here for trade or hired for a specific job that required rare spirit magics.

Amaya was lovely on the surface, like a living painting of an ideal concept. Also like a painting was the fact that if you scratched the surface, there was something less attractive underneath. Yoshiko was quite a way off when she heard the disgusted shouts from up ahead.

"See here, vermin, you are not to be anywhere near this place!"

There was a pause. Those to whom the woman was speaking were not yelling. Their low whispers came into Yoshiko's hearing only when she got closer.

"... no harm. We're just hoping for any spare food you might have."

The elven woman narrowed her eyes at the urchins. Both were human and neither was clean or well fed. It was true that they didn't fit in so close to the city center.

The princess moved to intervene just as the elf raised a hand. The woman's spirit was of air and the wind picked up quickly. The nearby flower box reached out with pale mycelia; the mushroom roots answered Yoshiko's call and they wrapped the wrist of the attacker. She didn't harm the elf woman; the law would be on her side after all. Even if that law was wrong.

"Peace, my lady. These little ones have done no real harm."

The woman's eyes narrowed and she growled. "They have stunk up my street and soiled my porch. You know well the laws regarding vagrant humans!"

It was clear this woman didn't know who she was. Even with the law on her side, no elf would address a royal so. Yoshiko considered putting her in her place, but that would complicate things and spread rumors of her outings. She decided on another plan.

"Of course, all good citizens do. Yet you would rub the children and the dirt they carry all over the street. Imagine how hard it would be to clean blood from white stone. No, they need to be escorted to the nearest guard barracks."

The look of anger faded from the woman as she considered the words. She probably hadn't thought of how hard blood was to wash from the ivory walkways. Yoshiko gritted her teeth as she waited to see if this would come to blows. Finally, the woman huffed.

"I don't have time to be guiding urchins to the authorities. I carry the words of the Alder King himself and we are preparing for the Contest."

Yoshiko waved a hand. "I'm going right past the one two streets up. It would be my honor to do a service for one so important."

The woman gave her a curt nod, then reached into her purse to pull out a thick copper coin. It was worth ten talons, much more than the little ones had asked for. The woman smiled and held it out.

"I wouldn't feel right asking another elf to work for free. For your time."

Yoshiko took the money and smiled. Outside the city, this might have fed both these children for a week. The irony wasn't lost on her, but she gave a courteous bow and turned her nose up in the direction of the children.

"Come along, I'll not abide my time being wasted."

The children both looked at her with wide eyes, but they had seen a hint of her power and neither made any effort to run or fight. They sighed and followed her up the street.

She led them down the path until they neared an alley. Tendrils of her mushrooms shot out of the dim alleyway and scooped up both of them. She followed them into the gloom.

The boy was older, maybe only a couple of years younger than her. He stared up with defiant eyes and started to scream. His mouth was wrapped up in an instant.

The girl was a bit younger yet. Perhaps ten or eleven springs and she had skin so dark it made her hard to see in the dim light. They weren't closely related and she wondered how they came to travel together.

Yoshiko held up the coin, placing it in the boy's hand. She would have kneeled had he been much shorter than her, but at her height few were.

"Listen to me carefully. I have no intention of turning you over to the guards. The coin will serve you better than I. I'm going to allow you both to speak; please don't scream. Trust me when I say the guards will take my side and I mean you no harm."

The mycelium unraveled over both of their mouths. The girl still looked afraid, but the boy mumbled in a low whisper.

"What are you going to do with us?"

The princess looked to the fear in the girl's dark eyes, then to the resignation in the boy's.

"That depends. Where are your parents?"

He winced and paused before answering. "Mine were taken by the guard months ago. I found her wandering around south of the mere. Girls... get taken there; I've been trying to keep her safe."

Yoshiko's jaw clenched. The slave trade moved through the southern docks, some of it even legal under the Alder King. The boy wasn't wrong about the girl's safety. She looked to the girl.

"Is all of this true?"

The girl was terrified, but gave a nod. The boy spoke again and Yoshiko turned to him.

"She never talks. I don't even know her name."

The princess looked to the girl again, as if testing his words. Sure enough the girl didn't move. Yoshiko sighed; she wasn't going to get those seeds.

"If you beg anywhere near the city center, you will be arrested. Or worse. When's the last time you had a meal?"

The girl still looked terrified, but the boy muttered an answer that broke her heart.

"A vendor let us have some of his unsold dumplings four days ago."

The rage that filled her almost pulled up the mushrooms that served her. Last time she had torn up most of a street and gotten admonished by the king himself. She took long deep breaths and got her temper under control. The children both found themselves free of the pale bindings.

"If you will both follow me, I know a place you'll be safe."

The boy looked down at the coin and paused. The girl moved over to take his hand. He looked back up and nodded. She thought of the stares they would receive.

"If anyone asks, I'm taking you to a guard outpost. Do not argue with me or try to run. We're going to a place you can get a meal and a safe place to sleep."

He gave her a nod, his eyes misting up. Her heart broke all over again, bringing her rage to a boil once more. She moved out of the alley, the pair following closely behind her.

It took almost two hours to reach the western edge of the city. In a clearing a way off the road was a camp. Battered tents stood around a central fire. Several dozen people milled around, none of them elves. Most were human, though a few were of other races. A plump older woman moved up to greet her.

"My lady, you know it's risky for you to be seen here!"

Yoshiko hugged the woman and shook her head.

"I know, but these two were in a bad spot and I didn't know what else to do. Do you have room for two more?"

The old woman nodded and knelt down to the little girl.

"My name is Keffi. Would you like something to eat?"

The little girl was staring at her feet, but nodded just enough to get the message through. The boy turned around, looking Yoshiko in the eyes.

"I can't stay here. I still need to find my parents. Thank you for helping her. It will allow me to move more quickly."

The princess raised a hand and shook her head.

"The coin is yours and will feed you for a time, but you are weak and tired. Rest here for a few days and then continue your search."

He hesitated, looking at the people there. All looked hungry and his pride was urging him to move on. His hand went through his filthy hair as he shook his head.

"I can't take from those who have nothing."

Yoshiko nodded and pushed her power down into the soil. There was a faint rumble as the ground all around the camp began to erupt with mushrooms. Most were white, but several browns and yellows were mixed in with an occasional red. It was nothing for her to do so. Honey aided her request and the realm gave more than what was needed for the rest.

A chuckle came from the old woman. "Well now... we'll eat well tonight!"

Yoshiko cocked an eyebrow at the young man, who shook his head and gave the first hint of a smile.

"I guess I could stay for a couple of days."

Yoshiko smiled back, accepting one more hug from Keffi before turning around to get back to the Beryl Gardens. Just as she reached the edge of the clearing, three flowers bloomed in front of her, each maturing to seed before her eyes.

All three were rare and beautiful. She reached out and took the pods, placing them in her pocket. She got her seeds after all.

It would seem the realm was on her side as well.

***

Claire walked down the path that would take her to the new school. Guards walked both in front and behind her, though she had little fear of attack in her own kingdom. The rumors of her harsh dealing with an entire invading army from Winter had spread both love and anxiety through the citizens of Autumn.

All took a strange pride in the terrifying woman who seemed to be genuinely making life better for them.

The school was a new addition to Autumn. It was a massive undertaking to get the facilities built, not to mention getting at least a few children from every race and village into the first round of classes.

Of all the potential she'd seen in her time as queen, this endeavor was the one that held the most promise. Once she believed, as had everyone else, that the most potent and rare powers were born into the great houses, royal families, and the military. She was wrong.

Among the orphans and more impoverished villages, Autumn was hiding some of the most powerful people she'd ever met. She wouldn't have been able to figure that out without her brother's ability to 'taste' spirit magic. He simply walked through the combat classes and tapped a shoulder or clasped a hand to sample the aura of each child.

Over a dozen children had abilities that would have been considered a gift for a queen. Many of them had been roaming the streets only a few short months ago.

Among them had been another Portal Master like Issabol, as well as a Mimic and a Battle Shaper, all maker magics of the change spirit. Now all three orphans were adopted by the Blood Keep, though they lived with Issabol.

The only woman among the guards had been assigned to help keep them safe and help care for them. Bilney had been kind to Claire when few would even approach her. She was well suited to the task.

Aside from the new family Issabol had received, Autumn had formidable users of earth, fire, water, and air. A girl named Edana from a southern town had the same Inferno spirit her father once possessed. Autumn had two young Tempests who could each wield the power of a thunderstorm.

It took some deft words to explain the need for a new roof on the east wing of the school at the end of the first day. Still, the boy said he was sorry. She'd given him and his fellow Tempest a gift to help prevent further damage to buildings.

Despite the worry of young people with incredible power, Claire was excited to watch the duels that would determine those who would represent Autumn in the Contest of Champions. Part of her was disappointed Gray wouldn't be here to sit with her. He always had a knack for seeing how each duel was playing out and would answer her questions when she got lost.

Claire's power was more frightening than most, but she had little wish to fight. Usually, she talked her way around conflict or let her brother deal with such things. Her abilities weren't good for pretend battles. Death wasn't served in half measures.

Now that she thought about it, all of her wished Gray were here. Despite her efforts to push him away, he remained focused on spending time with her when she would allow it. Though he had his own quests and objectives, he worked tirelessly to help her bring the change she promised her people.

If she had taken Joobel's advice, she would have married him already and had an heir on the way. Though gnomes saw relationships quite differently, Claire was beginning to think her adopted sister had a point.

It was hard being cursed. The prophecy Issabol shared weighed on her like a grindstone: heavy and burdensome. It was the fact that she cared for Gray that made her push him away. Her future would carry pain and sacrifice and he need not have to bear it.

At least that was her thinking before. Now, as she moved toward twenty autumns, she began to think that he was up to the task. Having his support might make all the difference for both her and the people who depended on her.

He was both powerful and creative with his aspect of air. Though the flavor of magic wasn't a concern in her lands, it would be seen as wise to marry air into the royal family.

She had already changed the laws that would have kept Jack from honoring his oath to Joobel. The people either didn't mind or were afraid of what Jack would do if they spoke ill of the gnome.

Gray was also everything she could hope for in a husband. He was hardworking, creative, and loved the people of her kingdom. The school she walked to now was his idea, as was the portal system and the public water supply. He was pushing forward even now. More importantly, she loved him so very much.

The effort of pushing him away had grown to the point where she had to either give a relationship a real chance or send him away for good.

Claire was so lost in her thoughts that she was startled when an arm snaked around her own and a mop of silver hair dropped against her shoulder.

"Oh, isn't this exciting? We get to choose the young ones who will come to Spring with us!"

Joobel had to be part cat, moving silently past the guards who would never keep her from joining the queen. The gnome would be hard to see as anything other than herself and was the only person who was nearly human-sized with wings similar to that of a pixie.

The gnome once thought to hide who she was and try to blend as if she were human. Jack asked her not to and Claire was glad he did. No one should have to live as something they weren't. Claire recovered from the startling presence and looked over as she hugged her friend.

"I only hope the explosions don't get out of hand."

Joobel scrunched her nose. "Oh, silly queen, the boy saved my life when he blew the roof off the school. Likely your brother's as well. I wouldn't worry about him doing it very often."

Claire knew the story quite well. The young Tempest had helped her brother and Joobel rescue some students being held hostage. There was also a slightly terrifying troll and a gnome who somehow earned the title of Dragon Slayer. All were rewarded with items forged by Issabol and herself and honored as heroes of Autumn. The roof was expensive, though.

Claire sighed loudly and laughed as she patted the gnome's hand. "*Often* implies how many buildings per year?"

Joobel shrugged. "It can't add up to more than a half dozen or so."

The laugh turned into a groan as the guards took formation around the royal box overlooking the training grounds.

Seating for the training field had been an afterthought. The number of people wanting to watch the students spar and duel kept growing. Before long, Claire's inner businesswoman stepped forward to expand the structure into an arena.

Tickets were sold and the money earned went into developing and funding the school while caring for the orphans who lived in the dorms there. Since the whole kingdom was less than a half-hour walk away, thanks to the portal system, the place was sold out during even the smaller competitions. Today was no exception.

Below, the first round of students was stepping out to be announced for the first phase of the competition. The Contest of Champions in Spring was to have three categories for both the junior and adult divisions. Hand-to-hand combat was the first and all races were allowed to participate, though the more sizable races had a distinct advantage.

The second was spirit casting, a competition that would exclude all who had no symbiotic spirit, so only humans and elves would be present.

Last would be the overall championship. Only the top contenders from the previous two categories would be able to move on. Claire's father was the last to hold the top title.

There was only a little showmanship in announcing the first two contenders in the hand-to-hand combat category. Both were tall, lean trolls from the Stone Spears, recent refugees from the Mountain Wyld who had become full citizens of Autumn. The smaller and much younger of the two was Tedar. He was the troll who had helped save many of the other students during the incident that cost her a roof.

In his hand was a long spear. It was made of solid stone, red like the heart of Blood Mountain, where the rock was mined. The heart of the weapon was of iridescent purple construction, forged in Issabol's workshop and infused by the queen's own power with gifted magic from a mighty sea dragon. It was called Tremor.

Claire frowned at the sight of the weapon.

Joobel giggled. "Silly queen... just wait."

The smaller troll took his place at the far side of the field. As they squared off, Tedar spun the powerful weapon and then thrust it into the ground, clearly channeling only a tiny bit of its power with the thrust. The pressure wave flowed through the hard packed dirt.

There was a rumble through the stone that held the seated audience, including the royal box. The crowd was silent for a short moment while the ground settled. Then a roar rose up as the people could see they were clearly going to get their money's worth from this battle.

The other troll smiled around his dark tusks. He was clearly older than his opponent but recognized that this weapon brought honor to the whole tribe.

One of the judges sounded the starting bell as both trolls grew. It was as if layers of thick muscle were being piled on the frames of both fighters. Joobel clapped and squealed.

"Oh, I love this. Some of the trolls can get all big and stuff."

Claire rolled her eyes. "It's called Boiling Blood... as you well know."

Joobel didn't look away from the combatants and only smiled in response to the correction. Claire looked out and squinted as if trying to see the red sigil on Tedar's arm. She even lit her eyes to see in the spectrum of Death.

She knew the Battle Shaper's mark was there, but could see no evidence of it. The younger troll was the only one who had been touched by Laris. The queen wasn't ready to have the girl start marking her soldiers. She might never be.

The two trolls circled for only a few moments before the larger of the two made his move. It was hard to follow his speed even at a distance. Claire's eyes showed her only afterimages as he moved. People had to track more where he had been than where he was.

Tedar caught the attack by grabbing wrists and rolling to the side, tossing the larger foe hard into the stone wall of the field. The crash shook the ground nearly as much as the spear. The troll bounced off and was moving before most had even registered where he landed.

The next attack was more cautious and managed to work around the defense of the smaller troll long enough to connect a powerful kick into Tedar's midsection. He, too, flew hard across the flat ground, bouncing once before sliding against the wall.

Just like his opponent, he recovered and moved as if he were made of lightning. The two trolls exchanged blows a few more times, though each blocked enough to keep from getting thrown as far.

Eventually, the match came to a grapple, each sliding around trying to get a solid grip while keeping the other from doing so. Then the bulkier troll locked on with a thick arm around Tedar's neck.

Just as it would appear the match had ended, the smaller troll kicked out with his legs, shifting the balance of both and forcing a roll. Then Tedar's head snapped back, shattering the taller troll's nose and loosening the grip on his own neck. In an instant, the hold was reversed, only a short few seconds before the Boiling Blood left the taller troll.

The crowd roared; the fight was spectacular, though it lasted well under one minute. Tedar stood and helped the other troll up with a clasped hand, quickly lifting the now lean body before shedding his own Boiling Blood. Each gave the other a salute, a clasped fist over the heart accompanied with a slight bow, before turning and directing the same to Claire.

She stood and clapped before nodding to each. From her spot in the royal box, she was able to see everything she could keep up with quite clearly.

Her informants and spies had given her some idea of what they would be up against. If this was the power level of the junior division, Autumn wouldn't feel any shame in the coming Contest.

***

The moment Gray left, Jack found his hands full trying to calm his cousin. He didn't have Raine's authority, Claire's tact, or Joobel's charm. The only thing that kept Myrin in check was knowing she couldn't take him in a fight. Jack had been sure she would never attack a friend, but the wild anger in her eyes brought an uncomfortable amount of doubt.

She immediately started searching for the manticore who had the nerve to try and poison her. The slight shake in the ground told the prince she was trying to feel him through the earth even now.

Maeve made a low growl. The hound could sense the earth spirit that once belonged to her creator.

Jack had taken the earth spirit to remove the man's control of the golems and hounds that threatened all of Faerie. He wasn't sure if Myrin was influencing the spirit, or if the reverse was true. Either way, she was dangerous in this state.

Some sprites were getting a bit close, curious about Myrin's shouts and the rumble of the ground. Jack lit his eyes a bright yellow and gave them a look that ensured they stayed safely away as his cousin fumed and paced. His words were a stern whisper.

"Calm down."

Myrin turned on him. "Calm! You want me to be calm?! He tried to kill me!"

Jack almost jumped back as her ire was now aimed at him, but at least he could hold her off if she lost control. A low growl told both humans that Maeve wouldn't tolerate any attack on her master.

Myrin seemed to deflate, her temper finally losing its iron grip on her thoughts. Even she wouldn't risk making Maeve angry.

Jack sighed. "We knew he would use poison. He was oath-bound to do his best."

"I thought I was going to die again." Myrin squeaked.

She shuddered, the tremor running from her head down her back. Her fearful tone replaced the strong and imposing woman. The spindly girl from Jack's early memories stood before him. Her eyes grew distant.

For a moment, it seemed as if she were reliving that night in front of the Black Citadel. The night she gave her own power to her sister to avoid a civil war. Jack saved her that day, binding her to a spirit that once belonged to a very evil man.

The removal and replacement of the symbiotic spirits of Fairie was dangerous. It was something only he could do naturally, though it could also be accomplished with constructs. The only man who knew how to do that was eaten by Harvest. Jack did know one thing for sure.

"Your spirit and mind are not linked like you believe; your choices are still yours to make. My mother gave her spirit to Claire and yet was still present as a ghost and helped us leave Heluvot."

Myrin wiped the wet streaks from her dusty face. Trails of lighter skin could be seen where the fine dirt was washed away. She turned to look at him, daring him to pity her.

Jack wondered if she ever felt pity. He knew what it was like to have trouble connecting. The prince didn't look away from her hard gaze, only stepped forward to put a steady hand on her shoulder.

"Afraid you're past redemption?"

She gave no response; only the slightest tremble of her lower lip confirmed his accuracy. He shook his head as he spoke again, wondering why he of all people should have to do all the talking.

"You were a victim in Winter. You helped Raine take on her rule. Since then you've saved many more from a slaver's collar."

More tears trailed as she shook her head. She now spoke in the faintest whisper.

"Perhaps I have done good things, but I... I don't want to be nice. I want to hurt people, I want to destroy things. I want to walk through the ashes and laugh at the weak. I am evil. Deep inside, I'm not a good person. Where does that leave me?"

The bark of laughter shocked the woman; she could have easily coped with condemnation or an attempt to console. He was laughing at her, though he was trying not to.

The little brown hound was wagging hard against his leg, trying to be part of the merriment without any idea what was funny. Jack held up a hand to hold her comment until he could get the words out.

"You think I'm called Demon because I can sing? We're not bad because we are violent. It's only when we lose sight of who deserves it. We need others to aim us where the real evil is."

For the first time since leaving the Blood Keep that morning, Myrin smiled. Jack was always thrown by her ability to look so innocent and weak with that smile. His tended to make people step back.

It was genuine, though; even when they were very young, he could always tell when she was hiding something sinister.

Innocently, she hooked her arm into his and laid her head against his shoulder. She then led him down the path through the nearby trees, giggling like a much younger woman.

"Do you think they have apples here? I find myself famished."

The little hound growled low as she followed.

***

"Thunderbird?"

Gray was a bit thrown by the word being used to describe the avatar of the great air spirit. He'd heard the term before as a deity of sorts from the chieftain of the Stone Spears. At the time, he assumed it was some sort of idol. Though the feather was a curiosity, he'd been so busy he hadn't paid it much mind.

The old man smiled widely, obviously excited about telling the story. Blowing steam off the tea, the sage continued.

"Yes, the thing you seek isn't the bedrock of our realm, but a feather from its avatar. To accomplish this, you must pass through the Wyld to the Cave of Cinders. There you will meet a flame spirit who can direct you to the ruins of Akash, an old desert temple that contains an urn that holds a scroll that can only be unlocked...."

Gray had zoned out when he heard the word *feather*. As the old man continued to speak, he dug through his pack and pulled out the piece of oilskin. He held it up as he pulled the stiff cloth open to reveal the long yellow feather. It crackled with power; the static charge made the hairs on his dark arm stand up. As the old man trailed off to silence, Gray held it up.

"You mean like this one?"

The sage looked shocked for only a moment, then seemed to deflate. Leaning back in his chair and waving a hand, he sighed.

"Yes... that's exactly what you need."

Gray looked at the feather, then up to the man. His gaze went down, then up... down... up. Finally, his face went red.

"I got ruby slippered!"

The old man looked confused. "I'm not even wearing slippers...."

Gray's eyes went wild. "For months, I've been training, planning, and trying to pass trials! All the while needing to get home. I get here.... It was in my pack the whole time?"

"Yes, I suppose that's about right." The old man crossed his arms and frowned.

"You seem upset...." Gray could only stare at the wrinkled face that seemed so disappointed.

"I just had this really great quest for you. It would have been really neat."

Gray glanced at the feather. "I'm kind of in a hurry, though I'm sure it was a nice quest."

The sage nodded with a grin. "Oh, it was! There was a summoning spell and everything."

"That does sound pretty great, but since I already have the feather...."

The old man waved a hand. "Yes, yes, it's fine. Do you mind me asking where you found it?"

"It was a gift from some trolls. They kind of kidnapped my friend and I blew their village away."

The old man smiled again, seemingly over his depression. He gave a gruff chuckle as he spoke.

"Ah, you and I are going to get along well. I love a good story."

Gray returned the smile. He had much to do. Despite his frustration, he knew that the opportunity to learn from this man was not to be wasted.

"How does the training work?"

The sage was sipping his tea to wash down a large bite of bread and honey. He swallowed most and spoke around the rest.

"Id es mor of a gif dan a trenin."

Gray stared blankly for a second. "What?"

The old man finished swallowing. "I said it is more of a gift than a training."

"What kind of gift?"

Now the old man shuffled over to a large piece of parchment. On it was a long clean script. Though the words seemed old and formal, he could make out most of it.

Gray's dark brow furled. "What is this?"

The sage smiled. "That is your contract."

He quickly read the document. The words were clear; it was much more straightforward than any legal material he had ever seen. Basically, he'd agree to serve as the sage when the previous sage dies. In return, he would get the power and control that comes with the Pakaa.

There were no bylines or subscripts. He even squinted at the edge to make sure nothing was hidden. The sage laughed at his meticulous inspection.

"I signed one just like it, a very long time ago. The role is a good deal of work and you hear things that will break your heart at times. You get a chance to help steer events down a kinder path. Many have come here hoping for the boon I would give to those who complete the trials. Others just want to test themselves. You're the first that has come on a quest to help people. That, more than your victory, is why you're holding that parchment."

Gray cocked an eyebrow. "If I had come for my own selfish reasons?"

The old man shrugged. "I would have given you something of great value and arranged another test. Passing power to a child is a silly way to find an heir. So many problems down below come when the unworthy are put in charge of more than they can handle. I think you are up to this."

His large dark hands trembled as he held the contract. He had so much to do. Yet if they defeated the Black March, if Autumn could hold out against the other kingdoms, what would become of him? Claire didn't want him.

How could he spend a lifetime on errands for a queen who didn't love him? She was worthy of service, but it broke his heart every time she turned away. Here he could make a real difference without facing his own rejection.

"Great sage, you honor me with your offer. I have made commitments that I cannot deny and need to see my quest to its end. If this offer is still here when I'm done, I'd like to discuss it further."

"Ah, my boy, that's a fine answer. Since the contract is on hold and you already have your feather, allow me to give you this to help you complete your task. You did win your trial."

Gray started to ask what he meant when a bolt of yellow light shot from the old man's palm and crashed right into his forehead. His head swam and he cried out, though no sound left his mouth. It was as if his whole body clenched up so hard that every muscle would be sore for days; then as quickly as it began, his body relaxed. Looking up, he stared at the old man.

"Herbegtuler."

The sage nodded. "Yes, I know, the power over lightning is quite a gift, but I like you. I think you will do good things with it."

"Jatburcelep."

"Of course, you will need to acquire control as you would with any skill. I just broke down the wall in your mind, set the basic skill up in your thoughts, and gave you a bit of a boost in overall power."

"Weth runge wit meh muth?"

"It seems obvious that you are grateful beyond words. Come see me when you have decided one way or another about the contract. You're always welcome in the realm of Dawn."

"Waith... wut?"

Gray's eyes went wide as the feather folded back into the cloth on its own, the parcel slid neatly into his pack, the pack moved into his lap, and he shot out the door. He flew faster than he had ever managed before. Backwards. His pack still in his lap and a warm cup of tea in his hand that wasn't even spilling.

In seconds he landed smoothly in the tall grass of a clearing. Jack and Myrin were sitting on a bench to one side, eating a couple of green apples. Maeve was about ten feet deep into a hole she was digging through solid rock.

His friends left the bench and walked over to him, Myrin swaying as she moved beside Gray. She leaned down over him, showing more than was respectable, before taking the cup and downing the rest of the tea in one gulp. It flew from her hand back in the direction Gray had come from. She laughed at the sight, then looked down.

"So, how did it go?"

"Eth em nod surg."

Jack shook his head. "Like I said... gibberish."

***

The life of a queen was busy. At least that is what Yoshiko once believed. She put in the request to spend time with her mother and Sayuri responded almost immediately. As a young girl she used to thrive on the woman's attention, savoring every second the elder Cerelia could set aside for her. Now as a princess she dreaded these visits.

It wasn't because she didn't love her mother. Yoshiko moved down the spotless hall leading to the queen's rooms. A guard posted outside gave her a pleasant smile and a gracious bow.

"You are expected; go right on in."

He moved to open the door and she entered the queen's apartments. Queen Sayuri didn't share her living quarters with the Alder King. He was known to visit this part of the east tower, but not often, and Yoshiko was careful to avoid having to deal with him directly.

Her mother stood at the balcony rail looking out at the flawless city of Amaya in the dark night. Lights twinkled out from the city dome below.

The queen was beautiful, but in an unconventional sort of way. Her hair was slightly darker than her daughter's and she had a pleasant face that seemed to have just entered adulthood.

To a human, they would appear much more like sisters than parent and child. Yoshiko had gotten her lack of height from her mother and she stood eye to eye with the queen when they were face to face.

"It's good to see you, mother."

The queen turned, seeing her and turning back to the view with no change of expression.

"Hello, daughter."

Yoshiko winced at the sound. The words weren't unkind, but the tone was distant. It was as if Sayuri barely even registered that she had a daughter. The princess set her jaw and pushed forward, hoping today would be different.

"I'm excited about the upcoming festivities. Have you heard from the other kingdoms?"

There was a long pause, the queen staring absently at the lights illuminating the streets below. Sayuri gave a sigh and turned to answer.

"It is good to have festivities."

Her mother's face turned back to the lights flickering below. It was like this every time the princess visited. It was as if she would scream at her mother across a wide chasm and the woman would barely notice the words.

Yoshiko wiped her cheek and leaned in, feeling the closeness of the embrace even if it wasn't returned. She fought through the fog in her own mind.

Things were not right. Yoshiko was home but never felt safe. Never felt loved or close to anyone. The entirety of the Beryl Gardens felt like this.

Her only reprieve was her outings to the city. Each time she would find her heart and plan on what she'd do and say upon her return. Then she would return and forget those plans. She was so much happier before: before she was a princess and before her mother ruled a kingdom.

Did her mother rule a kingdom? She wondered if the woman could even dress herself. Yoshiko leaned her head against the woman in her arms. She felt the willpower harden inside her and whispered into the queen's ear.

"Are you even here with me? Do you see me? Do you hear me? Do you even have the will to hug me back?"

Yoshiko felt a shudder in her arms. Her mother shook for a long moment and then turned to look her daughter in the eyes. A tear flowed down one cheek as Sayuri opened her mouth to speak. The words were silent, her mouth opening and closing with no air to make sound. Finally, she was able to get words out. They broke Yoshiko's heart all over again.

"Hello, daughter."

CHAPTER 5

Ruling was a great deal of work. Raine remembered what Claire had said and corrected herself. Ruling *well* was a great deal of work. Part of her wished she was less compulsive about making sure everyone was adequately cared for.

The tank was built at the top of a tower, just a few paces from the edge of Loch Mozeg. The progress on the project seemed quite slow despite Autumn sending several earth shapers to help get it complete.

Raine had no trouble giving the order for the project. Unlike Autumn, who had little experience with both hands-on rulers and the Black March, the citizens of Winter offered little resistance. Once she explained it would help protect them from the strange enemy that attacked them, no one objected further.

At first glance, the whole thing looked like a drinking glass. On top of the tower sat a large cylinder that was nearly thirty paces across and forty paces high. Gray told her it would hold over a million gallons of water. Most of that seemed like nonsense, but what he said would work usually did.

Every city in both Autumn and Winter would be connected. All the drinking water for every citizen of both kingdoms would go through this tank. Every drop of it would be infused by both her and her bonded dragon, Mist.

Gray called it an 'active deterrent,' and explained that anyone who was infected by the Black March would burn the corruption out every time they took a drink. Anyone who couldn't sip the water was likely affected.

Tonight, the last touches were being finished. Soon she would fill the massive vessel.

The tank was a dark grey, unlike the red stone used in the south. The top had a thick roost so the dragons could use it as a staging area. This would both give the high perch a secondary purpose and make sure no one dared tamper with the water but her.

The older man came up to let her know it was finished. He was a proper sort in his worn suit, though she had loaned him and the other workers some of the guards' warm leathers and furs. Mist landed just a few feet away and nodded once to let her know her words would be heard by all.

"Thank you all for your hard work. I have gotten notice that the portals for water flow are complete. Soon this will allow us to give everyone in both our kingdoms pure, clean water."

There was a muffled cheer. Most of those present were cold and tired. The queen didn't push for more pomp; she was also quite cold. Even more so when she used the toe of each foot to slide the thick boots from her feet. Raine would need the power of Winter's great spirit for this.

She closed her eyes as the flow of energy built up inside her, then she held a hand out to one side as the water began to push against the ice on the shore of the Loch. Then a large crack formed, allowing the liquid to rush through.

A thick column of cold water moved next to her; she infused her Purification spirit through every drop as she pushed the liquid with the spirit of Flood. One power she had been born with, the other was the last gift of a dying great spirit. She would use both to serve her people, one final tribute to a grand power.

Mist moved next to her and blew a thin fog of her own Purification into the flow of water. This allowed Raine to push a much larger stream of liquid, now as thick as her arm was long, into the reservoir.

She filled the tank after several unpleasantly cold minutes. Portals inside heated the water and the heavily insulated walls kept it warm. The liquid wouldn't freeze even in the frigid cold of central Winter. The whole process would have to be done about every three days, even more often as other people started using it

Once finished, she pulled her boots back onto her cold feet and accepted a ride from Mist.. Tired as she was, there was much to attend to before leaving for Spring.

The Winter Queen returned to her chambers to find yet another body on the floor. Cruor was slouched in a chair while flipping a pointed dagger high into the air and catching it on the tip of his finger. Each time the point would draw dark-red blood that would run down his hand, then work its way back into the wound before it closed up.

The queen groaned. "Another one?"

Cruor shrugged. "Seems so. This one was from Summer, I think. I made sure to keep the blood off the carpets."

"Well, I do appreciate that; I swear they never have time to dry otherwise. How many is that this week?"

"This one is only the second."

Raine lifted a white eyebrow. "Are you counting the one Puddle caught climbing the wall?"

He shook his head. "Well... only two for me."

Raine peeled off the layers and soon was in the functional clothing she wore to attend to things when she wasn't holding court. Despite the steps she took to help everyone in Winter, many didn't like her changes in policies, most of all the one regarding slaves. The assassination attempts started right after she announced the new laws.

It had been months now and at some point, she assumed they would just run out of assassins. At first, there were more than three per day. Now that was an average week. Cruor made a game of it, and he always made sure the cleanup was easy. She didn't want to know where all the blood went, but it wasn't on her furnishings. It's incredible what can begin to seem normal with time.

The lean man never looked up from his game with the dagger, but he did seem to want to know how the tank was coming along.

"So... is it working?"

Raine slumped at her desk and pushed parchment around. She looked at all the reports and sighed.

"Everything is in place. Claire said Issabol will activate the portals one by one tomorrow to check for leaks."

The lean man nodded. "I'm proud of you."

Raine was almost startled by his words. He seldom said anything serious, but when he did, it had a habit of catching her off guard.

It shouldn't matter what the man thought. Currently he only held the title of bodyguard, though likely it would be Winter's Champion before long. Still, his statement hit her harder than she'd have expected.

She recovered and evened her tone before she replied. "Why do you say that?"

Cruor sat up and tossed the dagger aside. It embedded itself in the thick wood of the table. He never carried a weapon; that would have belonged to the assassin.

He moved to sit across from her, the large desk putting them two paces apart. He hit her with a broad smile, his long canines just barely showing.

"I've never heard of a ruler walking barefoot in the snow for the sake of poor peasants in another kingdom."

Raine sighed, a shiver from the recent cold running through her. "The project protects us all. Autumn is providing us with enough crops to get us through until we can settle our new economy."

Cruor nodded slowly. "True. Yet our kingdom's side of the bargain is met by the one person who doesn't have to do anything she doesn't want."

Raine wanted to get caught up on the stack of papers Hurley left out for her. Yet, she couldn't help but look up every time he spoke.

"Believe me, if anyone else could do it, I would be happy to delegate."

"You knew that when you agreed to it. Few of the great families would work so hard. I daresay fewer rulers still. You do what is needed for the sake of others. It's why I decided not to kill you."

Raine was now well and genuinely shocked. Cruor had been her personal guard for months. As strong as she was, he could have killed her on any given day for the duration of that time. Despite his casual words, she still didn't feel afraid of him.

"Decided? That's quite decent of you. When did my life become officially spared?"

He leaned back as he put his boots on the edge of the desk. A red knife formed in one hand, an exact copy of the one on the floor. It flipped into the air and landed on the tip of a finger. He seemed to be doing so without thinking as he spoke.

"Do you remember when you summoned me from my home in the mountains? Those with my skills are trained from birth to fight. There's no doubt what spirit a child has with these eyes.

You claimed my service right after you made many enemies in Winter. My father instructed me to kill you the night I arrived."

Raine leaned back at the implication. "You're telling me the head of a great house ordered my death?"

He shook his head. "I'm telling you *every* head of *every* great house has ordered your death."

This wasn't really a surprise, though hearing it aloud stung a little. The queen had known that these changes would have a price, even as she agreed to them. Still, understanding that one of the people closest to you was ordered to kill you is a bit surreal.

"Well, it would seem the deck is stacked against me. How is it I find myself still alive all this time later?"

He absorbed the dagger on the tip of a finger and then reformed it to toss again.

"It started with the yeti."

Raine remembered that. A young yeti girl had cut her leg on a sharp piece of stone. The wound went to rot and she got sick.

Regular healers struggle with blood poisoning. Word reached the Citadel and Raine flew for almost two hours on Mist to get to her in time. It was the first time Cruor rode a dragon.

She nodded. "Kotin is her name. She's quite adorable."

"Yes... yes, she *is*." He put emphasis on the fact that the girl remained so and wasn't long dead. His red eyes went distant; he looked thoughtful for a long moment.

"My father isn't a good man. Sure, he's smart and competent, and he does an outstanding job of seeing to the needs of the family's coffers. Yet, if he thought you would be good for his interests, he would have told me to protect you."

Raine nodded slightly. "So, it would seem I'm bad for his interests."

He huffed. "Well... yes, clearly. Now that night, I realized that had I killed you, that little girl would have died. That would've been like me killing the child. If I killed you the next night, who would you not be there to save? It could be anyone. If I let someone else kill you, that would be like watching someone else kill that innocent child. Soon it became clear that you needed to stay alive. I found that much more to my liking."

She tilted her head as she worked it all out. "What of this father who ordered my death?"

"The night you saved the little girl, I sent him a message saying that if anything happened to you, I'd hunt him down myself."

"That's quite kind of you." She cocked an eyebrow. "Do you regret choosing my side?"

Cruor shrugged. "Like I said, I'm proud of you. I'll stand with you as long as you will have me."

Raine wondered just what he meant by those words. Before she could ask, two guards arrived to take away the body of the latest assassin.

She turned back to her papers and continued working until the others left. The cook had a kitchen boy bring up a platter of food.

Cruor took the tray and opened it far from her. He always did so in case it was rigged to hurt her. He really was the ultimate bodyguard. Despite his appearance, it seemed there was more to him.

He made his own plate of fruits and vegetables; he never ate meat. Then he brought the tray over so she could make a plate.

Another knock at the door found a guard with a foot bath. Wisps of steam rose from the warm water. Cruor brought it over and set it under the desk.

He took each of her feet, rolled up the thick hose, and placed them gently in the warm water. Then he went to eating silently, keeping her company while she worked. The bodyguard was ever alert to any dangers that might come her way.

He was a bit older than her, but not by much. She'd have been much younger before the time spent with Jack in the world of fast time. She found herself staring at him as he ate his dinner.

Claire, Gray is all yours, Raine thought to herself as she chewed and drudged through each document. Ruling well was hard work.

It seemed there were benefits.

***

Issabol was finally enjoying some peace and quiet in her workshop. Bilney had taken the children on a walk outside her hut deep in the Twilight Vale. There were once threats that would have made such an outing dangerous, but the trolls in the valley had pushed away most predators. The guard woman was far from helpless and the young ones were quite safe with her.

Now the ancient child was able to focus on the many tasks assigned by her young queen. Despite the constant requests for crafts only she could do, Issabol was glad to see Claire use her own power to assist whenever she was able. It was always a good sign to see a queen willing to work hard. In her thousands of years, she'd seen many queens come and go. The lazy ones tended to do more harm than good.

As she focused, Issabol realized the quiet bothered her. Areena had been gone for months, off on some personal matter. The laughter of the young ones was constant. Now the silent workshop unnerved her.

Bilney left half an hour ago in Fairie, but nearly half a day ago by the workshop's measure of time. The Portal Master adjusted the output on one of the water flow portals. She turned when there was a knock on the thick wood at the entrance of her shop.

A tall man with dark skin stood there, his broad shoulder leaning on the worn wood. A travel pack dangled weakly in his loose grip. He'd left early that morning in Fairie, but nearly a week ago for her.

Her eyes glanced up for a moment, then she was once again focused on her task. Her voice held the tone of one who was giving only part of her attention.

"Well... you're still alive; that's a good sign. How did it go?"

Gray moved to sit on a stool near where she worked. He reached inside and drew out a cloth, pulling apart the folds to reveal the long yellow feather. The man carefully set it on the table next to her. He then sat silently as she finished her final adjustment and wiped her slender hands on a clean cloth.

She looked at the feather, reaching a hand out, just short of touching it. There was a faint sizzle of energy passing through the air. Looking up with wide eyes, she asked the obvious question.

"So... this is... I mean, I'll have to reshape it, but this..."

The man's eyes narrowed. "Thet is meh stoopid ruby slibber."

Issabol liked talking to Gray because he was both polite and intelligent. After a certain age, you lose patience with anyone who lacks either. Now he seemed to be speaking gibberish on more than one level. She looked at him and then reached a hand toward his forehead.

Gray slapped her hand away. Instantly, she could see he hit her hand harder than he meant. He waved a hand in the air as he took two long strides back. He held an open palm in front of her, the fingers curled into a rough imitation of a claw.

Issabol was hurt by his gesture, but her curiosity won out over anger. She stared at his hand as a spark moved from one finger to another. It passed to the next. The frequency increased as arcs of yellow-blue electricity began to coalesce into a small ball of lightning in the center of his hand.

Sweat ran down his brow and he quickly let the power fade. He reached out for a table and slumped onto a stool. His dark eyes pleaded for understanding as he looked at her.

"Eh stull cond cuntrul id. Oo mide gud herd."

Issabol nodded as he stumbled through his scrambled mind. Twice she'd met those who were spirit touched. Some could gift power and skill to a chosen individual, but it had a way of shaking up the mind.

He would be as good as new in a day or so. Better than new. She rubbed her hand and nodded to show she understood, then looked back at the feather.

"I won't ask for details as you need to go rest. I assume you want this as soon as possible. There will be enough for the other project. Would you like me to work on what we discussed?"

Gray looked relieved that he wouldn't be expected to speak further. He nodded with a broad smile and then reached into his pack once more.

He pulled out a long-stemmed flower, the petals a light shade of lavender. The color was close to the streak in her hair. He laid it on the table next to the feather. Attached was a note in a neat hand.

Thank you for all you do.
I saw this and thought of you.
Gray

Issabol nodded once more at him and watched as he walked out of the workshop. Not to the portal room that would lead him to the Blood Keep, but to his small room here in her home. No doubt, he was exhausted.

Her small hand reached out to stroke the soft petals of the flower. It really was a perfect match for her lock of hair. She picked it up and slowly breathed in the light fragrance, sweet and clean.

Despite the time that passed in her life, she had the heart of a girl of twelve autumns. Who knew how long it would be before she could marry or have children of her own? The gesture was the action of a kind and thoughtful man. He would have done so for any number of the people in his life.

Issabol began forming a construct immediately. Despite the urgency of her other tasks, she took a few minutes to make something for herself. She created a tall orb of iridescent purple with a hollow inside. It shifted to clear glass as a slow stream of her power was trickled in. Once ready, she slid the flower inside the spell-woven container.

Tendrils of clear liquid pulled the shape into a perfect pose. She closed the opening and flattened the bottom. The spell of preservation was a simple one. Applied with her long-practiced hand, it was as near to perfection as any inspection would allow.

Finally, she set the globe on a shelf near her main worktable and took one more moment to feel appreciated. She sighed and looked to her other projects. There was much to do.

The ancient child took a pair of long tongs and picked up the feather, preparing to make something she alone was capable of. She was going to give Gray the key to his home world. Her nimble hands worked in silence for another hour.

When the sounds of the children returning drifted from outside the workshop, a small smile formed on the face of the world's oldest child.

***

Jack rested comfortably on one of the sofas in the sitting area of the royal quarters. Gray left to deliver his prize to Issabol while Myrin departed for a well-earned soak in her tub. His bare feet rested on the table in the center of the room.

Maeve lay rolled into a ball on the thick carpet below. A guard had informed him that both his sister and Joobel were spending the afternoon at the school. The man was secretive about the reason, but that just meant the news was to come from Joobel. Honestly, that was fine with him.

Still, he was under orders to report the results of the mission. The conversation with Myrin had shaken him more than he wanted to admit. Her desire for violence had felt too familiar.

Jack always tried to let others make decisions. He was too direct, always thinking of the heavy-handed solution. He'd never hurt anyone when he could avoid it, but in truth, he often wanted to.

His mind wandered to those excursions to find those who needed justice. The battles and killing flashed in his mind. He relived the night he stared down Winter's army. He had killed a soldier with a ball of pure heat. Later that same night, he took the lives of several assassins. Did he do it because it was needed? Or because he wanted to?

One assassin survived that night and revealed the circumstances that drove her actions. Makani was given another chance and now seemed to be thriving. Didn't they all deserve that chance? Did he kill because he enjoyed it? Was he evil?

Only one thing he could think of proved he wasn't: the way she looked at him. His gnome was flighty, stubborn, and often too excited. She was also the most compassionate person he'd ever met. Joobel could never love someone evil, someone who killed for pleasure. She was proof of his own goodness; she stood between what he was and what he could become. Jack needed to see her.

To pass the time and allow his thoughts to roam, he began to work through the exercises that honed his skills moving energy. When Fluvial gave him the stone of heart-dew, she allowed him an unforeseen ability. It was weeks before he saw the potential, months before he fully gained control. He could wield basic fire and water. Combined with his spirit of Transition, he also gained control over heat and cold.

Before, he could take energy, usually from the realm. Once in control he could focus it into heat, flame, or concentrate the power for an explosion. Now he could use the same magic to draw the heat away and create cold, turning water to ice. He could combine the two abilities to create steam, mist, or even more substantial explosions.

Being potent with basic spirits is mostly about drawing power. A simple ball of flame is a real threat when it's large and hot enough. Drawing power was his real talent and the amount of energy he could control allowed him to practice things no one else could.

Yet he still had to restrain himself; even the reserves of a great spirit are not endless. Everyone in the realm relied on that power. Now he could flex his power without taking any away from others.

As the prince sat on the sofa, his eyes glowed a faint yellow. His left hand formed a dense ball of heat, so well contained that the nearby fabric of his shirt never singed.

He pulled the heat from his own creation and formed an identical orb of heat in his right hand while leaving a blue orb of dense cold in the left. Gray liked to explain that cold was not itself anything other than a concept, just an absence of heat. Jack didn't need to be told this; he could feel the channels of energy and the movement of the heat all around.

He passed the hour doing this until Claire and Joobel arrived. He spent that time flexing his power, moving more and more heat from one hand to the other. The orbs of each type grew denser and denser with each exertion.

As he heard the ladies approach, Jack drew on his power, making a construct he'd mastered over the previous weeks. He formed a stem of dense ice; leaves of detail formed along the stem, and as the shoot ended, it flowed into a perfect rose of dark-red flame. He created a tiny grain of both heart-dew and heart-fire into the construct. The stem wouldn't melt, nor would the fire go out, for as long as he lived.

The door opened and a gruff-looking guard walked in. He stared curiously at the prince standing there with a strange flower in his hand, then seemed to decide it wasn't worth getting involved.

As the Queen of Autumn walked in and looked up, she immediately moved to one side. Claire had gotten in the line of fire before and sworn to never do so again.

"... just love watching the young ones hone such amaz...."

Joobel stopped speaking when her eyes landed on her love. In a short second she was in his arms, lifting him in the air as she planted a kiss on his face.

"Oh, Jack dear, I was worried! You won, of course, but who knows? You could've been hurt and I'd have been so upset, but you're here now and safe and...." Her eyes landed on the strange construct in his hand. "Ooohhhhh... what's that?"

Jack went into a long speech about how much he cared and expressed himself as only he could.

"It's for you."

Joobel lowered him to the ground and stepped back, taking the rose in both hands. Her eyes glimmered as she looked at the gift.

Claire and Issabol could use maker magic to create things, but constructs are tricky. Most users of basic spirits are never able to make much more than a simple knife or shield.

The construct was a perfect blend of two opposing magics, yet remained in form even when no longer in contact with the creator. Jack was the only person in the world who could create such a thing. He made it for her.

Thick tears ran down the gnome's cheeks; she realized how much time it would take to learn this. He'd spent all that time for her sake.

"When did you start trying to make this?"

"I realized I could while I was recovering and training with Raine. I wanted to get it to you sooner, but they kept melting. I wanted it to be perfect. It took me over a year."

She hugged him tightly and wiped the tears on his shirt. Claire walked over and held a hand out to see the flower. Jack watched his sister inspect his work while he embraced his future wife.

The queen turned it around in the air and then held a hand above the flames to feel the heat. Then she smiled and reached down to the floor. Her own Transmutation shaped a small piece of stone to form a base and carefully set the rose in the center of the table. She looked impressed.

"How did you contain the heat of the petals?"

Jack shrugged. "Magic."

Claire's eyes narrowed. "Little brother, when I say I can turn you into a rug, you know I'm not lying."

He sighed and tried to explain. "Light doesn't really have to create heat. You can make one with almost none of the other. It takes practice."

Claire nodded in admiration. "I'd guess that creation is worth more than a Winter estate. It's a worthy gift for our adopted sister."

"I'm not his adopted sister, only yours. Soon I'll be your sister-in-law."

Joobel's voice was still muffled in his chest. She wasn't quite ready to let go. Claire rolled her eyes; gnomes could make things awkward. She looked around the room and then back to Jack.

The queen took a tone of authority. "Are you alone?"

Jack gave her half a smile. "I'm here with both of you."

Claire's tone shifted to a low growl. "Big... Fluffy... Rug..."

The prince just shrugged. "Myrin went to take a bath. She fights dirty. Actual dirt."

"And Gray?" Claire's knuckles were white, face slightly flushed.

"We have the stuff he required; he went to take it to Issabol. He said he would just sleep there. The old guy messed with his head somehow."

Claire's hope faded as her concern rose. She lightly bit her bottom lip.

"What do you mean? Is... he ok?"

Jack shrugged again. "When he got back, he was speaking gibberish and holding a teacup."

Claire smiled wistfully. "He always talks gibberish, though the teacup is a new touch."

The prince shook his head. He wasn't quite sure how to explain.

"This was different. You'll just need to talk to him yourself. Don't touch him, though."

Claire cocked an eyebrow and took a fighting stance.

"You don't get to tell me how to act, brother. I'm the one in charge here."

He smiled. "Fine by me. Myrin slapped him on the back and got thrown about ten paces. He's sparking all over the place."

Claire seemed skeptical, but let it go for now.

"I'll let him rest. Don't stay up too late; the next round of tryouts will be tomorrow."

Jack tilted his head. "Tryouts?"

Claire nodded. "I'll let Joobel explain. There will be fighting and Raine is going to join us for some of it. I'd like you both to be present."

The prince smiled; he hadn't been able to visit his cousin in some time. He also was ready for a more challenging fight. This all sounded promising.

"Say... Claire, is Cruor coming with her?"

His sister turned as she was walking to her room, her mouth open in a broad grin.

"I hope so. You two are the exhibition match to start the trials."

Jack grinned ear to ear. "You're too good to me, sis."

"It's why you're not a rug," she huffed.

Claire retreated to her room while Jack sat on the sofa and Joobel snuggled in close. The gnome gave him the best news possible. He was going to get to fight in a tournament.

Maeve made sure to wiggle against Joobel's leg a few times and put one paw on her arm to remind her they were friends. Joobel finally gave in.

The little hound got her belly rub.

***

Claire didn't know what to say. She wanted to speak to the strange man from another world. She'd made a decision and waiting was the last thing she wanted. Seeing Joobel still hugging Jack wasn't making things better. Why hadn't Gray come back to the Keep?

She soon found herself worried that she'd waited too long; maybe he moved on. Despite the need for rest, the young queen lay awake for hours as her mind ran through all the possibilities, both good and bad. Part of her wanted to wake Joobel in the next room. Though there was a real chance that she could get slapped.

Eventually, even her overactive mind faded into a fitful sleep.

***

Naoki ran through the rest of the day and into the stillness of the night. A few ember sprites and glow-shrooms could be seen through the darkness, but to most it would be difficult to move so swiftly without running into things. Had he been moving through a land devoid of life, the elf would have the same problem.

He focused a trickle of his power into his eyes and the aura of life in the trees and grasses lit his view and allowed him to continue his pace through the realm of renewal. He was making good time and would reach the capital by late morning. Thoughts of being able to hire help in watching over the trees filled his racing mind.

Sakura's voice snapped him out of his waking dream. "We have a problem."

Naoki slowed to stop. He could run and speak to her at the same time, but her floating spirit would hurt his head and in the black night he didn't want to risk injury.

"What is it?"

Her form came into view, details still clear despite the darkness. The tone of concern in her voice wasn't reflected in her wooden face, ever free of emotion.

"The grasses whisper of axes. Cutters have been spotted just north of us."

The elf's jaw clenched. "Homesteaders, maybe?"

He hoped it was just people looking to build a home or gather deadwood for cookfires. The forests provide many with homes and he wouldn't fault them for harvesting enough to survive.

Sakura tilted her head to one side. "It doesn't appear so. Eight move carrying axes, all moving straight into the heart of the willow groves. They seem to be seeking heartwood."

Naoki cursed under his breath. His efforts to protect the forests had the unfortunate side effect of raising the price of the precious material to the sky. One dryad's tree could earn a man more than three years of honest labor. Even the Green Man's legend wouldn't deter all.

He gave her a nod and shifted course. From time to time she'd give him direction, correcting his course or steering him around rough terrain. It was a good distance out of the way, but his primary concern was always the wellbeing of the forest spirits.

Naoki moved on his new path for twenty minutes when her voice came once more.

"They are close, move softly."

He moved through the woods, the soft undergrowth reaching out to catch his footfalls and silence his movement. The elf began to hear the cautious whispers of the cutters.

"... no wish to meet the ghost of the forests this night. Are you sure this is safe?"

The man's voice was deep; his shape was broad and he had a thick beard and long hair. Human and older.

"It's as safe as any job that pays five thousand talons for a night's labor."

This voice less deep, still older. The silhouette was elven, tall and lean, the long ears shadowing the view of life aura around him. Naoki held back his growl as a higher voice spoke.

"I don't like this, uncle. I heard these trees are alive and can speak like you and me. Isn't this murder?"

Naoki looked at the shorter shape near the middle of the line. The girl was little more than a child. He measured the height of the others. Three of these were basically children. The realization came to him just as Sakura said it in his mind.

"I think they hope to shield themselves. Use your reverence of life against you. They think we will not slay children."

His hands formed into fists, tanned skin growing pale as he clenched them. He sent his thoughts back to her.

"They're right. I won't slay children and I can't kill the others in front of them."

He could feel her apprehension. The dryads accepted him because he loved them. They had mixed feelings at best for the other races and no love for any bearing axes into their forests. She seemed to test him.

"Will we allow them to butcher my sisters?"

He let his own anger seep through to her as he thought of the little girl.

"Would you ask me to butcher mine?"

Both were silent for long seconds as he continued to follow the group into the forest. Most couldn't feel the heart of the trees. Yet any spirit of renewal could sense heartwood.

The lead cutter turned and looked into the gloom. Naoki could see the willow spirit long before, a beacon of life aura among the dimmer light to his eyes. The man paused, then turned directly to his target.

The willow dryad was young, perhaps only a few decades old. She had the ethereal beauty of her kind, but her words were unintelligible to his mind. Sakura translated for him.

"She asks why you wait. Her fear overwhelms her and she asks if Midori O toko will guard his flock."

Naoki sighed. Sakura was right of course; he was oathbound to defend all the forest spirits. Three of the larger men were already readying axes when a sapling near one whipped out and took the tool from his hands.

The bronze blade flew back to stick in the ground by the cutter's feet. The snapping of the handle was preceded by several small pieces landing near the tool's head.

The men murmured and moved into a circle, each looking out into the blackness. A whispered voice came out from the group.

"We have come too far to turn back now. Cover me while I fell the tree."

The cutter lifted his axe. A branch reached out again, only this time the ax stayed behind. The man was wrapped in several limbs and couldn't scream. Another man grabbed the fallen blade and turned to strike the willow tree. He was also taken.

Naoki wove his power in the shadows, plucking the men one by one and wrapping them in the branches of the limber willow trees around them. Finally, all that were left were the children. Sakura appeared in his sight once more.

"They will grow up to do the same. They will try where their fathers have failed. Will you pity a pup only to watch the wolf kill your flock later in the flow of time?"

Naoki was torn. His knew these meant the forest harm, but his heart couldn't bring himself to hurt them.

He ignored the dryad and stepped into the dim lantern light of the three children. All whimpered in fear as he held up a hand.

"Who would steal from the Green Man?"

None of the children before him could speak. The ghost of the forests was probably the very tale their mothers told them to frighten them into good behavior. He didn't work very hard to dispel those stories. Naoki could see words weren't going to happen, so he made a show of power.

Branches wove together all around them. In moments the four of them were encased within a wall of slender branches and green leaves. Naoki sat on the ground, motioning for them to do the same. He spoke to Sakura in his mind.

"Ask the willow spirit to come to me. I will power her avatar."

He could feel her disgust. To appear to another race was a gift few would receive. He was going to offer it to those who were unworthy.

Finally, his stubbornness won out and the willow spirit slowly moved a couple of paces from her tree. She could only move as far as the roots reached, but it put her near those seated. Naoki pushed his power forward and she became visible to the children as well.

He smiled to her and asked his question. "What are you called?"

Her answer was all shifting leaves and creaking wood. Naoki waited as Sakura translated her words. He kept his gaze on the willow dryad as he replied.

"Yanagi is a lovely name. Your tree is wonderful and we thank you for this time to sit beneath the branches."

He turned to the children. Each was wide-eyed and full of confusion. The girl leaned toward the dryad, with more fascination than fear. Her small hand came up as if it were not under her control.

"You're beautiful...."

Naoki gave away a hint of a smile. His request to Sakura to translate was granted and the willow spirit gave a nod of gratitude.

A branch lowered down and caressed the girl's face, bringing a giggle to her lips. He turned once more to Yanagi.

"Does it hurt you when your tree is harmed?"

The words were relayed to her and she nodded slowly, her face still free of expression. Naoki followed up his question.

"These little ones were here to take the heart from your tree. They would have killed you, but I think perhaps they didn't understand what that really meant. Should I end them all right here and now?"

Yanagi jerked her head to stare at him. Another round of swishing leaves and creaking wood held a faint tone of horror. Sakura shared the response with a sigh.

"She's offended you'd consider it. Which is quite odd considering she was begging us to only moments ago."

Naoki nodded; he might be on to something. He asked one final question of the willow spirit.

"Do you think, now that they know what you are, that you could forgive these little ones?"

The wooden face moved in a jerking nod. Branches came down and caressed each small face as she offered her forgiveness.

He turned to the children. Every face was streaked with tears. Whether it was fear for their own lives or the realization that they nearly committed murder, he could only guess.

He allowed his power to Yanagi to diminish and she faded from sight as he addressed the children.

"You live by her will this night. I will not harm you, but know this is the only time such a pardon will be had. Tell others of the ladies of the trees. Each is a creature of beauty and worthy of your respect. Do not attempt to harm my forests again."

Naoki backed up as the branches allowed him to slide through as if they were but a thick fog. He gave the command and the five men were all lowered to the ground. He considered speaking a warning, then looked down to his wooden limb.

There was a sharp series of snaps as each of them received a broken arm. Cries rose into the night as they whimpered and cursed.

The axes were broken, the bronze heads set into his pack even now. With no tools and broken limbs, they would harm no trees this night.

He turned to leave them with nothing but a single lantern and a story few would believe.

He was moving swiftly to Amaya as Sakura finally decided to speak to him again.

"The big ones might try again."

He sighed; she wasn't going to let it go.

"They might. The price for the heartwood is high and greed is common."

He could feel her apprehension, the hesitation to speak the words. She managed to somehow mutter as she spoke into his mind.

"I'm glad we didn't kill the little ones."

His face broke into a wide grin. The dryad was silent the rest of the night. Naoki guessed they would make the city by late morning.

If he didn't have to make any more detours.

CHAPTER 6

Joobel wasn't a violent or angry person. Her spirit was one of life and joy, but she loved watching a good fight. It was a treat to get to spend some time with the Winter Queen whom she'd grown close to during the preparations for the Bitter Challenge. During that time, she feared the young woman's attraction to another recent addition to Autumn.

She wished Claire would just marry the man and be done with it. Sadly, Joobel couldn't force the queen to do anything despite her many efforts to do just that. The gnome could see the danger of Raine's attraction to Gray from a mile away.

Though she diffused the dangerous situation the last time the Winter Queen got him alone, the gnome dreaded it happening again. It almost annoyed her that Raine seemed to have fixed the issue with absolutely no help from her.

When Joobel had first met Jack, he wasn't quite fourteen autumns. Even then, the boy was strong, earning his title from the gnomes the night she first laid eyes on him. It was shortly after that he defeated his teacher Torg.

No one else had been a real match for him since then. Only Gray was able to beat Jack and then only on occasion, with the prince using only fire. There were times when he lost to multiple opponents, or a dragon, but never in a fair fight.

Cruor was getting closer every time they fought. The two young men were close to the same size, with Jack being a bit older and broader in the chest. Joobel knew well that if Jack used his real power, the fight would be over quickly. He never used that skill in a duel. He relied entirely on his ability with fire and it usually was more than enough. Cruor fought like a snake, coiled in defense until an opening presented itself. Then the young man hit hard and fast.

The first time she saw them test one another, she was surprised to see the younger man pull his gleaming red weapons seemingly from thin air. Cruor preferred to fight close range with living blades the length of long daggers.

Joobel looked at them through her power, her ability to see the aura and flow of life energies. They glowed with the same hazy red aura that emanated from the man himself.

She knew the nature of his spirit in that moment. Cruor was a Leech, a user of a type of water spirit that dealt exclusively in blood. The weapons he used were constructed from his own lifeblood, infused with his power and able to change at his will. It didn't really have to be *his* blood.

The blades shifted in size as the man fought, sometimes lashing out to strike at foes seemingly on their own. Even with Cruor's speed and skill, Jack was still able to best him in every fight.

Then one of those blades drew a small scratch on the Autumn Prince's arm. The wound was tiny, yet instantly Jack seemed to be fighting through a haze as if he were full of strong ale and wearing weights. As they continued, the Leech seemed focused on the wound, as if it were precious to him.

Through her eyes, she knew why. The flow of energy through the cut was clear. Only a desperate blast of heat had broken that focus and Jack cauterized the wound before more power could leak out. Jack might not have used his ability to manipulate energy in the fight, but he couldn't hold back his perception of leaking spirit magic.

That fight was close. This exhibition battle was closer yet.

Both men had stripped to the waist, with Jack wearing his preferred short trousers and Cruor wearing his black leather pants tucked into black boots. The prince's shaggy brown hair was combed haphazardly to one side, revealing the light tan of his face, his attempt to look nice for her.

By contrast, the younger man had pitch-black hair that was short all around except for the front. The longer bangs allowed it to hang down to hide those bright red eyes. The Winter guard had skin that was a little darker than snow, which wasn't uncommon in the frozen north.

Jack fought more cautiously now, keeping his defenses up and countering any incoming attacks hard. He was usually much more relaxed; his level of focus was a compliment to the younger man. Cruor was also keeping his defense up; the last time he challenged this man he'd gotten a good deal of that black hair singed off.

The prince moved in with a slash of heat and bright yellow flame which was blocked by the red daggers. The left-hand blade snaked out and thrust at the forward leg of the prince. Jack lifted the leg before impact and coated his right arm with a construct of orange flame to block the more subtle attack coming for his shoulder.

Jack pushed off with both legs to whip a wave of heat forward as he rolled back. Cruor turned to the left, letting the tide of blistering warmth pass him by, one boot now smoking from the near miss. Jack extended a staff of fire, then began to spin it around in his hands while Cruor's daggers slithered out to the length of whips.

The crowd, ordinarily loud and emotional, sat silent as the two fought. Rumors of the things the Autumn Prince had done were common gossip, and the chance to watch him compete in person brought the school no small amount of admission sales. The students were all allowed admittance for free. As Jack was an instructor, this was considered part of the curriculum. There were perks to being a student.

The staff of flame began to spin faster and faster, ripping the lashes of the red whip away before they could find flesh. Suddenly small orange balls started to shoot out from the staff. Cruor rolled to one side and smiled at his dodge when the nearest one exploded. Large pieces of dirt and grass pelted the younger man's flank as Jack returned the grin with a half-smile of his own.

The tip of a whip then shot up from the ground. The sound of movement alerted Jack to the attack, but it still drew a line of red blood up the side of his leg. Instantly he moved as if wading through thick mud.

A hiss of steam ended the development. Jack cauterized his wound as fast as possible. As quick as the stupor began, his head cleared. He pointed the tip of the staff at the Winter guard.

Cruor realized what was coming and gasped at his opponent.

"By the spirits, man!"

A constant stream of small exploding balls began firing toward the Winter warrior; he dashed and moved, trying to get his footing. Then they began to explode. Soon the amount of dirt and grass raining down made it hard to see what was going on. The final moments were shrouded in a haze of steam and dust.

Slowly the air cleared. Jack stood over his opponent, the staff of searing flame only an inch from Cruor's chest. The silent crowd broke into cheers and cries. Despite the defeat, many were cheering for the Winter guard. Few held out for so long against Autumn's Demon Prince.

Jack held out a hand and helped the younger man up. Both were wearing broad smiles as they walked off the field together. As they left, a tall man with a school staff uniform began using his earth spirit to repair the torn field and prepare for the next round.

***

Gray was exhausted and knew that he should be at the trials this morning. He even got a message saying that Jack would be fighting an exhibition match with Cruor, but he could hardly move. It took all he had to force himself to speak to Issabol before taking to his bed. He slept for almost twelve hours and still felt bone-weary.

He sat up, still in the clothes from the day before. He tried the words out loud.

"Meh nam es Greh."

It was an improvement. He'd hardly understood himself when trying to speak to Jack and Myrin. It had been only a bit better with Issabol. Holding out his hand, he formed a claw.

The sparks appeared more quickly and with much less effort. The electricity formed into a small orb. He tossed it up into the air, and it held together for just under a second before the energy dissipated out.

He was trying to look at a magical event with his logical mind. The best he could understand, the sage wrote a program and set it off in his head. It was rewiring his brain to give him access to parts of his power he might have never learned on his own.

As he wielded the new ability, he could feel the dry air moving and building a charge. His spirit could sense the static reaching voltages that allowed it to flow outside his fingers. He was surprised he'd not thought of it sooner, but wouldn't have known where to begin to actually do it.

It was like playing the piano. Anyone could play a note and most could learn "Mary Had a Little Lamb" in a couple of afternoons. This ability was to air magic what "La Campanella" was to the piano.

This would have taken many years of practice, yet he was doing it like he'd always known how. If he continued at this pace, he would be able to speak normally in a couple of days. Who knew what the power would become? Other than the sage, of course.

Gray forced his tall frame to a standing position, only stumbling a little. He moved to another gift he had helped make for Issabol. As far as he knew, the ancient child owned the only hot shower in all of Fairie. He found that it was easier to convince Claire to invest in infrastructure if he demonstrated the benefits with prototypes.

The exception was flushing toilets; those she agreed to immediately. He wondered if the distribution tanks were done and would have asked Raine if he'd been at the exhibition match. He moved the lever to allow the hot water to flow and then adjusted the cold to bring the steaming liquid to a comfortable temperature.

It felt good to wash away the filth of his battle with the sphinx, though most of the dirt was Myrin's doing. Gray was glad Jack was there. He wasn't sure he could have kept her from getting out of hand.

The hot water loosened his tired muscles. Dressed and drying, he entered the kitchen, only peeking into the workshop long enough to see the children all learning their craft.

Issabol complained of the imposition, but he could see from her smile that she loved them. The guard woman, Bilney, was there as well. She was reading a story to the little girl Laris, the one who seemed so far from reality. Gray had an idea about her he wanted to test eventually.

In the kitchen, he raided the cupboard and found some dried meat, cheese, and bread. He'd just begun to cram food in his mouth when a small girl with dark-brown skin, long brown hair, and eyes shaped like almonds came to sit across from him. She was cute and inquisitive, maybe ten or so. She squinted hard at him as he continued to chew. He assumed she saw him looking in on them. Finally, she smiled.

"Your skin is really dark."

Gray smiled back, pushing the bite of cheese down before he replied.

"Meh ancesdors luve in a plass with a lod ob sun."

She nodded as if that made sense, then she quirked an eyebrow.

"What place is that?"

"Meh fader's ancesdors er frob a plass called Afriga, my mudder's once libed in Cendral Emeriga. Dere is soom odder mix in, bud it es whad makez meh... meh."

"I haven't heard of those places. Also... you talk kinda funny."

"Few here woub hav, I am frob anodder worb. Meh talging wilb ged bedder."

This statement seemed to satisfy the girl. He hated the way he sounded, but she didn't seem to care.

Her tendency to squint seemed a bit off. This was the first time he had spent any time with her and he wanted to test something. He reached for a piece of paper and tore off a scrap. He drew a tiny but straightforward picture of a bird.

She tilted her head curiously. "What are you drawing?"

He held the picture back past his face but facing the girl.

"I woub lige you to telb meh wheb you can see whad ib is."

He moved his hand slowly to her face, and she looked hard at the picture. It was only a few inches from her face when she smiled with excitement.

"It's a bird, silly!"

He smiled back. "Veby gud."

Gray set the paper on the table and realized that she was extremely nearsighted. She would struggle to learn to read or recognize people who were more than a few feet away. He finished eating while answering more than a few questions from the inquisitive girl.

Despite her near blindness, she had a quick mind and seemed to follow sound logic with her follow up questions. Jack said that all three of the students staying with Issabol were having great difficulty before being moved here. This girl was far from stupid, yet she hadn't been able to keep up with the other children.

It was easy to make such judgments when you were dealing with large groups of kids. He was going to push for some one-on-one time for each student with people who could help find the cracks these children were falling into.

He wanted to help this girl today. He had an idea of how he could do that.

"Zay, Toba?"

"Yes, Gree?

He couldn't help but smile; she was making fun of him.

"Hob woub you lige to go wid meh to zee dah queeb?"

She giggled. "I bot nuddin elbse to doog,"

They both laughed and though his head swam, he decided there was no good reason to wait. If his idea worked, it would happen quickly. If not, he could have her back in short order.

Once he finished eating, he packed his things from his room. The girl shadowed him around until they got back to the workshop. Bilney seemed upset and scolded the girl.

"Toma! I've told you not to wander off; I was looking for you."

The tone seemed to have no effect on her; she squinted up.

"I was with Gree."

Gray nodded that she was with him. He then asked permission, a couple times, for her to go with him for a while. Bilney was cautious but finally agreed once she heard what the tall man wanted to do. He wasn't the only one who'd figured out the issue with Toma's vision.

Issabol moved over and held out a small disk to him.

"I was able to finish it early this morning. I assume you'll want it applied like we did with the last ones. Also, these are ready as well."

She handed him a slender box. He opened it to find two batons. Each had a slim grip that moved into a rod just shorter than his forearm. The whole of each was made of iridescent purple.

He set the box on the table and picked up one rod. He trickled air spirit into the handle and the rod crackled. He tapped his other arm, and the charge of electric energy would have been enough to knock him down if he didn't seem to just absorb it. He smiled as Issabol explained.

"Your idea worked out well. The bit of the feather alters any magic into that crackling stuff you make. It's a fine gift; I think they're a good idea. It's nice of you to help her."

"She deserbs dem."

The ancient child nodded and smiled. "I thank you for my gift too."

Gray looked up to see the flower inside the globe of what appeared to be glass. He'd picked it up because it was the same shade as the girl's lock of hair. It was an afterthought, yet it seemed to mean a good deal to her. He realized how lonely she must feel and was even more glad the children were here.

"Id waz meh pleasub."

He thanked Issabol for her work and promised to come back soon to visit longer. Bilney packed a small satchel for Toma and they moved into the portal room and stepped through to the Blood Keep.

He really hoped this would work.

***

Joobel flitted her wings as she watched her love exit through the combatant's entrance, then turned to the honored guest sitting next to her in the royal box.

"So, Raine... when did you fall in love with him?"

The queen sputtered only a little and then pushed her white hair behind one ear as she turned to face the gnome. It wasn't in Joobel to back down as her bright-blue eyes met Raine's with a challenge to deny the truth. The Winter Queen knew there would be no point in a lie and sighed.

"I'm not sure of that myself. I live in a dangerous land and most of those in power want me out of the way. When he is near, I feel safe. He makes me feel important." She looked away as she spoke, as if embarrassed.

Joobel gave a snorting laugh. "Being a queen doesn't meet that need in you?"

Raine shook her head. "I'd be surprised if there was ever a more thankless job. If things are going well, then you're largely overlooked. If things go poorly, you're always to blame. That man seems to care less about the result than my intentions. I do think I love him... really love him. It's a new experience."

Joobel was well aware of the nature of ruling. She'd spent more than enough time at court to know how people saw those in power. Raine's honesty was refreshing; Claire could learn something from her. The gnome hit the Winter Queen with her best smile.

"When will you tell him?"

Raine shrugged. "He was sent to kill me."

Despite her words, Raine didn't seem bothered by this. The gnome's head shifted slightly to one side. She stammered only slightly as she probed.

"I might... need some... context there."

"He told me his father sent him to execute me the night I met him. Gave me the whole story of how he simply decided not to. He's been protecting me ever since."

Joobel gave a slow nod. "Well, that makes this easy... sort of."

Raine gave a muted chuckle. "Easy? Please explain."

"Well, he went against his father and his family. He puts himself in danger constantly for your sake. It's safe to say he cares for you as well. So, it's mostly good."

Raine put her face in her hands and sighed. Then she looked up, parting the fingers of one hand to look out. "Why mostly?"

"I have a feeling you won't get along with your in-laws."

Both women burst into laughter as Claire moved into the box overlooking the field. She smiled at her companions.

"I won't be able to stay past midmorning, but I wanted to see our little Stormcloud fight. I asked them to move up the Tempest. Are Jack and Cruor not back yet?"

The gnome smiled up at her queen. "They just finished; should be up after they clean up."

Claire nodded. "Did either of them cheat?"

Joobel held up a hand and wobbled it. "Cruor tried a couple of times. Jack held back the right amount."

She made no attempt to hide the knowledge of Jack's real power. Raine was very aware of what he could do, but she was the only one from Winter who had such knowledge. Few knew that Jack was also the Man of Frost who aided in the Bitter Challenge that earned Raine her crown. His disappearance after the battle had grown into legend.

Claire only nodded; she knew he'd never reveal himself without good cause. The sound of the bell rang once again and all three women looked out to see two contestants beginning the first of the duels.

***

Only a little worried, Bayu readied himself for the match. His opponent was a girl named Edana. He hadn't spent much time with her, but she was incredibly sweet. She went out of her way to help people and was one of the reasons the school had pretty much no bullies by the second day of school or so. She had short brown curls and was curvy for being so young, only a few moons over fifteen autumns and slightly older than he was.

Both had perhaps the most potent flavor of spirit of their respective elements. Each was trained by the prince himself. Bayu was a Tempest, one of two in the kingdom. He could wield air and draw on the power of storms.

Edana held a scary form of fire spirit known as Inferno, the same as the queen's father, the previous winner of the Contest of Champions in Winter. She could move heat and burn things from the inside. For a fire aspect, she was also quite good with constructs.

Through mutual respect, they agreed to fight without using their most potent attacks, but each was planning on a bit of a display. He rubbed his wrist. The feeling of having his suppressor bracelet off felt a bit odd to him.

Bayu knew he didn't have to win to qualify; in reality, these trials were a way to show off what the students were learning. As long as he put up a good fight, he'd be on the roster. Edana was pretty much in the same situation.

As the bell rang, Edana began first. She drew an impressive amount of heat and focused it just below the top of the soil in the center of the field.

The moisture under the earth was instantly turned to steam and the pressure caused an explosion that shook the arena and shot debris high into the air.

Grass and rubble rained down on the crowd as they cheered with delight. The cheering waned, then abruptly halted as the sky began to darken.

Ominous clouds began to form over the arena; flashes of electricity sparked throughout the dark rolling mass. Just as the dust cleared from Edana's display, Bayu stepped out. His eyes and skin danced with the static charge of power. He pulled his hand into a fist and jerked his hand down hard.

The bolt of lightning brought a flash of light that left most blinded for an instant. The amphitheater style seating intensified the deafening thunderclap.

The shockwave that followed knocked the people back in their seats. The bolt struck dead center of the pit left from Edana's attack, the cup of earth holding some of the new explosion.

The fight hadn't yet begun. The field of battle centered around a hole that was about a quarter of the total space they had to fight in. The terrified crowd waited silently. Half were nearly deaf and had fallen out of the seats. These were children, not yet at their peak strength.

Bayu looked around and sighed. Perhaps they'd overdone it. He looked over to Edana and made a deep bow; she did the same.

Then one voice began cheering. It was light and melodic; he knew the voice. She taught his last hour statecraft class.

Joobel was clapping and shouting, all by herself, in the royal box. Both queens stood and started cheering as well. The Autumn Queen's voice then carried out through the arena.

"Well, I must say I'm glad these two are on our side. Autumn will be in strong hands for years to come."

Most of the crowd joined as well. A few still rubbed blinded eyes and looked a bit skeptical. The queen crossed her arms and continued.

"Now, if our students are done showing off... perhaps we can continue?"

Bayu and Edana bowed toward the royal box and then turned to face each other. He readied his defenses and tossed a small ball of air to get them started; the bell had long since rung. Edana slapped the ball aside without effort and they were at it.

He won in the end, though he was long past the battles where it was easy. He limped out of the circle with a few blisters and singed hair. Edana had a broken arm and what had to be some dislocated ribs, but she gave him a wincing smile as they exited the field to see the green dragon.

Far from where the two students could hear, the Autumn Queen addressed her counterpart from the north.

"So, Raine, what do you think of our students?"

The woman had gone even paler than usual. She shook her head slowly.

"I think Winter is going to start building a school."

Joobel clapped. "Oh, we know, dear. Claire said this would be enough to get you to do it."

***

Jack had been unaware of the contest brewing in Spring. While he was helping Gray in the realm of Dawn, everyone else was hastily getting ready. He didn't find out until his meeting with Joobel the previous night.

The prince relished that time, whether it be a stolen moment or an entire day. He'd come to rely on her more than he intended. She translated the feelings of those around them, allowing him to understand and empathize much more effectively.

Many tried to do so in the past: mother, Norim, Claire, and even Raine to some degree. While helpful, something was different when he was with Joobel, as if being close to her allowed him to feel more deeply.

The prince knew he'd been close to giddy as she told him they would be traveling across the world to be tested against the most powerful fighters of the four kingdoms. It was a relief to learn Claire accepted the challenge openly and he wouldn't have to try to convince her.

He was only slightly worse for wear after the match with Cruor, a fight he knew was to help solidify his spot on the roster for Autumn. Still, he would stop by to see Bloom later in the day to properly fix his leg. It gave him an excuse to check on the dragons, who were often kept far too busy.

Though he hated to admit it, he was going to need to work with Gray some more to stay ahead of the young man from Winter. Cruor was getting closer and closer to besting him. Jack also liked to fight close, but now he couldn't win if he didn't keep the Winter guard at a distance. At least not with fire alone.

Gray was the master when it came to fighting with strange techniques. The staff and the mass of exploding balls had been his idea. The oaf was a genius when he wasn't talking gibberish.

Cruor had left to join Raine in the royal box, as he didn't like having her out of his sight for more than a moment. The prince had stayed near the exit to the field to watch two of his students battle. Edana could already do things with fire that he couldn't, and she had the temperament to lead.

The boy, Bayu, worshiped Gray. In a couple of years, he'd be in control of more raw power. Had Claire not tested the children of this kingdom, nearly all these powerful spirits would have wasted away in obscurity.

The battle was impressive after the initial demonstrations of raw power. Even his ears were ringing as the bout came to an end. He greeted them both as they exited.

"You both fought well. Edana, you still need more control of your attacks, but you were much improved. Bayu, your match was clean, but I'm concerned about your ability to deal with close up threats. Keep your shields partially up when you are moving, or you can be surprised by your opponent."

The students bowed and nodded at his advice. They stood looking at him expectantly.

He sighed. "I'm proud of you both; now get cleaned up."

They smiled and moved away without a word. Jack knew how far that tiny spark of approval would go; he didn't shower praise. Having power wasn't something to be prideful of, but hard work should be acknowledged. Both of these young warriors had worked themselves to exhaustion.

Jack guessed he would see Edana moving high up in the military and Bayu a powerful soldier in just a few years. He had little interest in either, but he found his role of teaching quite fulfilling.

Other students were getting ready to move out and he walked through the halls until he was able to reach the royal box.

Immediately he could see Claire had run off, no doubt holding court and dealing with the details of state. He wouldn't want that job for anything. The idea of sitting with dusty papers while people complained grated up his spine.

He moved to sit by Joobel and found himself in the middle of an argument.

"Winter has enough dragons; we can take Mist and Brook and allow Puddle to represent Autumn," Raine argued, her face a bit flushed.

"Oh, it's a generous offer, but Bloom would be heartbroken if she were left behind. Besides that, she's a death dragon... sort of," Joobel replied.

Cruor scoffed. "I'm more of a death dragon than Bloom."

"Puddle is bonded to Depth, who's still a citizen of Autumn. You would break no law in taking him, and I'd bet the Citadel that pompous ass will try something if Bloom is there."

Raine's words were calm and even, but her frustration seemed to be growing. Joobel shrugged and smiled before continuing.

"Please understand, I've tried to argue the same thing. My Bloom sees being there as her duty. She has grown close with several of the children. The idea they could be hurt without her there to heal them doesn't sit well with her."

Raine shook her head. "Spring is covered in healers; there's no reason to risk a brood over her pride."

Jack was only half-listening. If Joobel started needing his help winning arguments, then blood would have to be shed. That last bit though, he wasn't sure he heard right.

"Did you say brood?" He arched an eyebrow at the Winter Queen.

"He doesn't know?" Raine gasped.

Joobel seemed to deflate a bit. She set a hand on Jack's arm and looked into his eyes. Her words were nearly a whisper.

"Bloom will drop a clutch of eggs in a few weeks. She means to surprise Claire."

Cruor chuckled. "Jack didn't even know? Well now I feel special."

Raine pushed her long white hair behind her ears and pushed for Jack to join her side.

"She will be a short time from laying when we're in Spring. You know this could go poorly. I disapprove of the risk."

Jack was still a bit in shock. His mind was running through many follow-up questions he felt were of the utmost importance. Then he frowned.

"Wait, is Harvest—"

The gnome slapped his arm and replied in an offended tone.

"No, my silly prince. She and Puddle have been mated for months now."

Jack had recently been in a fight with one of the most potent fighters in Winter, but this made his head hurt.

"Puddle?"

Raine stepped in, trying to move things along.

"All drakes can interbreed. Something about a common ancestor. It isn't common due to the conflicts between kingdoms. Bloom is the only female dragon in Autumn and Puddle adores her."

Again, the questions whirled around like a school of fish bouncing in a net. The next one swam to the surface.

"What will the eggs even be?"

"If she's hurt in Spring, we might never find out," Raine snapped.

Joobel squeezed his arm, all her frustration in her grip. He was reminded that gnomes were terribly strong and he'd have to have Bloom heal that bruise as well. Her words betrayed no emotion.

"Honored Queen of Winter. My Bloom is the size of a large house. She's proud and protective of the people of this kingdom, the children especially. So much more so as she's becoming a mother herself. The drake gives them rides and soaks up the sun as they play outdoors."

Joobel loosened her grip and sighed before continuing.

"True, she's no warrior and her breath would bring an enemy to greater power instead of hurting them. But don't assume that a mother of her size and power is helpless, or that she'd let her people be in danger without her. I'm happy to take you to her and let you ask."

Raine sighed, knowing she'd been defeated. All present knew that both Joobel and Raine could talk to Bloom at any time. Dragon-speak would easily allow it at this distance.

The only hope for keeping Bloom in Autumn would be a request from Joobel or an order from Claire. The Winter Queen gave up the fight with as much of her pride intact as possible.

"I will have her watched. If anything tries to hurt her, I'll bring Winter's might down like a hammer."

Jack processed that his kingdom might soon have more dragons. That hope was wrapped up in the gentle giant that healed the sick and watched over the school. The thought of anyone trying to hurt her made him want to wretch. His words brought a moment of silence from the box.

"Maeve will stay with her."

Both Joobel and Raine seemed to take this in, knowing full well what that little hound could do. Only Cruor seemed skeptical.

"That seems a bit underwhelming. I'm sure your hound is great and all, but shouldn't we think bigger? The pup is smaller than a hunting warg and we might be up against dragons."

Raine rolled her eyes and then elbowed his arm.

"Remember what Hurley said about the hound tearing through Spring?"

Cruor pushed his hair aside and cocked an eyebrow. "I thought he was joking. She's smaller than Joobel. How scary could she be?"

Jack smiled slightly but allowed Raine to handle the question. Cruor was her guard after all. She seemed to hesitate and then looked not to Cruor, but to him and Joobel. She spoke in a low whisper.

"I trust him with my life. It would be good for him to know."

Joobel only looked to Jack, his secret to tell. He decided that Raine vouching for the man was enough. He tried to explain.

"On the night of the Bitter Challenge, do you remember the Man of Frost and the rock warg?"

Cruor didn't seem to make the connection. Jack pulled a slim dagger of ice from the air and handed it to him.

Now both the guard's eyebrows went up. "Wait... this... this is impossible. You're the Man of Frost? So, then your hound is—"

"Maeve is... complicated," Jack sighed. "We don't know exactly what she is, but she's my best friend and can be trusted. She's fiercely loyal and will protect anyone she sees as family. Bloom is definitely qualified."

Cruor seemed to now be dealing with his own torrent of questions.

"Could she face a dragon?"

"She has already. Maeve is the one who killed River," Raine said.

The guard whistled low and shook his head. Jack knew Cruor would feel the lack of crimson power in the hound, that she wasn't what she appeared to be. This was still a lot to take in.

His red eyes flared beneath dark bangs. A smile crept across his pale face.

"Good to know. So, I guess Bloom is going to Spring then."

***

Yoshiko changed into a dark yellow sundress and brushed her chestnut hair down so that it came just past her shoulders. She hadn't taken the time to adorn herself with anything other than the pendant that was always around her neck. She made it into the city most days and today was no exception.

Her sandals clapped against the smooth white stone of the streets and she hummed a sad tune happily. She'd brought enough money to eat lunch at the markets and should have enough time to walk all the way to the shores of the Kessho Mere just south of the city.

The warm air blowing in from the south kept a few strands of hair always in her face. She spent much of her time pushing them back into place as her keen hazel eyes scanned the stalls for a suitable lunch.

It was the first time she heard that voice, but she instantly knew where it was coming from. It was just one word. It was in a language she hadn't heard spoken for many years, and then only in her history lessons when she was younger. Then the voice spoke again, the same word: 'Mikata.'

Yoshiko wasn't sure of the meaning. 'Friend' maybe? The mushroom that resided several feet under her sandals had chosen to speak to her for the first time, and all she got was one word. She couldn't even remember what it meant. It was helpful to not be shy in getting answers.

She looked around and saw an older woman selling warm dumplings filled with rice and seaweed. For an elf, "older" only meant she had fully developed features. Yoshiko approached and bought three. As she paid, she looked at the woman and smiled.

"Honored elder, if I may, could you translate Mikata for me?"

The woman smiled. "Yes, child, Mikata means ally. It is always good to learn the old tongue."

"You speak wisdom and your dumplings look delicious. Be well, elder."

"And you, child."

Yoshiko pondered this; Honey was saying the word 'ally' to her. She hadn't used words to talk with her before. It was still not difficult for her to know what the enormous mushroom wanted to convey.

Honey didn't like her new family at all. When she touched the tendrils in the garden and thought of Harumi or her mother, it would lie dormant. When she thought of the Alder King, it would feel hot and angry. She got a similar reaction about the king's son Ohkami. She had little contact with the king but could verify that the Wolf Prince was no fun to be around. Yoshiko avoided him at all costs.

She'd run through many subjects and people; Honey seldom reacted. For the mushroom to speak to her through her power was very much an oddity.

The first bite of dumpling burned her tongue, so she was blowing on the doughy treat when she heard the word again.

"Mikata."

It fluttered at the back of her mind like an insect landing on an orchid. Then she noticed the crack in the white stone of the walkway. Amaya was a pristine city. She wished resources could be more evenly distributed, but had to admit that the place was lovely.

It was odd to see a crack, yet it wasn't a coincidence to see a small white mushroom poking up through the opening. She reached down, not to pluck it but to trickle her power through the soft white flesh. At her slightest caress, the cap snapped off. The stem receded into the earth below. She shook her head in disbelief.

"Well, that was plain enough."

Bending over further, she picked up the white cap. Nothing. She felt no different, heard no new voices. She was disappointed as she looked up with a gasp. Every person on the street was surrounded in a faint aura.

It was like they had a small sun just behind them and the rays were peeking out on the sides in a rainbow of colors. She stood in amazement, looking through the throngs of people who each had a halo of light. Many were dim shades of green and blue, some brown, and a couple were shades of yellow.

She was confused. Honey was trying to lead her, but making people glow just made walking more difficult. She could see people just fine without—

Her jaw went slack as she saw him. Where all others were wreathed in the dim glow, this man had an aura of dark-green that stretched out around him. Even more strange, the dark-green pushed out like grasping fingers, ignoring the people of the streets and caressing the plants.

The grass at his feet leaned in toward him; the branches of a nearby tree were trickling power into him. Even the flowers at a market stall were gifting energy to his aura. The voice spoke in her head a final time.

"Mikata."

Yoshiko slowly shook her head. "I hear you, Honey. Guess I need to introduce myself to our new friend."

CHAPTER 7

It was only a short walk from the portal in the Keep to the royal quarters. Gray had a room there just up the hall from Claire and Joobel and right next to Jack's. He slept there less than half the time between his travels and overseeing the various projects of the kingdom.

The main chamber of Claire's quarters was a common meeting place and he was glad the guard recognized him and allowed passage without making him talk. It was getting old. Toma was holding on to his hand for dear life. He assumed she didn't wander much and she probably couldn't see much at any rate.

Gray moved into the room and grabbed a piece of good parchment, then one of the quills the queen always had lying around. He then began to draw a scaled-up version of a very tiny object. Claire was the only one he knew who could make this work.

The Autumn Queen had the ability to change the shape and function of living flesh or simple matter. She was also able to craft things with Issabol's help, but today it was the ability with flesh shaping he needed.

A few years ago, his father had blind spots appear in his vision. Gray drove him to the eye doctor many times and always read through the pamphlets when he forgot to bring a book. Glaucoma required regular treatments and so he had many appointments.

One of the things he read about was a procedure called laser eye surgery. It dealt with micro incisions with lasers and was far beyond what he completely understood. In essence, all they were doing was reshaping the cornea, the transparent layer in front of the pupil.

Claire would probably do more harm than good unless she knew what to change and how. He was drawing a diagram of the eye; the part showing the cornea would tell her what to shape. His vision was nearly perfect and Claire could look at his eyes with her ability, in order to see what to change in Toma's eyes, too.

It might not work, so he was answering Toma's questions without telling her what he was going to try. He was sure Claire wouldn't leave her any worse, but he didn't want to give the child false hope in case it failed. What he hadn't expected was for Claire to walk in the door several hours before the trials would end for the day.

They'd only been there for a few minutes when the door opened. The queen had her head down, reading a message and holding a quill that tapped furiously against her lower lip.

As the door closed, she looked up and locked eyes with him. She looked surprised, perhaps a bit cross, and even hesitant. She spoke before he could.

"I... We missed you at the trials."

"Eh wab feening tireb."

She seemed to pause, then accepted his odd speech.

"Jack said you were speaking more gibberish than usual."

Gray rolled his eyes. Jack never talked except to make his life more difficult. He nodded to save time. Claire continued.

"I was hoping to speak to you. I've been...."

The queen's eyes went to the girl. Toma had been so still looking at the drawing that only now did Claire realize they weren't alone. She seemed both flustered and charmed at the same time. The queen directed her words to the girl.

"Toma, isn't it? To what do I owe the honor of your presence?"

The girl was very much a child, but even she knew that you shouldn't be rude to a queen. She stood and walked over, giving an awkward bow.

"Gree said we needed to visit you. I think he was scared to come alone."

Claire couldn't help but smile. She turned to 'Gree' and winked.

"I suppose there are many who fear the Banshee of Autumn. Do you feel safer, Gree?"

Gray sighed, really hoping that nickname died horribly in an alley somewhere. He changed the subject and asked Toma to draw him a bird. She skipped back to the table and went to work on the drawing, leaning close to make out the lines. Gray gently pulled Claire aside and spoke.

"Eh thoub you woul be ad dee triabs all day."

She slowly worked through his words. "I will be leaving for Spring soon. I have to hold court or I'll get too far behind."

Gray nodded and began the long process of explaining what he wanted to do. She would need to use her power to study the shape of his cornea and then reshape those of Toma.

The conversation took much longer than expected.

***

Yoshiko slowly approached the young man with the strange aura. She took another bite of the dumpling, decidedly not burning her tongue this time. She pretended to be very interested in the bulky blue fruits the seller had on offer.

It seemed the merchant wasn't happy with the haggling. The young man wasn't a good negotiator. She took a moment to observe the interaction.

"You're trying to rob me! These fruits grow as a gift from the trees. You cannot charge me to eat what nature gifts us all."

The seller waved a hand. "The price doesn't change because you have seen a tree! Pay or be gone."

"You speak nonsense; the fruit should be free for all!"

Yoshiko stepped up next to the young man. She smiled at the seller while putting a hand on his lean arm. She gave a squeeze and directed her attention to the merchant.

"You offer wonderful stock; may I have two of your best?"

The merchant kept a close eye on the young man as he accepted her money and handed her two of the fruits wrapped in waxed paper. She sighed and turned to her *Mikata*.

"Oh, these are quite large; I should have only gotten one. Won't you help me eat the other?"

With that, she took his arm and dragged the man down the street. She led him through an alley and stopped at a stone bench sitting next to a thin sapling. There was a white marble fence and just beyond it babbled a brook of clear water.

She sat down and held out one of the large blue fruits. He looked around like he was afraid this was a trap. He looked for the ambush, pausing as if listening. Finally, he gave up and sat down. She smiled at him and probed for information.

"Did the plants tell you I was no threat?"

The man chuckled and took a bite of the fruit. He gave his reply around the sweet pulp.

"Actually, they said you're the most dangerous person I've seen all day."

Yoshiko smiled at this; most assumed her weak. She preferred it that way. He wasn't so foolish.

"I wouldn't have used the word dangerous, but I'm not helpless either. Care for a dumpling?"

She held out one of her two remaining treats; with the fruit she wouldn't need both. The man paused as he eyed the warm dough.

"What's in it?"

"Seaweed and rice, unless the old seller wanted to surprise me."

At this, he accepted it and kept eating. He seemed thin and very wiry. He was no doubt powerful. Honey said this man would be an ally. It was best to get to know him.

"So... does the price of lunch buy me a name?"

He gave a smirk. "Yes... I shall call you Apple."

Yoshiko sat in silence for a long moment, then made a groaning noise before trying again.

"My name, and yes I already have one, is Yoshiko. I assume you also have a name; may I know it?"

He smiled around the juicy bite of fruit. "I'm called Naoki, though I haven't heard it in some time."

He took another bite of the fruit as she tried to understand. She tried a third time.

"So, what do others call you?"

"Others, as in people, do not call me at all. Those who speak to me call me Midori O toko."

Yoshiko thought back to the old tongue for a moment before nodding. "Who are they? Why do they call you Green Man?"

"They are the life of this realm. The plants speak to me. In my experience, they are more worth listening to. I'm the Green Man; they call me that, for I protect them. Just as they protect me."

"Ok.... Well, I don't disagree that most people are hardly worth the time it takes to listen. If it's ok, I'll stick to Naoki."

He shrugged as he set the core of the fruit on the ground. The grass pulled it apart and the smaller pieces were pulled into the dirt below. There was a dent in the soil as some of it moved to one side of the bench, and then the ground tilled up as a slender sapling began to push toward the clear sky.

It gained mass as it reached further, more and more branches reaching out to embrace the rays of sunlight as it began to bud. In seconds, bright green orbs began to bud from yellow flowers. Then the branches started to sag with ripe blue fruit. Naoki reached up and plucked one taking a large bite.

Yoshiko was in awe. She'd never met a Nurture. It was considered an omen to have one born in a generation. All of the ones she had read about were part of the great families. This man couldn't afford to buy lunch.

Honey paved out a strange day for her. Yoshiko spoke once again.

"I guess I could have bought just one."

He nodded. "This one is fresher. I would guess sales will go down when others discover better fruit for free."

"So... Naoki, I'm guessing you haven't been in the city long?"

"Not since I was about ten or eleven. The last time I was here was to petition the last queen about the cutters harvesting the dryads. She was of no use."

Yoshiko tilted her head and cocked an eyebrow. "Wait.... I believe the cutters have all but gone. I'd say something must have been done."

"Something was done." He took another bite and swallowed. "It wasn't her that did it."

There was a long silence, and then she realized what he was saying.

"You're the ghost of the forests?"

"Not a name I claim, dear Apple."

"Apple is *not* my name."

He gave her a smile. "I'm not a ghost."

Yoshiko sighed again. This man was both difficult and strange. Yet Honey wanted her to speak with him, and he was obviously powerful. Her tactful questions were like swimming up the waterfalls of the mere. She decided if Honey trusted him, she should too.

"Naoki, I think it best that I tell you the story of why I bought you lunch. Then maybe you can tell me why you needed me to."

The young elf finished his second piece of fruit and then walked toward the sapling on the other side of the bench. It too began to grow and soon it was drooping with the weight of ripe red apples. He plucked two and took a bite of one.

The strange man the other out. "Apple?"

"That's not my name." Yoshiko smiled, but took the gift with a nod.

She told her story between bites from the best apple she'd ever tasted. How she was a Shiro and wielded the power of mushrooms. How she could communicate with the fungus that sat under most of the realm. Then how that being led her to him and called him an ally. He made no more jokes, nor did he scoff at her abilities. He seemed impressed and nodded along throughout.

"Everything you have told me is true. Most lie when speaking, even if they don't mean to. You have character and you respect the land and the life within it. I like you, Apple; I will share my story."

She almost corrected his name for her, but he grew serious. He started his story years earlier when he was born to a digger in the quartz mines to the West. His father died in a cave-in and his mother was taken by a sickness they couldn't afford to treat. Most in the village had little to eat and rather than ask for help from those who couldn't afford it, he went into the forests.

It was there his powers awoke. He was able to gather more food than he needed. He brought what he could into the villages as an offering to his own good fortune.

As he got older, the dryads began to speak to him and he learned of the cutters: harvesters of the heartwood of the oldest trees, ripping out the spirits within. He took his discovery to the queen, but she and her court were well aware of the crimes and profited from them.

Naoki decided to fight them on his own. He spoke of how he slowed and hindered them.

Then he told her of the time they caught him. How they took three swings to chop through the arm of a boy of twelve. How he bonded with the tree he tried to save, of the bargain with the forests of the realm. He told her of the justice he served to the cutters who hurt him and to all those since.

As she listened, Yoshiko was in awe of the strange young man. She hadn't noticed the nature of his arm until he explained how he earned it. The grain of the wood so closely matched his skin that she overlooked it at first.

Naoki saw the line of her gaze and held out his left hand. He rolled up the sleeve to show more of the arm constructed from the heartwood of an old cherry blossom tree, the living core of a dryad.

She started to reach out, then caught herself, ashamed of how rude it must seem. He grabbed her hand gently with wooden fingers. His grip was like iron, but he didn't so much as bruise her own calloused palms. Instead, he nodded to her grip.

"You work in the soil; it is good to have hands that are not a stranger to toil."

She nodded as she wondered at the living wood. "I enjoy time with life in the gardens."

"There is someone I would like for you to meet."

He held his arm to the side and stood still for a brief moment. A woman came into view, her hand resting on the palm of his wooden hand. She was only a little shorter than him, her skin a light red with faint lines across her flesh like the bark of a tree. She had long hair that was streaked with equal parts white and pink.

She looked at Yoshiko with wooden eyes. Despite her strange appearance, she gave a slight bow and spoke. It was now evident where the man got his peculiar sense of humor.

"Naoki, you spent all that time telling me you came to Amaya to compete for money. How you have no interest in winning a bride. Now I come out to look around and find you charming a princess."

The man's face went as red as his half-eaten apple. He glanced back and forth between them as his face fell into confusion.

"Wait... what?"

***

Claire was confused, happy, and frustrated all at the same time. What was a korneeyah? It was hard enough to understand this infuriating man without his words being jumbled.

Still, she was pretty sure he wanted her to do magical surgery on a child's eyes. Her only instruction in helping this girl was to be the confusing blather of an odd genius. She tried to follow along, but all she could think about was the fact that he smelled nice and that she felt whole because he was standing there with her.

Finally, she made out the general idea of what he wanted. The fact that this adorable child was nearly blind was heartbreaking. Once she realized what he was actually trying to do, she felt guilty for wanting to put it off. She looked at his drawing.

Claire didn't know the words for all the parts. Still, curiosity led to her scanning her own body with her power of

Transmutation. It was interesting to try and understand how everything worked. So, the *cornea*, she saw it written out now, was the clear lens in the front of the eye.

Really this shouldn't be that difficult. The thing was so small that the power would be nothing for her. Yes, this wouldn't be a problem.

Gray sat on the sofa and she stood behind him, closing her eyes and scanning his. She paid special attention to the lenses in front of them. Then she studied her own with her power. She altered her left eye to match his.

Well, it would seem her eyes were a bit off, too. Suddenly she could see the far wall much more clearly. She hadn't even realized this was an option. Claire quickly fixed the other eye, then slowly tweaked the new changes to acquire perfect vision.

She'd long ago decided to not change her own body for the sake of vanity. Sure, she could tone her thighs or have longer legs. She could straighten the curls at her temples or remove the three-lined scar that covered one cheek.

But she had seen first-hand what could happen if you did so. The mad Queen Wenette didn't even remember her own face. This was different; better vision wasn't a matter of vanity, it was functional.

She leaned forward and whispered in his ear. "Tell me when it stops getting better."

Her power shaped his eyes as well, already good but now perfect.

"Dats much bedder."

She smiled at his words and then walked over to Toma.

"So Toma, how's your bird coming?"

The girl squinted up with a frown. "It's ok... kinda has a fat head."

It did have a fat head. Maeve would like it though. She smiled down at her little patient.

"I was wondering.... I have a special skill. You know how you can make more of something, like copies?"

Toma nodded. "Yeah, I can make lots of something if I know what we are making."

"Well, I can fix eyes sometimes. So that you can see clearly from much further away. Would it be ok if I tried to help you?"

Gray stood and walked over, waiting for the girl to answer.

Toma bit her lower lip. "Will it hurt?"

Claire thought for a second, remembering the sensation.

"It will tingle a tiny bit and only take a second."

The little girl nodded, and the queen set her hands on both sides of her head, her fingers tangled in long brown hair. Once more she scanned her own eyes to get the shape of the lens and then went to work.

The girl screamed, a peel of shrill terror. For a moment, Claire thought she'd hurt the child, but the only thing she had changed was those lenses.

Then he was there, hugging the girl close. As guards rushed in, Claire held up a hand.

"It looks so different!" The girl was shaking with anxiety.

"Eh knowb, but loog agan."

Toma slowly peeked out from around Gray's sizable shoulder. She whispered into his ear.

"Is that what things always look like?"

He nodded. Toma continued to glance around. She looked up at Claire.

"Wow, you're really pretty."

Gray simply nodded again. Claire found herself blushing.

Toma let go and began to walk around the room. She looked at her own hands, her dress, then moved over to look at the bird she was drawing.

"Aww... its head was even fatter than I thought."

Claire smiled, the fear of having hurt the girl gone. She felt honored to be able to help. This child's whole life would be different. The queen decided they would be going to the school and checking on all the young ones soon.

As she watched Gray interact with the girl, she thought back to how her father would act with her. He was hard as stone to most and yet so gentle with her and little Jack. The man before her had a strange sense of humor and Toma was giggling as he drew another bird with an even fatter head. That was that.

If Autumn was going to have heirs, he needed to be their father. She loved him more than she could say. He stopped his whole day, went out with little to no ability to speak, and despite feeling so weak, came here to help this child.

He was smart, funny, brave, and quite handsome. What was she thinking, waiting so long? Prophecy to ash, she moped all this time for what? Joobel was right; she should have told him how she felt long ago.

Toma was drawing another bird, a feathered head so fat it took up most of the page. Gray was laughing and pushing two sheets together so as not to be outdone.

Claire grabbed his head and turned him around. She leaned in and put all of the feelings from the past few days into the kiss. She forgot about holding court, forgot about the upcoming trials, and forgot a little girl was sitting not one pace away.

Gray started to pull away in shock, then he too fell into the kiss. Only one voice could be heard for several long moments.

"Oooohhhhhhhh. The queen is kissing Greeeeee."

***

As he listened to the young woman tell her tale, Naoki found he really liked the princess. As much as he hated the previous queen, this pleasant woman disarmed him. He could feel her power, and with it her intent. The plants whispered their love of her and they never steered him wrong.

Her story was one he found even sadder than his own. Despite the hardships of his past, he was free and never alone. He could travel throughout the entire kingdom of Spring and never would there be a moment when he wouldn't be greeted by the trees, the grasses, or the various plant life of the land.

Yoshiko was born into the Cerelia family; some of Spring's most powerful elves were sons and daughters of that troop. Her mother, Sayuri, was currently the Queen of Spring.

While in most lands this would make her the one in charge, in Spring she was only the third wife of the man known as the Alder King. He was known to some as the Erlking or the Ellekonge, but his name was Zankoku Legerdemain. He had taken Sayuri as a wife to fill the link he lacked with the realm spirit.

Yoshiko explained that her position as the queen's daughter allowed her some protection. Still, both the king and his children hated her. What's more, she'd begun to understand how the tyrant was exploiting the land and its people, yet was unable to stop him. She needed help in dealing with both him and his offspring.

Naoki consulted the trees and plants around him. They whispered the relayed love and trust from the plants in the garden. This woman possessed love and respect for the life they coveted above all else. This more than anything convinced him.

"I will help you."

Yoshiko's face lit up. He expected her to break down or shower him with gratitude. Instead, she smiled and asked in an excited tone.

"Shall we test one another then?"

He tilted his head. "What do you mean?"

She smiled mischievously. "I assume your grass just told you to trust me."

"Well, it wasn't just the grass, but yes, the grass likes you."

Yoshiko nodded with a smirk. "Well, the mushroom sent me to you, so it seems we're in this together. We need a plan, and for that, we both need to know what the other is capable of. Shall we make a wager on the outcome of our duel?"

Now he was curious. "A wager? You seem confident. What did you have in mind?"

She put her hands together and brought them to her lips. Then smiled when she decided the stakes.

"I think the loser should buy dinner."

He shook his head. "Ah, yet I find myself without any funds to work with."

She chuckled. "Then you best not lose."

He couldn't help but laugh. She wasn't the least bit intimidated by him. She must know the stories of the phantom of the forests, the reaper of the dark places. The Green Man. If she did know them, she sure seemed not to care.

He needed to get on the roster for the Contest of Champions if he was going to compete. Perhaps she could help him do that.

"It seems to me that this wager is merely a devious way for you to get to have dinner with me. I refuse to be manipulated and so I decline the bet. That said, I need to register for the upcoming contest and that will no doubt take some time. Perhaps if you were so kind as to assist me, I would be happy to provide an evening meal for us to share."

She laughed at his banter and then put her chin on her fist and pondered aloud.

"It seems you ask for my payment upfront, yet I know you are but a pauper on these streets. Should I aid you... how do I know you will make good on your promise?"

He smiled as he reached into his pouch. In his hand was a variety of seeds. Some were copies, but there were dozens of different kinds. He looked meaningfully to the newly grown fruit tree, shading the spot where they sat.

"Well, there are still tryouts at the practice fields. The casting division is full, but there are tryouts for the melee tomorrow. You should be able to earn your spot."

"What of you? Why wouldn't one of your talent want to compete as well?"

She faked a swoon, bringing the back of her hand to her forehead, and leaned to one side.

"Oh me? Well... I'm but a frail young woman. Such dangerous activities would positively leave me in tremors."

He looked at her innocent eyes. Moments ago, she was willing to fight him, yet now she was backing out. The realization dawned on him suddenly.

"You're already on the roster, aren't you?"

She smiled widely. "Currently ranked first in my division."

"You could have just told me."

She gave him a shrug, then another smile.

"Mine is a boring life. I find entertainment where I can."

Despite her being somewhat more like Sakura than he would have liked, he found himself drawn to his new friend. She had plans for the evening, but they agreed to meet late the next morning to get him a spot in the Contest of Champions.

***

She kissed him! It wasn't how Claire wanted to start things off and she chided herself for the impulsiveness of it. He kissed her back. She shook away the distracting thoughts. They had set aside time for that conversation.

Claire already made her final decisions regarding who would accompany her to Spring and who would represent Autumn in the Contest. The dragons were a bit of a given as Autumn only had two.

There was, of course the matter of Depth and Puddle, who were technically citizens of Autumn but helped in Winter as needed. She and Raine agreed that the existence of the sea dragon was best left to rumor and legend. Puddle would be more accepted as Raine's dragon.

So, both Harvest and Bloom would fly the royal party over. Gray and Joobel would serve as advisors. Her guards would be Jack and a Stone Spear troll named Stoveg. These selections gave her access to no small amount of military might as well as a group she had perfect trust in.

As she sat at her desk on one side of her throne room, she awaited her next appointment. It was the last of the afternoon and she was already packing up the work she would continue later in the day. A guard approached with a tall woman dressed in leathers and wearing a long whip on one hip.

"Hello, Myrin."

Claire smiled as she spoke, but her cousin seemed distant. Jack explained she was struggling emotionally and that patience would be needed to complete the task before her. Myrin brushed back her long reddish hair and sighed.

"Hello, cousin. I assume this is about the selections for Spring. I'm ready when you are set to depart."

The queen inhaled, not looking forward to this part.

"I didn't select you to go."

The woman's knuckles turned white as she processed the words. She worked out her reply through gritted teeth.

"I assume you think you found someone stronger?"

"Jack and the troll Stoveg will serve as my guards, but it is your strength that made me decide I need you somewhere else."

The attempt to soothe the woman's wounded pride seemed to have little effect. Her hand went to her whip and the ground trembled through the throne room. Claire wasn't afraid.

Though none of her guards were any match for her cousin, she could hold her own if needed. Several ghosts had started moving closer to where Myrin stood. A small trickle of the queen's will told them they wouldn't be required.

"My queen...." The words oozed sarcasm. "You mean to tell me that guarding your life isn't important enough to warrant my time? What then would you have me guarding?"

Claire picked up the papers and nodded to the cautious guards, who began to walk with her toward her quarters. She left Myrin's question hanging as they entered the suite and Claire picked up a pack that was readied.

She looked her cousin in the eyes and said with total sincerity, "I need you to protect my children."

Myrin seemed surprised, yet remained skeptical. Claire waved her on and gave a slight whistle. Maeve hopped up from where she was curled up on the floor and moved to her side. The happy hound wagged as she followed the two women down the hall and through the portal to Issabol's.

Claire let Maeve go and greet the children as she and Myrin moved to the portal room. It was a much smaller version of the hub that connected all the villages and towns in Autumn. On the far side stood a portal that connected to a long-dead world.

It was a world of decay, the very air poison to any who didn't have a change spirit. That was the land that claimed her mother and had nearly claimed both her brother and herself.

"Myrin, the spirit you now possess once belonged to a terrible man. He was working with the mad crone, and in his quest to allow them to rule our world, he built an army. Golems and Helhounds were to serve as his soldiers."

A shudder went through the queen as she relived that moment.

"When my brother took the man's earth spirit, the ghosts left the golems and the hounds ran wild. Those hounds are bound to his power and his will. You have that power and I believe they might obey you."

Claire reached into her pack and pulled out a flight mask; at least, it looked very similar to one. She held it out to her cousin.

"I can breathe in this place, but it will kill you in moments. The mask will filter the air and your sister's magic will deactivate the miasma. It should allow you to breathe long enough for us to complete our task."

Myrin looked confused, her button nose scrunched up in disgust at the strange item.

"What do you hope to accomplish with these beasts?"

"With the hounds under your control, you will become the most powerful mortal in Fairie. Summer will almost certainly betray us while I'm away. It is Harvest and my brother that they fear. With them going with me, I believe the southern kingdom may attack. I need the strongest woman I know to protect my lands, my people, and my children. I'm here to give her the tools to do so."

Now the face of impatience and anger began to crack. Myrin's hard eyes had just a hint of moisture in the corners.

"You would trust me with the fate of Autumn? I would crush the weak people of this kingdom and allow only the strongest to rise up. Then build an army from the ashes and all would serve me in fear."

Claire shook her head. "You gave your birthright to your sister. You know there is a better way, though you are not gentle or kind. I love you, Myrin, but we both know you're not prone to mercy. I have those who serve me who possess those traits. I also have my brother. He's capable of terrible things, but he does them to protect our people. I trust *you* to do this."

Myrin moved so fast that Claire realized she'd been in much more danger than she initially believed, but the woman didn't attack. The embrace was uncomfortably tight; her cousin spoke her words clearly next to her ear.

"I, Myrin Anahita, a former Queen of Winter, hereby swear to serve and support you, Queen Claire Ashotok. Until my last day." Myrin backed up. Her gaze bore into the queen. "I fear losing myself, cousin. Your trust goes a long way in knowing there is yet hope for me."

Claire hugged her for a brief moment longer and then helped her don the mask. A low whistle summoned the little hound to her side. Myrin looked to the animal who never seemed to like her.

"If you don't mind me asking, why is *she* here?"

Claire shrugged. "In case this doesn't work. We will want to make it back alive."

With that, Claire adjusted the portal to allow them to pass through. The odd trio entered the land of the dead.

***

The skies were dark with smoke and the ground reeked of decay. Unlike Claire's first visit to this terrible landscape, there was no ward stone preventing her from setting a portal at the base of the mountain.

This towering mountain was hollow and held the workshops that birthed the golems and Hel-hounds. Maeve whimpered lightly, understanding where they had come. Myrin sounded otherworldly as she breathed through the mask.

Claire scanned the surrounding area, leaving the portal open should they need to make a quick exit. She had no real way to know how Myrin would communicate with the hounds, but she'd spoken at length with Issabol and walked through her best guess.

"Try to reach out with your earth spirit; you should feel the broken bonds with each hound. Try to mend them one at a time."

A distant howl told them that they wouldn't have long before the test would be very near at hand. Myrin kneeled to the ground and sent a pulse through the hard earth. This ground was already infused with the presence of power. Once Anwir's power, hers now.

She began to run through the pathways in her mind. Myrin learned to control her stolen spirit of earth quickly. Though she missed the offensive power of the Frost Fire she'd been born with, she was willing to admit that earth was more versatile. When she had the boundaries of the infused land sealed in her mind, she sent the pulse.

Claire watched as a fine mist of dust rippled only a hand's width from the ground. It moved in an expanding circle like water from the splash of a pebble. Another howl began, yet seemed to cut short as the power passed through.

Suddenly another cry began, followed by many more. The sounds began to move closer. A shudder ripped through her shoulders as the sound took her back to running for her life.

Claire remembered the feeling of watching these beasts take her mother from her and then almost kill her brother. This place made her feel small and weak, but she needed these monsters to protect her kingdom. She couldn't back down.

"Myrin, I don't mean to rush you. I was just wondering how it's going?"

Myrin was panting now, her hair streaked with sweat, and her breathing was coming in gasps. Claire reached over to Maeve and sent her a mental image of a large hound protecting them. Maeve immediately began to grow, transforming into a more extensive and cruder form of herself. She wasn't wagging; this place held terrible memories for her, too.

It was only a few short seconds before the first hound crested a nearby hill. Two more followed shortly after. Maeve sent up her own howl; the impact of sound from the massive throat thundered through the valley. The trio of beasts paused and waited.

Then Claire heard the steps behind her. As she turned, she could see a dozen more had padded up to that side. More began to cover every area in a large circle around them.

The low growl emanating from Maeve gave them pause. As their numbers grew, Claire knew they would find courage as a pack.

"Myrin, I think we might need to call the retreat. I'm only good to take down a few. While Maeve would probably survive a full-blown attack, we certainly wouldn't."

The scream of anger and frustration peeled the sounds of the pack away as Myrin stood and shouted defiance. The whip at her hip lashed out and chipped stone from the nearest hound. Maeve growled even louder, but Claire put a hand out to calm her.

The pack started to attack, then pulled back. The Autumn Queen watched in amazement as Myrin continued to shout and lash out. Each time the beasts seemed to want to move in, and yet hesitated.

For a few long minutes they hovered inside the stalemate. Then one hound went to the ground, its head low against the dark earth in submission. Then another, and then two more. Soon rows of the hounds went down in subservience to the tall woman who was snapping her whip and screaming at the top of her lungs.

More seconds passed and more hounds arrived, each fighting her control but eventually submitting to her authority. Finally, Myrin leaned down to put her hands on her knees while trying to pull air through the mask on her face. Claire let her rest for a moment as she looked around wide-eyed.

"There are thousands of them."

"Seven thousand, eight hundred, and ninety-three. All seem to think that our big friend here killed a good deal of the pack. You aren't loved either, cousin."

Claire cocked an eyebrow. "You counted them?"

"I... I feel all of them; I don't know how to explain it. I don't have any idea how to make more, either. It's not a skill natural to my earth spirit. The person who built these was a genius. Is he still alive?"

"He's, well... Anwir is dragon poop by now."

Myrin paused and turned to face her. "Wait... what?"

"He was a rather terrible man. He tried to kill Jack and then he attempted to steal my throne."

"How does that make him dragon poop?"

Claire gave her an evil smile. "Never cross me and Harvest will never have to answer that for you."

Myrin turned and laughed. She doubled over and had to put a hand on Claire's shoulder to steady herself.

"I didn't know you had it in you, cousin. No wonder no one ever questions Autumn's Queen."

"If only that were true. Jack makes sure to do so every day. Will your control hold? I doubt the mask will protect you much longer."

Myrin nodded. "They belong to me now; they will come when I call."

Myrin sent a pulse to carry her wishes to the assembled hounds, who dispersed as the odd trio walked back through the portal that would take them home. The whole task in Heluvot had only taken about fifteen minutes. It was well past dinner when Claire reached the Keep.

CHAPTER 8

The sun was glinting through his window when Gray finally left his bed. The apartment he kept in the Blood Keep was small and bare, with only the necessities to get by. Despite the fact that his speech was still somewhat garbled, and that he was preparing to embark on a mission across worlds, he found himself more cheerful than he'd been in some time.

Claire had feelings for him. He'd known his queen was special when he met her as the Autumn Maiden a few years ago. It was during her long absence in Heluvot that he realized he cared for her. Since that time, he'd been turned away time and time again. Just when he thought he was gaining ground, she would pull away.

He'd only gone to the queen to try to help Toma see correctly. Knowing how much Claire had going on with the upcoming Contest, he planned on departing shortly after. Yet she seemed opposed to leaving his side.

Claire came with him when he returned to Issabol's home with Toma. They had walked through the halls of the Keep together and even taken lunch in each other's company. She was gone the rest of the night but they had plans to talk things through. It was one of the best days of his life, even if he was nearly mute.

Now he was preparing to leave this world. At one point, he wanted only to return to his home world, to leave this strange place and the seemingly barbaric thinking that its people held. Now that he was near departure for a place he hadn't seen in years, it was like once again being torn from where he belonged.

This was his home now: his friends, the children, his queen. Possibly much more in the future. In the world he'd been born into, he was merely one man, smart and promising, but caught up in a world where his presence would be overlooked. A place where lesser men couldn't see past his skin color.

Here he had become a catalyst, an agent of change. Claire once gave him the task of helping her build a better world, and they had done much to see that happen. Yet hope balanced on a razor's edge. All the kingdom's accomplishments were held together with good intentions.

That and the backing of a handful of powerful individuals. Jack alone influenced countless people, his drive and power inspiring the people to follow the queen he was pledged to. The dragons also did much for Claire, who had a strange way of ruling a once desolate kingdom.

In this world, he was necessary. Now that he was going to leave, it hurt.

There was a checklist of things he needed to do in his home world. First, he needed to acquire help in the form of a very specialized scientist. Second, he needed to bring the required equipment back to this world to study the black ooze. Finally, he needed to bring whatever knowledge and tools would be useful for the future progress of Fairie.

To do all these things, he needed money. He'd pondered how to accomplish this for some time. It was an odd breakfast with a lovely curious girl that provided a possible answer to that question. Claire arranged a meeting that would allow him to test his theory.

The walk to the treasury wasn't a long one. The Autumn vaults were technically inside the Blood Keep, though he had to cross the courtyard to reach them. His jacket was more than enough to keep him warm in the fresh air, and he paused to soak up the rays of the sun.

He often wondered about the shape of this world. His guess was that Fairie was a continent on a planet, with Summer near the equator and the temperature dropping as you moved away from it. This planet would have to be smaller than his own to have such a change over a relatively short distance, which would mean some very dense matter at the core of the planet.

He shook his head and continued walking; curiosity could cost him precious time. Upon entering the vaults, a pleasant woman looked up and smiled at him. Despite the security, most knew of the tall, dark man who was close to the queen. More still knew of the only person to have beaten the Autumn Prince since he was a child.

She was a bit older, though still well within her prime. Her blonde hair had a hint of red and she had many freckles covering her arms and face. She paused for a moment to check her schedule and then nodded and stood to greet him with a handshake.

"Grayson Davis? You're set to go in to talk to the head treasurer. I want to warn you, he's... passionate. Also, we know of your issues with speaking. Think nothing of it."

Gray smiled back at the woman and shook her hand in both of his. Her warning was noted, but Claire had already filled him in on the odd man who oversaw the wealth of Autumn.

"I ab sure we will do fibe, thang you."

He stepped through the massive stone doorway. The room was protected by thick walls of red stone, the door balanced on perfectly crafted hinges. The room was filled with various sized piles of copper and bronze.

Fae currency was complicated when some could pull minerals right up from the ground. Gold and silver were present, but the most valuable metal in this world was copper. Beyond its use as a coin and the rarity of the mineral was the fact that Fairie was a world that never had an iron age.

Cold iron ate spirit magic and any world that had the metal in any significant amount would never develop the spirits needed for the higher forms of magic. So copper was often used in making tools and weapons, thus it always had value. It was over a large stack of copper coins that a tall man in grey robes leaned.

The old man had long grey hair and a neatly trimmed beard. He squinted over his ledgers and moved the small metal disks from one stack to another. Gray approached and stood a couple paces away while he let the man finish his count. It was only a few seconds before the treasurer spoke, his eyes still on the coins.

"I'm told you are the one who put strange ideas in our queen's head."

Gray smiled at the thought of that queen but answered without hesitation or apology.

"Wheb your queeb gives you a tasp, you either obey or come ub with a good reasob nod to."

"Couldn't think of a reason?"

Gray grinned. "Dibn't wan to."

For the first time, the man looked him in the eye. He was cunning and the appraisal was almost palpable in the air around the larger man. Finally, the treasurer smiled widely.

"Good. You have no idea how stressful this job was before our queen came in and started to get the wheels moving. People starved because we couldn't afford to get goods where they needed to go. Now the hardest part of my job is keeping the money moving."

He waved a hand at several piles of copper coins.

"Seems just when I think our coffers are going to fill, she comes up with another project. Then we start to empty until some previous endeavor pays off and we are back at it. I use wheelbarrows much of the time."

The man started walking and Gray had to almost jog to keep up. He continued speaking, moving his hands to add meaning to the words.

"This room is mostly for setting budgets for projects. Most big jobs get a pile. The big area over there that is almost empty was for the water tank we helped build in Winter. The taps are already working, and the water tastes amazing. I hear that was one of your little projects."

"I helbed shabe the idea. I woulb give the crebit to our allied Queeb of Winder."

The old man nodded. "Good alliance that, one less border to fret over. So... I hear you are to inspect the royal jewels. I hope you're not overly excited. Most of the gemstones we had were sold off by Queen Ornella to make ends meet. There are a few excellent stones left though."

It was a long walk through the mazes of the vaults to a small room that held a series of shelves. Each was sparsely populated with various gems in brilliant colors. Even in the low lantern light, Gray could see the glistening of emeralds, rubies, and sapphires. These were all both valuable and helpful, but they weren't what he was looking for.

A few years ago, he'd been at a trivia night in his dorms and he had missed a question about the most expensive diamond in the world. Red diamonds were made of pure carbon, but the structure was such that the color could make them look almost like a ruby. Claire mentioned that there might be such a gem in the vaults. Such a valuable gem comprised of a single element was the key to his idea.

The head treasurer loomed over him, protective of the treasures and curious about what the man was looking for. He asked if he could assist and Gray described the gem he was most interested in. The man led him to a small ornate box in the corner of the room. He reverently opened it and revealed what Gray had hoped to find.

A large cut gem the color of iridescent blood sparkled, even in the lamplight. The treasurer confirmed it was as he hoped. The red diamond was cut into a pentagon with odd angles that caught and manipulated the light around it.

Gray never really paid much attention to what a carat was, but this gem was more substantial than an acorn. In his world, such an item would be worth millions. He couldn't help but smile; he looked over to the treasurer and broke the man's heart.

"I wilb take et."

There was no small amount of protest from the old man. Luckily Claire ordered that Gray could take whatever he wanted. Soon he walked back across the courtyard with both the diamond and several small bars of gold weighing down his pockets.

***

The Queen of Autumn had given her word that she would inspect the warehouse Gray requested. To her, the idea of a large square building that would store stuff seemed odd. He insisted they have one ready for the things he was planning on bringing back on his return.

The earth spirit builders put the whole building together in only four days. In her quest to rebuild and add infrastructure to the kingdom of Autumn, she recruited stone shapers from as far away as Spring, with many being initially from Summer. Several of the men and women working for Autumn were little more than slaves in the Summer kingdom, where earth spirits are standard and work is scarce.

Autumn was a long way from running out of work for those talented earth spirits. She had plans for roads, public buildings in the towns and villages, as well as seasonal housing for the drifters who moved around to help the farmers during harvest. Not to mention there would be new townships forming to help establish the nearly constant flow of refugees from the other kingdoms.

The newest project was impressively done. Despite detailed instructions to keep the building functional and straightforward, the workers had outdone themselves. Even in such short time, they reinforced the corners, added eaves off the roof to help shed rainwater, and stamped the stone floors to add a sort of non-slip tile.

A gnome was waiting to guide her through the inspection. He waved and spoke in a loud, clear voice.

"Over here, my queen!"

Claire walked over and without pause, sat in the dirt and smiled. It was an old form of courtesy to do whatever possible to speak at the same level as the smaller races. Claire did what she could to show respect; it went far to endear her to many in her kingdom.

The gnome was broad and well-muscled for his size, with the beginning of a thick brown beard. Small hands held a tiny clipboard that he carried as if it were part of his arm.

"Oh, my queen, please! You'll get dirty—"

Claire smiled down at him. "Hush, I like dirt. Nothing grows without it. What may I call you?"

"I'm Barth, a designer by trade. I usually design tools, but my skills work well enough for buildings."

Claire nodded. "You're to guide me through my new construction then?"

She hoped the question would let him relax. It was always slow at first when the queen needed to work with new people. Answering simple questions put people at ease and allowed them to forget that the woman asking was both feared by most of Fairie and the monarch of the kingdom they called home. In this instance, it worked quite well.

"Yes, my queen, it should be ready for you. It was finished yesterday, but we wanted to get it swept out and adjust the skylights."

Claire began to stand. The gnome moved toward the edge of the outer wall. He began pointing out the features of the building.

"Ok, we tripled the stone mass on the corners. Otherwise, if we get a small quake or a strong enough wind, we could see cracking near the top. This will reduce the need for maintenance. We added high window slits for added light and airflow, as well as a curved roof. Shouldn't see leaks for decades."

She looked at each feature as the gnome subtly bragged at his design and the execution of its construction. She didn't mind; those who practiced a craft they were proud of did better work.

This was built quite well. The gnome finished his speech as they stepped through a set of sliding doors. She thought of something.

"Is the roof resistant to lightning?"

The gnome laughed and then nodded. She'd been speaking in jest, but now he really did have her attention.

"You're serious? Oh, do explain, my dear Barth."

"After the...um... incident at the school..."

Claire moved her hand in a circle. "I'm well aware and in a bit of a hurry."

"Well, even without... ah... special students, we get lightning strikes from time to time. We attached copper plates along the top of the roof and ran them deep into the ground with thick wire. It's not cheap, but it seems to be quite effective."

Claire thought for a moment, tapping her finger against her bottom lip. That didn't seem like something she'd heard of before. Then a knowing smile crept across her lips.

"Was this suggested by a tall, dark man that likes to float around?"

Barth nodded. "If you mean the Wind Walker, then yes. He said it was a safety issue and that the items inside would be sensitive to such things."

The queen shook her head; that man was all over the place. The thought of him leaving soon brought both joy and worry. She pushed her attention back to her task.

The building had seemed significant from the outside. Now that she was within, it seemed huge. No tricks or portals needed, only the impression of open space.

The inspection only took a few more minutes. The large empty room contained no other special features. The building would eventually be an auxiliary gym. Still, Gray insisted that when he returned from his homeworld, they would need to get a large amount of stuff moved very quickly and would need ample space to unload it all.

Her gnome guide moved out and back to his other projects. Just as she moved to the exit, a portal opened on the wall to one side. Claire dealt with even more complications before continuing on with her duties. She still needed to make rounds at the school and hold court before she could call it a day.

A queen's work is never done.

***

Yoshiko enjoyed watching the young man fight for his spot on the team for Spring. They arrived later than she guessed and had to work to get him a spot to even try out. Naoki had only the melee combat division for a chance at the top prize.

She worried this might be an issue for him. Nurture was a powerful spirit type and among the soil of Spring where renewal is the power of the land, it was stronger yet. But it was a spirit that generally required distance and time to work with.

Naoki brought up the tree quickly when they had lunch, but that wouldn't stop an ogre. Unfortunately, that was what he was up against now.

He could win in one of three ways. The opponent could surrender, be removed from the ring, or be unable to continue. This could mean a severe injury, being knocked out, or in more cases than anyone liked to admit, they could be killed.

She started to protest when they put him up against such a large foe, but the soldiers running the trials didn't like outsiders. Since he wasn't enlisted or a royal, they saw fit to get rid of him quickly.

The gong sounded as soon as both were in their starting places, and the ogre immediately began to charge. For such a massive creature, it moved like a horse at full gallop. Naoki didn't react until what she thought would be too late. Then he stepped to one side and set a hand on the ground.

The blades of grass on the very edge of the circle lashed out and wrapped around the head of the ogre. The long green strands then pulled until the brute was teetering at the edge of the ring. The elf walked calmly over and pushed the back of his huge enemy, sending him the last step over the side. He won, seemingly without effort.

Naoki walked back to the center as a roar of anger and frustration came from the recently defeated ogre. Yoshiko stood and, when she saw the soldiers weren't going to intervene, began to draw her power. She'd waited too long, though, and watched in horror as the ogre reached the elf.

Naoki turned and punched the creature in the stomach with his left fist, which she knew to be his hand of living wood. The heart of a cherry blossom had mimicked his skin so closely it would be hard to notice by looking, but it was like a stone when she touched it.

The bare skin of the ogre's belly made a loud '*whap*' at the impact. The ground shook as the ogre hit the packed earth of the field. Yoshiko stomped over to the soldiers, eyes filled with anger.

"You allowed that attack? He could have been killed!"

The man looked older, so perhaps several centuries for an elf. He looked up at her dryly, waved his hand once, and sneered.

"If some peasant wants to die trying to play with real fighters, what is it to me? He wastes everyone's time by trying to pretend, and I have better things to do."

Yoshiko's eyes narrowed. "You will do your job, or I will see you court-martialed! Do I make myself clear?"

He looked closer at the young woman accosting him. He still seemed unimpressed. In his defense, she never really acted, dressed, or spoke like a princess. But to his dismay, she wielded her power like a daughter of Cerelia.

"Listen, bitch, if you don't get out of my—"

Tendrils lifted up all around him, wrapping around his arms, legs, and neck. In less than a second, he couldn't move. Spore stalks slowly moved to a hair's breadth from his nose and mouth. His armor creaked as the mycelial tendrils strained the bronze joints. Yoshiko leaned over to speak in his ear.

"Call me that again. I dare you to say that word one... more... time."

"You cannot accost a soldier of the king!" His words were a faint rasp. "I will report you. You will not leave this place alive!"

The voice that answered came from behind the woman the soldier didn't seem to know was a princess. She was considering pulling him apart on principle. Who knew how he treated people who couldn't fight back?

"I bet she leaves this place and safely walks back to her home in the Beryl Gardens. If anyone reports the incident of the guard who called a Princess of Spring a... well, an impolite word."

Naoki made a point of sadly shaking his head.

"Still, when she tells the story of how she ripped the limbs from a guard who dared insult her in such a vulgar way, the report will read, '*Died of his own stupidity*,' I assure you, though, she'll leave here untouched and healthy."

Yoshiko turned around to see the Green Man leaning on a table, not even out of breath for having dropped the ogre. Several more guards were approaching and he waved and yelled at them.

"Never fear, O great defenders of the kingdom! Our princess was just coaching your friend on the proper etiquette for addressing a lady."

One of the soldiers stepped forward. Upon seeing Yoshiko, he seemed to recognize that she was indeed a Princess of Spring. To his credit, his voice only quavered slightly.

"She... she's the daughter of Queen Sayuri. Please forgive us, we didn't realize we had a royal audience."

The man bowed, followed by the others who approached. Yoshiko didn't know if she was angrier at the soldier who insulted her or at the young man who outed her as the princess.

She sneered at the man in her web of mushroom tendrils. He failed to bow, though it might be due to his inability to move at all. Finally, she spoke through gritted teeth.

"No one should be treated that way, princess or not. Do we have an understanding?"

The soldier nodded as best he could with his neck immobilized. She dropped him in a heap on the ground and looked around.

"Who else is in line to fight against my friend?"

One of the newcomers answered.

"If it pleases your grace, we all feel that his performance against the last contestant ensures him a spot on the roster. Is there anything else we can do to be of service?"

Yoshiko huffed; she hated nothing more than a double standard. In many ways, she looked forward to fighting those who wouldn't hold back for fear of the wrath of a royal. Why did her mother ever marry that horrible man? The elf took a deep breath and let it go. She was, after all, owed a dinner.

"Very well, see it's done." She glared down at the man who was trying to stand upright.

"Also, see that you treat our citizens with more respect. Next time I might be in a foul mood."

With that, she strode off. Naoki looked around at the men, shrugged, and smiled.

"Isn't she great?"

He quickly followed the furious princess.

***

After inspecting the warehouse, Claire moved on to make an appearance at the school. It was a good use of time and she liked to see the children and ensure that all was going smoothly.

She entered through the side gate, her guards nodding to the patrols at the outer wall. The queen moved to a large room at the center of the main building.

The new security system was turning out to be quite useful. A round man with a slightly grey beard was sitting at a desk with a pad of parchment. To most, it would seem he was simply writing random information in neat rows. To Claire's eyes, it was something else altogether.

After the attack that took place on the first day of school, she decided that they needed a better way to monitor the halls and entrances. To accomplish this, Autumn employed the dead. No shortage of ghosts chose to stay in Fairie, delaying moving on for personal reasons.

Many of the security ghosts had descendants attending the school. Each made rounds and reported information to the only other person in Autumn with a spirit of Death. This man had hidden his brand of spirit most of his life. Claire made it a bit more acceptable in her time as queen, and the man everyone called Fife was a beloved fixture of the place now.

Each ghost would swoop in and give a short report regarding each section twice per hour. Should anything occur, there would be news to her in the Keep in less than a minute. Fife could also use his power to let the ghosts be visible for a time.

If he needed to, he could alert every guard on the premises in seconds. Many instructors were battle-trained and could be called in to help as well. This included her brother, who was teaching combat classes at this very moment. All things considered, the school was perhaps safer than her own residence.

"Good afternoon, Fife. How are my children?"

He glanced up only for a moment and after seeing the person asking, he smiled widely.

"They are the best kind of trouble, your grace. I got two apples, a peach, and a pair of gloves from them just this morning. Some days I don't even touch my lunch."

Claire giggled and brought up another gift he'd gotten.

"I heard the trolls brought you a thank you as well."

He chuckled and patted his substantial belly.

"You know, everyone made jokes about the roast deer, but I think nearly everyone who works here had a bit. It was excellent."

Claire nodded. "I find the trolls have made an interesting and happy addition to our land."

Fife chuckled. "Very true, honest be. I'm glad they're on our side. Even the smaller ones are fearsome on the training fields."

She thought of the tryouts and nodded. "I'll not argue that."

The man began writing again. Claire took no offense; she liked how seriously he took his job. Wordlessly he slid one of the apples her way as she was walking out. She took it with a grin.

"Thank you, Fife. Look after my little ones."

He never stopped writing, but he responded with his own grin.

"Of course. Though half of them are bigger than you."

Claire walked out into the hall. Only the ghosts heard her whisper.

"They are still all *my* children."

***

It only took Gray a half-hour to make his way back to the portal near his room that would take him back to Issabol's. He only made one stop at a supply closet to grab a large bag of graphite. It was kept on hand to make the ink that Claire used so much of. His new friend was just the person he needed.

Bilney was sitting on the floor of the workshop singing and playing a clapping game with the strange girl Laris. The little Battle Shaper tapped her hand along to the beat but stared up at a point on the wall. Varam was reading a thick book of Issabol's and Toma was stacking blocks into a tower that fell long before it could be described as tall.

As he entered, Bilney looked up to smile but kept her song going, rhythmically clapping along. Toma squealed at seeing him and ran over to hug his leg. It was the highest point she could reach on his tall frame.

"My friend Gree was kissing the queen!"

Gray grimaced as he realized that bit of information wouldn't long be a secret. Even so, he was neither ashamed nor regretful.

"Ib is because I ab so hanbsome."

Toma smiled, then seemed to hesitate. She said in a whisper that was about the same volume as her normal voice.

"Issabol is asleep. She worked late and needed a nap."

"Id is you I wanteb to talk too. I hab a task for you."

Gray pulled out the box and carefully set the gem on one of the work tables. Then he took the bag of graphite and placed many of the pieces on the table as well. He carefully explained that the red stone was precious, but it was made of the same stuff as the large black flaky chunks of graphite.

This all came down to Toma's abilities. She seemed both excited and scared. Gray told her that her mistakes would still be helpful and to take her time.

Gray wasn't really knowledgeable about gems, but he knew red diamonds were incredibly valuable and that they were made entirely out of carbon. Carbon like that found in graphite.

The girl pushed her long brown hair behind her ears and squinted her almond shaped eyes. She picked up the stone in her left hand as she concentrated and took a large piece of graphite in her right.

A grey glow of light emanated from her hand and the graphite began to flake away. In her hand was a copy of the diamond. Gray took the new stone and held it up to the light.

There were a couple of flaws he could see even without magnification, but the gem was priceless even in this state. It could be recut or kept whole and still serve his purposes. He smiled down to the sweet girl.

"Toma, dis is perbect!"

The girl beamed before bragging. "I can do better, that's just my first try. I can feel the mistakes in the stone. Would you like me to take them out?"

The diamond he held was nearly perfect. If she could improve on it, that would make it worth even more. He nodded and smiled. The girl went back to work, only taking about an hour to make just over thirty of the gems.

Several of the early attempts were flawed noticeably, but the last dozen or so were more perfect than the original. He would have to make a very rough guess, but the stack would be worth hundreds of millions of dollars in his home world. He leaned down and hugged the girl who made it possible.

"Gree you're silly. So... I did ok?"

He couldn't believe what she'd pulled off. "You did so well."

Gray noticed he didn't slur any words. The spell the sage hit him with was almost done changing his brain.

He held out his hand. The arcs of blue energy came quickly. It was like he had learned to ride a bike in his youth. Now years later, he was stretching those muscles once again. The arcs moved and bent to stand higher in the air.

He held out his other hand, and with only a little concentration, the arc shot over to that hand. The crackling became loud and the air began to hold the aroma of a summer storm. Gray smiled before releasing the energy.

Reaching into a pocket, he pulled out a hair clip. It had a row of small jade gems inlaid in a silver base. He'd gotten it from Claire, who had worn it as a child. It was a long-ago gift from her father.

He kneeled down and took Toma's hand, setting the gift between her slender fingers. She looked down and then up again. She was one of many orphans Claire gathered and provided for. The girl even wore clothes that once belonged to Joobel.

The child had once known hunger and loneliness. Even at her tender age, she knew this was an item that cost more than she could have ever hoped to earn in several years.

Her cheeks grew wet and her mouth struggled to portray emotion. She began to sob and leaped up to hug him around the neck.

Gray had given several gifts to the girls in his life. This wasn't a normal reaction. Bilney stepped over and whispered in his ear.

"She has never owned anything. Please realize what this means to her."

Gray hugged her back and then stood, lifting her up. She held on tight, crying and keeping the clip tight in her fingers. He thought of the irony of her making a queen's ransom in gems and then losing herself over something worth so much less.

Bilney had said more than her words suggested.

'*She has never owned anything.*'

No one has given her a gift. He showed that he valued her and that he cared. His own eyes began to grow misty as he thought about how much more there was to do in this world.

He still had so much work left ahead of him.

***

Joobel looked at the bed, table, couch, walls, floor, and ceiling that were covered in clothes. How did one pack to visit another world?

She would be the lone companion to visit Gray's home world. Magic would be scarce even with the heart-crafted disc, and Joobel would be the only person who would have no trouble staying at full power.

The mundane worlds had a small amount of renewal energy, her flavor of spirit magic. She was also Named and would be able to absorb even more energy from her surroundings. This was aside from the fact that she could play the part Gray needed her to and was a trained diplomat.

Gray sent her the message that they would buy some clothes after they arrived, but she didn't intend to show up looking like she'd put no effort into her appearance. Paper-thin wings hummed loudly in the room as she rose to examine a cream-colored dress with matching hose. It just didn't seem to be enough.

She zipped over to her sketchbooks. Quickly looking through some of her designs, she saw what she wanted. The red dress would cover her arms and hang just below her knees. The darker cape would hide her wings and slippers of dark-red would match it perfectly. The gnome had the material and at the speed she worked, she could have it finished in less than two hours.

She wouldn't have it done before she would have to leave for her lunch date. A long glance at the flower sitting on her dressing table brought the gnome thoughts of her dear Jack.

Her betrothed was technically rich, being a prince and all. More so as the kingdom he served was becoming rather wealthy. Yet her prince never really spent money on anything for himself. He dressed in whatever she gave him, ate whatever was available, and preferred to entertain himself rather than going out. Anything he could have bought her would have been a passing gesture, taking only moments of his time and money he didn't value.

This present had taken Jack over a year of intense focus and concentration. The rose was a one-of-a-kind gift and was bonded to his very spirit. It was worth more than any estate and to her, it was priceless.

Jack struggled to express himself, but she never doubted he loved her. For him, it was a choice. For her it was as much a part of her as her blue eyes or thin wings.

The bards spoke of love at first sight, but for gnomes, it was much more real than that. Once a gnome imprinted on someone, they couldn't love another as long as that person lived. She had no choice but to love Jack. That suited her fine.

It only took a few minutes to change for a picnic in the tended grass of the courtyard. She chose a pink sundress of embroidered blue with laced sandals and a simple silver chain around her neck.

She quickly ran a brush through her long silver hair and left to find her prince resting on the sofa, the basket of food and drink sitting on the table. He was in the shorts and sleeveless shirt she'd designed. Though he hadn't bothered with shoes, he did made a meager attempt to comb his shaggy hair.

He greeted her as she approached. "You look nice."

She kissed him for the attempt.

***

The stack of paper wasn't getting any smaller. Raine skimmed through the ones that updated her on the various states of affairs throughout her kingdom.

The guards had come by first thing to collect two more bodies. Cruor had dispatched them without even waking her. She envied his ability to be up through the night and still look refreshed the next morning. Part of her wondered what happened to the blood. Deep down, she didn't want her suspicions confirmed.

Hurley was working with her and had given her the roster for Winter's contestants. She would be taking Brook and Puddle to serve as her dragons. Despite her bond with Mist, the dragon's power was too valuable to the kingdom to risk taking to Spring. The same could be said for Bloom, but Raine had lost that fight.

Her advisors would be Hurley himself and a division leader of the military named Shaw. Her bodyguards would be a talented Yeti named Gorn and her red-eyed shadow, who was currently inspecting the window locks near her bedroom. Cruor would also be competing in the games.

It would only be a few days until she would depart with her team. There would be a couple of meetings with Autumn to plan the contingencies that might arise.

Claire was to send a messenger with her roster and her selections for her royal party. Raine would learn she'd correctly guessed most of those choices but was shocked by the choice of messenger.

The knock on her chamber doors was coded and indicated it was a guard. Cruor was at the door before the last thud. As he opened it, he found two of the Citadel guards and one tall woman in leathers. She had long reddish hair and a whip on her hip. The guard spoke.

"She came through the, *ahem*... south doorway. Claims she has a message from Autumn and wants to give it to our queen herself. I assumed that with you here..." He looked meaningfully to Cruor. "We could let the queen decide if this was safe."

Cruor looked the woman up and down and then nodded as he opened the door wide. Hurley looked suspicious, but he didn't seem to recognize the person standing before him. Raine was curious and stood to greet her guest.

The woman stepped forward with her hands at her side. She bowed slightly.

"You look well, your majesty; I trust you've fully recovered from the cut on your cheek."

Raine paused for a moment, clearly confused. Then her eyes went wide. It took all the control she had to keep her words even.

"Leave us."

Both Citadel guards left upon hearing the queen's words. The number of bodies they carried away from these rooms made clear that when the queen spoke, you just obeyed.

Cruor looked to Hurley; neither of them made a move to leave. The Winter Queen looked around as if surprised she was still in the company of the men who served her.

"Gentlemen, I'm not weak. Nor am I accustomed to repeating myself. I'll send for you both when I need you. Leave us... Now." The last word moved through gritted teeth.

Hurley began to move to the side rooms. Cruor still seemed to hesitate. He didn't like being too far away to act. His vigilance had saved her life far into the double digits. He turned to follow Hurley out of the room, leaving only his words.

"I'll be close. If you need me, just make someone scream."

The door closed and Raine found herself alone with the sister she hadn't seen for months. She began to tremble as the pent-up emotion struggled to get free. She smiled as the other woman stepped forward and spoke.

"I missed you more than I thought possible... little sister."

Raine rushed around the desk and embraced Myrin tightly. She wanted to be stern and forceful, as she thought would be respected by the distant sister she remembered. But her body betrayed her emotions with abandon.

She laughed and cried all at once, her arms squeezing so tightly that the queen worried she might harm the woman she missed so much. Finally, she pushed Myrin away enough to look her in the eyes.

"By the spirits, Claire does good work. I'd have never known you."

Myrin gave a wry smile. Her eyes were dry, but she seemed genuinely happy to once again be in Winter. She replied in rare mirth.

"I still scare myself if I walk by a mirror in the night. It always takes a moment to remember what I look like now."

Raine nodded. "Your voice, too. I had to think about the cut you gave me before I realized—"

The mirth left Myrin in an instant. "I regret that.... There is much I regret."

"I'm just glad you're here. Please sit. Are you hungry? I can make sure it's not poisoned. I'm afraid some try."

"I know. We've found contracts popping up in Autumn. I swear you have a higher price on your head now than...."

Myrin seemed to find shame in her words. Raine put a hand on her arm.

"You have no idea how much I missed you. All is forgiven, and considering you weren't yourself, even that's not needed. Please just tell me you will visit more often and I'll make sure you can do so safely."

Myrin nodded and gave a slight smile. "I'd like that."

Raine was able to cherish the visit. Myrin had information regarding Autumn's roster and the party that would travel to Spring, as well as the news that she would be staying behind. Her older sister seemed to take pride in standing in defense of the kingdom of Autumn.

Then Myrin shared her fears of losing herself, of becoming more and more numb to the world and the people in it. Where Jack was able to relate to the feelings of anger and violence, Raine could only listen. She heard the words and simply replied.

"Dear sister, evil people don't go around worried that they are becoming villains. They run around doing horrid things with confidence. When you stop worrying about your mistakes, then I'll begin to worry for you."

In the end, Myrin stayed through the afternoon and long enough to take dinner in the Citadel. When the food arrived, Raine properly introduced Cruor as he brought the trays.

"Myrin, this is Cruor. My bodyguard." Then she turned to the young man.

"Cruor, this is my sister. The deceased Myrin Anahita, a former Queen of Winter."

To his credit, he didn't flinch. He did flip his hair out of his eyes to take in the figure before him. Then he shook his head.

"I don't see the resemblance. It's a pleasure to meet you."

He took his leave, only taking some fruit from the tray to eat in the next room. Myrin waited for him to leave and then smiled at her younger sister.

"My, my, is he single by any chance?"

Raine smiled, a twinkle in her eye. "No, sister, he's VERY much taken."

Both women shared a long laugh.

***

The seeds he chose to 'make dinner' allowed him and the princess to dine on some rich tree nuts and subtly sweet citrus fruit. The shells were quite strong, but he gave them a squeeze with his wooden hand and cracked them before handing them to Yoshiko.

The sun was just beginning to set over the tall mountain in the distance that housed the realm of Dawn. The air was lightly brisk with departing warmth and the tall grass was soft as they sat to eat. He looked to his unlikely companion.

"Does this suffice for payment in helping me make the cut earlier?"

The young elf woman was peeling the large round fruit and chewing one of the richly flavored nuts when she looked up.

"I suppose. Do you have anything to make a good glass of wine?"

He thought for a moment.

"I have grape seeds and you could speed fermentation... but I don't have any glasses."

She laughed at this. Despite the incident with the soldiers, in which he knew they were trying to get him killed, his time with this woman was quite enjoyable. He'd gotten entry into the contest and spoken more to another human being than he could ever remember.

Yet, he felt like something ominous was happening. The trees and grasses spoke to him as well. Not specifically, but as if they sensed something. He decided to ask his new friend.

"Say, Apple...."

Her nose crinkled. "Not my name."

"Has your mushroom seemed on edge as of late?"

She used the sleeve of her dress to wipe the fruit juice away from her lips and paused before nodding.

"Honey seems to be building power as if she sees a fight coming and wants to be ready."

It was as he thought, the spirits of the land were on edge. They would always grant power at his request. Now he felt as if they were trying to force-feed him. He was their champion, and as the land grew nervous, it wanted a strong protector. He moved to another thought.

"You say this 'Honey' led you to me. Called me an ally. I was thinking of what that implies."

Yoshiko was still eating; the exertion at the tryouts had given her an appetite. She seemed to have the same line of thinking, though. She finished chewing and looked over to him.

"Common enemy."

He nodded with a sigh. "So, who is our common enemy? I'm not a fan of your fath... um, the king. Still, it seems odd that the land itself would be worked up over some old guy who is full of himself."

She hadn't missed his almost calling the king her father. She put it out there but refrained from acting offended.

"My father was a soldier. A sub commander in the southern legion. He died in a skirmish with some bandits."

He tilted his head. "Bandits killed an officer? How did they even reach him?"

Yoshiko looked down, eyes scanning the grass. "He was off duty when he came upon a robbery on the road on his way from a meeting. He tried to stop them but was outnumbered."

Naoki nodded his respect. "Sounds like a brave man."

"Bravery is overrated. He was a good man and I'm proud to be his legacy. The man who married my mother isn't worthy to speak my real father's name."

He grew wistful for a moment. This was a rare chance to speak of the past that haunted him.

"I don't remember my father's face. I can picture him from my memories, but I don't know if it's what he looked like or a face I saw somewhere that I mixed up. I was so young."

She patted his arm, only then realizing it was the wooden limb. She pulled her hand back and looked away. He gave her a smile and waved away her worry.

"It feels real, you know, my arm. I often forget it's not the original. It doesn't really have disadvantages. Except Sakura maybe hurting my self-esteem."

Yoshiko laughed again. She tossed the shells and peelings around for the land to reclaim and laid back beside him. Together they watched the sun fall away, the horizon layering reds and purples into the distance.

"Apple?"

She sighed. "Not my name."

He grinned at her frustration. "Do you think you will be queen one day?"

"It's possible, but I'm not getting fitted for a crown anytime soon. Why do you ask?"

"I have spent most of my life hating the Queen of Spring. I was wondering if I might have to rethink that."

She almost held back her smile.

***

Gray had a busy day in preparation for his trip to his home world. One bit of time was set aside for something else. Claire worked her schedule around to allow them to take the evening meal together in the gardens of the Keep. Lantern light lit a stone platform, casting tiny shadows on the surface around the modest fare.

Claire often ate light in the evenings, preferring a substantial breakfast and a snack at midday. Sliced meats and a small block of sharp cheese were surrounded by steamed vegetables and some sliced fruit. She'd even had a bottle of wine chilled, a treat she seldom allowed herself.

He now walked out to the meeting place dressed in some of his nicer attire. Like many in the Keep, he'd been gifted several sets of clothes by the resident gnome seamstress. He even shaved and combed out his thick hair.

Even from a distance he could see she'd already failed at putting her work aside. Those lovely brown eyes were focused on a piece of parchment, quill tapping her lower lip.

He paused to watch her for a moment. For so long, he tried to prove himself up to the challenge to be with her. Only the previous day, she'd kissed him without warning.

His heart pounded loudly in his ears. The queen was quite lovely. Perhaps more to him than others. Joobel was doubtless more charming and Myrin was sexier, but Claire had an air about her. She seemed to have an aura of quiet authority, confidence, and comfort in who she was.

Perhaps it was the flaws that made her so attractive. The three etched scars on her cheek, the curly hair at her temples, the slight hook to her nose.

These all were things she could change with a small effort of her will. Yet, she embraced them. Just as she embraced her spirit of Death for the protection of others. To him, Claire was the most beautiful woman in the world.

Her words moved through the garden though her gaze never left the pages before her.

"If I were going to eat alone, I wouldn't have wasted so much lantern oil."

A smile crossed his lips as he moved to sit with her. No doubt ghosts were milling about all around them, all protective of the queen.

"If I'm not mistaken, I've been accepted to court my lady. It's now my privilege to gaze upon her beauty."

Her smile was just starting to slide off to one side.

"Sit down, you silly man, before I have you dragged away."

He smiled back, but shook his head.

"It would take more guards than you have in your employ."

She looked up and started to speak, then realized there was a good chance he was right. She paused and changed the subject.

"You have your tongue working much better. Are you feeling up to leaving tomorrow?"

He held each hand away from his body as if he were balancing himself. Blue energy crackled from one side to the other. The air snapped and popped loudly. When he stopped, the after images of the bright lights slowly waned from sight. Ozone filled the night air.

"I feel amazing. I think perhaps your kiss is better medicine than our green dragon."

"I truly doubt that. Either way, I won't be kissing every sick person in the kingdom," she chuckled.

He laughed and sat down. "Please don't think I was suggesting it. This all looks very good; thank you for making the time. I... I'm glad you had a change of heart."

She seemed at a loss for words, a rare look for the queen who used language like a blade. Finally, she let the mirth leave her voice.

"I didn't have a change of heart. I had feelings for you before I even came back to claim my throne. I've loved you for some time. I was afraid; that hasn't changed."

Gray shook his head. "Claire, I fear only three things. Fairie's demise, Jack's dog, and your rejection."

Claire sighed. "The prophecy will not allow me a happy life, Gray, you know—"

He slammed a fist against the table. "To hell with the prophecy! It says you will make important decisions. You do that every day. Why do you have to be alone while making them? I need you. I need you to be who you are, only to do so with me by your side."

Claire wiped one eye, "It isn't an argument you need to make anymore. I cannot go on like we have been. Every time you go off on some task, I stay here to hold things together. I'm surrounded by people all the time, yet I feel so alone. I turned you away to protect you, but I can't do it anymore."

Gray nodded slowly, eyebrows furrowed. This was good news and yet he sensed there was more as she looked away from him. He asked the question.

"I feel like there's more to this story."

She swallowed the emotions.

"Queens don't court, Gray. They take consorts, often husbands, and they produce heirs. Those men give up their lives outside the kingdom to become servants of the queen."

Her tone was dead serious, her face like stone. He began to laugh, trying very hard to contain the chuckles. She looked as if he'd slapped her. He held up a hand.

"You're worried about what you're supposed to do? *You*? Who have broken every rule and tradition that stood between you and what you think best? You honestly expect me to believe that this is the one thing that you are going to draw a line through?"

"Well, I—" she stammered.

"You must be joking. So what if I'm called your servant. You can't enslave those who serve out of love. Just ask any ghost. Honestly, I've worked for you for years and I'm yet to get a salary."

She paused, and then she too laughed. "I suppose you are a bit underpaid."

Gray looked into her eyes, the color of falling maple leaves. He loved those eyes.

"Actually... I think I'm going to get everything I always wanted."

Claire's cheeks reddened at his words. She wiped away a tear and then spoke the words he had been waiting to hear.

"Yes. I suppose you are."

They continued to speak the words that would define the relationship and what they both wanted from their futures. It wasn't a whirlwind affair; both were prone to planning and pragmatism.

It was now official, though. The nerd from another world was dating a queen. Finally, things moved on to the events to come.

Claire finished chewing and looked up. "Have you made all your preparations?"

"You've seen that the warehouse is ready. Issabol says the disk will sustain me indefinitely. If all goes well, I can visit more in the future. I'd like to see my family and let them know I'm ok. Oh, and this seems to have worked out."

He pulled out a pouch and poured the red gems onto the flat stone surface of the table. Each crimson diamond sparkled pleasingly in the dim light. Claire reached down and picked one up between her fingers.

"These are rare enough but not unique. Are you sure this many will buy everything you require?"

"Claire, one of these gems would be worth more than a person could hope to earn in a lifetime. In my world, this amount will be greater than ever found in our history. I think we will have enough. I have this as well for some starting cash."

He slid the small bars of gold beside the gems. "Plans tend to change, but I think we've done what we can to prepare."

She nodded in agreement. "I can only hope you're right. Please be careful and hurry back. Both you and our gnomish friend are part of my escort into Spring."

"I intend to, but we don't know how time moves there. I think it wise to have your second choices made in case this takes longer than expected."

She nodded slowly, as if deciding how to proceed. After a brief pause she met his gaze.

"I have things well in hand and will have people I trust at my side when we depart."

He sighed, truly wanting to be that someone. His hand reached out and gave hers a gentle squeeze.

As often happens in these moments, both spent way more time than initially intended, each hesitant to leave the other. He knew it would be some time before they would be together again. Finally, the tall man took his leave.

Gray said goodnight with a slow parting kiss.

CHAPTER 9

The gnome was quite proud of fitting everything she would need in one medium-sized case. Gray was very clear that while her wings were beautiful, they would draw immense amounts of unwanted attention. She was leaving most of her magical gear behind and anything that had materials not found in the other world.

She'd memorized descriptions of the various items they might run across made of iron or steel. These would be the biggest dangers to both of them, but to her especially.

Once again, Jack was sitting on the sofa outside her room, meditating and moving energy around in the form of heat. As he heard her door open, he looked up and snuffed out the white-hot ball of glowing warmth.

"You look lovely."

She'd trained him well.

The gnome leaned in to kiss his dimpled cheek and handed him the case. He slumped with the weight of it. She had packed small, not light. Despite his burden, he said nothing of the equipment she needed to look so pretty for him.

She'd trained him *very* well.

It was a short walk down the hall and to the portal to Issabol's home. There they would depart from the portal room that led to so many wondrous places. As they arrived, she found that they were the first to do so. That was until they could hear voices from the workshop.

Gray was playing a silly game with Laris and Toma. A ball of smoky air was being bounced to each as they sat in a circle. If it touched the ground, the ball made the rather rude noise that all children find hilarious. Gray looked up and smiled.

Both children 'awwwwed' as the game ended. Toma hugged the tall man's leg before heading toward the kitchen. Issabol was sipping tea on a stool next to a workbench. Joobel curtsied and greeted her friends.

"Aren't you just so excited? I know I am. We will have such fun. I will bring back presents, some for everyone. Then we can —"

Gray interrupted her with a raised hand. For a moment, she thought he'd changed his mind, and she would be staying here. Instead, he reached over and picked up a slender box. He handed it to her and allowed her to open it before he spoke.

"You're a good friend. Many times, you have put yourself at risk, yet you have little in the way of defensive magic. You have learned some skills in fighting, but weapons are beyond your nature to use. I have worked with Claire, Issabol, and Jack to make these. They will stun but shouldn't permanently harm those you would use them on. They are our gift to you for your courage."

Joobel looked at Jack, who only nodded. She picked one baton up with the tips of slender fingers. She scrunched her nose.

"How do they work?"

Gray nodded and held out a hand. She handed him the baton. He held it up like a dagger, and the end began to spark and zap.

"The core is part of the feather we were gifted by the trolls. In the core lies some of Jack's stored power, his *real* power. Channel any magic, even yours, through the handle and the end will produce the energy to stun someone."

She picked up the other baton, then held it out to her other hand.

Gray frowned. "I wouldn't—"

There was a spark and the gnome dropped to the floor, baton flying from her fingers. It was several seconds before she could get her legs to cooperate, both men helping her up.

Jack seemed alarmed. "Are you ok?"

The gnome's eyes were alight with excitement. "That was awesome!"

Joobel started to do it again, but Gray caught the end before she could zap herself a second time.

"We're in a bit of a hurry, but you can practice with them later."

She looked at his hand; he should have gotten the same shock. Maybe it was his size? Gray saw her confusion and held out a clawed hand. Sparks bounced around his fingers.

"Hitting me with one of those is like trying to burn a flame drake. It just won't work. Other than possibly a few other aspects of air and myself, no one else should be immune."

She looked to each of the men and hugged them both, then hugged Issabol, who nearly spilled her tea. Gnome affection could be dangerous, big gnome affection even more so.

Issabol showed her a belt that allowed her to keep her new weapons hidden at the small of her back.

Then with a few goodbyes, Joobel walked with Gray through the portal. The pair stepped into the world of Gray's birth, a place he hadn't been since his abduction years earlier.

It was time to go home.

***

Gray looked around the streets of New York. It had taken Issabol some time to find the location that would allow them to get started on their task. Part of him wanted to land directly near his home in Missouri, but the mission of the Black March had to come first. Who knew how long it would take to find a way to fight back?

Moving between worlds causes a strange sort of jetlag. Though moving through time zones can mess up the body's natural rhythms, moving between planets could just leave you a mess. You might land in a different season or climate. Different makeup in the air or gravity could also play havoc. There was also the concern of the rate of time flowing between this world and that of Fairie. They could only hope this wouldn't be too big of an issue.

Joobel looked around in wonder as he walked over to a newsstand and leaned down to see the date. His knees hit the pavement in shock. The gnome moved up beside him. There were thick tears forming in his eyes.

"What's wrong?" Joobel whispered.

He looked at the date on the paper: April 14th, 2016. Time didn't flow at a different speed; it was flowing in reverse. He and his friend had gone back in time. His voice whispered through his anguish.

"You can never go home again...."

Joobel didn't understand the months and dates on the paper. Many of the words were odd to her too, but she could feel her friend hurting. She leaned over and hugged him tightly. A voice came from over his shoulder.

"You people ok? Do yeh need me to call sumbody?"

A shorter man with dark hair was standing next to them. Gray started to wave him away, then paused and wiped his eyes.

"Could you direct me to the nearest gold buyer?"

"Sure, just two blocks thataway. Big letters out front say gold, yah can't miss it."

He nodded and pulled himself up. "Thank you for your help and your concern."

Gray picked up their bags and moved in the direction the man had pointed. Sure enough, it only took a few minutes before they saw an older building with the 'GOLD' sign out front. There stood a pawn shop and the promised sign assuring the best gold price. They stepped inside.

The man in front looked both of them up and down, obviously more impressed by the most gorgeous woman he had ever seen, despite her strange clothes and having dyed her hair silver.

"How can I help you?"

Gray explained he had a small amount of gold to sell. The man got out his scales, and though he seemed curious about the shape of the bar, he weighed it out and offered just over eight thousand dollars.

He tried to figure out if that sounded right, then just assumed the vendor was starting low. He countered at nine thousand five hundred.

They went back and forth, but soon agreed on eight thousand, seven hundred. After some convincing, the man paid in cash.

Shortly after, they were moving toward the hotels in the better part of town. Gray wanted to get a place to work out of. If the movies he watched growing up hadn't steered him wrong, finer hotels could help a person find what they were looking for, assuming you could afford to stay there.

Once they found Times Square, they steered into a grand looking hotel. It was later in the day than in Autumn, but there was plenty of time left to work through the tasks they had before them. He needed to get clothes and access to a computer and a salon. The next phase of his plan required both him and his companion to look the part they needed to succeed.

The hotel asked for a credit card, but after a two hundred dollar tip the clerk informed him that they already had Sam Jones on file. The name was common and he'd always liked the name Sam.

The clothes they would need were only a short walk away. Gray packed some of the money and half the gems into the safe in his room. He included the few magical items they had, minus Joobel's new batons. She was quite attached to those.

Upon entering the clothing district, Gray had a nice suit picked out in minutes. After an hour, it was clear Joobel was going to need more time.

He thought the salesclerk might 'Pretty Woman' them, but everyone was helpful and courteous. The woman helping Joobel promised to keep his friend in the store and Gray whispered a reminder to his friend to hold her wings out of view while changing.

Soon he entered a bank just up the street and went through the steps needed to open an account. He set it up in an LLC with himself holding controlling interest. Joobel was named full beneficiary. He had to give a last name.

Since Joobel was to be married to Jack soon, he chose the last name of the prince. Soon Autumn Equities, LLC was set up to receive money with the partnership under the names Grayson and Viviana Ashotok.

It would be easier to pose as a couple. Besides, his name was already taken by a boy in Oklahoma who was finishing his second year of high school.

He used five hundred to open the account and got the needed numbers to transfer funds. When he got back to the store, he found Joobel sitting with several stacks of boxes and his bagged suit.

He chuckled at her fun. "Did you find anything you didn't like?"

She stuck out her tongue. "They said I could come back for the rest."

Her smile lit up the room. She'd obviously charmed everyone around her. With a sigh, Gray handed about half the remaining money to the cashier.

Once they unloaded at the hotel, he grabbed more cash and changed. Joobel switched to a pair of stylish jeans and a red blouse. A lighter red jacket hung low enough for her to hide her wings and her new weapons.

They walked several blocks to an electronics store. He bought a laptop and a couple of software packages. Joobel bought some trinkets such as a penlight, a frog that croaked when you got close, and a little stuffed Pikachu.

He was glad to have her childlike wonder to cheer him up. His inability to see his family was weighing heavy on his mind. At least one of them was enjoying this trip.

There was plenty of cash left and he still had more gold. There was little reason to be frugal, so he took his friend to a posh restaurant with a balcony that overlooked the streets. He ordered his first steak in several years and Joobel learned that she greatly enjoyed a dish called pasta.

It was late by the time they got back. He had asked both Jack and Claire if it would be ok for him and Joobel to share a room. Both laughed, neither even considering the type of betrayal that was common in his world.

He intended to take the couch. After looking at the small piece of furniture, Joobel insisted he was much too tall. She was curled up and asleep before he got out of the shower.

Despite the elegant bed and smooth sheets, his sleep was restless throughout the night. The words repeated over and over in his mind.

"You can never go home again."

***

Gray's home world was awesome! The gnome had spent less than a day in the strange world with no trees. Shaped stone covered everything she saw, and she couldn't begin to describe her love for the clothes!

There were some notable downsides, though. Early that morning, after she had breakfast brought to her room by a man in a funny hat, she bumped up against a railing and burned her arm pretty badly. She had several small vials of Bloom's healing mist and it took all of one to get her back to normal.

Why would you build things out of iron? She could feel it in the walls and even inside the stone she walked on. Even with her substantial reserves of energy, it made her feel sleepy. The whole thing seemed very poorly planned.

Also, she longed to stretch her wings. She looked every time they were outside and not once had she seen anything in the air but birds, insects, and some odd fan that floated around with flashing lights. No sprites or pixies darted around, no dragons flew in the distance.

Oh well, if you had to hide wings, at least do it in style. Today the world's *only* gnome wore a lacy white top with a dark-blue skirt and matching jacket. She put her belt on under the shirt and slid the batons inside. They were so well thought out and intricate in design. She had trouble thinking of them as weapons, so touching was the gift.

Joobel tried some odd shoes that had heels that rose so high she couldn't walk. Gray said they were supposed to make you taller and were considered sexy. She just thought they were a broken ankle waiting to happen. Instead she put on stylish shoes with a much lower heel.

Now she was following her tall friend to a place called a gem importer. Gray spent hours in front of an odd folding box and had chatted with the friendly woman at the hotel. He found several traders who might be able to pay for the gems in his coat.

The first was only a short walk from the hotel. She was given a part to play, now a rich heiress from a place called Europe here on family business. In these hard times, she must part with an heirloom that had been in her family for generations. They were going to do this several times.

The Gem Society was a posh building just off of Times Square. The front room had a marble desk and a well-dressed man taking calls. She realized why it was so important that they come in dressed the part.

The man finished his call and stood, arrow-straight. With a nose that never dipped to look her in the eye, he questioned their presence.

"Do you have an appointment?"

Gray gave a slight nod and answered respectfully.

"No, sir, we just had some merchandise we were hoping to have apprai—"

A shake of his upturned head. "No one gets seen without an appointment."

Joobel stepped forward. Most things in this world confused her. Half the metal burned like fire. Everyone was in a hurry and shoes had gone mad. People who were full of themselves, though, this she'd dealt with all her life. She flipped back her silver hair and pouted her lips.

"Sweetie, I told you we shouldn't bother with this place. I doubt they even have enough on hand to put a deposit on the Devil's Eye. Let's go to that place across town; I can take a nap in the limo."

Gray smiled with his eyes at her perfect impression of a spoiled rich girl. He turned back to the attendant.

"I told George I'd allow his company to make an offer." He shook his head and sighed, then looked to Joobel. "I'm sure you're right. We can get some sushi on the way."

She gave him a childish grin. "Oh, and a drink with a little umbrella?"

He faked a grimace. "I'm sure we can find you something."

Both of them started to leave, but the man stepped forward and cleared his throat.

"Ahem, you say George sent you? You mean George Atkinson by chance?"

Joobel looked annoyed and retorted with a sniff.

"Does your little business have more than one George?"

"No madame, my apologies. Please, right this way. You said you're selling the Devil's Eye; I'm afraid I haven't heard of it."

Joobel tossed her hair and added about three handfuls of insolence to her words.

"I wouldn't think you had. It hasn't been bought or sold for over three hundred years."

The man who started out so rude was now fawning over the two of them. They were led to a small but plush waiting room and given hot towels and champagne.

It was only a few minutes before a well-dressed man with dark, slicked-back hair entered the room. He smiled and bowed low.

"My name is Ingram. I'm afraid George isn't working today. Perhaps I can assist you."

Gray stood and shook the man's hand and grinned.

"I'm not sure he ever does. Sure, you can give us an appraisal."

Joobel swished the amber liquid in her slender glass. The bubbles fought their way to the top and popped with a low sizzle. She never looked up and gave her impression of Laris.

"I am teeeeelling you; they can't affooooorrrrrd it...."

Ingram never let down his smile, only stood to the side and held out a hand to walk ahead of him. Gray waited for Joobel to stand, down the champagne, and saunter down the hall.

He had never seen the gnome woman act this way. If he was forced to judge, Joobel had an even better saunter than Myrin. He shook his head slightly and walked behind her, letting Ingram follow along as his voice guided them.

"The second door on the left. It has my equipment."

While Ingram got his lenses in order, Gray reached into his coat. Inside a numbered envelope was one of the thirty red diamonds. This one was specially chosen; it had only one tiny flaw.

Gray weighed it out back at the hotel and found it to be just under six carats. As far as he could tell, this might be the most valuable gem in the world.

If the man offered anything less than twenty million, they would walk out. Joobel continued to be annoying, childish, and sexy. It was an effective blend to distract poor Ingram.

"What are we looking at today? I'm afraid I have never heard of the Dev—"

Gray set the diamond on the desk between them. The man stopped talking and stared with mouth agape. His eyes widened slowly before he looked up.

"That isn't a ruby... is it?" He didn't accuse them of bringing him a fake, but the man knew that if it was real, then it was quite a find indeed. He almost touched it, then looked up to Gray.

"May I?"

Gray nodded and Joobel rolled her eyes. "Waste of tiiiiiime...."

Ingram spent several minutes while Gray made attempts to appease the beautiful annoyance at his side. Joobel got out of the chair and walked around looking at things. She made sure to touch everything. Finally, Ingram just whistled.

"It's genuine, as I am sure you know. At just under six carats, it's the largest red diamond I have ever seen, or even heard of. I'm sure you know it is valuable. Do you have a price in mind for its sale, or are you looking to auction?"

Gray hid his relief while Joobel broke a lamp. She tisked at the object that dared to get near her.

"What a pitiful thing, it seemed poorly made. Have someone clean up the glass; I might want to take my shoes off."

Ingram called for someone to come pick up the glass and make the floors safe for spoiled girls. When he finished, Gray pondered his intentions.

"We have several quotes and one more stop to make. If you can give me a number, I can let you know what we decide."

Ingram seemed worried about letting them out the door, but eventually gave them a quote on the diamond.

Gray was smiling ear to ear as he walked outside. Joobel had no idea what the numbers on the paper meant. She was good at math, but Autumn didn't really ever go into figures this big. Plus the word 'dollar' really had no context.

"Is it a lot?" Joobel asked, now back to her merely excitable self. Gray was relieved to have a break from the spoiled version of her.

"It's twice what I hoped. Almost forty million dollars."

"I have no idea what that means."

"It's more money than a smart person would need in several lifetimes. It alone would get us close to everything we need."

"How many of those do we have?"

"My friend, right now, I have more red diamonds in my pocket than the rest of this world combined."

"Why not just offer to sell them all?" She was genuinely confused on this point.

"The reason they are worth so much is the fact that they are rare. Once I reveal them all, the price for each goes down."

She tilted her head. "Ah, won't they know you sold the first one?"

"Most of these guys are pretty greedy. I think we can sell all of these off at a premium, then move on to the next step of our plan."

Joobel was happy to see him so focused. She couldn't imagine what it was like for him to be so close to home and yet not be able to see his family.

She thought of her own family in Blood Mountain, and what it would be like to never be able to visit them. She wiped her eye and pulled out a small mirror to make sure she hadn't ruined her appearance for the next appointment.

The day went smoothly. Joobel was surprised how much better people treated you when they thought you were both wealthy and terrible.

Also, out of seven different gem sellers, all but two had an old guy named George. What an odd name, but then she was going to marry a guy named Jackalane.

They let the sellers stew for a day, then they went back and accepted each offer and gave them the gem each had examined. The funds were wired to Autumn Equities and the money was signed for by Grayson and Viviana Ashotok.

The little company now had well over two hundred million dollars and twenty-three gems left unsold. The gnome pushed her arm through her friend's and leaned her silver hair against his elbow.

Joobel was confident she'd earned pasta.

***

Gray breathed the morning air in deeply. He rented out a small office space and set up computers to search for the next part of his plan. A man named Emmet was parked out front, paid well to be their transportation around the winding streets of the city. The scents of bagels and fried dough filled the air and his mouth watered.

For the first time, at least in his home world, he didn't worry about the price of anything. It felt surreal to be so terribly rich, even for a short time. He entered the building with his petite silver-haired companion in tow.

He had been excited to let her try doughnuts. To his dismay, she didn't care for them.

The gnome wrinkled her nose. "Ugh, they are way too sweet."

Gray tried a couple of other local favorites. In the end, the gnome just ate some fruit. Turns out, she really liked pineapples. He went another direction, the glazed sugar sticking to his fingers and lips.

He'd been looking all morning and narrowed his search to two candidates. He was looking for an infectious disease specialist but didn't want to do what had been done to him. They needed someone very good at their job, but with little family to speak of and a reason to negotiate with him.

The first he checked up on was an older man named Dr. Harold Greenburg. He was single, no living children, and had a brain tumor that would kill him in the next few weeks. Sadly, when Gray called the hospital to see if he could get in to see him, the man had already died of complications.

His second option was a widow in her mid-seventies. The woman had a rare form of blood cancer and was in her final days. She had no children on record and was top of her field. Currently, she was staying in a hospital on the other side of the city.

He wrote down the info and turned to his companion, who was flapping her wings and bouncing around the room.

"When you get done being crazy, I have a lead."

Joobel flipped in midair, spun, and landed perfectly on the balls of her feet. Her smile was wide. He knew it wasn't the same, but he also missed flying. She asked about his discovery.

"Is it the old guy?"

"No. Sadly, he passed away. The woman is still a possibility."

She waved a hand and zoomed into the next room. They paid top dollar for so much wasted space, but it was clear the gnome needed to work her wings. It wasn't like they could go to the park.

Only seconds later, she emerged again, wearing a short red skirt, a yellow blouse, and a long red jacket that hid her wings. She had pink sandals with sequins and a handbag that matched the shoes.

Gray wore his only suit. It was much easier to be a man and stay in fashion. Emmet pulled up the car as he saw them approach. He was being paid well to be both available and discreet.

Despite the short distance, it took almost an hour to reach the hospital. The main desk attendant seemed surprised when they named the person they wished to visit. She was genuinely cheered up at visitors coming.

"Oh, you mean Mini. She's such a sweet lady. She doesn't get many visitors; only a few grad students have dropped by. Are you... family?"

Gray had to smile. Say what you will about race, a tall black man and a tiny white woman weren't going to be the children of a Chinese lady. He tried to tell a version of the truth.

"It's about her work. There may be an application of her research that might help a good deal of people. I work with a not-for-profit that wants to make medications for free distribution."

The woman seemed torn. Obviously, she wasn't supposed to let them up, and to lie that they were family would be counterproductive. It might have been Joobel who helped her decide. Gray noticed the small woman looked like she was falling apart. Her eyes were red with tears.

His friend was shuddering as if she were holding back sobs. Then it hit him. The gnome was at least a little empathic. Joobel felt the pain of others and it was anathema for her to not help. This was a hospital, and the pain and suffering of so many in such tight quarters was overwhelming her.

Gray saw the attendant looking at his friend as he spoke.

"It would mean a good deal to *many* people if we could speak to her."

She typed something on the computer and then slid a tag over to each of them as she explained.

"Fourth floor, elevators are down the hall. Room 417. If anyone asks, you are here for final arrangements. Be nice to Mini; she's a wonderful person."

Gray thanked her for the badges and promised that Mini would be a big help. He worked to hold the gnome up as they walked. He needed Joobel for this part of the plan, but it was beginning to hurt him to see his friend in such a state.

It wasn't unheard of to see people upset in a hospital, so no one asked about her obvious distress. He hugged her in the elevator; polished steel all around made it hard to avoid touching a wall. The proximity of so much iron made him feel weak.

Then she whispered to him, horror in her voice.

"There are children. Oh, Gray, there are so many and they are so sick."

The hospital had a cancer ward. There would be no shortage of sick kids. But they had to complete the mission.

He guided her off the elevator and down the hall to Room 417. In the bed lay a petite Asian woman, her skin only lightly wrinkled.

Her pallor revealed a long, losing battle with disease. The room smelled of strong disinfectant. Once black hair had more than a touch of grey and hung lank and thin. Her eyes were closed in a drug-induced sleep.

Gray looked at his friend. Joobel could barely stand, but she nodded at him and began to do what they came for. As he moved to stop the flow of morphine, she clipped her silver bracelet to the woman's wrist.

He had explained that drugs were pumped into patients who were in pain. They made them sleepy and made it hard for them to concentrate.

The bracelet worked quickly to purify the drugs from her system and the old woman started to grow restless. Joobel clasped her hand quick as a snake. She took away the pain and gave this woman a moment of clarity.

Gray moved to close the door. He pushed a dense wedge of air behind it, blocking anyone from walking in.

He moved back over and addressed the woman whose wide eyes were darting around to the strangers in her room. He held up a hand to assure her he was no threat.

"Dr. Minzhu Zhang. Sorry if I failed the pronunciation. My name is Gray and this is Joobel. We have a proposition for you. We require your skills and it would seem you require ours. Might I discuss this with you further?"

The old woman seemed oddly calm as she lifted a weak hand up to peel back the oxygen mask. Her words were slow and deliberate. There was a faint hint of an accent.

"What are you using for the pain? It's marvelous. I haven't been able to think this clearly for months."

"I'm afraid it's not something we can really mass produce. My friend has some talents, one of which is giving us this chance to talk."

The doctor seemed confused by this. She looked to Joobel, who had a firm grip on her other hand, holding back the waves of agony that would leave her unable to speak.

The old woman whispered, "You're helping me?"

"I wish I could do more." Joobel was choked up by the tears forming in her bright-blue eyes.

Gray moved forward and sat beside her on the bed. He began to tell a story that he only hoped she could believe.

"I would be happy to go in-depth with you later, but time requires us to move swiftly. I'm from this world but have spent the past few years in another. Joobel is from there originally. It's a world where spirits bind with mortal bodies and magic is possible.

"That world is under attack by a threat that I can only describe as a sentient disease. It has destroyed many worlds and ours is next. We need your help... and you need ours."

She looked back and forth and then, with a great effort of will, sat up to face him.

"If you cannot face your disease, how can you help me?"

He nodded in understanding. "If you agree to come to our world to help us in this fight, I have been authorized to offer you three gifts."

Her tired eyes squinted and one eyebrow lifted. "What could you possibly offer a woman with days left to live?"

He shrugged. He"Time, for starters. The other gifts we'll discuss later. Right now, I think we can heal your body and give you more time to do your work."

Joobel was still falling apart, and the woman showed her own empathy at the younger woman's pain. She gripped the gnome's arm with a weak hand.

"What's wrong, child?"

Joobel wasn't able to speak, so Gray answered for her.

"One of her talents is empathy. She has others, but this one allows her to share the pain of those hurting. This place... is a bit much for her."

The old lady shook her head. "I have to admit that you tell a good story, but I'm a woman of science. How can I possibly believe what you are telling me?"

"I thought you might feel that way." He nodded to Joobel.

Though she was hurting and distracted, she was the best proof they had of what he claimed. She stood and removed her long red coat. Four paper-thin wings shot out to the sides. She worked them with a loud hum and hovered off the floor, floated over the old woman, and then landed back where she started.

Old eyes went wide with surprise. "Well then..., that is evidence."

Gray nodded. "If nothing else, we would hold up our side of this agreement first. You would walk out of here with us today. If we cannot do that, you will have agreed to nothing. Understand though, we are leaving this world. If you join us, you will not be able to come back. You will be leaving here forever."

She glanced around the room, then down at her worn body.

"Hospice is a good thing, gives people peace. Time to say goodbye, you understand. I have given my farewells and am ready to die. Whether with you to a land of magic or as an empty shell in bed, I'm not long for this world."

"So, you accept my offer?" he asked, his voice soft.

She smiled weakly. "I do, though I'm not sure I believe you. If nothing else, this will be interesting."

Gray nodded to Joobel, who reached into the small handbag. There were five of the vials of Bloom's healing mist left. She handed one of them to Gray. He popped the plug and looked to the old woman.

"Breathe in deeply."

She did so, and with a wisp of his power, he pulled the air from the bottle and pushed it deep into her lungs. She gasped loudly and tensed up as the magic entered her bloodstream. Her blood was cleansed of the cancerous cells that made her body work against itself. Then she relaxed and looked up once again.

"That was quite an experience. I feel better but still quite weak. What's next?"

He gave a wry smile. "As I said, we walk out of here."

The old woman worked to stand and took short steps in slippered feet. She walked across the room and then back again. As she moved, her joints limbered a bit, and she gained some confidence. Gray nodded with satisfaction.

"As we leave, you will feel like you are being held up some. That will be me; just go with it."

Tendrils of soft air moved to her hands and shoulders, giving her support and helping her move. As Gray dropped the barrier to the door, Joobel walked over and turned, her look pleading. Through her tear-filled eyes, she begged him to understand.

"I cannot leave so much pain. Please understand why I have to do this."

Before he could act, the gnome was moving down the hall.

***

Claire looked around at the gathered allies around the wide oval table covered in maps. It sat in a world that had an altered flow of time. Gray made something up about gravity wells or some such nonsense when he tried to figure it out. Whatever made it work, it allowed long planning sessions that would take little time from her duties at the Blood Keep.

At her side sat her brother and Norim. Just across from them sat Hurley and Cruor, who were seated on either side of Raine. All the planning and preparations had been made. All that remained was choosing a path of travel and staggering arrivals to ensure the best advantage should there be an ambush.

While it was sometimes frustrating to work with Raine, mostly because the young woman didn't have to obey her, Claire was grateful to have such a powerful ally. The Winter Queen was breaking down her intentions for travel.

"Our dragons are our best defense should we be accosted. I think we should portal to here."

Her pale, slender hand moved to point out a line of low mountains just on the Winter side of the Spring border.

"From there, my retinue will leave and arrive just over an hour before you do. It will not seem odd for you to come from the direction of an ally and they are unlikely to insult Winter. Also, we have Puddle and I doubt they would have any good way to deal with him."

Claire could only see a couple of small risks in this. Hurley would have worked out the success rate of the strategy. She looked to the older man and he smiled, knowing what she wanted.

"It has a 97% chance of getting both groups there unbothered. Beyond that I can only guess."

Claire smiled. "Raine, I want you to make copies of him."

The Winter Queen put a fond hand on her advisor's arm. Her smile beamed.

"We have been looking for another like him. Should we find one, we can negotiate. This one is mine."

Hurley cocked an eyebrow as the two queens who'd banned slavery joked about trading him off. He cleared his throat and Claire continued her line of thought.

"They are good odds but I don't think separating is wise. Our strength is in the alliance between us. If they can pull one party away, the other is vulnerable. Consider we each land here and here."

She indicated two spots, each perhaps a ten-minute flight apart, again on the Winter side of the border.

"We would never be more than a few minutes apart and would arrive from slightly different directions. With dragon-speak we would never be out of contact."

Hurley paused as he wove his power around the words in his mind. All watched him for a response.

"It's over 99%. I think she has a point. I support this plan."

Raine nodded, having long ago accepted that Claire was crafty to the point of annoying. Cruor stood and looked down at the map, his hand hovering over each route. He looked at Jack.

"I see seven ambush points; we would need to have some way to scout them. Any ideas?"

Jack stared silently for several seconds, then shook his head.

"I see nine. Harvest can scout for dragons; I'm sure the others know how as well. If anything else comes at us, we can just wipe away all traces of them. I don't have to hold back if we don't plan on leaving witnesses."

Cruor began to nod as he too saw the other two points where they would be vulnerable. Then he registered Jack's words.

"He can see them far out?"

Claire stepped in to answer for her bond-mate.

"Harvest learned some things from the sea dragon, Depth. He kind of pulses out his dragon-speak. Other minds that can use the ability pulse back. He can get a good idea of who is there and where they are."

Cruor seemed both impressed and concerned.

"Could he see my queen right now?"

Claire shook her head. "Not across worlds. If she stepped through the gate and he was looking, then yes."

Cruor's red eyes narrowed. "Not sure I like that."

Jack could see his worry and stepped in. "Harvest guarded Raine the night she hatched Mist. If our death drake wanted

Raine dead, she would be dead."

Cruor didn't seem satisfied, but Claire knew he was fierce in his protection of the Winter Queen. She didn't fault him, only tried to give him perspective.

"One of the downsides of powerful allies is you get a good look at how they could hurt you. Even Harvest has those he fears."

The Leech gave a bitter laugh. "What does a death dragon that big fear?"

"Maeve, Depth, Claire choking on something," Jack said abruptly. The room fell silent before Claire ushered them forward with planning.

They collectively set times and roles for patrols. Claire made sure Raine knew that even now the dead of Autumn roamed Spring looking for traps and dangers. The Alder King limited the number of dragons and guards, but he said nothing about ghosts. Hospitality would allow it.

When all was decided, Claire looked over the plan and nodded.

"Ok, that should do it. Messengers can carry last-minute details. We will all meet up in just under three days."

***

Gray had heard of Joobel's ability to affect emotions with a song. It was something she used sparingly as it cost her to sing it. She was willing to pay the price to ease so much suffering in this place.

As the gnome stepped into the hall, a faint melody rose up into the air. Even with his protections, he could feel the effects of the magic. Moments of joy from his memories started to push their way to the surface of his thoughts.

He read a favorite book with his mother, hit a slow pitch from his dad. He accepted his diploma from high school. A young girl could see correctly. He turned to receive a kiss from the woman he loved for so long. The joy bubbled up inside and he found himself laughing.

Beside him, the woman who had so recently been at the edge of death began to giggle as well. The song moved through the halls, into each room, and through the nursing stations. The faint sounds of distant joy and laughter echoed back through the corridor.

Then the gnome was moving. Gray knew where she was going. The children's ward was on the third floor. He moved as fast as he could to follow, the old woman plodding behind him with her magically braced limbs.

Joobel couldn't take the stairs with the steel handles on the door and he just missed her on the elevator, baton in hand to push the buttons. He caught the next one and went to the third floor.

As the door opened, the song came back in volume. A doctor was laughing happily in the hall, reliving a precious moment, no doubt.

Gray moved to the hall with the rooms for the children. They were all empty. Joobel walked straight past them, not bothering to look inside. Drawn by the pain in the small bodies, she moved directly to the source.

A large sitting room had rows of chairs and beds. A woman was laughing while holding a storybook she was no longer reading. Over two dozen children were in various spots around the room, each bald and wearing breathing tubes. Tiny bodies were thin and weak.

These little ones were what put his friend over the edge. Her song grew louder and she looked at the children, then to him. As her song ceased, she threw the last four vials of the healing mist to the ground hard enough to shatter the bottles.

He only had a second to react. Bloom could make a seemingly infinite amount back in his world. Here in this place, that mist was worth far more than any gem. It meant time for those who had none, and he caught it with his power.

As the children laughed, he broke up the portions and pushed the magic into each of the tiny lungs, allowing the energy to flow through them.

Joobel walked over to him and hugged him tightly, strong gnomish arms almost bruising his ribs.

She was close to sobs. "Thank you, we can go now."

They turned to see the old woman staring at them in shock and awe. She was a person who had dedicated her life to healing and saving lives. What she'd witnessed had told her more about these strange people than any words could have.

The old woman wiped her eyes. "Let's get started. You can call me Mini. All my friends do."

It took a bit of time to work their way back to the front entrance. Even with the aid of the air helping to hold her up, the old woman moved very slowly.

Finally, they reached the main desk. Mini walked over to speak to the woman, glancing at her name tag.

"Hello, Sarah. I need to check out. These folks need my help and I'm afraid it will take some time. Do you have a form for me to sign?"

The woman named Sarah almost fell out of her chair.

"Mini, what are you doing up? You could fall and... are you ok?"

The old woman nodded. "I'm fine, though a bit hungry. I'm sure we can stop for something. Do you have that form?"

Sarah looked for a moment and then frowned. She turned back to them.

"You have a power of attorney set up. Only your agent can make those decisions. You're not supposed to be able to move."

"Oh, ok." She looked up at Gray. "Is there anything I need to bring with me? I'm afraid I gave most of my stuff away."

Gray leaned forward and whispered in her ear. "I have over two hundred million dollars to spend and we are leaving in two days."

The old woman cocked an eyebrow before her lips widened into a broad smile. She waved at Sarah.

"Goodbye, sweetheart. Thank you for all the company."

With that, they walked out the front door. The desk attendant watched them go and couldn't help but smile.

Later that week, the sweet woman named Sarah would find out that other oddities happened around the same time as the strange case of the old woman's departure.

Doctors and nurses blacked out for several minutes. The sick people throughout the whole hospital all reported feeling better for a while. Twenty-seven young cancer patients all went into remission.

At the exact same time.

CHAPTER 10

J oobel was starting to snap out of the daze she'd been in since the hospital. The frail doctor came back to the little office with them. The gnome flew around for a bit to clear her head. Sadly, they got a noise complaint, so she stopped for now. She wanted to see them fly quietly in such a small space! Right now, she was pestering Gray.

"I'm getting hungry. Can we get pasta again?"

He winced. "We picked up lunch on the way back. Can we wait a couple hours?"

She pouted and laid back in her chair. "I might waste away by then."

Gray wondered if his small friend might have picked up some of the habits of her spoiled rich girl character. He was sitting at a table with Dr. Minzhu Zhang, or Mini as she liked to be called. The old woman said it had a double meaning, indicating her size. Joobel noted that was kind of insulting since the woman was taller than she was.

Right now, they were making a list of the equipment Mini would need to study a strange disease. Gray had done his homework and ordered most of the things earlier, but some would have to be added to the list and rushed for delivery.

Joobel now understood why they needed so much money to start with. It seemed building a lab from scratch wasn't an inexpensive task.

The old woman kept talking about air samplers, analyzing equipment, sterilizing equipment, dee-in-ay sequencing, and something called an infrared spectrometer. Not to mention she wanted access to machines that could see inside the body.

Gray insisted on buying duplicates of some of the most expensive equipment as well as manuals for repair and the parts to replace various pieces. Already the price tag was in the tens of millions of dollars. Mini seemed quite confused about Gray's insistence that they couldn't come back again.

Joobel was also confused by the whole time issue between the worlds, but up until now, it was something they were able to exploit. Now it made this a single endeavor.

After a couple of hours of discussing delivery options, Gray began ordering the additional equipment. A large warehouse just outside the city would be stocked with all the things they had ordered.

Gray had been up late arranging rushed delivery for the items. A small group of workers staffed the warehouse at all times to take deliveries and watch over the things inside.

Joobel was surprised that large and expensive items could be moved so quickly, but for the right price, things were finding their way to the building in record time.

Her stomach finally getting the best of her, she walked over and used all her charm on her big friend.

"Feed me!"

He grimaced. "Ok, ok. Let's go out and have something special. Mini deserves a good meal."

Though she was a little thin from her illness, Mini wasn't much taller than Joobel. The gnome shared her wardrobe and Mini found jeans and a blouse that fit her pretty well.

Soon they were walking to an elegant Italian eatery just up the street. It was an odd group, but the old woman was taking her change of circumstance in stride.

The evening was a nice break from the urgency and stress of the tasks they had set out to complete. Gray and Joobel shared stories of Autumn and the friends they had there. They even discussed the queen Mini would meet once at the Blood Keep.

Mini immigrated to the United States long before Gray had been born. She was born in China in the late nineteen forties and gotten her doctorate in medicine there. When she moved, she specialized in infectious medicine and studied several viral outbreaks in Africa, South America, and Europe. She'd been married to a civil engineer for over 40 years.

Joobel found it was easy to overeat in this world. She patted the bump at her waist in satisfaction. Mini had eaten much more than she had at lunch and seemed to have more energy.

After dinner, they bypassed the office and went back to the hotel. This time they moved to a suite where the two women could share a room. Gray would be only a dividing door away.

Perhaps it was the relaxed dinner that lulled them into letting their guard down. Maybe it was the presence of the sweet old lady.

Either way, learning not to flash your wealth is a hard lesson.

***

Gray awoke to the sound of the hallway door slowly clicking open. Three shapes moved in and stepped through. The last one closed the door behind them. Gray pushed through the fog of sleep, just alert enough to avoid giving away his own wakefulness. The figures were quietly whispering to each other as they moved toward him.

The nearest was carrying a thick cloth that smelled of sweetness and disinfectant. It was doubtful they were there to scrub down his room.

His mind quickly darting around, he assumed that these people knew about the funds he'd been moving around and so would know who was staying in these rooms.

Without knowing just how strong and fast Joobel was, they would assume him to be the only real threat. They both went through great pains to nurture that illusion.

As the forms grew closer, he could see that only two of them were coming toward him. The third must have moved through the suite to the room where the women were sleeping.

Gray forced himself to hold still and keep his breathing even. Despite his size, two against one would be a struggle. He hadn't tested his limits in this world but could feel his control over air was much weaker here. Even Mini had seemed heavy when he helped her.

The nearest man leaned over him and pushed the cloth toward his face. Gray kicked out against the further man, just as he grabbed the hand holding the cloth. A loud '*oof*' let him know that he had knocked the breath from his intruder. He grappled and twisted, pushing the fabric to the face of the man nearest him.

In only a few short seconds, the man went limp, just as the other pulled in a lungful of air. This man was now ready and pulled out a long blade.

"You shouldn't have woken up. This won't be clean now."

Gray didn't bother trying to banter. He always thought it stupid to duel with words when you could just punch. He faked to one side and then threw a quick jab into the face of the knife wielder.

The sound of a muffled crunch spoke of a future with a crooked nose, but the man shook it off and crouched low, swaying with the knife in front of him.

Backing up, Gray felt behind him on the nightstand, grasping for something he could use as a weapon. He was desperate to get into the other room and find out what was going on with Joobel and Mini.

He felt a plastic box covered in buttons and switches: the alarm clock. He grabbed it and tore it from the wall. As he pulled back to throw his makeshift missile, the knifeman lunged forward. Gray took the slash on one arm as he swung the clock down with the other.

The sound shook the room, knocking pictures from the wall and knocking the TV from its place on the desk. Gray looked down in amazement, wondering how he'd done it. Then he heard the scream.

Frantic to help his friends, the large man tossed the mangled clock aside. He pushed the knifeman away to the floor. He was out for the count.

Running to the other room, he could see Joobel on the floor leaning over the third intruder. She was desperately trying to get the man to move, muttering over him as she tried to push her power into him.

"Please be ok! Oh no, just please don't die! Please, I didn't mean to. I'm so sorry...."

Gray looked to Mini, who was sitting on the bed, looking stunned. He waved in her face.

"What happened?"

Mini stared up at him. Her eyes were still vacant in her shock. She paused for long seconds before speaking.

"That man came in and asked where we had all the money. I didn't know what to tell him, but she..." Mini nodded to the gnome. "She jumped in front of me. Then the man pulled a knife and started to stab at her. She just tapped him with a stick of some sort and he flew into the wall. What was that?"

Gray realized he had miscalculated. He tried to make the batons with Joobel in mind. He had pushed magic through them and Jack did the same. Jack even let Gray use it on himself to make sure they worked as intended.

But Joobel's magic was way more potent than he'd guessed, even in this world. The gnome had no real way to wield her power directly; she could take pain or sing her siren's song. She could fly and was faster and stronger than should be possible for anyone her size.

Claire had Named her Viviana. She was life. In this world, her power of renewal was the only spirit magic present. His power was weak in this world; hers wasn't. When he channeled magic through the baton it flowed like a gentle stream. But Joobel powered it into a jet of force that threw a full-grown man nearly through a hotel wall.

Gray leaned down and put two fingers on the man's neck. He felt for a pulse while eying a large wound on one side of the man's torso. It was where the baton made contact. The heat from the shock flash boiled the moisture in his body. The contact point exploded at impact, rupturing his torso and burning away the cloth.

There was no pulse. This man was dead beyond hope. Perhaps if they had several bottles of Bloom's healing mist it would be different, but they were gone. They had given a new chance at life to the children at the hospital.

He felt a pull on his arm. Mini was binding the slash from the man's knife, her doctor's training bringing her out of her stupor.

"You will need stitches and you are going to have a nasty scar," Mini chided.

He didn't care about the arm. As long as he didn't bleed out, Claire could fix anything that didn't outright kill him. His heart was breaking for his friend.

"Please don't be dead. Please. Please. Please!" Joobel begged, before breaking down into heaving sobs.

He laid a hand on her shoulder, pulling her into a hug. He whispered into her ear.

"This isn't your fault; I miscalculated your strength. You were protecting Mini. Please don't put this on yourself."

He stood, picking up the gnome. She was light despite her strength. He laid her on the bed and asked Mini to try and help her. Then he went to the task of dealing with the situation.

The sound against the wall was loud enough that he had little doubt the police would be called. They needed to leave.

They were the ones who were attacked, but he was a large black man in New York. His only witnesses were an old Asian woman who was supposed to be dying and a silver-haired supermodel who happened to have wings. For two of them a set of steel handcuffs would be deadly.

Gray pulled the men and the body into his bathroom and closed the door. He'd finished ordering the equipment before bed. All that was left to do was make one stop to sign the forms for the remainder of his funds and make the arrangements for his final goodbye. Then they could go home.

Fairie was indeed his home now; this world was only a stop on his quest. He quickly packed everything up. They would have to leave some of Joobel's clothes, but most of what she'd bought was already at the warehouse. Mini had nothing other than her borrowed clothes and some toiletries from the hotel.

The clock next to Joobel's bed read just after three in the morning. His clock was no longer able to argue. Mini carried the lighter bag with her along with Joobel's things. Gray grabbed his own case and scooped up his blanket-wrapped friend.

They didn't bother checking out, taking a side door onto the street. They saw the flashing lights and the police going through the front as they moved up the road.

Gray was glad to have the old woman walking with him. Wrapped and in the blanket, the gnome looked like a sleepy child.

He let Mini hail the cab and soon they were at the warehouse. The guards stopped him out front, but he knew all the passcodes. More importantly, he controlled the accounts that paid the men.

They spent the rest of the night in the large open building. Stacks of boxes, supplies, and equipment were piled up all around. More arrived as time passed. Many of the items had cost more to move in such a short period than the price of purchase.

He moved some boxes and set the gnome on a sheet of cardboard. Mini laid next to her and they shared the blanket. Soon both were back asleep.

Gray moved around the place, checking on the various items he'd purchased. He knew he wouldn't sleep again tonight.

The cut on his arm began to ache and the man found himself wishing Joobel could take the pain. Just before seven, he went out and asked a guard to have a meal brought. They outdid themselves and brought a catered breakfast, setting up just outside. It was enough for the guards as well.

Gray snuck out and made heaping plates for himself and his companions. It wasn't what he would had envisioned for his last meal in this world, but it was delicious and filling.

The smell of food woke Joobel. Though she was able to eat, she didn't speak a word. Mini made small talk, but seemed worried about the gnome as well.

Gray left in time to make his nine o'clock meeting. He transferred the remaining funds at his disposal into a trust where the money would sit invested in one of the few stocks he was familiar with. The tall, dark man bought just over a hundred million dollars' worth of Bitcoin.

He made the arrangements for letters to be delivered to his family at set times. He signed some papers and a large donation was made to the same scholarship fund that once helped him get into college. He shook hands with the attorney overseeing his case and walked out the door. It was time to go home.

The only home he would ever know now.

***

Raine had just made the final run through her packing list when she heard a knock at the door. One of the six guards watching over her moved to answer it. Usually, Cruor would be here alone. When he left he insisted on no less than six guards, and then only if she was both awake and armed.

She never slept without him a room away, a concept she thought silly at first. There were two more dead assassins the day before. Now the young queen found she slept better with her Leech on watch.

The door swung wide to reveal her other bodyguard for the trip to Spring. Her former companion and bodyguard, Sroto, was a Yeti of the air spirit who gave her own life to save the then Winter Maiden.

Now a Queen of Winter, Raine had few she could trust with her life. The vast form that ducked to step into the room was the older brother of her previous guard.

The Yeti of Winter had been the first to pledge themselves to her upon taking the throne. She would do anything for them and they honored her in the same way.

You would expect something as vast and broad as a Yeti to 'lumber.' Despite the expectation, the towering figure covered in thick white fur moved as if he'd spent his youth learning to dance. His motions were full of grace and his bow to the queen was a smooth fluid gesture.

She smiled and ran to hug the visitor. "Bulroc! It's so good to see you."

You would expect the voice of something so significant to be deep and gravely. In this case, it was just so. The words rumbled low as the yeti spoke.

"You as well. I haven't seen you since my sister's sending."

Raine's blue-grey eyes went distant as she remembered her friend.

"It was a lovely service. I miss Sroto every day."

The room grew quiet with the shared sadness. The yeti picked the queen up and hugged her back. The guards all readied for a fight, but he gently set her down and ignored them. Between the thick fur and layers of muscle, they would need much larger blades to actually harm him.

"I carry little, but what I need is packed. If I might stay in the Citadel, I will attend to you in the morning."

Raine scrunched her nose and pushed her white hair behind her ear.

"Nonsense. I have a room near my own quarters for you to sleep in and you must join me for dinner tonight."

The yeti shook his head. "I need not impose. I have my own rations."

"I have three deer from the Twilight Vale spit roasting below. If you would rather eat jerky...."

Bulroc smiled widely, sharp white teeth visible through the fur only by the gleaming shine.

"I suppose it would be rude to leave you to eat alone."

Raine nodded as if offended. "Yes, I think it would."

She hugged the furry figure once more and then began to explain their travel plans. Before she'd covered their route and the precautions to safely travel it, Cruor strode into the room carrying a small pack.

He stared at the yeti for a long moment, seeming to choose how best to dispatch the intruder should it become necessary. Once he decided, he turned to Raine.

"Are you all packed?"

She nodded. "Of course. Have you met your fellow bodyguard? This is Bulroc."

The great ball of white fur rumbled as he looked to the much smaller man.

"You must be the queen's infamous Leech. It's an honor to work with someone who has protected our honored lady so well."

Cruor nodded once and then moved to stretch out on one of the sofas. It could be argued that he drifted off to sleep, but the more astute of the guards noticed his head shifted slightly as the queen moved around the room.

The dinner was delicious. Bulroc ate two of the small deer by himself. In contrast, Cruor ate the salad and dried fruit that always accompanied the meals served to the queen's quarters.

With both capable guards so close, the rest of the soldiers moved to patrol the Citadel. The Queen of Winter took an early night to be rested for the next morning.

***

The portal popped into existence on the far end of Autumn's new warehouse. Despite his request to have trolls stationed to help unload the goods, only one person stood inside the large empty space. He entered alone to see the woman he loved.

"Gray? I thought you were getting ready to leave. What are you doing here with...."

Claire saw the state of her adopted sister through the doorway and gasped. He held up a hand and said the words he'd been thinking over for the past few days.

"My world doesn't move the same direction in time. Joobel is upset and we have a new guest, but I don't know what will happen if we cross paths with our past selves. Please send the trolls to help move things early and act as if nothing has happened."

He knew she would say yes. From his point of view, she already had. Claire shook her head, looking past him into the portal on the other side.

"Please, Claire, send a ghost the second we leave and we'll come straight to you. We need the things moved quickly. I don't know how a portal between these worlds will react if left open too long."

She stared at him for a long moment, her need to ask questions at odds with her trust in him. Then the queen simply nodded.

"I trust you. Watch over my sister. I'll have food sent to you."

He shook his head. "I have some from the other world. Mini can't eat the food here just yet. We will be fine; it's just one day."

Claire sighed and then gave him a curt nod. "One day."

Then she was gone. His queen must have sent ghosts to request help from the trolls, because they arrived in minutes. Many carried long poles and tools for moving the merchandise from the adjoining warehouse in another world.

Trolls were incredibly sturdy and these were among those who could boil blood for even more amazing feats of strength. They knew the task ahead and without instruction began working to move everything into Autumn.

The tall, dark man moved back in and carried Joobel across the threshold with a small old woman at his side. His face was a mask of concern. Hers was one of wonder.

Mini lived a remarkable life and loved her dear husband until his passing. She'd enjoyed her work right up until she'd been forced to stop. Then at the brink of death, a bit of wonder entered her life. Now she was walking into a world of magic.

Tall men of dark green were moving boxes and smiling to her as they passed, their tusks making the gesture unnerve her a bit. She found herself in a building made seemingly of a single piece of blood-red stone. A tiny man was running around with a clipboard and squeaking instructions to the movers.

Gray pulled her to one side. "We have to sorta quarantine for a day. Time moves backwards between our world and this one. If we roam around I might meet myself, which didn't happen before I left. I'm great with multiverse theories, but don't feel the need to test them."

To his utter amazement, Mini just nodded. "Ok, I'll need to keep our winged friend comfortable. I have camped in much worse conditions. Will there be food? I find I've been really hungry since that green bottle stuff."

Gray smiled and moved to get the crate of dried food and bottled water.

One day.

***

Mini followed her host as he carried the winged woman through the building and outside. It had been summer when she left New York. Now she found herself in a brisk fall afternoon. She continued as he led her to another large building, a school by the name on the entrance.

They moved through the halls until they came to another strange doorway. Another step and her stomach lurched as they moved into yet another building of the same red stone. Soldiers in brown and gold walked the wide halls.

Then they stood at a solid, ornate entryway. Her host wasn't asked to knock; the doorman merely nodded to him and opened the thick wooden door with a nod of respect.

"She's expecting you."

The door shut behind them. Mini was surprised to see that the room was cozy. Couches circled a low table; small biscuits were on a large copper platter. Little jars of jam and a steaming pot of tea sat in the table center.

At the noise, a young woman came into the room. She was little more than a child. She had long brown hair that curled at the temples, skin only lightly kissed by the sun, and brown eyes that reminded Mini of jumping into piles of leaves as a little girl.

She wore well-made clothing of gold and brown, her leggings topped with a skirt that was a nod to the form that had given way to function. In her hair was a silver circlet, the only real evidence that she was the queen of Mini's new home.

The young woman ran and hugged the tall man, kissing him on the cheek. Her face then wrinkled in concern over the trauma and state of the gnome as he moved to set Joobel in her own bed. Finally, she turned to Mini as Gray spoke.

"Claire, please let me introduce you to Dr. Minzhu Zhang. She prefers to be called Mini."

Gray then looked to Mini. "Mini, this is Claire Ashotok, Queen of Autumn. Also, my girlfriend."

Mini watched as the queen blushed and squeezed the man's arm. Then the young woman moved to stand before her.

Claire was a queen and taller than the old woman, yet she wasn't the least bit imposing. She took the old woman's hand, giving it a gentle squeeze.

"Thank you for coming here to help my people. This world is in danger and I fear that we might not be able to win out on our own."

Mini was a bit confused. The girl was way too gentle and sweet to be the infamous woman who gave people nightmares. To hear Joobel tell it, Claire was feared throughout the world and had faced down an army. This Banshee of Autumn was seemingly quite pleasant. Mini shook her head.

"You aren't what I expected. It's a pleasure to meet you."

The queen laughed, holding a hand over her mouth and nodding.

"I'm many things to many people. I have been known to be... *protective*... of my children."

Then the queen's eyes began to shift to an eerie white. Figures appeared all throughout the space. The young woman's brown hair shifted to move and float in the still air of the room. Her voice became otherworldly.

"I'm long past the shame of who and what I am. Power is defined by how it is used."

Then as quickly as Claire had called on her ability, she released it. Before the old woman stood the pleasant girl once again. Mini was a bit shaken, but now she understood.

"Well, now. That's still not the strangest thing I have seen this week."

Claire laughed again, though she glanced toward the room where Joobel lay unresponsive. It was clear she wished to go to her. Mini felt it polite to give her the opportunity.

"Please, your majest... your queen... I don't know what to call you."

"'Claire' has worked in the past. Though if we're in public, then 'my queen' or 'your grace' is preferred. Appearances and all."

"Claire, I'm concerned about Joobel. She seems to have something we call post-traumatic stress. I can wait if you need to —"

The queen shook her head. "I have waited a day already. I intend to spend a good deal of time with my sister, but I'm afraid you need some attention first. Are you familiar with how spirits inhabit our human bodies?"

Mini received some brief instruction from Gray, but they had spent most of their time getting ready for her work in the lab.

"Only a little."

"I have some food laid out." Claire gestured to the table. "Once you eat from the bounty of our world, I'm afraid you will go through the rather unpleasant experience of having a spirit bind to you."

Mini winced. "It's painful, then?"

Gray sat down across from her and gestured for her to do the same. He described the experience.

"It's a different sort of pain. Stressful might be a better word. The spirit fuses with every part of your body and mind. Once you are bound, you can never return to the world you came from."

Mini cocked an eyebrow at him and he corrected his assertion.

"It's possible but difficult and dangerous. I won't be going back."

Claire sat next to Gray and leaned gently against him. She took one of the biscuits and spread some jam on it as she interjected.

"To be blunt, when a person enters this world and eats the food, they become bound with a spirit. There is always some risk, and some don't survive. The younger the person is, the safer the transition. No offense, but you're rather old, Mini."

The old woman crossed her ankles and set her hands on her knees. She didn't cheat death just to come here and die in a strange land. Her eyes narrowed at the tall man.

"That's something I had *not* been told."

Claire held up a hand to allow her to explain.

"You are here to do us a favor, and we will repay you in any way we can. Much was risked for us to bring you here. I won't allow our efforts or your goodwill to go to waste. I'm offering you youth, Mini."

Gray smiled and nodded at the old woman. "Your first gift was being healed; your youth will be the second. The third is the ability to do incredible things."

Mini was more shocked by this than by any of the things she'd seen. Did she even want to be young again? Her assumption was that she would work here for the next five to ten years and then give in to age. This really was an offer of a fresh start.

"What... do you mean?"

Claire reached over and picked up an apple from a bowl on the end table next to her. The fruit was just a bit on the green side. As she held it, the color began to redden until it was perfectly ripe, then proceeded to soften and wrinkle. Moments later, the apple moved back to ripe and then it was a light green. Claire set the now bright green apple on the table and explained.

"You *must* survive the spirit binding. You *must* help us understand this enemy and save this world. I will give you youth and health and you will bind to a spirit. You will have a home here, as well as the respect and love due to a hero of Autumn. Once you have helped us, you may live out your life however you choose within our laws. This I offer you as queen; you have my word."

Mini was naturally suspicious. This sounded too good to be true. Yet here she had a unique skill set. They had already offered more than she could have hoped. The man risked his life to bring her here. The silver-haired girl might have risked more.

"I accept your offer."

Claire had Mini lie in her own bed. The queen didn't often use her power of Entropy. It brought back memories of her mother. Yet she peeled away the years from the old woman.

In only a few minutes, the fragile old woman was transformed into a youthful girl, perhaps in her mid-teens. Claire paused for a moment and then laid a hand on the now young woman's forehead. A moment of concentration was followed by a satisfied smile.

Gray grew suspicious of the last gesture. "You fixed her vision?"

"Yup." Claire's smile held a hint of pride.

Mini blinked. It's one thing to dream of reclaiming one's youth. Yet the transition from a young body to an older one is a lengthy series of subtle changes. This was like being a whole different person.

The thick glasses now felt wrong. Her general shape was similar, though she was slimmer around her chest and hips. Part of her felt the boundless energy of youth, but the transformation did nothing to repair her atrophied muscles.

She set her glasses down, then looked at the smooth skin of her hands. Mini glanced up to the odd young woman, then back down to her soft skin.

"I think you are missing the real money; do you know what some people would pay for this?"

Gray winced, his brow furrowed. "The ones who could afford to pay aren't often the kind of people we'd want to keep forever."

Mini nodded slowly. Claire pulled Mini's face to hers. She examined her work and tried to see if there were any lingering effects. She spoke absently to her patient.

"How do you feel?"

Mini thought how best to sum up her confusion and elation, but decided to keep it simple.

"In a word: Hungry."

Gray smiled and then left for only a moment, returning with some of the biscuits and jam. A cup of steaming liquid sat beside the plate. He sat next to her on the bed.

"Our queen was bonded before she was born. Our winged friend in the next room has a different sort of spirit. I went through the process a few years back."

Gray sighed, running a hand through his hair.

"It will wear on you, like your whole body cramping up for several hours. Your very essence will be altered and you'll never be the same. Our old world will most likely not be able to sustain you; we can never go home."

Mini nodded. She respected his honesty, his lack of sugar-coating the harsh experience. Yet she'd already received her side of the bargain. She gave her word and would see it through.

She reached down, took a big bite of the jam covered treat, and took a long sip of the hot tea. Gray really had sugar coated the experience after all. For the next several hours she endured searing pain and the cramping of every muscle in her body.

It was worth it.

***

The Alder King often held banquets to honor various people, events, or institutions. During these feasts, he mostly acknowledged himself. It was clear that in the absence of constant fawning and praise, the man became unbearable.

Yoshiko avoided the king as much as was possible. Still, she was the queen's daughter and until it was declared otherwise, the assumed successor to the throne. This wasn't a prospect she cherished, though the power to get rid of the pompous fool and his kin was tempting enough.

As she had intended many times before, she aimed to speak truth to him this night. In the past, Yoshiko held her courage until the moment her lips parted. Then at the last possible moment, she gave in and sang the praise of this tyrant.

The banquet hall was an impossibly large room, with a long table sitting a step higher than the others. The royal family, top military leaders, and honored guests sat around it. The higher the honor, the closer you would be seated to the king. She was technically in the royal family and the assumed Spring Maiden, so she was sitting next to her mother.

Queen Sayuri was an extremely powerful Thorn Weaver. Yet, since she'd become the Queen of Spring, she had turned timid and frightful. The once proud and willful woman now deferred to the whims of a blowhard.

Yoshiko turned as the king began his rant.

"Fellow citizens of Spring, we sit at the eve of beginning the next Contest of Champions! It will be a tremendous undertaking with numbers like you have never seen. When you have such a prestigious..." he trailed off with a self-satisfied smirk. "You just have never seen anything like it. My own son, who is undefeated, will be competing!"

The people clapped and cheered. Yoshiko noticed that there was no mention of *her* competing. She glanced about. Much of the clapping was half-hearted, but no one seemed brave enough to refrain from applauding at all.

The young woman was surprised to look down and see her own hands coming together. She set them in her lap and held them firmly in place. The king looked over to her mother.

"Perhaps the queen would like to add something?"

Queen Sayuri stood and seemed to struggle for a moment. "It is a... great honor to be a part of such an event." She sat back down, her face red and head bowed.

Yoshiko stood so fast her heavy chair slid back. "I have something I would like to say."

She started to say that the king was a fool. He'd hurt people for the slightest crimes, he persecuted the other races of the land. He was a tyrant. She'd rehearsed it so many times. What came out of her mouth was something different.

"We're fortunate to have such a great king and leader."

Then she pulled her chair back into place and sat down. Those around her began another half-hearted clap at her words and she again noticed her own hands joining her mouth in betraying her heart.

Yoshiko fought to put them down again. These events always wore on her mind and body. She knew something was wrong but couldn't put her finger on it. Why did her mother marry this man?

The feast stretched into the night, many others taking the time to talk about how great it was that Spring was to host the Contest and how fortunate they were to have such a leader.

As soon as it was allowable, she escaped the festivities, making her way through the towers of the Beryl Gardens. She was near her quarters, close to a hot bath and a good book, when a voice came from behind her.

The Alder King had two children from his first wife. Harumi was his daughter and believed by many to be the loveliest woman in the kingdom. She was a horrible person as far as Yoshiko was concerned, always finding a way to insult and demean others. She was still by far the sweeter child.

Ohkami Legerdemain was tall, well-muscled, and a truly handsome elf. Many a woman swooned as they viewed him from a distance. None felt the same after meeting him.

His face was angular and his cheekbones were seemingly crafted out of marble, topped with well-styled hair the same dark shade as his sister's. His clear skin was evenly tanned and he radiated power.

As Yoshiko turned, she almost forgot why she hated him. Then he spoke and it all came back to her.

"Well, little princess.... It seems you have lured me out here. Perhaps you and I can have a bit of fun before you—"

He reached a hand out to pull her close to him. He stopped speaking as the slim dagger point came within a finger's width of his left eye.

She growled through clenched teeth. "I thought I made it clear you keep your hands to yourself."

He only grinned. "Oh, dear sister, it was only a little jest."

She lowered the point as he backed away. His smirk made her want to gut him.

"Something tells me that you don't speak that way to your *other* sister."

Then he moved, knocking the dagger out of her hand, his body pinning her to the wall of the corridor. She struggled to move, but her hands were down at her sides.

"You should be a friendly little princess."

He moved his tongue over his lips, moving around teeth that were now too long. Yoshiko reached her hands around, trying to free them. Then she slid her hand against the little mushroom cap from the market. His aura flashed in her eyes.

Ohkami didn't share the hues of the people in the market, nor the bright green of her new friend. His aura was a mottled grey and black mess, the undertone of green distant and shaded. She could feel his intentions, his aspirations, who he really was. It was more than she could stomach, in the most literal sense.

The banquets were boring and repetitive; the fawning over the unworthy was sickening. However, the food was excellent. She'd eaten until she had to stop, both because it was delicious and because it was something to do.

The feel of the terrible man pressed up against her, with his rotting aura, was overwhelming in her mind. It caused her to refund all of dinner and what might be some of her lunch right into his handsome face.

He jumped back, dumbfounded by what had happened. Looking up at the princess, his eyes filled with rage and disgust.

She'd used the dagger to caution him; he caught her off guard when he locked her hands in place. Now, as he rushed her, she was ready.

Right before his fist found its mark, a tendril caught his hand. Another wrapped around his chest while a third grabbed both ankles and locked his feet in place. Her eyes blazed with barely suppressed anger.

"If you *ever* touch me again... if I hear of you touching the servants or a guest in this place... believe me when I say... they will *never* find what is left of you."

He began to transform, his hands and face seeming to melt into thick grey fur. His nose elongated, and the teeth grew even longer to fill his growing maw.

Yoshiko knew that if he completely transformed, this would be more fight than she wanted to have. She decided to simply throw him out the window at the end of the hall.

Ohkami was a Fawnin, a spirit of renewal that allowed him to share the shape and abilities of a beast, in his case a wolf. It made him fast, strong, and deadly.

It didn't give him wings, however. Several stories to the ground would leave him unable to bother her anymore this night. Yoshiko almost swore she heard a howl growing faint as she opened the door to her rooms.

***

Jack paced back and forth in Claire's sitting room. He'd spent the last couple of hours trying to get his betrothed to give any hint of the spark she always had. He looked to his sister and the big man at her side.

"You *swear* no one hurt her?"

Gray shook his head. "I wasn't in the room, but from what Mini described, the man attacked with a knife but never got the chance to reach either of the women. I never realized how much power Joobel has; it was like lightning struck the guy."

This was a difficult thing for the prince to cope with. The person at fault was a world away. From Gray's description he was also quite dead.

Yet that was the problem, wasn't it? Joobel was so akin to life that the act of killing had broken something in her mind. She retreated within herself and even he couldn't bring her back out.

Claire stood up and walked over to her brother. "You need to give her time."

Jack shook his head. "We leave for Spring in the morning. I can't leave her like this, and she can't go as your advisor while she's lost in her own head."

He stomped back into the room that Joobel kept right next to Claire's own. Shutting the door behind him, he walked over to where his gnome was curled up on the bed, staring at the wall. He sat just above her pillow and pulled her head into his lap.

He always struggled to put his feelings into words, yet he'd grown to care for this woman more than he thought possible. Her long silver hair was mussed and hung over her eyes and face. He slowly pushed it aside and sadly smiled down at her. To her he was able to form more words.

"You know, I don't think I would have ever married. I don't think like other people. It's hard to feel like I know they want me to. I fell in love with you, though. You're my link to the world outside. You translate what others need from me. I can't be what this world needs me to be without you."

The flood of her emotions rushed into him like a dam had burst. She'd once given him a blessing to help him recover from a terrible wound. Her power had developed to such a state that her gift had grown into an unbreakable bond.

Jack felt flutters of the link and often wondered how she was always able to find him no matter where he was. Now his side of that bond was being torn open. The man who felt so little suddenly shared the overwhelming emotion that the gnome carried always.

In his mind he stood in an open meadow. The sky was clear and the sun shone warm light upon a field of flowers. The rainbow of petals and the crisp green of the grass contrasted with the storm cloud of grief on the face of the tiny girl sitting among them.

Joobel was minuscule, smaller yet than his beloved was the day he met her. This was how she often felt, small and vulnerable.

He moved to stand before her in the grass, then sat and leaned over to her, careful not to loom. He felt the words enter the air though he never moved his lips, trying to convey his concern through his dark-brown eyes.

"You brought me into your mind through our bond?"

Her voice sounded normal to him despite the size of her avatar.

"You're always welcome here; I keep nothing from you."

"That's not completely true. I was never told of this connection."

Her face scrunched up, worry clear on her features. She gave a long sigh. "You were hurt so badly. I was afraid of losing you. I did what I had to."

He nodded, holding no anger at her actions. "What if we hadn't worked out, had grown apart? What if you were meant to be with another?"

The tiny girl's eyes rolled. "For my part, there was never any chance of that."

Joobel hesitated and then decided to share the secret she'd kept from him for so long.

"Gnomes imprint on the one they will love at first sight. I did fear you might not feel the same, though."

He smiled down at her. "Well, put your fears to rest. I need you. You have to snap out of this."

She shook her head, lip quivering. "I killed him, Jack. I pushed the power forward and it destroyed him. I'm a murderer."

Jack almost laughed but thought better of it. He tried to give perspective to her actions.

"Murder is a strong word. Did you hunt this man down to take his life?"

Her tiny eyes narrowed. "Of course not!"

"Did you see he was weaker than you and use your power to destroy him?"

Anger darkened her tiny face. "I would nev—"

"Did you try to protect someone by keeping violence from reaching them?"

She was silent, her mind back in that room.

He put a hand over his own heart. "Joobel... am I a murderer?"

The little girl began to weep. She sobbed into her hands and the shudders shook her tiny frame. He didn't let up.

"I need you to answer me."

She looked up, cheeks wet. The gnome slowly shook her head. He spoke the words that long weighed heavy in his own mind.

"You know what I am, what I'm capable of. I want to be good, to do good, but part of me wants to burn it all down. I focus my violence into a shield instead of a sword. If what you did was murder, then I'm so much worse. If you're a murderer... then I'm a monster."

She leaped to him, her tiny arms stretching out around his neck. The body that was so small now held a more familiar embrace. She was with him as he saw her now. Two sides of a coin, each helping to balance the other. Together they held both shadow and light. In the middle was clarity.

Jack blinked as he was once again in a dark room. The woman lying in his lap reached out and took his hand. She kissed it once before holding it tightly to the side of her face. The prince smiled in relief.

"Welcome back."

***

The bonding finished late in the night. Cries of pain and exhaustion kept them all up until a seemingly typical Joobel slipped into the room. The gnome put a hand on the now young Mini's forehead and they both fell sound asleep. Claire had then taken Joobel's bed.

Both Gray and Jack slept on the couches in the sitting room. Each of the men had rooms just down the hall, but wordlessly agreed to stay close as the feeling of unease in the area had them on edge.

As expected, Mini woke feeling sore and moving slowly. The bonding process left her with very stiff and painful muscles. Still, she insisted on moving around and this was something to keep her busy.

As Gray watched her, little puffs of mist formed around her hands and face. Jack had taken her now smooth, slender hand before they even had breakfast. He tested the spirit within and explained to the others. Mini held a spirit of water, the power of Healing Mist.

Gray was astonished to hear the tiny woman tell a story that was a first as far as he knew.

Most outsiders are brought to Fairie as prisoners. Summer almost certainly was still doing so, to his dismay. The bonding is done without warning or care to people who are usually quite young. The physical burden of the task is more survivable for those who aren't yet adults, but it's a process of pain and fear.

Mini was in her mid-seventies; her mind was full of a lifetime of willpower. Though her body was made young to ensure she would survive the process, she was also warned of what was to come and was ready.

When a spirit of fire began to bond with her, she tasted destruction, the violence of its power, and simply rejected it. Another spirit of earth showed her the power of stone, but she had no use for crafting rock.

Many spirits came and tried to fuse to her body and soul, but Mini knew who she was. She was a healer, a doctor, and a woman who had given up the chance to have her own family to help others remain whole.

In the end, a spirit of water showed her how the mist could ease pain and speed healing. The old woman with the young body approved and they became a single entity. Her pain would bring relief and healing to many.

Gray wondered at her story, almost disappointed that he wasn't able to do the same.

There was still much to do. The sun rose slowly on the last day before leaving for Spring. Thick clouds covered the horizon and rain would blanket the Blood Keep by midday.

Gray moved through the boxes and equipment as a newly youthful Mini moved slow and steady to take inventory of her lab equipment.

As they began moving around the warehouse, the now young woman moved much as she had in her older body. As time passed, the movements would become faster and more confident. For now she still showed the stiffness of her ordeal, but her actions matched her appearance.

He almost thought Claire made her too young. Many would say those of her country aged more slowly, but Mini couldn't be more than sixteen in this body. His musing was interrupted by a large troll holding an even larger box.

"Is this the one?" came the gravelly voice, only slightly jumbled as it came around mammoth dark tusks.

"It is!" Gray took the box. The large yellow lettering on the side indicated that it was a state-of-the-art laptop computer. He placed it with the stereo equipment and case of wires he'd set aside. Mini looked up from her industrial centrifuge to cock an eyebrow at him.

"Young man, I believe you're up to something."

Gray smiled widely as he moved a large stereo speaker to see how much it weighed.

"Have you ever been to a rock concert?"

Mini chuckled with a nod. "I was at Woodstock. I've seen the Beatles live and once got backstage passes to see the Doors."

Gray was outdone and he knew it. If she liked music, then she was going to enjoy the first of several surprises he had planned for Spring.

It took a couple of hours to set up the things being transported to various locations. Several crates of seeds were heading for long term storage. The medical equipment was going to be set up in a lab that would join Issabol's.

Countless books went to the library, a home theater system was headed to the Keep, and a generator that he hoped would work as intended went with it. A laptop filled with music, movies, and TV shows he wanted to share with his new world was on its way to Issabol's home.

He finished his work and took Mini with him to have lunch with Claire and two individuals Mini hadn't yet met. She almost fainted as the giant black dragon leaned his head down to look at her with a yellow eye the size of a table.

"Hello, little one." The voice bounced through her head.

Mini fought the urge to run. "H... h... hello. My, you're a big one."

Harvest smiled, a not altogether comforting sight. "You should meet my Elder."

"I'd like that." Mini quickly accepted the dragon as a friend, though she found Bloom to be less intimidating. This was universally true.

Gray kissed Claire goodbye and let her take Mini to tour the school. The woman would have the odd role of being both teacher and student there eventually. For now, he was going to set up his surprise for Spring.

***

Claire loved watching people meet her dragons. Though Harvest was one of the most dangerous beings in Fairie, he was like a little brother to her. Come to think of it, her actual little brother was also one of the most dangerous beings in Fairie. The realization amused her greatly.

Mini seemed to take it in stride, though her previously much older heart might not have made it through the experience.

It would have been much faster to use the portal network to get to the school, but Claire took every chance she could to fly with her bond-mate. Mini wore some of Joobel's warm clothes and a flight helmet.

The queen wondered if the woman would be able to handle the trip at first. About thirty seconds later, Mini was cheering and having a genuinely grand time of it. For one so small, she seemed to fear very little.

Part of the purpose of the school was to help the people of her kingdom learn to reach their full potential with the various forms of spirit magic available to them. Mini was probably as smart as any teacher in attendance, but her power would be entirely new to her.

With her reduced age, she would fit in among the students. She could train with the other water spirits to better learn her abilities. Eventually, she might help teach her own brand of wisdom to the younger generation.

Harvest touched down in the courtyard, just outside the administrative offices. Both women climbed off. Mini jumped up and down and hugged a giant black foreleg.

"That was amazing! Oh, I loved it. Please let me go again sometime."

Harvest seemed a bit put out at the new girl not even acting a little intimidated. Still, he eventually agreed to take her up again sometime.

Claire thanked her giant friend and moved inside the building. She smiled up at the round man making notes in a ledger.

"Hello, Fife."

The man looked up, though not at her. He nodded, wrote something else down, then stood, giving a bow.

"Good morning, my queen. I trust all is well?"

Claire shrugged. "You know better than me, I'm sure. Are the contestants ready?"

The man nodded and checked his ledger, flipping pages.

"They went home about an hour ago to make final preparations. Some of those children are terrifying... and I talk to ghosts all day."

Claire smiled back, nodding knowingly. "You and me both, Fife, I want to introduce you to my newest advisor, Mini."

The man bowed, then looked confused. Claire explained the woman's appearance.

"Mini is much older than she looks. She will be attending some classes here soon. Should she need anything, she speaks with my authority."

"Of course, my queen. It's nice to meet you, Mini." He looked back at Claire. "Are you ready for your trip?"

Claire could hear the concern in his voice. Most accepted Winter as an ally and all knew Summer to be a threat. No one liked the idea of such a beloved queen so far from home in Spring.

"You have met my dragon?"

The man's face grew grim. He could see her deflection and remained worried.

"My queen, if anything happens to you... it will mean war. I will help fight it."

It took some effort to hold back the emotion in her voice. She put her hand on his shoulder and looked into his concerned eyes.

"This must be done; know that we have planned well and have taken every precaution."

He nodded and bowed once more and then sat down and focused on the ghost relaying its latest patrol. Mini followed out into the hall, a look of concern on her face.

"You're leaving?"

Claire explained the Contest of Champions and the political dealings surrounding it. It was a delicate balancing act and she wished it could be avoided altogether. Mini nodded, absorbing the information.

Mini frowned. "It's a trap; I mean, you see that, right?"

Claire shrugged. She didn't know what form all this would take, but she wasn't blind.

"We have done our best to prepare for it and if they do try something, we will respond... *harshly*."

"I like you, Claire. You're good to people, which is rare in those with power. I once lived in a place where that wasn't true. Chances are slim that your replacement would be just as kind. These people know it."

"It's nice of you to say, but for now, let's show you around before I leave. You still need to see your new lab."

The two women moved through the campus, children excitedly squealing and running up to hug the queen. Mini got to meet some of the teachers and see the training fields. It was crude compared to some of the schools she'd seen.

Still, she knew that only a few short years ago nothing was supporting the wellbeing and education of the young in this land. Mini was impressed and said so. Claire was proud of how far they had come, despite how much was left to do.

CHAPTER 11

D espite his confidence that there would be an attack on the way to the Beryl Gardens of Spring, Jack was relieved to find that the trip went rather smoothly. He was now dressed as a guard of the Blood Keep with long sleeves and pants that wore on his patience. The solid black leather boots constricted his feet. Though he had little concern for temperature, he found it was only moments before he was tired of the uniform.

He rode on Bloom along with Joobel and a tall troll named Stoveg while Harvest carried his sister and Gray. They were traveling light as both Autumn and Winter had portals that would allow them to step back and forth between the Beryl Gardens and their respective homes.

The use of the portals would be subtle. Now that Autumn had a network in place and Winter was in the process of setting one up, they would be no secret to the rulers of the other kingdoms. It was still wise not to flaunt them.

The Autumn dragons were using dragon-speak to communicate with those of Winter. Raine's group would arrive first as it would be less likely to be attacked or insulted. Autumn would land only a few minutes later. Jack felt the unease of going into an unknown environment with unfamiliar threats, but his real concern lay with Joobel.

She'd come out of her depression but still seemed to be quieter and more introspective. Her batons were strapped to his own back as she wasn't ready to carry them just yet. He loathed leaving a weapon so matched to her out of reach.

He let the cold air drift by him as the massive green dragon carried them to the Spring capital of Amaya. The words entered his mind like an echo, the voice that of the strange water dragon.

"We are landing now. There's a contingent of soldiers and several well-dressed figures. There are two large dragons on the ground. All seems as expected."

Jack smiled inwardly. If there was an ambush, Harvest and Bloom would still be in the air and would be able to cover a retreat. The dragons of Spring were only a little concerning as all but Raine were wearing a silver bracelet that would give some protection against the spores they breathed. Winter's Queen was naturally immune.

For the first time since they began this endeavor, the prince began to think that the invitation was merely politics.

They cleared the peak of low hills, the dragons now flying low. Joobel tensed and let out a slow gasp of wonder, her words the first she'd spoken in some time.

"Oh my.... It's beautiful."

She wasn't wrong. The troll behind him grunted and even Jack nodded agreement. The Beryl Gardens were a wonder of the Fae world. Four tall spires climbed into a clear blue sky. Walkways crisscrossed the balconies and reached over a dome of the same material that shimmered with panes of crystal cut in geometric shapes.

Planters and outcroppings of wonderous flowering trees and bushes were arranged as if the whole of the building were a bouquet of color and wonder. Atop each spired tower was a cone of shining jade. The morning sun illuminated the whole of the structure. It was breathtaking.

Most would have seen the portrait as a genuinely prestigious sight. Jack's mind went to what his sister would see. More than a few of the villages they flew over were pitiful and sparse.

Claire would see the opulence for what it was: a show of wealth for the sake of pride. Jack felt the beginning of a smile. He was looking forward to seeing Claire meet the famed king of this place.

Jack hugged Joobel tightly for a brief moment before standing up and walking out to the edge of the dragon's neck. Bloom was seconds from landing, but only the troll feared the prince might fall.

He bent his knees and jumped right as the massive green form gently touched down on the green lawn. He lightly landed, taking the extra energy and absorbing the power to add to his stored magic. His control over various forms of power was becoming much more refined.

The prince turned to assist the gnome, who needed no such help but smiled at the gesture. She was also dressed in finery of sorts, and had made new clothes for Raine and Claire for this occasion.

Joobel wore layered silks of deep green, the skirt hanging low but allowing full movement. The tunic was trimmed in a lace of lighter green. Claire had her own outfit of golden brown and Raine wore one in a radiant shade of blue.

Gray wore a uniform identical to Jack's own, while the troll wore a sash and loose pants in Autumn's colors. When you tend to change size, it is wise to dress accordingly.

Cruor and Hurley both wore uniforms of Winter's blue and white. A man named Shaw was wearing a suit with a bit of adornment, indicating his rank in Winter's military. The towering white figure Jack knew to be a yeti was wearing only a loose blue vest, his fur serving to add white to his uniform.

Both groups had arrived close enough in time to allow the royals of Spring to greet all at once. As Puddle described, a couple dozen soldiers stood to one side of the landing grounds. Two dragons of impressive size stood to each side of the troops.

Claire had schooled him on the differences between the drakes of Autumn and Winter and the wyrms of Spring and Summer. The dragons of Spring were colored a pale yellow-green, and they didn't possess wings... or rear legs.

Two thick limbs stood out a quarter of the total length of the beasts down from a broad head that was packed with muscle. The jaws would be genuinely terrifying in strength. They weren't much smaller in total size than Harvest.

Jack assumed that since they couldn't fly, they would be built more robust. In the air, Autumn's dragons would have a clear advantage, but close up and on the ground.... Jack found himself wishing he had Maeve at his side. The hound would arrive later as she tended to draw attention.

A tall man strode out from the others. He was adorned in an almost comical amount of silks and jewelry. Despite the general theme of Spring being green and tan, the man seemed to have an unhealthy tendency toward gold.

The attempt to prove wealth and power came across as desperate to Jack's eyes. Autumn's Prince knew well that power was a tool more than a badge of honor. Wealth unearned was more shame than pride.

The man stepped forward and spoke, seemingly confused about the dragons that carried his guests to his home.

"Welcome. I erm... I was under the impression that Autumn's dragons were short of three years old...."

Claire stepped forward, Harvest leaning his head protectively over her. She smiled innocently.

"Yes, you're correct. We feed our dragons a special blend of slaver and tyrant. As you can see, it does wonders."

The Alder King seemed to bristle at the queen's implications. While his sister's words weren't what he had predicted, Jack didn't blame her for taunting the man. Things were wrong in this place. There was magic in the air, seeming to emanate from the people before him. The man who called himself king stepped forward and continued.

"What a nasty thing to say. These dragons must be over a century old." He huffed and pouted. "No matter. You're addressing King Zankoku Legerdemain. As you're in my kingdom, you may address me as *Your Majesty*."

Then Jack understood what he was feeling. All around him, people started to kneel before the man. He felt only a fraction of the compulsion, just an inclination to bow to the so-called king.

The source was clear to the Autumn Prince, who could taste the power flowing through the air. The king himself was pushing his will on the visiting royals.

For one queen to bow to another is to make her whole kingdom subservient. Only Joobel, already bonded to the only person who could give her a command, seemed immune.

Jack reached out with his own power, not bothering to push back the weave of spirit. Instead, he absorbed it. No outward motion gave away his interference. He pulled every wisp of aura from the air in a wide circle around his people.

Claire almost seemed to stumble, but regained her composure and then tapped a finger to her lips as she nodded.

"I'm the Necromancer of the Blood Keep, the Banshee of Autumn, Death Witch of the Western Lands, Eater of Souls, Sister of Dragons, Giver of Names, and the Mother of the Motherless. You can pick whichever best suits you."

Claire smiled and nodded to Raine, who stepped forward. The dragon Puddle leaned around her protectively. He wasn't the Winter Queen's bond-mate, but his clutch-mate was, and he'd crush anyone who threatened the woman. Literally.

Raine gave a slight stiff bow and spoke. "I have far fewer rumors about me. I'm Queen Raine of the Kingdom of Winter."

Both queens introduced their chosen guards, advisors, and—to the king's surprise—all four dragons. It seemed that Spring looked at its dragons as less than human.

Jack wondered at that idea. Any being who could think was worthy of acknowledgment. He thought back to a mighty sea dragon who chose to carry two lost children in a dead world.

The Alder King began to introduce his own party.

The tall, slender woman with dark hair was his eldest child, Harumi. Jack was absorbing the power she was sending out as well. By the taste of it, she had some control over men.

The elf was pretty enough, but not on par with Joobel. She seemed to be upset that the only male of either Autumn or Winter to even give her a second glance was the troll Stoveg. Jack was pretty sure the green warrior liked her earrings.

Next, the king introduced a shorter woman with dark blonde hair and a silver band of flower petals. Sayuri was the Queen of Spring and should, in truth, be the one in charge of all of this. Jack could feel her power as well; she had control over the brambles of the plants here. Not a very versatile ability, but her spirit aura was dense and strong. She would be a formidable fighter.

The shorter woman beside her was named Yoshiko. The king almost seemed to mention her in passing, though her aura was also dense. He couldn't tell without making contact, but he thought she dealt with plants or something similar.

Finally, they came to a tall, lean man. He was young and quite powerful. Autumn's Prince had trouble reading his ability. It was somewhat akin to Claire's power of Transmutation, yet more narrow. It was a spirit of renewal; his aura was tight around him and could only affect his own body.

The king spoke with evident pride at the man he called his son. "This is Ohkami, my son and the undefeated Prince of Spring."

The young man stepped forward, walking past Jack. Ignoring the queens, the Spring Prince stood before Joobel. He smiled widely. Jack had to admit Ohkami was striking in appearance. His face seemed to be chiseled out of the same marble as the palace. He gave a slight bow to the gnome and spoke.

"We have stories in Spring, of the great beauty of the west. A strong spirit of renewal lost in a land of the spirit of change. Here they call you Akiko, the one who tamed great Tatsu, the lost dragon of Spring. As the prince of this land, I must insist you dine with me this evening."

Jack was a bit surprised by the man's nerve, not that he could blame anyone for being attracted to his Joobel. He never faulted people for staring at the lovely woman or even working up the courage to ask her out. There was a line though. As Joobel replied, this man found it.

"I'm flattered, Prince Ohkami, but I'm afraid I must decline. I'm already betr—"

The handsome face devolved into anger. "You would deny a prince?"

Before anyone could react, he grabbed Joobel's arm and began to pull her along with him. Things moved so fast that few could even make out what happened.

Two things should be noted about the world's biggest gnome. She was still on edge from the events of her last night in the mundane world, the attack and her response a sensitive issue.

Also, gnomes are strong for their size. A typical gnome can lift several times their own body weight, and with more magic they are even stronger. Claire Named Joobel and with her increased size and magic, she also grew in strength.

Joobel never showed off this skill. At heart, she liked to pretend she was a maiden who needed saving. She wasn't. She was a strong-willed woman who was more powerful than most knew. Only Jack really knew of her physical strength. He'd still never beat her in arm wrestling.

When the man abruptly grabbed her and jerked her forward, she reacted like lightning and slapped Ohkami. Not a frail slap like one would expect from such a tiny woman, but a blow that threw the Prince of Spring several paces away to land on his back.

Ohkami jumped back to his feet and let out a low growl as he lunged back at the gnome. His claws sunk deep into the face of a Winter guard who never flinched as the long nails tore through his flesh.

As Ohkami threw another blow, Cruor caught his strike in his free hand and twisted it hard, making an audible '*pop.*' The Prince of Spring winced pain.

"You would stand between me and my revenge?" Ohkami roared.

Cruor calmly pointed up with his free hand.

"You just laid hands on the sister to the Banshee of Autumn, the betrothed of the Demon Prince, and the bond-mate to a pissed-off dragon. A dragon who is even now trying to figure out how to get around me so she can bite you in half. I stand between you and your death."

Even as the Leech spoke, the long line of blood running down his face retreated into the wound on his cheek. The edges of the claw marks sealed themselves.

Ohkami looked up at the dragon and paled. Bloom was one of the kindest beings in Fairie, but she was still more massive than a house and fiercely protective of her bond-mate.

Jack could see tears forming in Joobel's eyes. He moved over and took her hand. He spoke softly to her, but he now understood the Prince of Spring's power. The elf heard every whisper.

"It's ok. I promise you if he touches you again it will be the last thing he does while drawing breath."

Jack saw Ohkami's eyes move to him then. The orange glow that met him spoke of unforgiving flame. Cruor released his grip and was back at Raine's side in an instant.

The Alder King moved forward to save face, speaking in only slightly frantic tones.

"Now, now, there will be time enough for testing your skills at tomorrow's games. Come, let us feast this night."

Jack could feel the waves of power flowing out at the king's words. He was giving off a compulsion to forget the incident: Ohkami slipped and it was all a misunderstanding. Jack absorbed the weave of power; he would remember the truth.

So would everyone else.

***

As the group moved to follow the king, a young elf woman was watching closely. She walked to the side of the gathered individuals. As she looked around at the strange people from across the world, she slid a hand into her wide belt and touched a small white mushroom cap.

She glanced out at the powerful people and noticed two of the women, each having three distinct auras. One had shifting shades of white, blue, and turquoise. The other moved between grey, brown, and tan. The whisper entered her mind as she marveled at the sight.

'*Mikato.*'

Yoshiko smiled inwardly. If it were true, these people could help her. She and Naoki had a real chance of making a difference.

She glanced around at the group assembled with the two queens. There was the man who had stopped her stepbrother and his aura of deep blue. A substantial furry form held the pale yellow of an air spirit, while a troll held the pale orange of inborn fire.

The woman Ohkami tried to attack had a luminous green so bright Yoshiko needed to squint her eyes. Then she looked at the young man with shaggy dark hair who held the woman's hand. His aura seemed to devour the light and magic around him.

The Autumn Prince was said to be a powerful user of fire, but this was something she couldn't comprehend. It was like staring into the void, into nothing and everything all at once. It frightened her and she looked away.

As she fought the urge to run, she heard the whispered voice again. This time it spoke another word.

'*Kinan.*' This word she knew.

This word meant disaster.

***

Mini walked out of the lab that was forming under her supervision. Four hulking trolls assisted her in moving the heavy equipment. She was learning that despite their appearance, they were all very polite and quite curious.

Half a dozen gnomes were working on hooking everything up, pouring over the manuals, and learning how everything worked.

Twice someone touched exposed steel components by mistake. She marveled at the effect such a metal had on the spiritual power that was at the core of everything in this world. It had a result similar to strong acid.

Now she moved over to the workshop that was owned by a girl who looked younger than herself. Issabol was older than she could ever hope to be. The ancient child was currently sipping tea and pouring over an old book.

Another woman sat on the floor, setting blocks with letters on them in front of a pretty little girl with dark hair and eyes. Mini smiled at her new neighbors and sat on the floor next to Bilney and Laris. She spoke softly, long accustomed to working with fragile minds.

"I'm looking for a wonderful girl named Laris."

The child looked up at her, dark eyes seeming to stare through her. Finally, she spoke in a sing-song tone.

"Some call meeeeeeeee Laris.... Some caaaaaaaall me other things...."

Mini ignored the creepy vibe the girl gave off. Gray told her this child was haunted by a spirit power that let her see layers of power and potential instead of a regular face. It made communicating complicated and friendship with the other children almost impossible.

She set a box on the floor and opened it up. Inside, the camera already had a full charge on its extended battery. She pulled it out and pointed it at Laris. The contraption made a soft '*click*' as the image was captured. The small screen on the front showed a perfect picture of the beautiful girl.

Mini turned the camera around and showed Laris her own face. The girl looked long and hard at it.

"Is thaaaaaaat the girl... they call Laaaaaaaaaaaris...?"

The doctor nodded. "It is. You can use this to see people as they are. As they would be if you didn't see power through your eyes. It will take some time to learn how to use it, but it will help you understand people better. It is a gift for you."

Bilney smiled widely at the gift and added her seal of approval.

"Oh Laris, this is wonderful. I spoke to you about how people look without your power clouding them; this could be a big help. What should you say to the lady?"

"Thaaaaaaank you... Laris says to the laaaaaaaady...."

Mini suppressed the shiver. She tried to not judge based on what couldn't be helped. She showed her some of the primary functions and then left a booklet with Bilney. The staples had been removed and replaced with a plastic ring binding. There was iron in everything, at least where she was from.

Finally, she let the guard take over and moved into a little room covered in wires and sound equipment. On one wall stood a large screen; at least it appeared to be a screen. In truth, this was a portal overlooking the arena of Spring. It was set to allow a small amount of light through to enable remote viewing.

Two smaller portals were set to allow sound to pass, and each had a large speaker positioned in front of them. A cluster of portals was assembled in front of another set of huge speakers, another project Gray set in motion. The man stayed busy.

Sitting at a desk was a small girl, perhaps ten or eleven years old. She had brown skin and long brown hair. Her eyes were shaped like almonds and she was adorable. Gray had taken a liking to this girl and given her a computer and a job of sorts.

Mini agreed to teach her how to use the laptop and access the music stored inside. A handful of solar panels were collecting power for the upcoming performance. They kept the computer running and charged Laris's camera.

Toma looked up at the old woman who only seemed to be a few years older than her.

"Oh, hi Mini. Is Gree coming today?"

Mini shook her head. "No, sweetie, Gray went to Spring with our queen. He asked me to help you get everything going."

Toma sighed, then smiled. "We also have a nom to help."

Mini cocked an eyebrow. "A '*nom*'?"

Before the child could answer, a tiny girl in a yellow-flowered dress jumped onto the desk. She looked surprised to have company but gave a perfect curtsy. Mini laughed as she understood.

"You must be our '*nom*.'"

The gnome smiled widely. "Why, I'm from the greatest sept of '*noms*' in all of Fairie. Wemwi of the Sept of Fallen Leaves, at your service."

Toma beamed. "Wemwi is a dragonswayer."

Mini sighed and started to ask, but the gnome waved a long copper screw.

"Dragon 'Slayer,' and it's a long story. I much prefer books and gadgets."

"Well, Wemwi, I'm pleased to meet you. My name is Mini. I guess we're all here to help our friends put on a show."

Toma clapped and hit a button on the keyboard. The speakers strained as the sound poured through.

"AHHHHHhhhhhhHHHHHHH."

The opening of the song shook the small room and Mini was forced to cover her ears. Wemwi hopped over the girl's arm and moved the volume dial way, way down. The newly young doctor just grinned.

"Led Zeppelin, Nineteen Seventy. Oh, this will be fun."

***

Growing up in the Black Citadel was often a depressing affair. The Winter Queen's natural optimism and joy didn't always win out against the harsh realities of living in a kingdom where food was scarce and the weak didn't survive long. When the time came for celebration, Raine relished the event.

Never in her life had she seen such a lavish banquet. The hall stretched out to the edge of her vision. Long tables of polished white marble were trimmed in gold and silver. Dotted down the middle were living centerpieces of ivy, flowers, and live songbirds chirping in time with the band.

Sprites in servant's livery darted around, taking orders and refilling the wide bowls of a deep red wine. Chairs of carved wood moved independently to help seat the occupant comfortably, and tall, slender elves brought trays of food around to fill plates of delicate porcelain.

The whole affair seemed to step out of a storybook. She felt no less unease in this place, but would admit that the elves of Spring had great taste.

In the center of the room stood a tall platform that held up a table for the Alder King and those closest to him. While the rest of the furniture was tasteful and refined, the solid gold table and matching chairs seemed garish and overdone. The king sat on an ornate throne of the same metal.

Across the room stood a group of minstrels. They currently sang of the founding of the Beryl Gardens and the taming of lands of wild creatures and dangers. She found it prone to flowery prose, but the music itself was skillfully played. The melody exuded a strong sense of wonder and joy.

As the song ended, there was a brief pause and an instrumental number began. Some of the elves stood and bowed to others, then moved to the large square of the dance floor.

Raine smiled and wondered what it would be like to be whisked away to spin and dance the night away. The voice at her shoulder brought her out of her daydream.

"My queen, it would seem wise to scout out the room. Perhaps you would agree to dance with this lowly guard?"

She looked into his bright red eyes. Unlike Jack, Cruor's eyes never completely dimmed. His long bangs worked to cover the revealing beacons of crimson, but not at this distance. Soon enough, all would know what he was. She was more interested in *who* he was.

The Winter Queen pushed her long white hair behind one ear and then blushed in embarrassment.

"I'd love to, but...," Her voice lowered to a whisper. "I never learned how to dance."

He smiled widely, giving a glimpse of sharp teeth. He took her hand and gently lifted the queen to her feet.

"Just let me lead, I'm quite good. Think of it as dueling with good intentions."

She let him lead her onto the dance floor, trusting he could protect her if anyone should try to attack. Not that she needed all that much protection.

The music carried a subtle bass beat, and she could see the young man begin to sync his movements in time with the tune. He took one of her hands in his and wrapped his other around her lower back. In moments they were moving around the floor with grace.

He wasn't wrong. The motions weren't unlike fighting. Though Raine felt like everyone was watching her, when she looked up, she could see that all eyes were focused on someone else.

In Winter, dancing was considered frivolous and wasteful. However, some of the great families still threw parties that allowed it, Cruor's seemingly among them. In Autumn, it was more frequent.

She could see Claire and Gray were also moving around the floor, though clearly the Autumn Queen was leading the larger man. Both were laughing, so she assumed embarrassment wasn't an issue. They also hadn't gathered much attention.

On one corner of the dance floor, her cousin was moving in time to the music with Joobel in his arms. Jack was quite good and adeptly led her around the floor. While he was talented, she was terrific. The gnome not only used her feet and legs to move in time, but her wings aided her balance and allowed her to literally float around the dance floor.

Raine looked to her partner to see that even her unshakable bodyguard was smiling at the spectacle. She enjoyed the moment, finding herself moving closer and closer to the warmth of her protector.

As the song ended, she was nearly hugging the man. Then she felt him tense as if a cat ready to pounce. She looked up to his face, then followed his red-eyed gaze back to where Joobel and Jack were dancing.

Ohkami was approaching.

Jack must have felt the man's aura because he went from moving to the music to poised in a fighting stance in an instant. He pushed Joobel behind him and light began to leak from his tightened fist.

Raine let go of Cruor and took three long strides. She was stepping up to the Prince of Spring before he could get close enough to speak to the gnome. She spoke with more confidence than she felt, her words attempting to prevent bloodshed.

"There you are, Prince Ohkami. Perhaps you would suffer to dance with a queen?"

The man looked at her with anger, but he could see the lean guard who'd stopped him before. The elf nodded slowly.

"Yes, it would be an honor to take to the floor with Winter's Queen."

Raine took his hand, fighting off the cringe she felt. She didn't like this man but was well aware that Jack would kill him long before he pondered consequences. She faked a smile as they stepped into the dance.

"I'm afraid I just got my first lesson. Feel free to lead."

Ohkami only glanced at her for a second. "Yes, of course."

Raine kept a good deal more distance throughout the rest of the tune, looking to see that Cruor was now only two steps away and dancing with a lovely elf maid. She often felt he was too overprotective, but then remembered just how many times he'd saved her life.

Ohkami hardly looked at her, his eyes never leaving Joobel. She tried a few times to make awkward small talk, but he never engaged. Finally, the song came to an end and she gave a brief word of thanks and moved to sit back at her table.

Cruor joined her side. She leaned over to his ear.

"Your partner seemed quite lovely."

His smirk was not one of mirth. "Yours seemed like a real winner."

She shuddered. "The difference is, mine was a monster."

Cruor shrugged. "Monsters tend to get slain."

Raine knew that he wasn't making banter. Her guard would kill without hesitation. Cruor spared the horrible prince before to keep his friends blameless. If he killed Spring's Prince, it wouldn't be in a crowded ballroom. It would be in a dark hallway and they would never find the bloodless body.

Just as she sat down, she could see that the band had wisely moved to a different form of entertainment. A bard sat on a low bench, his feathered cap low over his face. He was an elf, and his nimble fingers danced across his lute with the grace acquired through decades of practice. He looked out to the crowd with a confident smile and began to speak.

"Many honored guests join us this night and many songs I could play to further praise them. Yet honor will be earned on the field of battle, and so I offer a mystery. One that only a single person in this room could bring to light."

He looked straight at Raine as his tune increased in tempo. He continued building up to his song.

"It was only a few months ago that Winter had a Bitter Challenge. A legendary fight between queens for the frozen throne."

The bard paused his words as his fingers graced the strings, building the tempo to add to his presence.

"The mighty Queen Raine brought with her allies of vast power. A monster of the deep waters, a dragon that breathed magic, and a warg of immense size and power.

"Yet, my friends, perhaps the most mysterious was the man who froze the very blood of her enemies. I speak tonight to this assembled merry gentry, of the Man of Frost."

He leaned over his instrument and began to shift the melody to repeat his rhythm.

"Lords and ladies, sit back and listen to the tale of the hero unnamed, the man who served a queen for but a single night. The Winter Warrior...."

The tune stabilized. His high and melodious voice began to sing. Raine almost laughed and looked to her cousin out of the corner of her eye.

> As Winter faced its longest night,
> And shadows crept with vile delight,
> A man came forth to set things— 'TWANG'

The lute popped as not one, but all four strings snapped at the same time. The bard looked up in horror as the assembled crowd looked disappointed. Raine could see Jack looking a bit too innocent.

He was quite a shot with his little heat blasts. Raine sighed and once again decided to save someone from unseen consequences. The Winter Queen stood and slowly clapped, a grin forming on her face.

"A mystery indeed, good bard, yet did you not know that to speak of the Man of Frost is to incur his wrath? You're lucky you only gave up a few strings to his ire."

Raine looked out to the crowd and gave the musician time to escape the fury of her host. The Alder King seemed displeased that the bard had failed to sing his tune. She pushed her power into a nearby pitcher of clear water and pulled the liquid into the air.

It began to shape into a field of battle. One of the servants saw what she was doing and the radiance in the hall started to dim. A beam of light shone down on her creation.

Across the glowing liquid dragons fought, a mighty warg ran and jumped, two women dueled with long swords, while a man pulled ice into walls and locked down his enemies. Raine continued speaking.

"In my time of need, I begged the great spirit of Winter to lend me the overwhelming power of water. To my great relief, a man of frost rose up from the still waters of Loch Mozeg and fought on my behalf."

The liquid figures battled and fought as she concentrated on her construct. Raine brought her eyes up to slowly scan the crowd before smiling.

"As the battle was won, that man of snow and ice left my side. No one was able to catch him as he moved through the hills of snow. He hasn't been seen since. Perhaps he will be back again someday."

At her words, Gray snorted a laugh and almost drowned on his own drink. He really was a strange man. Raine ended her story and the water flowed back into the pitcher except for a small fraction that flowed into the glass in front of her. She took a sip, bowed, and sat back down.

The crowd began to applaud the display and the band moved to play the next song. It was another that would have many on the dance floor.

She glanced nervously to Joobel. Claire also saw the impending issue and stood; her voice lifted through the dead only Autumn's Queen could see.

"Good people of Spring, this has been a truly wonderful evening. I find I'm overwhelmed by your generosity in hosting us this night. I must admit that between the excitement and our long trip this morning, I require respite. I shall retire with my people and be well-rested for the events of tomorrow."

With that, she turned and followed an elf servant who led her away. Gray walked just behind her, followed by the troll Stoveg. Immediately Joobel stood and left as well, Jack walking protectively behind her.

Raine looked and saw the anger on Ohkami's face. He'd meant to settle things with an audience; now he'd have to find another time. She was tempted to just let Jack kill the man, but Claire's plan required them to remain blameless in the eyes of the people here. Raine sighed and leaned to Cruor's ear.

"We shall wait for half an hour and do the same."

Her guard raised an eyebrow. "Shouldn't we gather more information?"

Raine thought of the ghostly spies moving all throughout this room, the Beryl Gardens, and out into the capital city of Amaya. Claire would know anything of importance long before they could gather anything.

"I think we will be plenty well informed. You know, the band is still playing. I wouldn't mind a second lesson."

Cruor stood and made a slight bow. Taking her offered hand, he led her back onto the dance floor. Despite the tensions and intrigue, it ended up being a rather pleasant evening.

CHAPTER 12

I f she had awoken in Autumn, Claire would have thought it a
rare sunny day. She could only assume most days here held
blue skies and warm light. The accommodations were more
opulent than she could have imagined. Her rooms were on the
top floor of the western tower. Actually, every member of her
party had rooms set aside for them. All were staying in hers.

Gray and Stoveg slept in a spacious sitting room that had
several large sofas. She and Joobel shared a big bed in an
adjoining bedroom while Jack made a pallet on the floor. All
agreed they would sleep better in safety rather than comfort.

Raine and her group were in the northern tower, though
using the dragons as a relay kept them in contact. All were safe
and well rested.

The dragons had a vast haven just outside the city. They too
gathered together rather than spreading out. Bloom might not be
much of a fighter, but Brook was fully grown. Both Harvest and
Puddle were terrifying in their own right.

The sunlight poured into the windows of the main sitting
room and lit up the morning. Autumn's Queen had no sooner
dressed in the beautiful clothing Joobel set out for her, than a
soft knock echoed about. Jack was at the door before she could

adequately turn around. A tall elf with a cart came into the room. His voice was proper and respectful.

"Your breakfast and that for your party, my Lady. I hope you find it all to your liking. Please do not hesitate to ask if you have... other requirements."

The last he said while looking to Stoveg with disdain. Autumn's Queen didn't miss the slight.

"I'm sure the meal provided will be sufficient. Please give our thanks to our hosts."

The man left the cart and made his way out. As the elf left, she looked to Gray and nodded. He leaned down and activated the orb cluster at his feet. The doorway popped into life and in moments an opening was carved through space to the Blood Keep.

Inside the room, she could see nearly two dozen people, all ready to take part in the games. The first through the door was a happy little hound who almost knocked her brother through a wall. Maeve would be led down to the dragons to help guard Bloom.

The junior division had a dozen young fighters who would be taking part in the contest this very afternoon. Ten more adults would be fighting along with both Gray and Jack.

They streamed inside and she doted on them as they entered. Autumn had a good deal of diversity, with a few trolls, one ogre, and several humans set to take part.

A few of the younger fighters could likely hold their own in the adult contest. Jack were still young enough to fight in the younger division, but chose to compete for top prize. He was only thought to be young enough because he'd two years in the world of fast time that few were aware of.

The young queen grabbed a plate and began filling it with the various foods provided by Spring. She could have food brought from home, but the blue bracelet would protect her from the most potent of poisons.

She admittedly didn't dine with much royal dignity, but she did fill her stomach. Gray and Joobel also ate, and Jack stayed alert and inspected Autumn's fighters. Stoveg paced the room, ensuring that they stayed safe.

Claire appreciated the dedication of the troll. Chieftain Rakash recommended him highly, and she'd been quite happy with how the Stone Spear trolls had settled into her kingdom. Her builders were already preparing the empty lands on the western border for more refugees; there was little doubt they would come.

Now she focused her eyes on her other citizens, not of Autumn's living, but of the dead. The invitation was clear as to whom she could bring, but there was no prohibition stated for the ghosts of her homeland. The royal party contained only seven, including herself, and another twenty-two counting her fighters. In truth, several hundred residents of Autumn were in attendance.

The vast majority wouldn't need to be fed, housed, or entertained. All had answered her call, and all were pledged to her service willingly.

An unwilling ghost was a significant drain on her spirit. Even now, as strong as she was, she could only hold maybe three in thrall. Autumn's Queen had earned the respect of not only the living, but also of those who had passed, but not passed on. They were willing and this meant they cost her almost nothing.

The girl who was briefing her on the state of things was maybe in her early twenties. Her color was hidden by the ghostly pale light of her nature. Claire thought she would've been pretty in life. The woman spoke in the fast but precise speech common in Autumn's Capital.

"As far as we can see, there's nothing out of the ordinary. We have kept a close watch on all of the royals of Spring. The queen seems like she's unaware of her surroundings, and the king plots to embarrass you this very morning. The Wolf Prince intends to kill your brother in response to the perceived slight of your advisor, though he plans it for the arena. The spore dragons are jealous of the regard the king holds for Bloom. Please be wary, my queen; you tread through a den of vipers."

The woman faded away. Claire noted nothing she hadn't already guessed, though she'd let her brother know to be on his guard. Despite the danger, few could pose any real threat to Jack, and Cruor had managed to deter the horrid Ohkami on the previous day.

She finished eating and focused her sight on the living world. Jack completed his inspection and was stuffing his face while Gray took over so Stoveg could do the same.

Another knock sounded at the door. This time the elf almost fell down at the sight of the suddenly full room.

"My lady, the opening of the Contest of Champions... will begin shortly. Please, erm... follow me."

It was a long walk down the stairwells and she was nearly out of breath by the time they reached the courtyard. She noticed the Winter party streaming in as well. Claire looked around. There was no sign of Summer. They had been assured all four kingdoms would be present.

She tapped a finger on the shoulder of the servant leading them. "Pardon me."

He turned and looked annoyed. "Yes... your grace?"

"Where is the group from Summer? Surely they would have arrived by now."

The elf paused and seemed uncomfortable. "Many of Summer's combatants arrived late last night. I'm told the royal arrival will take place later in the day before the Contest begins."

Claire's brow furrowed. The absence of such a hostile kingdom made her nervous, but she carried on as if it didn't matter. Her group split as the fighters were taken below, while she and the remaining members of her group were led to an ornate box of seats overlooking the Amaya arena.

She hated that some of the more powerful members of the group were separated from them. However, her seating was next to Raine's, and between them they still had a good deal of protection. As she was motioned to her place, she looked again to the servant.

"Say... is there any way we could share a box with the Winter Queen and her party?"

The tall elf seemed to be fighting an eye roll.

"Winter's viewing box is right next to yours. You may, of course, send messages if needed."

Claire looked to the wall separating the two groups. She nodded to the elf and turned to Stoveg with an evil grin.

"Please give the message to the Winter Queen that I'd like her to sit next to me. Please be *completely* direct." As the queen finished, she looked to the wall with intent.

The troll focused for a second and then began to swell. Lean muscle gained mass as the hulking figure walked over to the wall. He put both hands on the white stone and began to push. Red veins began to protrude through his dark-green skin as he strained.

In moments the wall started to crack. The thick stone collapsed, revealing a very surprised yeti. Claire waved through the new door.

"Hello cousin, won't you join me for the festivities?"

The Winter Queen smiled innocently.

"Why yes, it would be lovely to have the company of friends as we enjoy the contest."

The elf paled at the raw power of the troll and the general lack of hesitation in breaking things. The servant cleared his throat nervously and stepped back as he finished speaking.

"So glad you are satisfied with the accommodations.... Um... please let me know if you need anything."

Claire glanced about the arena as preparations were finalized for the opening ceremony. She watched curiously as the flat-packed dirt was covered with various stones and trees. Before her eyes, a small fort was set up and meager defenses were arranged around it. A wide wagon entered through one large door on the north end of the field.

As they sat down, there was a slight hum as a barrier moved into place. The transparent dome was powered by dozens of spirit weavers. The shield would allow no living thing to pass through without losing its very life force.

It would also block most spells, a precaution she was assured was to both prevent interference and stop any participants from harming the spectators.

The Alder King stood on his high platform and puffed up, looking down at his audience. His voice carried through the arena. An air spirit was amplifying it, if she had to guess. Claire found herself tired of listening to him instantly.

"Many years have passed since the last Contest of Champions. They are, of course, our way of testing the very best of each generation. This year's games will be a tremendous affair, with battles like you have never seen. My own son competes for Spring this time around. Before we begin the games, I have prepared a special presentation for our guests from the other kingdoms."

Off to one side, a band played an upbeat battle hymn. The large wagon pulled away from the center of the field and the huge gate at the south end of the arena opened. A wide swath of soldiers began marching into the stadium. The Alder King spoke once more.

"You are all familiar with the great victory over the Ardon tribes on the very spot the Beryl Gardens now stand. Today we have recreated that battle. Rest assured, the defenders are all convicted criminals and no innocent blood will be spilled."

Claire turned her head slightly, looking out in confusion. There was a short pause before her world went crazy.

A loud pop sounded to her right. She turned to see Joobel slamming against the side of the shield, trying to get inside. The gnome was hurting herself in her mad rush to enter the field of battle.

Then a ghostly middle-aged man with a limp appeared before her, speaking in earnest.

"I'm sorry, my queen; we didn't see until they opened the wagons...."

Claire ignored him while she turned to shout at Stoveg. "Grab her before she hurts herself!"

The troll swelled in size once more and tackled the gnome just before she hit the barrier a fourth time. Claire heard Raine speak in soft tones to her advisor as she turned her own attention to the ghostly scout. Her words came through her mind, carried to him by her power.

"Out with it; what's going on?"

"My queen, there are several children in the fort below. We think they mean to slaughter them."

Then she understood. Criminals. The children were likely caught stealing or trespassing. Whatever they did, she couldn't allow this.

Claire spoke through the scattered dead, her voice for all present in the arena.

"What is the meaning of this? You would have us sit by and watch as you kill innocents in the name of entertainment?"

The Alder King smiled widely and held up both his hands, replying through the air weave that amplified his voice.

"As I said, these people are all criminals. If they were not to die in honor of our history, they would only await a different form of punishment."

Claire was shocked. How could he think this was ok? She felt a firm hand on her shoulder and heard the whispered words of the Winter Queen.

"He knows the rumors coming from Autumn and now Winter. A better life for the common people. He means to create a kind of equivalence. Show everyone we're no different. I don't think I can do much. The barrier will stop my power and none of our guards can pass through."

Claire thought for a moment. No *living* thing. Jack had mentioned that the shield would be no issue for him; he could rip it open without effort. He wasn't here, though, and even if she got the message to him, he'd almost certainly lose his temper and save the children while killing half the crowd.

No *living* thing....

Claire was the master of Death. A slight smile covered her lips as she realized how she could turn this to her benefit. It would be messy and she couldn't save everyone, but she *would* save many.

Autumn's Queen spoke once more through the unsettling voice. "I understand. It seems I will have to let this reenactment play out. I suppose I might even learn some of your great histories."

The Alder King smiled and shouted to the troops below. "Let us begin!"

To the eyes of the crowd, there was a small stone enclosure surrounded by a few sparse trees and rocks. It was meager cover considering the dozens of well-equipped troops marching to besiege the place. Just over thirty defenders stood on the low walls and none had more than a dull bronze blade.

Claire could hear Joobel weeping at the coming slaughter. She put on a grim smile and turned to her adopted sister.

"Trust me, I protect my children. As of now, I claim these as mine."

She turned her focus back to the spectacle. As the first of the soldiers made the walls, the defenders began throwing stones and swinging to try and hold them back. Strong armor deflected the attacks and it was only moments before the first of the defending men fell from the wall, stabbed through the heart.

Claire pushed her power down below. To her eyes, the field was much more crowded. The ghost of an elderly Autumn Champion slid into the body of the slain man. There were murmurs through the crowd as the clearly dead defender stood tall.

With a skill born of decades of experience, the zombie quickly dispatched two of the soldiers climbing the wall, having forgotten the corpse behind them. Each soldier fell to the ground, convulsing for only a moment before they too rose and began fighting against their former allies.

All around the defenses, the dead rose to continue the fight. Almost a dozen of the defenders were slain. To their credit, they secured the group of children with two women in the center of the enclosure.

More and more soldiers were beaten back. Those that fell then rose as new defenders with much better armor and weapons. The murmurs began to change into a cheer as the crowd began to understand what was happening down below. More than a few felt a creeping fear at the sight of the dead walking.

Some of those present were supporters of the king and were none too happy with the spectacle playing out. Most were either relieved to see hope for those sentenced to death below or just excited to see a twist in the battle playing out.

In only a couple more minutes, it became clear that the remaining attackers couldn't win this fight and they began to retreat. Claire exhaled the breath she hadn't known she was holding. She looked over at the Alder King and her heart sank.

The man was smiling. A ghost appeared before her to let her know how wrong this was about to go.

The south gate opened once more.

***

Yoshiko watched as the battle raged below. It wasn't a surprise for her to see that prisoners were to be used as live defenders. They were sheep so outmatched they could only feed the wolves. Yet she was holding the small white cap and watching Autumn's Queen as much as the battle. Her aura of grey had flared and tendrils of that power flowed from her to the field.

That she was responsible was never in doubt, but the cunning of this woman! The young elf was in awe. She was enthralled in her observations as the whispered order came from the Alder King to one of his guards.

"Send in both. I want this to end as we discussed."

Both what? What could he be up to? Her brow creased, then her eyes went wide as she realized what he intended. Dragons. They could enter the field through the gate. No number of dead soldiers could stop the dragons from executing the prisoners below, children included. Her stepfather really was a monster.

There was a low rumble as the gates opened. The serpentine figures of two giant spore dragons entered the arena. They were heavy and built like long thick snakes. They had two stout front legs allowing the head and neck to lift and release deadly spores into the air.

The first dragon roared in excitement and lumbered out into the fray of soldiers. Its neck lifted the huge horned head into the air, the bright sun glistening on pale yellow-green scales. Then it blew a blast of deadly fungal spores into the defenders fighting before them.

Those men showed no signs of the debilitating effects. She'd been right; they were no longer alive. The spores couldn't stop them. They began to slow as small yellow mushrooms sprouted all over their skin, making it hard to move, but the advance never ceased.

The second dragon moved swiftly in a wide arch, flanking around the fighting and heading straight for the enclosure. Yoshiko focused her power and let it flow into the ground below the stands. Unlike most, she could push her energy around the barrier.

She held the power of renewal and life, but she didn't need to go through it. The princess pushed her power into the soil of Spring to the giant mushroom below. Honey heard her call and granted her request.

Large tendrils of mycelium, the roots of all mushrooms, burst from the ground of the arena. They grasped at the slithering form of the second dragon, slowing his movement and making it hard for him to spot his prey.

Despite her efforts, he broke through and sighted the children inside the makeshift fort. A blast of spores poured from its pale green snout and slammed against a large red mushroom cap that sprouted from the ground between him and the gathered prisoners. White spores burst forth, neutralizing the dangerous yellow ones.

Yoshiko was sweating with exertion; doing so much at such a distance drained her power quickly. Who could face a dragon? She was almost ready to pass out when a large shadow passed over the field of battle. The princess looked up to see a huge drake flying through the sky.

Scales of a bright green glittered in the sunlight. A roar of rage and challenge echoed from the clouds. Instead of charging against the barrier, the dragon dropped a light-brown stone near the peak of the dome.

The stone fell from high in the sky, gaining speed as it drew near the ground. From the great height it began, it reached such a speed as to send tremors through the entire arena as it slammed the hard dirt with a '*thud.*'

The vibrations came to her through the floor of Spring's royal box. Her exhaustion was too much, and the tendrils holding the dragon loosened their grip as she slumped in her seat.

The stone left a small crater in the packed soil of the field. As the dust cleared, a little hound stepped through the thinning cloud.

Two of the animal's legs were crushed and broken, yet it moved out and shook as if damp with water. As the whole of the crowd stared breathlessly, the legs stretched and popped until the creature righted itself. Yoshiko held the white cap as she studied the animal.

It held an earthen aura, faint in its color while blinding in intensity. The whisper from Honey wasn't much help. '*Kimyona.*' The word meant weird or strange. She could see that on her own.

The hound showed no fear, only walked to stand between the remaining prisoners and the nearest dragon. The little creature sat down and stared at the colossal wyrm looming above. It barked once and went perfectly still.

For a moment, the whole of the arena was completely silent. Only the whispered voice of the king could be heard in her ears.

"What in the world is a little mongrel supposed to do to stop a dragon? Why not swing a stick at it?"

Yoshiko wasn't convinced this was in any way a hound. If it had been alive, the barrier would have either deflected it or killed it on the way in.

The dragon near the soldiers roared and began to once again tear apart the undead troops stabbing at it with short spears and bronze swords.

The second dragon seemed to smile as it inhaled deeply and poured a thick stream of yellow spores onto the hound. The cloud of death roiled all around the poor creature. The crowd gave a disappointed 'awww,' but when it cleared, the animal only gave an annoyed sneeze.

A few in the crowd laughed at the sight. The dragon roared again and began to move forward, taking slow lumbering steps and rumbling out a challenge.

The small brown figure charged, and with every lunging step, it grew. The packed earth of the field flowed into its shape as it became more and more massive. When it hit the dragon, it was every bit as large as the beast and the impact once again shook the entire stadium.

The savage growl that escaped the snapping jaws sent chills down the young elf's spine. What seemed moments ago a comical mismatch of opponents now seemed just as one-sided in the other direction. The huge hound of earth and stone used its immense weight to push the spore dragon to the ground.

With a loud wet snap, it tore the pale green head from its thick neck. The hound stood, tall, broad, and terrifying. It looked directly at the Alder King, horned dragon head still in its jaws. Then it bit down with a sickening crunch. The thick bone of the wyrm skull collapsed in its jaw under impossible pressure.

No one dared speak. For several long seconds, thousands of people sat in terrified silence. Then a small boy sitting in the front row jumped up and cheered. The sound spread and began to rise from the people gathered around.

Yoshiko felt part of her mourn the loss of a dragon, but she wasn't nearly as sad as she would have been to watch that same dragon kill those children. Then came the woman's voice again, seeming to come from everywhere and nowhere all at once. The eerie tone made her shudder.

"This has been quite a show, but it seems wasteful to lose dragons in a reenactment. Perhaps you should call in your troops?"

Yoshiko could hear the angry stammering of the Alder King. He collected himself before his voice came in reply, carried through the stadium on a weave of air.

"Yes, it has been... quite a show. Let us take a short break and then proceed with the Contest. I will see to it that these prisoners receive their sentence later on."

A peal of laughter came in eerie tones, that same otherworldly voice.

"Oh, you need not worry about the remaining prisoners; they belong to me now."

In the distance, she could see the Autumn Queen hold up one hand and snap her fingers. A moment later a loud gasp rose from the crowd. A slight shimmer of purple glowed at the feet of the two women and gathered children.

Without further warning, the ground swallowed them whole.

***

The ancient girl had been taking a break from her work when she heard Toma's scream. Bilney reached the small viewing room before she could and the woman was clearly angry.

As Issabol looked to the viewing portal, it was clear that there was some sort of fight going on in the arena. It couldn't be anyone from Autumn. Those fights weren't to come until later in the afternoon. Her eyes locked on the group of children standing inside a small enclosure.

Toma was crying, believing the little ones about to die. She wasn't wrong to think so, but then a slain defender rose and returned to the fight. More and more did the same. Clearly it was the work of her own many greats niece. Claire did have a way of making a spectacle.

Then a ghost stepped into the room with them all. Toma squeaked in fear, but Bilney was no stranger to the queen's abilities. The specter looked around and saw Issabol, speaking in that eerie tone.

"The queen asks you to ready a ground portal, to deposit where both safe and convenient. She will give the signal when she is ready. Can you do this?"

Issabol thought for a moment. She was typically put out by urgent requests. Looking once more at the frightened children and the fighting going on all around them, she pushed the lavender lock of hair from her eyes and nodded to the specter.

"It will be ready; I'll need ten minutes. Then give the signal any time."

The ghost bowed and disappeared, no doubt to carry the message across multiple kingdoms in a breath. The dead need not concern themselves with distance.

It was too big a job to start from scratch. The ancient girl pushed the view of the portal to focus on the children. They were packed reasonably tight together. It would still require a larger opening.

"Bilney, get Varam and meet me in the portal room. We need to move and adjust the door the dragons use to visit Depth; it's the only one big enough close at hand."

Then she was off and running. They set the large portal to open on the ceiling of the room. Varam was able to adjust the output since he was familiar with the portal room's location. At the same time, Issabol used the viewing portal to get a lock on the huddled prisoners.

When finished, the opening would appear a finger's width under the soil beneath their feet. The people and a decent amount of dirt would pour into the room. She'd only need to keep it open for a couple seconds.

The ancient child finished her task mere seconds before Toma yelled that it was time. Almost two dozen frightened people crashed to the floor in a cloud of dust and dirt. Several were injured in the fall since there was no way to warn them.

Issabol felt it was a good trade. A better fate than the one that awaited them where they had been only moments before. Bilney stepped forward and held out her hands.

"Please don't be afraid. You are guests of Autumn and are safe. If you are hurt, please let us know. My friend here can help."

Mini stepped forward, cloaked in a thin layer of light blue mist. She gave them a sweet smile.

"Welcome to your new home. Immigrants are welcome in Autumn."

Once the group was calmed, the ancient girl returned to her tea. She sighed and anticipated taking a long drink of the hot bitter liquid. Instead, she choked and sputtered at the thickened mess.

The cup was about half full of Spring dirt.

**

His breaths came in desperate gasps. The troll had held his blood in a boil for over three minutes. Tedar couldn't afford to stop moving; the Summer girl's strength and speed were too much. His coarse black hair was slick with sweat and his torso hissed as the latest blow rapidly healed. He rolled hard to one side as a fist slammed the ground where he had been.

The troll had spent much time learning of the various spirit powers he might face. He watched this tall girl in her previous matches. In the final round, he faced her might himself.

He'd tested a few devastating blows against her. Still, the thick layer of rock coating her skin made everything completely ineffective. Tedar discussed this battle with Bayu earlier and they worked out a plan. He only had one hope of winning.

His dark-green foot slid in some loose soil and he had to catch the quick jab with two crossed arms. He could feel bones crack and skin split. The exposed blood sizzled with a hiss in the cool air. The healing of another wound drained his power.

Exhaustion wasn't far away, and the barrier on the outer edge limited him to what energy he could store in his typically lean body. There was a time when he couldn't have hoped to win this battle, only holding this state of strength and speed for less than a single minute. That was before the little Battle Shaper had gifted him with a sigil of fire. He liked to think all his hard work helped as well.

Now he could boil blood for half an hour or more with little effort. Well, he could when he wasn't continually healing the damage to his body and moving with his full strength.

As he blocked the most recent strike, he began to hope. The blow wasn't as solid and he could hear the girl panting through the thick layers of stone.

Tedar faked a lunge to one side and leaped at the back of her armored form. His opponent was tall, he could see that even from a distance, but the armor of rock and hardened earth made her nearly as tall as he. He clamped down with sturdy fingers, making her carry the weight of both fighters while careful to avoid getting pinched in the joints.

For a few desperate seconds, he shifted his weight. He breathed hard while allowing his mass to push her down. She roared in frustration, her rasping breath now even louder.

Then came the first sign of faltering, a literal crack in her armor. Pieces of stone began to crumble away from her arms and back. Tedar smiled around his dark tusks.

Encouraged by signs of weakness, he began to shift his weight, keeping her off balance and forcing her to exert even more of her precious energy. His only chance of victory was to force the young woman to use up all the power she had stored and allow her protective shell to crumble. Only then could he strike.

It was a close thing. The girl faded to nothing only seconds before the healing and exertions forced him to drop the boil of his blood. As the shell of rock and dirt crumbled, he put one hand on her shoulder and pulled back for a vicious punch.

Without the energy required to hold her shell, the girl looked weak and fragile. Tedar lowered his strike and gently set her on the ground. She was too exhausted to even try to stand, so he dropped the boil and bowed low to his opponent.

She had fought well, with honor and dignity. He wouldn't take that away from her. Then he did something that brought more pride to his queen than his victory. He reached down, taking her tan hand in his, and helped her to her feet. Having others carry her out would rob her of what was earned.

Tedar walked out with the young warrior of Summer. As he moved, he noticed a mark on her brow. It was a symbol, a tall tree with one low hanging branch. He knew the character.

Some of his tribe had escaped bondage in the south and once bore the same mark. It was applied with a type of fire spirit and couldn't be removed until recently. When asked, the Queen of Autumn only said she had a tool that could break any spell and unravel any weave.

This amazing girl was a warrior slave. The troll gritted his teeth but held his tongue; he would report this to the prince who was to stop in later in the afternoon. He walked to the exit gate to the cheers of the crowd.

The tired young woman spoke faintly, "Thank you... for not finishing me. You fought well."

Tedar felt her start to slump, almost ready to pass out. Her pride pushed her to get her legs under her as they made it to the gate. A short man with a shaved head stood with fury in his eyes.

As the gate moved into place behind them, Tedar allowed the girl to lean on the wall. The man approached and began to scream.

"You allowed yourself to lose to... that... thing? You've disgraced your kingdom and your queen. You're not fit to—"

His hand was coming down at her face. His strike and his words were interrupted by a hand with three fingers catching his arm. The man turned and saw the troll was swelling in both size and anger. Now past the barrier Tedar could draw power again. Dark eyes held murderous rage that caused the little man to sputter over his words.

"See here, troll, you dare lay hands on—"

Tedar thumped his head against the stone wall. The little man's eyes rolled back and he sank to the ground. The troll leaned over and once again helped the girl walk. They moved into the barracks.

The troll stepped up to the administration desk. "I want to inquire if a price has been set for the loser of the last round?"

The man never looked up, only moved to his ledgers. When slaves fought, it wasn't uncommon to set a price, either inflated or discounted, depending on whether they won or lost the fight.

After a few moments, he nodded and stated, "The girl known as Avani is owned by the Sont family of Summer. Her price was on the rise, but with her recent loss and the families' need for coin.... You see, she won't earn any more now that she's been eliminated. Let's see... Ah, she's up for two thousand, four hundred eighty copper talons."

Tedar thought for a moment. "My winnings, how much do I have?"

The man looked up and seemed to jump as he just now registered it was a troll standing before him.

"Um... well, let me see. You've earned a total of three thousand, six hundred forty-three, but you understand that trolls cannot receive coin. Your funds will go to your kingdom purse and the treasury of Autumn, so—"

"I accept the offer to sell this young woman. Put the funds down and send for approval from the Queen of Autumn. She leaves with me now." He motioned to the tall girl.

Avani just now seemed to understand what was happening. Her eyes welled with tears as she realized she was being bought by the hulking troll. She began to tremble as several scenarios played through her mind. Tedar leaned down and whispered around his tusks.

"Peace, friend. I'm purchasing your freedom, not your life. Play along for now and I promise you will choose your own path."

The little man was taking notes as he looked up.

"I'm afraid if you try to take her before the sale clears, she will be deemed a runaway and you a thief. Rules, you see."

The troll growled as he bent and picked up the young woman, carrying her like a small child. He leaned over the desk, his voice a low rumble.

"Move it along as fast as you can; I will be sitting over there against the wall. I'll not abide anyone abusing my property until then. Do we have an understanding?"

The man nodded and began filling out forms and sending for approval. Tedar set Avani down in the corner of the room, then moved a seat down to give her some space.

He was quite tired; the fight had done a number on him. Two other young fighters moved over, seemingly cautious. He started to protest, but Avani smiled weakly at them.

"How are you both holding up? Your matches will begin tomorrow if I'm not wrong."

The boy was a bit bigger and nodded. "Yes, the next phase begins shortly. Are you... are you going away?"

Tedar listened as the trio whispered back and forth. His anger rose as he pieced together the situation of Summer's young combatants. When he could take no more, he leaned over and whispered in the tall girl's ear.

"How many of Summer's fighters are warrior slaves?"

Avani hung her head, looking at the others and then back to him.

"All of us."

***

Alder King Zankoku was fuming as the messenger from Summer stepped into his chambers. The whole day was a complete disaster.

Despite his attempts, Ohkami had been unable to get the strange gnome woman away from the Autumn group. The spectacle that was planned to make the western and northern queens look just as detached as the other kingdoms backfired spectacularly. The strange hound made a show of force the people wouldn't soon forget. To top it all off, a loyal dragon had been slaughtered in front of the entire kingdom.

Of course, his assistance from Summer never showed, only the fighters to represent them. He looked to the woman standing near the door wearing the dark-green and brown of the southern kingdom. She didn't even look afraid.

"I assume you have come to tell me the Queen of Summer will be here by morning?"

The woman tilted her head to one side, her shaved skull glistening slightly in the lamplight. Her dark-green robe of fine silk trailed behind her as she moved smoothly across the room.

Standing before him, she held his gaze with neither fear nor apology. She spoke slowly, stretching out every syllable of each word out of her mouth.

"Plans have changed. My queen will not be in attendance. She has sent an emissary and her fighters to participate."

Zankoku slammed a fist down as he raged. The his face darkened to a flushed red and he threw a lamp across the room.

"You back out on me now? I brought disaster into my home. I held up my side of the bargain. I lost a dragon today and half my people want to defect to the rotting swamp of that creepy wench and her demon. Did you see what that monster did? It would have tried to kill me! Do you understand? How am I to—"

She held up a hand, calmly halting his rant. Then she once again spoke in her slow rasping voice.

"We do not back out of the agreement; times have required us all to seek power in unfamiliar places. You are correct in saying that dangerous powers have been let loose in your house, but it is also true that that same power is no longer protecting its home. The Banshee is strong, but her real power is the loyalty of her people and the potential to attract others."

"She's not what I am worried about! You saw the size of those dragons. Something is going on in the west. Even the gnomes are as big as elves. That hound took out a full-grown spore wyrm as if it were a mouse."

The woman nodded, head slightly tilted to acknowledge his words. "The Banshee is both loved and *feared*. What if she were to fail in protecting her people? Even now, Summer moves to the City of Blood, the heart of her power. Once it falls, we will attack Winter on two fronts and it too will fall. Spring and Summer will split the land and the spoils, then all will once more become as it was."

The king sighed aloud as he seemed to deflate. This whole plan seemed to risk more for Spring than Summer. Still, admittedly, his armies would face significantly fewer battles in the coming weeks. The presence of the Summer Queen would have gone a long way toward easing his mind. The emissary spoke once more.

"When can we expect the gnome? We cannot properly understand the power of Autumn until we see how they grow in strength so quickly."

His face reddened again, his words through gritted teeth.

"She's well protected. Can we not capture someone else for you?"

The emissary lifted an eyebrow. "She grows in the same way those dragons do. If you would rather bring us a dragon of Autumn, that would also work."

Zankoku knew that was an insane proposition. He started to move to confront her, to scream in the woman's face. An idea hit him just as he stood. Moving frantically, he went to a shelf of ancient texts. Pulling out a large volume of green leather, he set it down.

The ancient laws held old remnants of power, imposed by forces few had any hope of understanding. He saw it, just as he remembered. A wide grin crossed his face as he looked back to the Summer messenger.

"A dragon will work, then?"

***

The news of what the king of this wretched kingdom had done didn't sit well with the prince. The act itself stoked the flames of his temper more than enough, but the impact it had on his already fragile gnome had him enraged.

He fought that battle inside. It took all the will power he had to focus on helping her and not on killing the pompous monster in his ivory tower.

Jack gave her a few minutes, some time out in the night air to be alone with her thoughts. When her sobs slowed to the occasional sniffle, he moved to join her on the balcony of Claire's sitting room.

Joobel sat on a bench, looking out at the stars in the night sky. It wasn't the first time her beauty took his breath away. Long silver hair flowed over her light brown skin. The flowing silks of her green dress swayed in the gentle breeze. She was humming again, a sad melody that seemed to flow out from her in waves.

The prince took a seat next to her and put an arm around her slender shoulders. He brushed the silver hair away and leaned into a sideways embrace. He wanted so badly to help her, but words were never his strength. This attempt was no exception, his speech slow and awkward.

"I heard what happened, what you tried to do.... Are... are you ok?"

She shook her head, thick tears still flowing down her cheeks.

"How could anyone do such a thing?" she sniffed. "In many ways this is my home. This is the realm of my spirit. Why do I feel so out of place?"

Jack tried to come up with a good answer, a way to give her comfort. He took her hand and traced slow spiraling lines on the smooth skin. Words were not his gift, but he did his best.

"There are monsters in this world. Not all live in caves and eat villagers. This world needs people like you to show the path forward." His eyes narrowed. "And people like me to clear it. I hear the children all survived?"

Joobel nodded as she squirmed deeper into his arms. She leaned hard against him and sighed.

"Issabol was able to pull them through safely. They now belong to Autumn and many will soon be at the school."

Jack already knew as much. He wanted her to say it out loud. She needed to draw hope from their better future. Her sobs had slowed and he felt her breathing become even. He tried one last time to comfort her.

"We only see what the blowhard wants us to. There is evil in our home as well, but we also know of the hope for something better. I'm sure it's no different here."

She sniffled and lifted his hand to kiss it. Her bright blue eyes stared out at the stars twinkling so far in the distance. After several long minutes of closeness, she gave his hands a squeeze and stood up.

"We should get some rest. Who knows what tomorrow holds? Thank you for being here with me."

Jack looked up as she stretched and hopped into the air. She hovered around for a few seconds to work her wings and then landed. Joobel took his hand and pulled him toward the door. They moved back inside until he tasted an unfamiliar flavor of power.

He reached his aura out further and picked up more of the spirit. It tasted like a silver coin. Now that he was picking up on it more, he found it wasn't so unfamiliar. It was very close to the spirit of the revolting prince of this kingdom.

Jack took a deep breath and waved Joobel inside. She shrugged and headed toward the door. He turned and held out a hand, feeling the source of the spirit so near and yet unseen.

Aquamarine eyes met his own glowing orange as he looked over the rail. Sitting on the ledge in a faint shadow was a large cat. Its face and ears were black as Harvest while most of the body was a light brown.

He could feel the spirit inside. This wasn't just a cat. He wanted to simply kill the creature and throw it from the tower.

Jack thought of how disheartened his gnome was at the moment. He couldn't hurt her anymore today. Jack met the feline gaze, then shook his head as he spoke.

"I don't know what you thought you were going to try to do...." He sighed and rubbed his temple. "It would be best if she didn't have to know of any more killing today. Whoever hired you, they didn't pay you enough. Go now and you can live. Do *not* return."

He let his eyes flare orange and held up a ball of flame. The cat found its way back down the tower. Claws dug into the hard marble and scrabbled so fast it almost fell several times.

Jack snuffed out the flame and moved back inside.

CHAPTER 13

The Winter Queen was a bit disappointed that her kingdom didn't hold out well in the melee phase of the junior games. One of the young yetis made it to the final four, but that earth girl was just too much and it was a short fight. Smart move for that troll to wear her down.

Raine was happy to see one of the new additions to Autumn had earned prestige and coin for his kingdom. She hoped Winter would fare better in the adult competitions.

Next, there would be a presentation of the various dragons, a rare chance to allow the protectors of each realm to make a show of strength. Already moving into the arena were two giant wood wyrms, the dragons of Summer. Each was nearly as long as the field. Like the spore wyrms, they had two stout legs on the front to allow them to move thick necks and enormous heads.

Each moved to the far end of the field and were followed by the dragons of Spring. One was as large as the wood wyrms. The other would have been almost as big as Depth.

Raine gasped and looked over to Claire, who also seemed shocked.

"Do they get that big naturally?"

Claire just shrugged, in awe of the mass slithering across the packed dirt.

Shadows moved over the arena, circling slowly in a gliding descent. Brook landed first, seeming small next to the wyrms. Puddle also joined her, looking proud but showing none of his strange abilities. The iridescent blue of his scales shimmered and changed shades in the bright Spring light.

Two more shapes began to circle, one black as pitch and seeming to absorb the sunlight as it tried to reveal him. Harvest landed with a tremor, not as large as the biggest spore wyrm but perhaps the biggest to take flight in the Fae world.

A glimmering emerald form that resembled her ebony brother in shape yet was nearly opposite in power circled him. Raine still hated that Bloom was here in her condition, perhaps only days away from dropping a clutch of precious eggs.

The dragons were all positioned in a wide circle: four drakes and four wyrms. Each type of dragon had advantages and weaknesses. The Alder King's voice floated out of the air as he spoke for the ceremony.

"We stand witness today to a fantastic display. Before you are dragons from all four kingdoms, each able to perform feats no person could ever dream of, all bound to the great spirits of their home."

He continued on for some time, the words moving in slow circles. From time to time there was a round of cheering for the dragons below. Puddle looked up at the Winter Queen and sent his words to her mind.

"Harvest wants to know if we can eat him. He doesn't like the taste of people, but I'd swallow the man whole if it would stop the rambling."

Raine smiled slightly as she sent her thoughts back.

"Please don't. Even I couldn't purify that poison."

Puddle chuffed visibly, his scales glinting little bits of scattered light all over the field.

The king continued. "These are the most impressive dragons in all of Fairie, here to add prestige to the Contest of Champions."

The crowd roared this time, shouts and clapping ringing throughout. Raine wondered what they would think if Depth had shown up. That was a card best kept inside the sleeve. She'd just resigned herself to the guy making even dragons boring when his words caught her attention.

"We have a special showing for you this day. The ancient laws still hold sway, and here in the realm of the great spirit of renewal, a challenge must be met. A dragon of the same aspect may challenge another for Dominance. Bear witness, my countrymen, as two titans will fight for control."

Raine jumped up, eyes wide. Renewal. Spring's aspect of great spirit. Dominance was a way for dragons to work out a pecking order within their own number. His words could only mean one thing.

The colossal spore wyrm began to unravel and move to the center of the field.

She could see Claire's hands gripping the rail overlooking the spectacle. The Autumn Queen's knuckles were stark white in her fear and anger. The dragon's words came like a crashing wave into the minds of the crowd.

"Kaiju of Spring challenges Tatsu, the Autumn dragon known as Bloom, to a battle of Dominance under the ancient law. The winner will hold authority over the loser."

The Winter Queen was surprised once again. She heard laughter from the last person she would ever expect. Joobel was giggling and at first, Raine thought she'd completely lost her mind. Then the gnome spoke.

"He doesn't know! That foolish blowhard doesn't understand. This really will be a show!"

Raine thought of the ancient law; all royals had to learn them as children. Dominance was designed to prevent infighting among the dragons. They were too powerful to battle just anywhere; cities could be leveled.

Dragons were too rare to risk excessive losses. They were precious to the land they served. So, no dragon who carried a clutch could be forced to fight; her sire could stand in her stead. Bloom's sire was sitting on the field, a strange dragon with abilities this world had never seen.

Claire looked at Joobel as if she were mad, tears already forming on her face. Raine stepped forward and took her cousin's hand, giving it a tight squeeze.

Raine then spoke through her dragon-speak. She relayed her words through the powerful Puddle who was close enough to help. All present heard the Winter Queen. She smiled as she spoke.

"The ancient laws cannot be ignored. The challenge must, indeed, be answered. Alas, the dragon Bloom is mere days away from dropping a clutch of precious eggs. She's the only female dragon in Autumn and her health cannot be risked. So, under the law, I hold authority over her mate and the sire of the eggs. I accept this challenge and the water drake Puddle will do battle this day."

The squeeze on Raine's hand ground her knuckles; Claire whispered harsh words in her ear.

"What! My only female dragon is going to brood? Why was I not aware?"

Joobel stepped forward and hugged Claire's other arm, still giggling a bit. She cooed in her queen's ear.

"Bloom wanted to surprise you. She's been mated to Puddle for some time now. As you know, drakes can interbreed. We are going to have cute little dragon babies!"

Raine was also excited. A more substantial dragon presence in Autumn would help Winter as well. Despite her joy at sharing the news with Claire, there was still the matter of the challenge.

The Alder King was silent, standing on his platform and fuming with impotent rage. The tone of his words didn't manage to hide his frustration.

"The law demands battle. Let us proceed."

***

The other dragons began to move to the far sides to bear witness to the duel. Bloom stepped over to push the top of her head against that of Puddle. They held for a moment, drawing various cute noises from the crowd. She moved over to stand next to her brother.

The black drake put his voice into the air, not for everyone, but only for those who could speak the words of dragons.

"Should any interfere, I will end them. As is the law."

Brook added her agreement, as did both of the wood wyrms. Kaiju moved into place across the field from Puddle.

The thunder of the gong rang out and the wyrm released a mighty blast of yellow spores. They shot across the field and slammed against the barrier at the far end. The people on the other side jumped and squirmed, but the shield held and they began to cheer. Puddle simply dashed to one side, evading the attack. The water drake roared his fury.

The arena had been part of the plan for the Alder King. Fighting with the barrier up would make flying nearly impossible. The only real way Bloom could have held her own would have been to attack with her claws from the sky.

He could also fly, but it wasn't his only skill or even his most dangerous one. More than that, he was angry. He and the other drakes agreed to keep out of the politics of the land, their actions only serving to undermine their queens. Yet he'd witnessed much in his exploration of this place.

Puddle had watched the way people were treated from up close. His observations as he took the form of a strange fog rolling through the city of Amaya didn't encourage him. He scouted this place and found it wanting.

He'd only ever lived in a world changed by the Autumn Queen and spent time in Winter as Raine ruled it. He wasn't used to seeing people mistreated. On top of all that, the fool of a king plotted to take away *his* mate.

Bloom was the kindest creature in his world. Loving, beautiful, and so full of compassion. She carried his future with her. They wanted to take her from him. In his anger, the typically mischievous dragon was now all steam.

Twice more, he let the huge wyrm fire off his deadly spores. Then when his opponent was gathering power for another attack, he let loose his own 'unique' form of dragon's breath.

The crowd shouted in confusion as the strange blue dragon released a blast of mist that shot not at the wyrm, but at the sky above him. The thick cloud moved high as the form of the drake below became translucent until he was completely gone.

The roiling cloud shifted and rolled until it came together and sped toward the ground below, the field right below Kaiju. The cloud crashed together into a ball of solid ice, slamming against the back of his massive opponent.

A roar of pain and confusion erupted from the wyrm as Puddle shifted into water and streamed to one side. He released a small explosion and four ice shards launched into Kaiju's side; a fifth shattered on the shield right in front of the Alder King's face, causing the man to fall out of his chair.

A few muffled laughs came from the crowd, though most were so focused on the fight they didn't notice. The shards evaporated and the mist rejoined the form of the drake.

The massive wyrm whipped his thick tail around, right as Puddle reformed. The hit thundered through the arena. The blue dragon rushed to meet the stone wall, but instead of a thunderclap, a loud splash was heard. Several streams of water rushed across the ground, some lashing up to become blades of ice that slashed at the wyrm's sides and stomach.

Roars of pain and frustration rose up, before one of the streams snaked around to flow up the thick front leg and up onto the neck of the spore dragon. The water ringed into a thick collar that began to use Puddle's other ability, that little bit of Pressure gifted to him. His master and the one who hatched him had given him a part of his own power.

The ring of water flowed around Kaiju, growing tighter and tighter. Strong forelimbs scratched at the collar; sharp claws slid through the liquid and tore at the flesh beneath. The wyrm couldn't see his opponent; he couldn't fire his deadly spores. Kaiju couldn't draw breath.

This was the moment that the other spore dragon made a deadly mistake. Seeing the might of Spring gasping on the ground, the dragon let loose a blast of his own yellow spores. The blue drake shifted to one side, avoiding the shot, just as Harvest let loose a thunderous cry of rage.

The death drake lunged across the field and slammed into the wyrm. He clamped onto its thick neck and ripped the throat from the interloper. More bloody chunks were torn out as both wood wyrms tore into the dying beast.

Puddle turned his attention back to Kaiju, who was slowly losing consciousness. The water drake began to shape the rest of his mass into his standard shape. Though instead of a solid mass of blue drake, he created a shell. He formed a construct of turbulent foaming water that was bigger than his standard size, bigger than Kaiju. It looked more tremendous than even Depth.

The construct looked like a frothing dragon out of nightmares. As his opponent lay unconscious on the hard earth, growing red with the spilled blood of the other wyrm, the construct lifted its head to the sky and let loose a roar.

It had no lungs, no real throat; no sound came from its mouth. The cry entered the minds of every man and woman, king and queen. Every slave and lord in the city of Amaya cringed as the sound assaulted their minds without bothering with ears.

Then the construct slowly turned to the platform. To the man who sat on the other side of the barrier. The foaming behemoth spoke in a low tone, now for Zankoku's ears only.

"The law is met. Do not attempt to take her from me again."

Then the water stilled and reformed back into an iridescent blue drake, his scales shifting color as they glinted in the sunlight.

Despite his ire at the plot, he recognized the huge wyrm had broken no law. Puddle bowed his head in respect to the massive spore dragon. He was pretty sure this creature belonged to his mate now.

He moved to Bloom once more, putting the top of his head against hers. She whispered to him through her mind.

"You are a wonderful protector, my love."

Then she did what her very nature compelled her to do. Other dragons had been of Spring, of the spirit of renewal, yet they tried to bring death and pain. Bloom held a pure spirit, and it offered something else.

A slow and steady stream of green-tinged mist left her throat, spreading out across the ground to the enormous Kaiju. The cloud entered his gasping lungs and formed around the slashes on his sides. Wounds closed up and his breathing evened out. In moments he was both whole and no longer in pain.

Bloom looked to the other spore wyrm. No amount of healing would help him now. Harvest stopped at one devastating attack. If that had been all, she might have saved him. But the wood dragons ravaged him way past any hope of life.

She felt a wave of sorrow pass through her, a slight shudder at such a loss. Puddle wondered at her compassion, her love the open hand to his sword. He loved her all the more.

Then the water drake heard the heavy stomp of feet and turned to Kaiju. He stood before Bloom, the challenge over. Puddle couldn't say if it was his honor, fear, or the ancient magic, but the wyrm bowed low to the green drake of Autumn. He spoke for all to hear.

"The challenge was met under the law. You hold Dominion over me, Bloom of Autumn."

The crowd was still in shock from the terrifying display of the water dragon and the brutal death of the other spore dragon, but slowly the clapping began. Gradually it moved to a cheer, and finally a roar from nearly all present at the display of might. Puddle heard only one voice, a whisper deep in his mind.

It came from the young woman who Named him. She shared her home with both him and his master. The drake had seen the spark in her, just as Depth had on the shore of a dead world when she was young and vulnerable. She set four words in his mind and he treasured them.

"Thank you... my friend."

***

The afternoon held few surprises for the Tempest, who was working his way through the ranks of the junior casting division. Bayu had spent his days sparring against fighters like Edana, Tedar, and many of the adult warriors. He'd even gone up against the prince a couple of times. He didn't win, but he lasted a couple seconds longer than most.

The fighters he went up against today were either lords and ladies that were sheltered from real training, or slaves that had no passion for winning, only a fear of losing. Granted, he was blessed with more power than most, but he also put tremendous effort into his training.

Bayu had eaten lunch with his friend Tedar, who already won the top prize in the melee division. He was quite shocked to find out that the troll purchased a slave, a Summer fighter named Avani.

The news that Summer sent nothing but slaves to compete concerned him in more ways than one. For one thing, his queen wasn't a fan of the practice. For another, he knew that he could have fallen into such a life quite easily had he not been adopted by the Keep.

Tedar carried a letter from the queen. She hadn't just approved the purchase of Avani but arranged to have Gray buy all the others who completed their trials. Some were already being quietly transported back to the Blood Keep through portals.

Avani decided to stay and help calm the others so they could do the same as each became available. The tall girl was well known among the Summer warriors. When she spoke to them with the slave mark missing from her brow, they were quickly convinced.

Edana was brought into the conversation as well, and Tedar asked both her and Bayu to help with the plan. As each of the fighters from Summer was eliminated, they became available for purchase. The better they did, the more expensive they became.

Of course, the faster and more embarrassing the loss, the more quickly each could be bought and, in turn, kept safe. Edana had been handling her role in this endeavor admirably.

Bayu's job was also to make sure his opponents lost and did so as terribly as possible. He'd have taken pride in his ability to defeat opponents with so little effort, except most were in on the scheme now and were throwing their matches.

The only challenge he faced now was a handful of Winter fighters Raine declined to share the plan with and a few spoiled lords from Spring. As each fight was completed, both he and Edana rose through the ranks. By the time the final four came up, they were both among them.

Edana had last gone up against a Spring boy who used a type of water spirit that allowed him to move blades of liquid about. She fought well, but in the end was outclassed and lost. Bayu could live with that, but the young man sliced her over a dozen times after she tapped out.

His friend was bled nearly to death and had her clothes turned to ribbons. Bayu wasn't feeling his usual calm. He ended most fights quickly out of compassion. This one was to be something else. He still intended it to end quickly, though.

Looking across the field, he could see the smile on the young man's face. He'd nearly killed one of the sweetest girls in the world. The boy took her dignity when it gained him nothing. *That stupid smile, on that foolish face!*

Bayu gritted his teeth and reached down to his wrist, unclasping the bracelet that allowed him to control his anger. This time he relished and fed it.

Tiny sparks of yellow light began popping around his hair as the static began to build all around him. Dark clouds formed in the sky above the dome shield.

People in the stands were getting ready for the show as they began to notice the hair on their arms stand up. They stared in awe as the boy with the curly blonde hair started to arc energy all around the ground at his feet. The young fighter from Spring stopped smiling and suddenly looked around for something to hide behind.

The gong rang, a light appetizer for the deafening crack of thunder that immediately followed. The bolt of lightning crashed from the sky, ripping through the top of the dome that had taken hits from a dragon's breath only hours ago. The energy overloaded the casters powering the shield, shocking them and throwing them away from their work.

There would have been no hope for the Spring fighter had Bayu wanted him dead. The bolt struck the ground three paces away, sending up a burst of burning soil and melting the rock underneath. The Spring warrior was thrown hard toward the crowd and would have hit the barrier if one had still been in place.

A rather large woman found a singed water warrior landing in her lap. The fight was over less than a second after the gong. It was the shortest match in the history of the Contest of Champions.

Bayu reached down and snapped the bracelet back into place, embracing the calm that came with its power. He straightened his collar, walking calmly to the gate with only a hint of pride on his face. After all, he was now the champion of the junior casting division.

As he walked, he risked a look to his queen. She had her hands on her hips and was slowly shaking her head. He sighed as he stepped out. His only hope was the words that came from the ghost appearing just inside the gate. The face was a young woman, but the voice was his queen's.

"At least this time, it wasn't *my* roof."

Bayu smiled slightly as he moved to join his friends.

***

Zankoku grabbed a small table and flung it across the spacious office. It slammed against a wall, breaking into splinters. The emissary from Summer had left, telling him only that all was under control.

All his ally from the south would do to support him was send a bunch of warrior slaves. Most of them proved little more than fodder for his enemies. He looked to his soldiers standing next to the door, and yelled his frustration.

"They humiliate me! Me! That nasty woman would trick me into a dragon challenge!"

He threw a lamp at the door, shards of crystal flying everywhere.

"Then she has another of my dragons killed and steals my pride and joy!"

He shattered a half-full pitcher of wine against the wall. The crimson liquid clung to drapes and the marble around them.

"That drake threatened me! Oh, I saw it.... He doesn't know who he's up against!"

The fuming elf picked up a book and tore it in two.

"I will *not* be bested in my own home! I will see them pay. If I cannot give Summer the dragon, I *will* get the gnome. I'll see them sorry they ever challenged me!"

He threw each half of the thick volume at the door one at a time.

Naoki listened to the man rant, careful to remain motionless in the terrace garden outside the Alder King's office. Yoshiko had been clear that he wasn't to confront the king. Those around him lost their will and the ability to think.

Except the foreigners. They seemed to be immune somehow. His friend was clear that the western and northern queens were allies in this, though she hadn't yet met with them. This would be the night, though. He was to help her with that particular introduction.

The elf had hoped to gain some information from his observations, but the Alder King was in a fit, and little more of use would be obtained.

Naoki released the branch of the tree that had grown several feet to allow his eavesdropping. Long blades of grass and vines wrapped around his forearms and ankles and lowered him down a couple of stories. There on a bench sat the princess.

Yoshiko was nothing like what he would have expected. She was more grounded and compassionate. Even though she might someday rule this kingdom, she clung to humility.

The girl had changed out of her elegant dress from the festivities and now wore a fitted white uniform, like that worn by servants all throughout the Beryl Gardens. With her hair pulled back and makeup and jewelry gone, save her ever-present pendant, she could pass for one of the staff. Her curvy form was evident through the fabric and he wondered why he found her more attractive in this humble state.

The soft soles of his boots dropped silently onto the landing. The grass and vines moved back to their normal position. He walked up and began to speak, yet Yoshiko somehow detected his presence and beat him to it.

"I'm afraid."

Naoki hadn't expected that; she always seemed so confident. He moved forward and sat on the bench, looking up at the tiny flecks of white fighting the void of black that dominated the night sky. She took his hand and he could feel a tremble.

"What is it you fear?" He tightened his grip around her small fingers. It had been so long since he felt alone and afraid, but he could still remember the feeling and wanted to offer what comfort he could.

"The king, the state of my mother, the fate of our people, and... the dark prince."

"Your step-brother? I think we both know he's no match for you."

"No, Ohkami is dark in his own way. Evil is a good enough term. Autumn's Prince isn't so much evil as he..."

Yoshiko paused, trying to pull the words from her mind.

"He has too much power. The potential to do great things, both good or evil. I fear what he could become."

"You and I aren't strangers to power. Not all who wield it abuse it. Perhaps our introductions will put your mind at ease."

He felt the squeeze on his hand tighten, then she let go and stood. Spring's royal family took up a good portion of the eastern tower. The pair would need to cross over to the north end to make their way around the skyways between the spires to visit Autumn's quarters to the west. He stood and they began walking.

It wasn't uncommon for the princess to walk the skyways in the evening, though once they reached the northern spire, they needed to move undetected. Patrols of three or four men moved lazily back and forth.

The guards were so accustomed to the ease of the duty that they didn't notice the brush along the side rustle as it reached over and carried two elves silently along the outside edge of the platforms. The white marble walkway hid them from the insides of the towers and the distance would make them nearly impossible to see from the ground.

At the speeds the plants carried them, they reached the western tower in only a few minutes. From there, it was a simple matter to climb to the top floor in the same way he'd reached the garden ledge outside the Alder King's study.

Yoshiko sighed. "I hope they don't attack us; we won't hold up well against so many."

Naoki pondered her words and began to think of a way to let the strangers know they meant no harm. His planning was interrupted as they came up under the ledge to the Queen of Autumn's rooms. As he and his passenger came around the rail, quiet as whispers, a lean young man with shaggy brown hair greeted them both.

"Everyone's waiting. Let's get inside."

***

The ghosts of Autumn informed her of the pair and their plans shortly after arriving in Spring. Claire not only knew when to expect them, but how they would get there, their basic spirit abilities, and the character of her guests.

Sometimes she wished her skills were more useful in a direct fight. The Banshee of Autumn rarely had to do so. Preparation was everything.

Claire knew the two elves meant no harm, so she sent only one person out to greet them. The fact that she sent the Demon Prince was evidence of her need to leave no room for error.

With some help from Stoveg and Gray, the place had been arranged in a semblance of the war room. Chairs and sofas ringed the center of the room, allowing all to hear and be heard.

Raine and her envoy of Winter arrived by portal over an hour ago. Most were tired and the next round of games would start early the following day. It was time to get started.

Claire stood just inside and greeted the princess first, as was the custom. She gave a slight bow as she spoke.

"It's an honor to host you, Yoshiko Cerelia, assumed Maiden of Spring. I'm Claire. You may address me as such in these casual circumstances."

The princess stood dumbfounded and after a few silent seconds, returned the bow.

"Pleased to meet you.... How did you..."

"It's always wise to be well informed when in unfamiliar places, wouldn't you agree?"

The elf woman nodded and moved aside for her companion. Claire couldn't help but notice her working hard to keep a safe distance from Jack. As the other elf entered, she gave the same bow of respect and greeted him as well.

"Naoki, I presume. It's a pleasure to meet the one called the Green Man. You are welcome here as well."

He only nodded and returned the bow. Then Autumn's Queen beckoned them both into the room. More introductions were made, and soon the niceties of conversation gave way to the reason the two had risked the visit. The elf maid began by confirming that which Claire already suspected.

"We think Summer is moving against your border. So much of your power is here, I fear your people are in danger."

Claire nodded at this; plans were in place. It was true that without her dragon patrolling the border, they could find themselves in trouble. Much was at risk, but there was much to gain as well. She nodded at Yoshiko in thanks.

"It's kind of you to bring this to us. We have taken precautions against most outcomes, but appreciate the warning."

Yoshiko looked hesitant, afraid even. Claire had been careful to make her guests feel at home, yet something was bothering the princess. The elf glanced around, eyes wild.

The Autumn Queen gave a concerned nod. "My dear girl, I assure you there is no danger here. What has you so shaken?"

There was a long pause before Yoshiko bit her lower lip, meeting Claire's eyes. Her words were a whisper.

"May I ask you a question?"

Claire smiled widely and nodded. "Of course, I welcome the candor."

Yoshiko grabbed Naoki's hand and then looked across the room to Jack. The prince was eating a honey cake and looking bored. She pointed to him and then looked at Claire.

"What *is* he?"

Claire cocked an eyebrow and tilted her head to one side slightly. Sure, Jack had a reputation as a bit of a hothead, one that was literal and well earned. Still, he offered no violence. If you didn't know who he was, there would be little to be intimidated by.

In the room was a Winter guard with glowing red eyes, a yeti the size of a large horse, a rather scary looking troll, and two queens of Fairie. Yet the princess picked out the one who was by far the most dangerous in her group, if not the world.

Her mind worked through the risks and possibilities of revealing the true nature of her brother. Every indication pointed to these elves being good people who may yet help her. However, Jack was a card she wasn't ready to play. Perhaps she could deflect.

"My brother is a bit... overzealous, but I assure you that he—"

Yoshiko shook her head. "His aura is eating away at the magic in the air even now, all while radiating power like waves against the shore. He wields more energy than anyone I have ever seen. It frightens me."

That was more than Claire expected the elf girl to know. She focused the conversation on the ability to perceive such things.

"You can see auras?"

Yoshiko nodded and pulled out a small white mushroom cap. It looked a bit limp and worn.

"It's a gifted power, one I gained recently. The land is... dissatisfied. It hopes to bring about change. It led me to him." She nodded to Naoki. "It spoke the same of you, calling you an ally."

"The land spoke to you?" Claire asked.

The elf shrugged. "In a way. I'm not claiming to understand it all."

Claire nodded; she was no stranger to playing catch up with the powers of this world. She leaned back in her chair, tapping her finger to her lips as she pondered the best way to proceed.

"My brother is... complicated. I assure you none of us mean any harm to either of you."

Yoshiko looked pensive. Claire could tell she wasn't satisfied, but she didn't bring it up again.

The meeting was short, considering all that was to be discussed, but the Autumn Queen was pleased with the encounter. As the two elves left the room and worked their way down the tower, Raine moved to her side at the balcony rail.

"Can we trust them?"

Claire sighed and relaxed, revealing how tired she was. She put an arm around her cousin and leaned her head over to rest against Raine's.

"Trust is a bit like copper. Hard to come by and much too easy to part with. Those two have an agenda and our wellbeing isn't their top priority."

"Yet we will work with them?" Raine asked with a tone of sarcasm.

Claire gave a nod. "We are far from home, with enemies on all sides. I don't have so many friends as to start turning them away. Our goals aren't so dissimilar."

Raine shook her head slowly. "I hope you are right. Personally, I'm starting to miss my cold black castle with a constant stream of murderers."

Claire chuckled at the words, then turned to face the white-haired queen.

"Yes, I hear the assassin's guild has started recruiting again. It seems they're running low."

Raine rolled her eyes as the pair moved back into the tower.

CHAPTER 14

The lab was nearly up and running. Mini moved through the winding halls and rooms of Issabol's home. She saw Varam working the settings on a portal orb in the workshop and walked through the kitchen to see Bilney baking something sweet.

The bright flash blinded her for a moment, drawing a gasp. As her eyes readjusted, the doctor looked down to see a cute little girl with black hair and caramel skin. The child spoke not to her, but to the picture of her on a small screen.

"Oh it's Miiiiiiiiiiiiiiini.... Hi Mini.... I'm going to help make coooooooooookies.... I like the Miiiiiiiiiiiiiiini...."

The child skipped away, humming something and giggling. Another voice came from the kitchen.

"She's doing quite well, wouldn't you agree?"

Bilney ran a finger over a copper whisk and stuck the digit in her mouth, nodding. Then she handed the utensil to Laris, who cooed and began licking it clean. Mini nodded and smiled. Where she was from, there was little need to worry that a patient might be ill adjusted due to the power to see the spirit magic flowing through others. Still, Gray's camera seemed to be doing a grand job of helping the girl adjust.

Mini spoke briefly to the guard and moved to the small room that held her other project. Another beautiful child sat clicking away on the computer.

Toma was a bit older and seemed to have the aptitude of the young with computers. Only a few days ago she couldn't turn it on; now she was clicking and typing away. Another girl was hard at work, this one both a bit older and much smaller. The gnome was testing the wiring on the soundboard.

Mini moved over to stand behind Toma, but the girl was so focused that she never noticed the old woman in the young body walk in. Wemwi stopped her task and welcomed her.

"Hi, Mini! We are just rechecking everything and will be ready to open the Spring portals for the noise boxes."

"They are called speakers. That's great news. You hardly needed me at all."

The gnome wiped her brow with a small yellow kerchief. She wore little overalls over her dirty tunic. Mini was a bit thrown by the gnome who held the title 'Dragon Slayer,' but she enjoyed working with her. The girl was quite intelligent.

Toma snapped out of her screen trance and looked up.

"Oh, hi Mini, when did you get here?"

She rolled her eyes. "Just now. Is the playlist set?"

Toma nodded. "Yep, we're all ready. How is your labridory?"

Mini smiled. "Laboratory... and it's just about done."

Upon the wall, there was a large viewing portal. A vast arena held thousands of people. In the center, two combatants squared off for battle.

The next round was beginning.

***

The wind whipped through the barrier on the edge of the field, stirring puffs of dust from the dry earth underfoot. Despite the heat, Cruor wore his Winter guard uniform. The only alteration was the removal of the sleeves.

The youngest applicant in the adult melee division, he had to sign off to compete. His pale arms writhed with tense muscle as he took his stance. He cocked his head as he heard a sound, faint at first, and just starting to grow as his name was announced, the words amplified with air magic.

"Representing the Kingdom of Winter. Cruor Mira!"

The crowd started to cheer, then hesitated as the sound blasted seemingly from nowhere. Gray had said that he wanted to gain some momentum as the final four fought.

Cruor had little trouble making it this far. He hadn't lost many fights in his life and all the recent ones were to one man. That was only with Jack keeping him at a distance.

This was the fight he looked forward to. On the other side of the arena stood Prince Ohkami. They announced his name with the fanfare of trumpets meant to lift him up in front of his people. Now another fanfare began from an unseen source.

'Ah-aaaaaaah, ah!'

The music blared loudly, and the crowd began to respond to the energy of the sound. A song from another world was blaring through the arena. A song that spoke of snow and ice. A song of victory in battle. Then some started clapping to the beat. Gray arranged for him to have his own introduction.

Led Zeppelin's "Immigrant Song" echoed through the stadium. Cruor wasn't familiar with the tune, but he smiled with his fangs fully out as the crowd fell into the rhythm. Then he could hear them begin chanting.

"Cruor! Cruor! Cruor!"

Finally, the music died down, lingering in the cheers of the crowd for several long seconds. The guard looked to his queen, the woman that inspired him to follow a different path. She smiled down at him and he felt a pool of warmth begin to form in his gut as he pulled on his power. He looked out to the elf prince, who was licking his lips as he began to transform.

Cruor had observed Ohkami's fighting method several times and knew this match was inevitable. The brackets would put him against the prince and that winner on to the final round. Both Jack and Gray would be fighting in the casting division and he alone was left among the fighters from Autumn and Winter.

Ohkami used overwhelming force to put his opponents on the defensive. The Wolf Prince pushed relentlessly until they gave up or were hurt badly enough for the match to be called. One fighter from Summer had died from his injuries.

Despite his own ability, the Leech knew this would be a close fight. He had to admit that the prince was faster than him, so he decided to take a lesson from a young troll.

As the gong rang out, there was a blur on the other end of the field. The prince had taken a hybrid shape of man and wolf. He sported a long snout full of razor teeth and thick brown-grey fur covered his skin.

Cruor tore the blood from his own veins, formed a long spear, set the back end to the ground, and waited a long second until the wolf reached him. As the distance closed, he pulled the spear into place and let the speed of his foe push the point home while he jumped straight up.

There was a loud howl as the beast cried out in pain and frustration. Ohkami turned just as the spear changed into a hook and the Leech ripped it from the beast's shoulder. This time the wound was extensive and blood flowed onto the hard dirt below.

A claw swiped toward his pale face and he jumped back. Not fast enough. Both men stood a few paces apart. Both the scratches and the shoulder gained months of healing in seconds. Ohkami smiled and spoke in a guttural voice through his misshapen mouth.

"Was it not kind of me to pity your queen and let her dance with a real man?"

Cruor stayed focused on his opponent, not willing to take the bait. He pulled the spilled lifeblood from the ground back into himself. The Leech gathered power from the blood on the spear and his own face. He drew more from the wolf's open wound even as the beast healed.

With every encounter he pulled more energy. Blow after blow was traded. Cruor knew he was just as strong, but the speed of the prince was insane.

He worked to hold himself out of reach, bleeding the prince drop by drop. Yet the elf, or whatever he was, didn't slow. It got harder and harder to avoid the incoming attacks.

The Leech was bleeding hard when Ohkami tried again to break his focus.

"Did she tell you she offered herself to me? A bit skinny she is, but pretty enough."

Cruor felt his resolve slip. A long-curved sword formed in his hands and he reared back for a wicked slash, leaving himself open only to a fighter who could move in a blur. A deep slash tore open the Leech's chest, opening him up from left shoulder to right hip.

The blade in his hand shortened and he fended off a second blow, trying to gain back the lost power spilled on the ground. Even as he opened up several small slashes, the wolf healed them much too fast to allow him to siphon much energy.

Now he was victim to the trap he saw close several times already this day. He was barely able to fend off the vicious attacks, never able to gain footing or prepare a counter. For several minutes the wolf laid into him, bleeding him of both his blood and his energy.

The stamina of his opponent was astounding, yet Cruor fought on, long past exhaustion and pain. Then someone in the crowd began the chant again. He couldn't spare the time to look up, but he heard the voice. Her voice. Even now Raine was cheering him on.

The Leech would have scolded her for making the same mistake. Falling into such a trap. Cruor would have told her that such errors were fatal, yet she was even now urging him forward.

He redoubled his efforts, but still the beast pushed him back. Then he felt the wall behind him and could retreat no further. A pair of daggers formed in his grip and he slashed with one and thrust with the other.

Ohkami blocked both hits with one hairy arm. With the other, he drove his claws deep into the chest of the Winter guard. The crowd that had taken up the cheer let the echo fade away. The prince ripped his shimmering hand out of Cruor's chest with a wet pop. The wolf turned and lifted his arms to the sky and began to walk to the center of the field.

Cruor strained to hear her voice, to stay conscious. He could typically heal even this, but he was all but drained of power. He needed blood and the only source was walking away with not a scratch left on him.

The ground flew up to meet his face. He lay gasping on the hard earth. The Leech felt a slight tingle where his skin touched the dirt located way out in the corner of the field.

Only a day before, a dragon had been ripped apart on this very spot. The body of the dragon was removed. The crimson stain tilled into the soil by an earth spirit. The only barrier between him and that power was a bit of soil. Cruor reached out his will as his own blood pushed into the ground. As it met the dragon spilled lifeforce, he felt the rush of power.

His chest knit closed and his crimson eyes gained a brighter glow. The lifeblood of the magical beast held more power than he could contain, and he stood feeling better than he had at the start. The crowd gasped and murmurs went up around the arena as he tore away the stained remnants of his shirt.

Ohkami turned to see an opponent who was all but dead walking confidently toward him. The chant rose from the crowd once more. Among the chorus, he could still make out her voice. He wouldn't fail his queen.

Once more, the beast rushed at him, yet he didn't prepare a weapon. There was no last-second dodge. As the prince approached in a blur, Cruor lashed out and thin streams of blood shot out from his bare chest and arms. Hundreds of tiny blades dug into the beast, not cutting, but boring past the fur and deep into thick skin, into the pumping blood of the creature.

Ohkami slashed and tore at the streams of red death, but as they were cut, more formed. Despite the efforts of the beast, he couldn't break enough of them to gain freedom. Cruor stole power; countless tiny streams of raw energy left the creature and flowed into him.

For several long seconds the prince fought to escape. Then Cruor could feel the last breath of spirit, the point from which his opponent could still recover. He wanted to kill this pitiful creature. This man was a beast and it had nothing to do with the transformation.

The prince's death would cause trouble for his queen, though. Despite his anger at Ohkami's words, the Leech could do nothing to hurt her.

The wolf faded with the loss of power. The handsome face of the prince landed on the ground with a thud. The crowd roared once more, but over the din could be heard another voice.

"You! You cheat! My son cannot be beaten!"

Cruor didn't stay to argue. He stretched his freshly healed body and calmly walked off the field of battle. He looked up only once to see the smile of the only person whose opinion mattered to him.

It was right where it was supposed to be.

***

Naoki wondered if his own abilities were technically cheating. As far as he could see, the matches were mostly decided by strength or endurance. Where others had to store power and carry it in with them, he could draw it from the roots of the plants deep in the earth under the field of battle.

Despite his spirit abilities being better suited to the casting division, he was doing quite well. In addition to the significant enhancements he got from his bargain with the plants of Spring, his wooden arm could be made harder than stone, giving him quite a punch.

His original plan was to participate in the Contest to earn money to help him protect the forests. Yet now his goals had become something more. He had worked his way to the final round of the melee division.

Part of him really wanted to face the Prince of Spring, more so after finding out how the man treated Yoshiko. Yet he'd been glad to see the Winter guard not only survive but win with such spectacle. Now Naoki faced the Leech.

Once again, the music from nowhere played at Cruor's introduction. Despite Naoki representing Spring, no trumpets played a fanfare for him. The Alder King was so enraged by his son's loss that he seemed to care little for the Contest now.

What Naoki hadn't expected was a tip of the hat from his opponents. As he was announced, a tune played for him as well. He didn't know the song, but the beat was played with strange instruments. The words spoke of the jungle, the power of life, and wild things. The music came through clearly, and the crowd reacted much as it had for his opponent.

The words continued and the music picked up in tempo. There was no hesitation as people clapped and cheered. Finally, the singer called for the people to scream. The audience took it literally and as one all cried out.

"Naoki!"

His new allies had included him in the festivities. Naoki had lived most of his life without friends, save the plants and Sakura. Even now, he struggled to believe he wasn't alone. Her voice snapped him out of his revelry.

"Something is wrong."

The dryad appeared before him, only seconds before he was to fight. He was curious how he would fare against such a strong opponent. Sadly, he wouldn't get to find out this day. Her words shook him.

"Spring's Princess is going to betray the outsiders."

Despite his newfound trust in Yoshiko, he knew better than to question the dryad. Sakura *never* lied to him. As the gong sounded, he looked to the Winter warrior, kneeled down, and tapped the ground. His feet were moving to the gate even as he said the words.

"I surrender."

He had to get to Yoshiko.

***

Raine walked with Claire and Joobel as they returned from lunch. As they approached the boxed seats set aside for Autumn and Winter, the yeti passed them. He moved ahead, making sure the area was clear before stepping to one side and allowing the three women to proceed inside.

A tall elf woman approached and greeted them, congratulating her on Winter's victory. She seemed familiar somehow, quite lovely and courteous. She even greeted the guards and thanked them for watching over her guests, shaking each man's hand as he entered.

That's right, Raine thought, she is one of the royals. She couldn't quite recall the elf's name, but it was nice to see her make an effort.

She was quite happy to see Cruor win the melee finals. Though she was a bit confused about why the young elf had fought all the way to the last round only to drop out at the last moment.

The next round of fights would be the casting division, then tomorrow would be the finals. Winter had already placed for the adults, and both top spots at the junior level were held by Autumn. So far things were going well.

Even with all the stress and danger, or perhaps because of it, Winter's Queen was enjoying herself. The next fighters were announced and she settled in to watch the show. A Summer earth aspect would be fighting a water spirit from Spring.

She felt Joobel bobbing up and down on the polished wood of her bench and turned to see her fidgeting with excitement.

"Jack will be up next round. I can't wait. He has *so* been looking forward to this!"

Raine smiled as she thought of Jack. He was in the barracks preparing for his upcoming fight, along with Gray, who had a match coming up as well. Cruor was done for now and would be back with her as soon as he got cleaned up. She leaned forward to inspect the fighters.

As the gong sounded, their trip to Spring deteriorated in a single instant.

She heard a squeal and turned to see her own yeti guard grabbing Claire, cutting off her scream with a large white hand. Joobel started to protest just as the troll Stoveg grabbed her and likewise stopped her from crying out. Raine was terrified and confused, but unlike her friends, she trained to fight relentlessly. She rolled forward just as a rapier stabbed into the wood of the bench where she'd been sitting.

Raine knew of no friends within shouting distance. Even if she did cry out, no one would hear over the roar of the crowd. Claire had prepared for poison gas, an outright attack, even the air getting blocked, forcing them to suffocate. Never did any of them considered the attack might come from their own guards.

She spun and landed against the rail overlooking the field. Hurley was pulling his sword from the bench and preparing for another attack. Shaw was moving to flank her. Raine looked into the eyes of one of her oldest friends and reconsidered a betrayal. She parried his thrust with her dagger and pulled the short sword. The two halves of Frostbite served her fighting style well in this way.

The troll stumbled as Joobel got purchase on a wall and kicked out with her legs, but he was too strong and she couldn't break free. Raine parried another strike, slapped her advisor hard with the flat of the blade, and slashed at Shaw. She nicked his arm and the magic of her dagger instantly saw a sheen of frost move across his body. She had no time to mourn him.

Claire was starting to slump, gasping for breath as the yeti blocked her mouth and nose. The troll walked out of the box, holding the still-struggling gnome. Raine hated having to plan on the fly.

The guards were attacking them and they seemed to want Joobel alive. Unfortunately, they clearly wanted Raine dead.

All three women were attacked at the same time, but her old advisor was slower. She was supposed to be dead but was still very much alive. Her words made no sound as she called on the only beings who could hear and might be able to help.

"Dragons of Winter and Autumn, your queens need you!"

Then she focused on staying alive. Hurley was an old man, but a master of the sword. His power allowed him to weigh each attack and decide on his best course.

She knew his weakness; each use of his power took time. Only a split second, but enough to overwhelm him if his opponent was swift and attacked relentlessly.

The Winter Queen focused her breathing and concentrated on her time with Cruor. He was cold and calculating. A harsh teacher and cunning opponent.

Raine moved fluidly, pushing her strikes with force and speed. Her attacks were routine, practiced, and smooth. The old man began to fall back, but already she felt herself tiring. She was far from the source of her power and couldn't land a crippling blow with her powerful blades.

Even a scratch from either weapon would freeze the blood in her advisor's veins. She blocked a flurry of attacks and countered with a spinning slash followed by a kick to his knee. He faltered and stepped back, already calculating his next move. She saw the pitcher of water on the table, refreshments for the visiting queens.

Raine took a defensive stance and whipped the water out hard, shattering the glass holding it. She wrapped the man's sword arm in a band of the liquid and pushed it back against the far wall. He let out a '*whoof*' as the air left his lungs.

Then she pulled Hurley forward, past her and against the rail overlooking the field below. The band of water kept his arm in place. She couldn't stay and hold him, and he'd likely follow her if she left him alive.

Her dagger sheathed, she held up her left hand and let loose a blast of Frost Fire. The bitter cold froze the water and locked him in place. She doubted Hurley would get to keep the hand, but his life was spared for now.

Raine looked around; Claire and Joobel were both gone. She ran out of the box and down the hall. The voice that came to her brought hope to her fevered search.

"We're all in flight; what do you need us to do?"

Harvest! He'd come and brought the others. The Winter Queen tried to think of what she could do, what they could do. Her anger and frustration were starting to cloud her thoughts. The queen stopped and took a slow, deep breath. She pushed the words to her friends in the sky.

"Spring has bewitched our guards. Stoveg the troll has Joobel and the yeti Gorn has Claire. I have no idea where they are going with them. They seemed to want them both alive. I'm supposed to be dead, I think."

The queen knew she was leaning on them to help decide how to proceed. Although all but Brook were quite young, they were wise beyond their years.

Even without words, she could feel the rage from Harvest. Bloom was worried about her bond-mate and Puddle was frustrated at the whole ordeal. The reply came after the long seconds she spent running down and out of the arena. It was Bloom.

"My brother and I are each bonded to one of the women. We will split up and follow the bond, Puddle with me and Brook with Harvest. Are you in danger?"

"I'm fine as of now; they probably think me dead. Just find our friends."

Raine resolved to allow the dragons to search while she got to the one person who could beat whatever spell was holding the guards. Jack was in the lower levels of the barracks. Gray and Cruor would be with him.

Spring made its move and she was going to make sure they paid. Raine rounded out of the arena seating and ran toward the barracks, sliding to a stop as a contingent of soldiers stood in her path. One stepped toward her and spoke for his fellows to hear.

"There she is. Ready yourselves, men. The water witch needs to die."

Raine rolled her eyes as she drew her blades. This day just keeps getting better and better. She could hear the distant roars of dragons as she readied for combat.

***

Naoki moved like the ghost he was often compared to, weaving through the people and stepping up to the edge of the royal platform of Spring. Yoshiko sat next to Queen Sayuri, who, in turn, was to the right of the king. The elf knew from listening to the Alder King the previous night that his own recent surrender would have the man angry.

As he glanced over to the tall man, he found that instead of fury, the king seemed pleased. It was as if he were in total control, as if he were winning, though Spring hadn't done notably well in the Contest so far.

The words left Naoki's muttering lips as he decided how to get his friend's attention.

"I'd have felt better if he were angry."

The elf leaned down and pulled a small seed from his pouch. It had the potential to become a flowering vine usually seen in the forests of Summer. He stooped down and held the tiny thing.

A slender vine peeked from within the hard shell, a shoot of pure, vibrant green. It wove through the feet of the guards and around the leg of Yoshiko's chair, slowly moving up until it hovered next to her hand. A single red and yellow flower bloomed and brushed the elf princess's fingers.

She looked down with a start and then brushed the flower in acknowledgment, her words only faintly audible.

"Mother, my fight is quickly approaching and I'd like to warm up down in the barracks. Wish me luck."

Yoshiko stood and followed the vine until she saw him. She was obviously trying to avoid drawing attention as she slowly strode to where he stood. Her words were an angry whisper.

"Why did you forfeit? What are you doing up here?"

He explained what Sakura told him, working hard to avoid the impression of an accusation. It was difficult to portray his sense of urgency while appearing to have a casual conversation. Before he could finish, Yoshiko interrupted him.

"The Princess... Harumi! We have to get to them. She left the king's side a while ago."

He nodded and turned, glancing across the field to see a woman with white hair and a blue dress fighting hard against an older man in a Winter guard uniform. He growled low as he took in the sight.

"We might be too late; it has started!"

Naoki took her hand. They abandoned the impression of calm and casual for a frantic and hurried demeanor. The two rounded the stone pillar of the lower floor of the arena when an angry roar shook the levels overhead. Yoshiko grimaced.

"The dragons know about the attack; how could they react so fast?"

He shook his head. "I don't know, but I fear your father has planted more than he can harvest."

"He's not my father." She spoke with disdain, but he was too frantic to notice.

The pair moved quickly through the levels until they came upon a group of soldiers gathering at the base of Spring's section of the stands.

Yoshiko marched up to a soldier. "What is the meaning of this?" she demanded.

He seemed to recognize her and bowed.

"King's orders; we're under attack. Autumn has betrayed us!"

In the distance, she could see four giant spore dragons making their way toward the arena. The Beryl Gardens were also bustling with activity in the distance. All of Amaya was beginning to enter a state of panic. Naoki was shocked at the sight, only brought back to his senses by Yoshiko's whisper.

"The king is using a fake threat to unite Spring's factions under himself. We might be too late."

As if to punctuate her words, a dark shadow passed over them. The mighty drake was the color of pitch and let out a cry that seemed to push him toward the ground.

This would mean war.

***

Gray was stretching out and speaking with Jack as they both prepared for their upcoming matches. He was looking forward to a test of skill, but the prince was so excited he was almost shaking. Cruor walked out of the baths and joined the conversation as he changed into clean clothes. The taller man was happy to see the Winter guard win out and smiled widely as he greeted the man.

"There's our champion. Well done! Your kingdom must be proud."

Cruor shrugged but smiled to accept the compliment.

"There was only one person I fought for. She seemed pleased."

Jack formed a sphere of orange heat, tossing it up and then reabsorbing the power as he caught it. All three were in good spirits. The prince would be called any second and Cruor was just beginning to move toward the royal box in the stands.

Gray saw Jack suddenly go from anxious excitement to near panic. His eyes flashed bright yellow with hot flame and he spoke in a desperate tone.

"She's gone! Gray, she's gone! I can't feel her!"

Confusion crossed the big man's features and the Leech turned to see what was happening, Gray grabbed the prince's shoulders and turned him around.

"Who's gone? What are you talking about?"

"Gray... Joobel is gone. I can always feel her. Always. She was there and then.... I can't feel her!"

Gray's eyes grew wide. He looked to Cruor.

"I think someone attacked Joobel. She's with Claire and Raine."

Gray started to turn back to Jack, but the prince was already running toward the door. He was only a couple of paces behind Cruor who understood enough to know Raine would also be in danger. Gray pushed a burst of air behind him to help him keep up.

Even though he was just as worried, he understood that if Spring was making a move, the three of them wouldn't be enough. Gray moved through the barracks. Seeing a familiar young troll, he slowed enough to give hurried instructions.

"Tedar! Spring is moving against us. Get the younger ones through a portal. Those who can fight need to head outside. Hurry!"

He saw a Winter warrior prepping for the casting division, repeated his message, and kept sprinting. Once more he rallied his people as he saw a group of Summer slaves they had purchased to freedom, directing them to their escape. He finally made it out of the barracks and looked out onto the hill outside the arena.

The battle was already underway.

***

The rush of soldiers was nearly overwhelming. The Queen of Winter parried and took every opportunity to flank around the dozens of fighters. Her blades moved in a fluid motion, blocking thrusts and deflecting the projectiles coming from the group.

Even with her power and skill, the odds were overwhelming. Her one positive was that she wasn't nearly as attached to these people as she was to the old advisor. Raine wasn't sure how many frozen bodies lie on the ground, but it was in the double digits.

Her movements had doomed her, though. She still felt getting to the barracks was her best hope of survival. Several more men came from her other side and in seconds she was pinned down. Now she had only one option.

Moisture pulled up from the ground as Raine whipped a thick layer of water around herself. With a flourish, she sprayed a blast of bitter cold against the swirling mass and froze a layer of protection several inches thick. Jack used a similar ice dome as they traveled once.

All she could do was wait and repair the cracks in her shell as they formed.

***

Jack reached the outer doors to the barracks only a few seconds before Cruor. He looked out on the fighting and was a bit thrown to see one of his little ice domes sitting in the middle of a large group of soldiers using various means to try to break inside.

Reaching out with his aura, the prince could feel most of the men were relatively weak in their abilities. Still, three strong spirits of water were actively at work inside the dome. Raine was with him the last time he made one. The occupant could only be his cousin.

The prince was loath to delay in searching for Joobel, but he couldn't leave Raine to this mob. As Cruor stepped behind him, he decided perhaps there was a third option.

An orb of dark orange formed in one hand, compressed into an explosive ball of force. He wrapped layers of jagged ice around the globe and then yelled to the crowd of troops.

"Look up!"

Jack tossed the sphere high into the clear sky. Just as dozens of men looked up in a reflex response, the blast went off.

Hundreds of tiny, jagged pieces of ice sliced and stabbed into the gathered men. A couple were blinded, but most shook off the attack and looked over to the prince. A soldier close to him even laughed and taunted.

"Is that all the Demon Prince can throw at us?"

Jack shrugged as he simply ran off to one side. He was moving toward the sounds of the roaring dragons. The soldiers laughed at the cowardice of Autumn's famed Demon Prince.

***

Cruor stepped forward as his friend left to continue his search. He took a long look at the large group of men fighting to hurt his queen. Every single one of them was now bleeding openly in front of him. A couple of the men realized what was about to happen. They began to run.

The rest charged at the Leech. Red eyes flared brightly as he pulled the lifeblood out of the two nearest men and forged gleaming dark-red twin longswords. Several more were drained similarly and giant bat-like wings began to grow from the center of his back. Cruor let out a battle cry of rage and charged into the men.

The blades were now so charged with energy that his blows sliced through armor, shields, and whatever else tried to offer resistance. As crimson life spilled from the enemy, it too was drawn into the hunger of his fury. Dozens of men were drained in mere seconds and the Leech began to form dark-red armor around himself.

As the final soldier breathed his last, the bodyguard walked over to the ice shell. He lay one armored hand on the cold surface of the dome and pushed. His power was now so overwhelming that as his hand moved forward, it shattered the frozen barrier. A large chunk of ice tumbled onto the ground inside. She was there with murder in her eyes. His beautiful queen, so exhausted and afraid.

Then he remembered what he'd done, what he must look like. Shame filled him as she looked down at the crimson armor covering his face and body. He dropped the swords and began to speak.

"This is... what I really am. I understand that you—"

Cruor couldn't finish his sentence as Raine crashed into his arms and kissed him. Her pale lips met the dark-red of his own. He paused in disbelief and then fell into the embrace. As their lips parted, she held the hug, feeling safe for the first time since the attack at the arena.

As she whispered, her voice only quavered slightly.

"It took you long enough."

***

From the sky, it was easy to see that the forces rallied against them were overwhelming. Even Autumn and Winter combined had only a few warriors here to hold the lines. Gray was trying to make her proud, to lead in her absence.

Claire was still lost. He didn't even know if Raine was alive. With the way Jack had acted, Joobel might be dead as well. No queens were here to lead and the prince was in no state to take over. Without direction they would be overrun in short order.

This wasn't going to be a real battle; Amaya was the heart of Spring's power. The only thing keeping this from slaughter was the fact that Spring's soldiers hadn't gathered fully. The best he could hope to do was buy time, as much as possible, before they would be forced to escape through the portals and leave Claire, Joobel and Raine behind.

Amid the fighting, he saw two individuals that he'd met the night before. Elves who had come in friendship. Princess

Yoshiko and her companion walked below.

Gray barked out orders as he set a barrier covering the flank of two Winter fighters who were pushing back several soldiers.

"Tedar, I need a front line to the east; lead those who can defend there. Bayu and Edana, throw some fear into the middle of the approach to the north. Make them hesitant. Those who can hold shields set up a perimeter."

As his orders were followed, Gray moved with the grace he'd earned through years of practice, dropping the last couple of feet to land right in front of the two elves. He spoke urgently but without malice.

"What's going on here?"

The young woman stepped forward, cautious of the tall man but confident enough considering the fighting all around.

"The Alder King has betrayed his guests. He ordered the queens killed and the gnome woman captured. We didn't realize his plan until it was already happening. I'm so sorry...."

Gray nodded slowly. This wasn't good news, but there was hope for Joobel. For Jack's sake, he hoped they could get her back. Before he could return to the fighting, the young man stepped forward.

"The Autumn Queen was taken by a yeti. The Winter Queen was alive last we saw, fighting through toward the barracks. Many of those against you are in thrall to the king's power. If we can stop him, I think order can be restored."

Gray cocked an eyebrow. "In thrall?"

"His power allows him a form of mind control. Yoshiko figured it out late last night. His daughter has a more powerful form of it but can only use it on men and she needs physical contact. We need to stop them."

Gray looked out to the fighting. If he left to chase down the king, those people wouldn't hold out long. Even if he did, he had no defense against the same power that affected so many others.

When they first come to Spring, all felt that need to kneel before the king. It had faded. There was only one person he knew who could break a spirit weave so easily. He was already starting to take to the air as he shared his idea.

"Yoshiko, was it? Remember the prince who you found so... worrying? I think he's the key. Do you have a way of finding him?"

The woman bent down and put her hand to the soil. She paused, then looked up and nodded.

"I can get to him."

Gray was already in the sky. "Find the prince. Tell him I sent you and that the Alder King is the key to finding Joobel. That last part will get his attention."

Then he left the pair, near strangers responsible for maybe saving them all. He moved back to the field where his sparse forces were working hard to hold ground.

"Claire... where are you? We need you."

CHAPTER 15

The sun had risen to its peak and the heat would have been oppressive if she hadn't been so accustomed to the humid warmth of the Great Arborium. General Kakshi was the youngest of Summer's military leaders. Her genius in battle brought her honor that was far ahead of most her age.

The conquest of Autumn was a prize she lobbied hard for. She would be recognized for many years to come for what she accomplished on this campaign. The invading force of Summer was maybe a third of the southern kingdom's military might.

The goal was simple. Autumn had gone too far with its policies of protection toward those who were not worthy. It must be crushed before Summer's economy began to collapse. In this, the problem was Winter.

The north made an ill-conceived alliance with the pathetic western nation and doomed itself to the same fate. Today she would invade Autumn while her fellow generals moved through the southern roads of Spring to hit Winter from the eastern border. Spring and Summer would force Winter to choose between supporting Autumn or defending its own lands. A predictable and straightforward choice.

Kakshi looked out at the marching forces from atop her strider, a large flightless bird with razor beak and vicious claws. Nine huge wood wyrms, two hundred bugbears, dozens of sasquatches, and three cavalry units of armored centaurs were at her disposal. Countless redcaps and satyr made up front-line infantry and some of the kingdom's finest spirit casters rode striders and other mounts in the back.

It had been over a century since such a force had marched across the kingdom's borders. The young general rode at the head of her army and could just make out the waters of the Shinez river. Its waters ran from the lakes of Winter far to the north.

The currents were swift and deep, running down along the western edge of the Mountain Wyld until they split to either run into Summer's northern lakes or flow west to the Forbidden Sea. Somewhere in the middle of those swift waters was the border between the realm of earth and that of change.

A water crossing would be difficult for all but the dragons. The Shinez bridge would carry her troops across the rapids. From there, they would follow the road that led to the township of Thera. She had memorized the maps made by her scouts. Her campaign would be both efficient and ruthless.

It would be generations before Autumn would even qualify as a kingdom after her job was done. The slaves and spoils from her campaign would bring her honor. Summer would gain resources needed to stabilize trade.

The young general glared out at the wide stone bridge and saw a single figure laying stretched out on a woven straw mat. She had dark-red hair atop a lithe tan body. She wore a strange garment of bright blue and yellow that covered only the bare minimum as she lay on the bridge. The stranger seemed to be soaking up the sun's bright light and warmth.

Kakshi hopped off her strider and moved to the foot of the bridge, her words spoken loudly so as to be heard.

"Hail, traveler. Be you of Summer, you must move aside to avoid being trampled."

The woman smoothly sat up and stretched like a jungle cat, her lean body flexing wiry muscle. She rubbed her eyes for a moment and then looked out at the army approaching her resting place.

Shaking off a yawn, she looked down at the general and stood as she buckled on a wide leather belt with a long whip to one side. Several silver bracelets were slipped onto one arm, and a bracer inset with green gems on the other. She asked a question of similar volume while applying her ornaments.

"What if I'm not of Summer?"

Kakshi tilted her head as she tried to understand the question. The troops were almost upon her and she wouldn't be slowing her procession.

"What do you mean?"

The woman continued attaching bracelets. "You said, '*Be you of Summer,*' yet I'm not. What must I do if I were, for example, here to keep invading armies from entering this land?"

A quick glance back confirmed it was time to move forward. The general remounted her strider and shouted the last warning.

"Begone or be flattened; I've no time for peasant riddles."

Kakshi waved her arm to give the order to proceed. Then she turned to see the odd half-naked woman had uncoiled the whip and lashed it through the air. The tip created a sonic boom that cracked as loudly as the splintering of a falling tree.

The general raised a hand to call upon the stone that would crush this bug, her power strong as she was still standing on the realm of earth. Before her woven spell could activate, the water started to move. The low grumble of a forest wolf growl came to her ears. Not one, but a chorus of low, angry snarls.

As the forms came up out of the water, she could see they were each encased in a shell similar to that of some earth spirit users. Yet the shells didn't leave them bulky or clumsy, and the eyes of the beasts seemed to glow a strange shade of tan.

Her eyes adjusted to see that there weren't just a few. Not a pack as wolves like to form, but a horde of hundreds or even thousands of the beasts stretched into the distance on both sides of the bridge. She looked up to the odd woman still holding her whip, smiling a wide grin that promised violence. The bizarre stranger spoke from her place on the stone structure.

"I've been trusted to hold this border. You cannot afford to pay the toll for this bridge. Be gone... or I *will* have my fun."

Kakshi felt her anger rise. She hadn't even crossed the border yet and already she'd lost time. She completed her weave and launched a nearby stone at the woman as she screamed.

"Kill her! Take the bridge!"

The sound of battle horns blared out behind her as she mounted her bird and urged the strider forward.

***

"I did promise Claire I'd give a warning." Myrin grinned. "Now we dance."

Her whip lashed out at the incoming rock. A boulder the size of a small man spun through the air. Power flowed through the whip as she snapped the earthen tip and reduced the stone to powder.

Myrin took three long strides and slammed her left hand down to the dirt on the Summer side of the Shinez bridge. There was a loud '*WOMP*' and a cloud of dust rose into the air just as the Summer army charged forward. The thick powdered earth was enough to slow the momentum of the charge. Snouts, beaks, noses, and lungs were quickly filled with thick powder and the subsequent mud.

She could feel some fighting her weave, trying to force the dust back down. A smile formed on her lips; she really liked this particular technique and had practiced holding it long and hard. It fit well with her plans.

The Hel-hounds charged into the cloud of powder. They felt like an extension of her, bound to her gifted spirit just as the dust was. Through her, they could move as though it were a clear day. Her power revealed every form from within the cloud. It was a clear advantage the army before her didn't have.

Howls and snarls went up as the first of her pack reached the enemy. The sickening crunch of bone and the screams of the satyrs and redcaps rang through the air.

Myrin pulled a dome of dense earth around her. It was an intensive task to keep the pack focused and hold the cloud in place. She would add little by joining the fray.

The smaller troops were going down like wheat before the harvest scythe. Some of the sasquatch and centaurs were going down slowly and taking her own forces with them, but the real problem was the dragons.

She hadn't expected more than a couple of the massive serpentine wood wyrms to have joined this force. Even one dragon would be difficult to hold off for long.

Myrin could feel the wyrms fighting toward her, the hounds ripping and slashing at the thick green scales. They were gaining ground and though she was thinning the enemy quickly, the hounds were taking heavy losses.

On the bright side, she hadn't expected to feel so much stronger. Standing on the soil of the great earth realm spirit was almost like having Jack keep a steady stream of power flowing into her.

Blows started hitting the sides of her rock dome, cracking the stone and requiring her to change tactics. The original owner of this earth spirit had learned its nature and Jack recently helped her do so as well. Burrow.

Myrin loathed the name of the spirit, but today she was grateful for its abilities. She began to fill the dome with solid packed soil while she moved more than ten paces straight down. The troops would hammer at the shell only to find she was long gone.

Through her link with the dust cloud, she could feel that the satyrs were all but wiped out. The redcaps and their useless poisoned blades were nearly gone as well. Half the cavalry had been brought down already, and the mighty group of sasquatches was forced into a defensive ring. The tall furry figures looked to be retreating from the advance.

Only the bugbears, wyrms, and casters were still trying to push the attack. The bugbears were proving more of a hindrance than expected, their thick hides protecting them from most of the attacks the hounds were capable of inflicting.

Myrin was forced to use Burrow on offense as well, pulling bugbears into the earth one by one. She could sink them far enough down without spending too much of her energy, and it freed up the hounds for other targets.

Even two of the dragons had been killed, each making the mistake of breathing petrifying fog on her minions. The constructs were immune to such attacks. How could you turn stone into stone? The hounds would just leap into their open mouths and tear the wyrms up from inside.

Sweat poured off her face as Myrin juggled the three spells. Soon she would have to cycle new air into her makeshift bunker and the strain was taking its toll. Some of the casters were using earth spirits to counter her dust, pushing it down to allow better sight and more comfortable breathing for Summer's forces.

Another dragon died as a group of hounds tore a big enough hole in its flank to literally rip their way inside of the beast. The sasquatches completely abandoned the fight and moved back into the trees.

Two dozen bugbears kept pushing forward, but she couldn't afford the energy needed to pull any more of them into the soil. Over half the casters were still alive, though none were still mounted. Six dragons remained and her pack was well over half destroyed, the spirits animating the constructs released to eternal rest.

Her air was running out and she felt pressure as two, no three, earth spirits were beginning to push on her small hiding place. It was time to go.

She rolled her power through the rock and soil under the river itself, popping up on the Autumn side of the bridge.

As she entered the light of day, she could see two more dragons going down under the weight of the pack. She wore a grim smile and muttered to herself as she took in the grisly scene.

"Four to go...."

Myrin knelt down low and put a hand on the stone bridge. It had survived for well over a thousand years, allowing trade and travel between kingdoms. Now it was a path of invasion for Autumn's enemies.

There was a shudder as she began to dissolve the rock supporting the structure deep in the river. The flowing water slowed her progress, but she had the supports gone in less than a minute. Then she heard an angry shout from the top of the bridge.

"You!"

The leader of Summer's army was covered in blood. Most of it was clearly not her own, as she could still walk upright. The woman gave her a look of contempt as she ran toward her.

Myrin had used most of the power she had available and was no longer on the earth realm. She was weak and tired, and all of her hounds were on the other side of a bridge that wouldn't be upright much longer.

Even so, she knew that any sign of weakness would work against her. She gifted a vicious grin to the woman.

"As you might have figured out, I dislike being disturbed while sunbathing."

The Summer woman screamed as a large chunk of rock was torn from the rail of the bridge and hurled toward Autumn's defender. Myrin conserved the power it would take to counter it and simply stepped aside.

There was a stomping rumble as the first of the dragons began to crawl up onto the bridge. She worked to buy more time.

"Perhaps we might talk this over? We both hold earth spirits. Could we bond over that? We might be friends. I'll buy you an ale and we can talk about boys."

The woman slung another large stone. Again, Myrin jumped to the side, now holding up both hands.

"Well, before you kill me, I think you should know something."

The leader wiped blood and dust away from her eyes. The woman sneered as she took the bait.

"What's that?"

As the wood wyrm lumbered up next to the woman on the bridge, Myrin smiled widely.

"Dragons are *really* heavy."

Before she even finished her sentence, the stone structure began to groan as the keystones buckled. The bulk of the bridge crashed down into the river with a mighty splash. The woman, the dragon, and some of the bugbears coming from behind all splashed into the raging cold water.

Myrin slowly walked forward and waved to the remaining casters, bugbears, and the last three dragons.

A few hundred hounds were still circling the remains of Summer's army, but they lacked the numbers to attack dragons. Angry scowls glared back at her, but she shrugged.

As she started to turn, something caught her eye that she didn't expect. Her stomach sank at the sight.

The wood wyrms moved into the raging chill waters and began to make steady progress to the shore where she stood. The remaining casters were riding on top of the dark-green shapes and moved toward Autumn's side of the river.

Her muttered voice came in a whisper, horror spreading over her freckled face.

"They can swim?"

The explosion of water rained cold droplets onto her as the first wyrm lunged out of the river. Myrin didn't have time to react or dodge. She had no energy with which to sink into the ground. Only the brief chance to send a final command to the hounds and whisper three words before the vast jaws clamped down on her.

'*Stay on that side of the river.*'

"I'm sorry, Claire."

The hound master was no more.

***

The room was dark and cold. The smell of old paper and wet stone filled her nose. The chair she was tied to was sturdy wood; the bindings dug deep into her wrists and ankles. There was movement to her left and she heard voices arguing in muted tones. She couldn't make out the words, but there was anger in the voices.

Autumn's Queen stayed motionless and though her head pounded, she focused on clearing her mind and taking note of her surroundings. She had been sitting in the arena. Joobel was been excited. Someone grabbed her. That was all she could remember.

Claire had no idea who attacked, but had little doubt as to who was behind it. She took note of her weapons. The dagger in her belt was gone, not that she could have really used it. She mostly opened letters with the thing.

Her energy was low as if drained somehow. Her power over the dead was always a benefit, but she could feel no vessels she could use nearby. Her mouth was bound with a rag that didn't taste fresh from the laundry, so her Banshee Wail would be of no use either.

Strangely, Claire wasn't nearly as afraid as she was angry. Partly at herself for not having prevented the situation, mostly at those who couldn't stand for any sort of hope for the people of this world. There was a time that such a situation would have her in a panic. Less so now.

She had secrets. Her spirit of Death was famous, or infamous, depending on who you spoke to. Her powers of Entropy and Transmutation were known to only a handful of people she trusted. The power jewel that sat against her breastbone refilled her stores of energy even now. Those were all comforting, but the faint pulse of energy she now sent out was of her original power.

Before she made a move, she wanted information. The Banshee sent her call, using energy they didn't know she had, and it was answered.

At first, all she could see was spectral feet, but the ghost seemed to understand her situation and sank into the floor until the ethereal head sat in front of her own face. Her long brown hair fluttered through part of the man's features as he gave her the information she needed.

Claire was deep underground, low inside the shafts of an old mine used to gather the marble for the Beryl Gardens. Raine was alive, but fighting. Joobel was gone. The ghost explained it twice, saying the gnome had been taken through a mushroom portal. The troll that had captured the gnome was executed. Stoveg was dead.

The queen felt a tear move down her face; she'd been quite fond of the quiet guard. She had even taken the time to get to know him. He loved carving and was a candidate to lead his own hunt.

Shaw was a frozen corpse. Hurley was alive, though injured and a captive of Spring. The yeti Gorn was barely alive, his body sitting across the room in a heap by the door. There were five other people down here with her, all men and elven. One of them was Prince Ohkami.

Claire thanked the ghost with intention, since words weren't an option. She asked him to stay near should he be needed.

A plan formed in her mind as the energy flowed through the jewel. She was going to hug Issabol again for the thing. After a few minutes, she'd allow the men to see her stir.

They had an appointment with a *very* angry Banshee.

***

Wemwi was doing her best to stay focused on the list for the intro songs Gray had selected. When the ruckus started at the arena and no fighters came forward, she sent Toma to go get Issabol. The ancient child moved some dials around and began scanning the combat field with the viewing portal. She finally came to an area not too far from the barracks.

There the two could see the Wind Walker hovering around. Gray was giving orders to a quickly tiring group of Autumn and Winter fighters. They were trying to hold the meager high ground of a hill outside the arena grounds.

Wemwi had studied military strategy some, mostly in her quest to work as an emissary of her kingdom one day. The gnome wasn't an expert, but it was clear that the small force was surrounded, outnumbered, and wouldn't hold out for long.

Issabol gasped and muttered under her breath, her pale face showing she could see it as well. Wemwi looked around; the house was filled with a healer, a crafter, one guard, and several children. Also, a gnome. A gnome who once slew a dragon.

Wemwi refused to watch her friends be killed, but she was no warrior. She covered her eyes with her palms. She could do nothing. If Gray, Tedar, Bayu and Edana weren't enough, what could she add?

The gnome looked up and around her. The stereo, the playlists, and the microphone stood out before her. Also, the array. Issabol called them micro-portals.

Toma had enabled Issabol to make lots of small portals, only as large as her own tiny gnome hand. They now opened up to all the gathering places. There were openings for the sound to pass in her home, the main halls of Blood Mountain, as well as the tribal fires of the Stone Spear camps, the Blood Keep, the streets of Southharbor, and all the other cities and towns.

The system had been designed by Gray and some of the gnomes. It was a way to warn of emergencies that might happen in the kingdom. Autumn's people were in danger; this *was* an emergency. She turned to Issabol, her words filled with hope and urgency.

"Issabol, can you activate the portal grid? I need to get this thing working."

The ancient girl nodded once and moved to start it up. Well, she hit one switch. Had the gnome been aware there was an on switch, she wouldn't have needed help.

Wemwi moved to the soundboard and plugged in the microphone. It activated with a long wide button; it took all her weight to keep it pressed down. She took a deep breath, set aside her self-doubt, and did what one so small could do to help.

"I hope you're all able to hear me. For those who don't know me, I'm Wemwi Dragon Slayer, of the Sept of Fallen Leaves. More importantly, I'm a citizen of Autumn, a place that has been trying to make our world better."

She pulled in a deep breath and continued.

"Some of our people are in danger, fighting a battle they cannot win in a place they cannot hold. There's a portal open to them; it sits just outside the Autumn school. Our queen has worked tirelessly to protect us, to keep us safe. To give us a home. She needs us. If you can fight, if you can heal, build, or help, now is the time to act."

The tiny gnome stepped off the transmitter, her message sent into the aether. Tears ran down her cheeks as she paused and looked back to the sight of the hill, the fighters there exhausted.

Seconds went by, then minutes. She put her head in her hands and began to weep, her failure evident before her face.

Issabol's voice brought her eyes back to the screen. "Look!"

Wemwi's eyes were bright with hope as she stared at the wall showing her the battle. A tall, lean troll stepped through the doorway. Battle paint on his arms and chest, he raised a long spear and roared his defiance. Then two more trolls came over the threshold.

A few of the shaper's guild stepped through and immediately started setting up walls to funnel the enemy.

A pretty blonde woman moved into sight, copper discs in her hands and a vicious smile on her lips. More of the teachers, students, and combat instructors from the school started streaming through as well.

Several men in Autumn's colors, guards from the Keep, followed. Then a wave of people all milled about, taking direction from the tall, dark man in the sky.

Wemwi's voice quavered. "We did it.... By the spirits, we did it!"

The gnome wiped away her tears and flipped on the speakers to the arena. She cranked up the volume to make sure they could hear it from such a distance. Small hands adjusted the microphone and spoke not to Autumn's towns and cities, but to the hill that so few had been fighting to hold. Her voice was no longer one of fear and pleading, but one of hope and triumph.

"Autumn stands united! Our people may fight against all odds. We might not be the biggest kingdom or the strongest, but we stand as one! Though we have been betrayed on foreign soil, and fight to get back what was taken, our enemies will not soon forget the day they challenged OUR kingdom!"

Then she switched over to the playlist. Not to the intros for the fighters, but to the songs. The gnome had been listening as she worked in the little room set aside for the stereo project. She scrolled down, her tiny hand working the pad. Then she picked a tune, an anthem from another world.

Thump, thump, clap.

Thump, thump, clap.

The listing on the screen identified the song by name. "We Will Rock You." The name of the band was 'Queen.'

It seemed appropriate.

The gnome didn't know if her efforts would make the difference, but she could see the people so far away react to her words of hope. As the music played, she could see a boy with curly blond hair pulling lightning from the sky.

He was moving in time with the beat, a smile forming on his face. Behind him approached a pretty girl with long red hair.

She stepped up beside him and took his hand.

***

The great thing about using the power of a storm to charge your attacks is that you can pretty much do it over and over. The power comes from the air and the clouds; you only need to supply the intention and a target. The ability to do it was said to be rare, but Bayu wasn't alone in the skill. Not even as he stood on a small hill that was just up from Spring's arena.

The queen's advisor and his hero, the man named Gray, had ordered the younger children and the slaves from Summer to be evacuated. Tedar had done as instructed and some moved through a portal to the courtyard between the school and the Blood Keep. Many had chosen to stay and fight.

The story that the queen was in danger somehow got out in Autumn. Before the troll could close the portal, a stream of people came back through. What was once to be a slaughter was now starting to look more like a battle.

Makani, his own instructor, was slinging small copper disks to devastating effect at any of the Spring soldiers who looked like they might be weaving spells. Old Fess, another teacher, was slicing through the front lines with blades of curved water. A tiny girl named Tass was laughing maniacally and sending small tornados into groups of attackers who started to get too close.

Tedar was now holding the line just below him, using the enchanted spear the queen had given him. Every time the power of Tremor was activated, there was a slight rumble that shook the hill they fought to hold.

With the others had come someone Bayu wished was with them the whole time. A young woman he shared many things with. Not the least of which was an air spirit known as Tempest. She held his left hand as they channeled their strikes together.

Zephyrina, or Zef, was his classmate and friend. They learned that they could weave in concert for more effect. The storm winds blew her long auburn hair out to one side and she was beautiful. The bracelets that suppressed the emotion that fueled both spirits were in his pocket, and both young people allowed their emotions to run free.

Bayu was smart enough to know what his life would have been if the queen hadn't shown compassion on a dirt road several years ago. He had a good life, one he had no way to earn back then. She'd given it freely and he was going to tear this place apart until they gave her back.

He raised a hand and his counterpart channeled to the same target, an opening in the road where soldiers poured through. The flash of light reached his eyes a brief moment before the crashing '*BOOM*' reached his ears. A small crater stood in the center of the devastation and several small fires burned in the grass around it. No more soldiers passed that gap.

Overhead flew the Wind Walker, the queen's man, and now the general of the impromptu army. He flew about, setting shields to allow time for his troops to adjust position, giving orders, and picking targets for the casters to focus on.

Gray sent a small ball of dense air spiraling toward a wagon the enemy was using as cover from the Autumn casters. Bayu's hair began to spark and his eyes had yellow lines of energy arcing through them as he focused. Zef moved her hand to the same spot and they built the charge.

'*BOOM.*'

The wagon was cinders. The deterrence of the strikes was doing much to hold back the attackers. Spring still had more than enough troops to push the siege, but they hesitated. He liked to think it was due to the devastation he and his friend were raining down. The sight of three giant spore dragons gave him some doubts.

They weren't approaching in a smooth, organized fashion; they were charging with a level of speed and ferocity that made him want to run. He would hold his ground, though. He got his bearings and used his air spirit to channel his words to Gray.

"Dragons from the east!"

Bayu could see Gray look in that direction, but distance hid the man's expression. He did notice that a small orb went in the direction of the beasts and it was understood they would be his next targets.

The Tempest began to build energy. It took time to build the charge needed for a bolt, and it took longer to make the kind that would stop a dragon. He squeezed Zef's hand.

"Think of something that makes you angry. This will take a good deal of power."

She nodded and bit her lower lip for a second. Looking at him with those deep blue eyes, she brought up an observation he too had noted.

"You know et seems that meh power works with just about any kinda feelins."

Then Zef grabbed his neck and pulled him in. Lots of couples have a memorable first kiss. If it's with the right person, it is hard to mess it up, even if it's terribly awkward. If it's on a battlefield with rapidly approaching dragons, with someone you really don't want said dragons to eat.... Well, it has quite an effect on a teenage boy's emotions.

This kiss was powerful. Bayu's eyes were sparking yellow power before her lips left his. When she let go, he turned and grabbed her hand.

The nearest dragon was almost two hundred paces away and moving fast; the wide arc of yellow light that shot through the beast cut the creature in half. The sound of the blast was enough to knock people down twenty paces from impact. A wide grin spread across the young mans face as he looked over at the pretty girl holding his hand.

"Two more to go...."

***

The soldiers seemed to be less in number now, but to the troll's thinking they were getting stronger in skill and power. As the spear pulled enough energy, Tedar would slam it to the ground or against a shield to create a devastating effect.

Once he'd done a service for the Queen of Autumn and she had gifted him Tremor. It was said to possess the power of an ancient sea dragon. Tedar never met the dragon, but the spear was awesome. It was the envy of every troll in the tribe and he recognized the need to learn to wield it properly.

Other trolls had arrived, most carrying slings. The group quickly set up a rotation to be more effective. Those in front would fight while boiling blood, and others who were rebuilding strength would take on the role of ranged attacks.

Tedar had yet to need to switch out. The sigil on his arm amplified his power and the spear allowed him to conserve energy in most encounters. He was a fierce and enduring fighter.

The troll had just finished pushing back a group of armored soldiers who charged the southern flank of the hill when he heard the Wind Walker's call from above.

"I need a solid line to the east; we have dragons incoming."

Tedar spun Tremor around and leaped toward the fray. At heart, the troll was more of a scholar. He much preferred books to battles and was vocal about it. Yet here in this place with so few of power, he knew that his absence would cost lives. He wouldn't sleep well thinking himself a coward. He cleared the hill and moved to a position on the exposed side.

It wasn't only dragons that were approaching. The beasts were at the head of an army of troops coming from the city of Amaya. Spring's main force was minutes away and they would almost certainly be overrun.

Hope flickered in him as the closest dragon was hit by a bolt of terrifying yellow energy. The beast was torn asunder by the blast and the troll knew he wouldn't want to have to advance with that raining down on him.

Tedar set the base of the spear down as he looked around. Several others had come to stand toe to toe with dragons. These people deserved his respect and he theirs. Autumn had lost lives in this place and the dead would be remembered in song.

He still hoped to be the one singing and not the subject of the tune. The ground began to shake as the two remaining wyrms roared and charged. His dark eyes narrowed at the sight.

The troll brought the boil of his blood back up and stood his ground until the closest beast was only a few paces away. He jumped to his left and spun hard, slamming the side of the spear into the wyrm's thick leg like a club. As it hit home, he released the power inside.

Tremor sent a shockwave through the joint that shattered the spot the leg bones met. The dragon was lunging forward to bite down on a Winter girl who was holding a shield of air. The now injured leg caused it to jerk to one side and spared the young woman's life.

Tedar turned to see the second dragon decided he was a threat and lunged for him with broad jaws snapping. He was off balance from his attack and wasn't going to make it. At least not until a stone form knocked him to one side and caught the bite.

The young woman screamed as the creature bit down hard, cracks already forming in the stone armor covering her body. He was quite familiar with the person who fought in that form.

"Avani!"

She continued to scream as the dragon shook and chewed, like a hound with a toy. The troll panicked as he thought about how to help. Then he saw the scales on the neck flex at each shake, opening up just a bit. He ran in a circle, building speed and timing it for the distance and throw.

He launched his prized spear at the wyrm's neck. The spear sank home, deep for any normal creature but only a pinprick for the colossal beast. The troll leaped, his blood-boiled muscles straining to make the distance.

His hand grazed the bottom of the spear, only a light touch but enough to do the job. He activated the remaining power. Tremor sent a shockwave into the beast's neck, too far out to break bone, but the vibrations wreaked havoc on the creature's inner ear.

The troll landed and reached forward, catching the girl inside the crumbling rock as she was thrown to the ground. She was bleeding from dozens of wounds and he could feel bone grinding as he moved her. The dragon's bite had crushed her through the armor. She wouldn't last more than a few moments.

Tedar rushed to the top of the hill, a shockwave pushing him forward. The dragon was being dealt with by the Tempests and the blast nearly deafened him.

Gently he set her down, the girl grimacing at the pain of so much damage. He felt thick tears run down his cheeks, drip down his tusks, and fall onto the bleeding form. His words were broken and his voice cracked.

"You saved me.... You brought honor to us both."

The girl reached a firm hand to his chin. She smiled with blood-coated teeth.

"I die... free. The honor is... mine."

Avani coughed, the pain causing a convulsion. Her eyes rolled back as she went limp. Tedar lifted his head to cry out in grief, but a voice that entered his head through his mind and not his pointed ears shouted out.

"Move, little one!"

The shadow at his back was another dragon, just as big but familiar. This dragon often stayed close to the school, watching over the children. He turned and obeyed, leaping to one side as the cloud of green-tinged fog rolled out of the dragon's maw.

Bloom held the stream of power until the girl began coughing. The sound became louder and clearer with each second.

Tedar looked over to see the dragon whose leg he'd broken was now losing a fight with an angry shape-shifting water drake. The one he'd stabbed with Tremor was a smoking crater, the spear nowhere to be seen. Bloom's voice boomed in his mind.

"Gather the wounded and bring them to the peak of the hill. I will swing by to assist every few minutes."

The troll had never seen Bloom angry, never seen her anything other than sweet and kind. He could feel it in her voice and see it in her eyes. The dragon was furious.

She beat her wings twice, roared, and went straight for the soldiers now reaching the hill. Bloom shrugged off attacks as she used her huge green claws to help hold the lines. A voice from the ground spoke up as he watched in wonder and terror.

"I'm sorry you lost your weapon."

Avani was starting to stand and he helped her up. She was a bit unsteady but was improving by the second. He was glad to see she was ok and smiled around his tusks.

"It was a tool. There's no dishonor in fulfilling your purpose."

He looked at the young woman, her slave mark gone. Her eyes looked at him without fear or disgust. Perhaps she saw the real him. He continued.

"I would say it was a worthy trade."

Avani moved forward, stood her tall frame on tiptoe, and gave him a tight hug. The embrace was fueled by her earth aspect and he felt his ribs creak. Then rock rolled up her legs and began to coat her body as she moved back to the front lines. Tedar looked at his empty hand, his prized spear gone. It really was just a tool.

He followed the *former* gladiator back into the fray.

***

It took Raine longer to find her people than she would've liked. She had started going the wrong way after Cruor had arrived. Still, they fought their way through several encounters, and she could finally see the flashes of lightning from the other side of the barracks.

As they approached, she expected to see the slaughter of her friends. Relief swept over her as she glimpsed the man she once proposed to soaring above the battle. He looked tired and ragged from the constant exertion. Yet, below him there was a makeshift shelter, ground defenses, and a healing area that currently had a giant green drake putting troops back in the fight.

Another crack of lightning blew dirt and mud into the air. A group of soldiers retreated from the flanking position they had been setting up. A light squeeze on her shoulder made her jump.

The Winter Queen turned to the guard. Cruor was still covered in blood armor, his twin long swords held to his sides. Crimson wings flitted in anticipation of more battle.

"We should set you up into the shelter above. You can direct the fighting from there."

She considered that, as she was now the only queen here. Gray was an advisor to Autumn, a capable warrior, but he held no military rank. Yet she watched as his orders were obeyed without question. He artfully prepared each maneuver to protect and counterstrike.

Raine doubted she could have done this, rallied the forces and created safety in such carnage. She looked back to the Leech, so much more powerful than she'd imagined. It wasn't even his power she was interested in.

"I will check in with Bloom, let her know we're safe. You will take a position on the front lines; I will add to casting support.

We will be soldiers today until we find out where Claire and Joobel are. Then we will rescue them and leave this spirit-forsaken kingdom."

Raine watched as he realized that she'd ordered him away from her side. He started to argue and then looked out to the fighting. Many of the fighters were junior contestants, risking everything in the hopes of recovering their queen. He looked back to her and spoke, his voice the rare tone of sincerity he seldom used.

"I chose to follow you because you make decisions in the hopes of helping others. It's my curse that any attempt to argue would undermine why I love you."

She leaned in and kissed him. Brief as it was, it held the promise of more. She winked.

"Never forget that."

He tilted the crimson armored head. "My words... or the kiss?"

"Exactly," Raine quipped with a wicked smile.

As expected, he immediately took his place where the danger was most significant. Cruor was so full of stolen power that he began to leap in and out of the fray, securing one location and then moving to where his help could best be used. All the while he grew even stronger as he robbed his enemies of crimson energy.

Raine spoke through her mind to the mighty green drake who was healing a young Winter woman. She felt safe enough to use the ability now, afraid to draw the wyrms to her before.

"Bloom, it's good to see you well. Cruor and I are here and safe. We're adding our strength to your fight. Any word of Joobel or Claire?"

The dragon jerked up and glanced around. After a moment she gave up on picking one person out of the fighting, and spoke back. The green drake held a mix of worry and anger in her voice.

"I'm happy you made it back safely. No word of either yet. Puddle left the fight to search. I'm not sure we can stay here through the night. Raine, I'm so scared."

"I know, my dear. You're serving the children of your kingdom. Know Winter will stand by you in this fight, and we will see Claire's vision through. Even if she and her sister are lost to us."

The drake continued her work. "Thank you, Raine. I... I need them to meet my babies."

Raine felt the tear roll down her cheek. She had nothing to respond with and took her place in the fight.

The power of Winter's Queen tore across the field of battle.

***

Books and ledgers flew around the room as he frantically rummaged through his study. Alder King Zankoku Legerdemain had done it. Under his watch, he'd killed not one, but two enemy queens and captured the strange winged woman!

Some of the most potent forces of Winter and Autumn were trapped and would all be destroyed. Sure, he had some very unhappy dragons flying around, and some clean up to do as far as public perception went, but his power made that simple enough. He found the letters Summer had sent; the plan was underway. He'd done it!

The knock from the guards outside startled him; he felt on edge with excitement. He opened the door, but before he could speak, a cry of pain escaped his lips. His left arm felt like it was on fire! As quickly as it began, it was done. Rubbing the forearm with his other hand, he took his anger out on the soldier.

"What is it? You know I'm busy!"

The man was pale, even for an elf. "My k... king, people are coming up... the side of the tower."

"Then kill them or greet them, whatever is appropriate."

The soldier shook his head. "We can't seem to slow them down, sire. One of them is... well, sire... he's... on *fire*."

The king rolled his eyes and slammed the door. He pulled up his sleeve and saw what had burned him. In old flowing script, his skin was branded with a message. He dropped the sleeve as his face went pale.

There was a booming sound below. He closed his eyes and sent out his power into the minds of the strongest people in the Beryl Gardens. The message was clear and the compulsion absolute.

'Get to the main garden. Protect your king!'

CHAPTER 16

The dragon felt her stir, wakeful from whatever had knocked her out. He tried to get his words to her, but Claire didn't respond. He'd done his best to follow the bond and then ping his dragon-speak to narrow his search. Brook was flying just off to his side and he pushed his thoughts into her mind instead.

"My bond-mate is near. At the base of the mountain... I think."

Harvest landed and paced around while Brook kept to the skies, patrolling for danger. He sniffed and scratched until he picked up her trail. His bond-mate was below him, deep underground.

He explained the situation to the frost drake while he roared and ripped vast chunks of rock and soil from the opening of the mine. They had her! She was so close and yet Claire was out of his reach! He fully intended to dig all the way down if needed, but Brook's voice came to him with urgency.

"Something is moving through the trees. Get to the sky!"

He turned just as the spore dragon charged from the thick undergrowth and whipped a tail toward the black drake. Harvest didn't move; his yellow eyes focused on the strike until the last second and then he caught the thick tail in his mouth. A wet crunch echoed through the clearing as the wyrm writhed in pain and anger.

"More are coming! Please, we need to go!" Brook spoke into his mind.

Harvest was a soldier and a protector. The woman held below wasn't just his queen. She was his bond-mate, the first friendly presence he'd perceived from within his egg. Claire Named him and loved him. She'd saved him from the curse that killed all but one of his brood mates. He wouldn't abandon her. Not now. Not *ever*.

When fighting multiple opponents, it's essential to keep a solid defense. When the opportunity to strike presents itself, do so hard and fast. You don't want to have to deal with the same threat twice.

As three more wyrms pushed through the trees of the clearing, Harvest flapped once, leaping high into the sky. His bulk slammed down hard on the wounded attacker.

Dark talons sank deep into the pale yellow-green scales with the force of a falling boulder. One winged foreclaw grabbed the wyrm's snout and pulled it up, exposing the spore dragon's lighter throat. The death drake tore out a chunk the size of an ox. Dark blood soaked the earth beneath them as more enemies came into view.

The wyrms were nearly as big as him. On the ground he lost his advantage of flight. The first wyrm lunged at his left flank as a sweeping strike came from a long serpentine tail to his right. Harvest spun, caught the tail whip with his front claws, and pushed the blow harmlessly into the dirt.

In one flap he dodged the snapping jaws just as a stream of Frost Fire flowed across its flank. The thick hide allowed the spore wyrm to shake off much of the hit, but it would hurt terribly as it thawed.

Brook swung around for another pass as the three wyrms squared off with the death drake. Harvest jumped and flapped once to give himself a height advantage and breathed a thick cloud of Miasma onto the attackers. Two dodged and held their breath while a third took in enough of the fog to slip into death in seconds.

The frost drake loosed her breath at the closest wyrm. It dodged and rolled, whipping its tail up just high enough to clip her wing, sending her into a spin. Brook crashed hard into the mountainside.

Harvest roared again as he leaped to the spore dragon and dug in deep with his talons, his black maw ripping out vast chunks of the beast's hide. Then the last wyrm lunged and the strong jaws clamped down on the ebony scales of his throat.

He tried to roar or use his Miasma again, but he couldn't breathe air, much less his deadly fog. He tried to get a hold with his talons, but the long body began to wrap around him. In seconds he was helpless.

Great muscles strained against the thick body that crushed him. His scales kept the teeth from breaking through, but the pressure would soon accomplish the same end. He pushed out the words that needed no breath, his apology for failing her.

"I'm sorry... my queen."

Harvest saw only darkness.

***

"Look there, she's starting to wake. Did you see it?"

"Yeah, I saw it. I'm only two paces away. How could I not?"

"Best get the prince; he will want to speak to her."

There was a shuffling of feet as one of the men left the room. A few seconds later, a familiar voice whispered in her ear. The sound made her want to vomit.

"Did you miss me?"

Claire looked up slowly as if she hadn't been awake for close to half an hour. Long brown hair hung in her eyes as she took in the smiling face. The prince allowed his sharp teeth to stand out just a bit, an impressive effect. She was genuinely intimidated. He grabbed her chin and she tried to speak through the cloth.

Ohkami shook his head. "Now, now, I know about your little death squeak. Let's not allow that. You're dead, did you know that? Father asked me to make sure both Winter and Autumn lost a queen today. The white-haired wench was polite to me and I allowed her a quick end. You have embarrassed me, my family, and my kingdom. You... need to suffer."

He pulled up her sleeve and his finger shaped into a long claw. He cut deep into the top of her arm, slicing through muscle and tendons. The pain was intense, but she held his gaze and never faltered. If he liked to see people squirm, he would need to look elsewhere. His expression went from smug to annoyed.

The Wolf Prince sighed. "Yes... you seem like the type. I have run across them from time to time. Some people can't be hurt directly. Yet you can still feel pain."

The prince took three long strides and with a clawed hand, stabbed deep into the side of an unconscious Gorn. The yeti stirred and sputtered for a few long seconds as life faded from the heaped white form. Claire's temper flared as she took in the sight.

Throughout the kingdoms, the temper and power of the Demon Prince of Autumn are well known. Despite the fame of his father's ability in battle, Jack's anger issues were a trait he got from his mother. This family line spent generations in the harsh lands of Winter. The prince inherited much of his mother's tendency toward outbursts.

It was lesser known that this temper was passed down to both children. Ornella's daughter was slow to anger, more prone to planning and diplomacy while working to resolve things peacefully.

Yet she also had a limit. A point where she ceased to negotiate and just went for blood. Claire tried hard to be patient and kind. But she was still her mother's daughter. The heir to the Ashen Lady. She truly was the Banshee of Autumn.

As the life spilled out of Raine's friend, Claire felt something snap. She knew what would happen if she died in a dank hole somewhere in Spring. She knew what would happen to her people, her friends, and the children of Autumn. *Her* children.

These people had taken her sister and killed her troll. Even now they were likely trying to do the same to her brother. Good luck with that.

It was clear that no bargain would be reached. This man simply needed to pay.

The leather bands holding her hands to the chair aged a thousand years in an instant and she stood as fine dust left her wrists free to move. The cut on her arm pulled together and left unblemished skin while the cloth in her mouth aged into dust as well. She spat the dark rotting threads on the floor. Her voice held the otherworldly tone of the afterlife.

"You shouldn't have done that."

The two men beside her reacted quickly, grabbing her arms. Both elves went from young men to dead of old age in a second. Ohkami's eyes grew wide as his mouth grew long and teeth filled the snout that let out a snarl. Two more guards ran into the room and started to rush her, but the aged bodies rose up.

Glowing white eyes looked to the soldiers and boney hands grabbed them as they screamed. In a moment, the two men stood back up, flesh mostly intact, but gaining the same glowing white eyes. The prince growled loudly and spoke in that snorting voice.

"You might have power. Even so... I will tear you apart!"

Ohkami lunged in a blur of motion, slamming to a stop only inches from her. He strained and squirmed, but he couldn't reach the woman.

He turned to see the furry white form of the yeti holding his arms. The brute was red with blood and his eyes glowed that same pale white. The queen leaned close to the prince and whispered in that otherworldly voice.

"Don't worry, little wolf. I won't kill you. Gorn really wants to; he came back just for you. Yet death holds honor... I would know. I sentence you to live a long life of shame. You will learn what it means to be humble. To be poor. To seek mercy. Perhaps you might even find some."

The Banshee leaned even closer, her whispered voice sending chills up the man's spine.

"But not from me."

She grabbed the sides of Ohkami's skull and poured forth her power. His ability wasn't dissimilar from Transmutation, just a shift from one form to another. A handsome elf with sharp features or a grey wolf complete with teeth and tail. One form and then another.

The angry queen rearranged the two sides of the coin. On the one side, the prince became a much shorter man, basic features on a pudgy middle-aged body, not elven but human. On the other side, she chose the humblest animal she could think of. Ohkami still remained in his halfway form, but the intimidation was long gone.

Claire took a step back, tapping her finger to her lip as she examined her work. She nodded and started to walk toward the door. Her voice was back to normal now and she waved a hand in dismissal as she left.

"Let him go. He can choose his own path from here."

Zombie Gorn dropped the prince to the floor and moved to follow his necromancer. Ohkami jumped to his feet and screamed at the woman who was almost out the door.

"You turn your back on *ME*? I will eat your heart, you wench!" He howled his anger and rage. "Baaaaaaaaaaa!"

Ohkami froze, then looked at Autumn's Queen as she stood at the door and shook her head.

"I'm going to assume that it would take more time than I have. What are you going to do, snuggle me to death?"

Claire moved up the mineshaft, leaving the half-man, half-sheep to wallow in self-pity. It took a few minutes to reach the surface. She would have gotten lost if not for her ghostly guides.

Just as the hint of sunlight became visible, she felt an ordinarily confident and friendly voice say something she never expected to hear.

"I'm sorry... my queen."

The word echoed out from her mind. "Harvest!"

There was no response. Claire ran for the bright light as fast as she could go and entered the clearing through an opening that looked as if something substantial had been trying to get in.

Her dragon was maybe thirty paces away, his long black neck clamped in the jaws of a pale green shape. She screamed out loud this time.

"Harvest!"

The zombies rushed at the wyrm, grabbing and pulling with inhuman strength. The yeti could unravel some of the long tail, but few things were as strong as a dragon, even undead things. Claire panicked as she thought.

What could be tougher than a dragon? How could I...?

She thought back to the day she'd called upon the dead of Autumn. Hundreds answered her call; all traveled to this land with her. Not all were human. She'd seen gnomes and ogres, humans, and a few brownies. There was one who showed up that she hadn't expected, a face she hadn't seen for years.

Deadfall, once the last death drake, answered her call. The mother wished to see the fate of her kind, to see life play out for the hatchlings she never got to meet. Claire had helped save them, Bloom and Harvest.

Deadfall pledged to her service, a ghost of the most powerful beings of her kingdom. She now appeared before Claire, eyes pleading for the power to save her son.

Autumn's Queen looked to the edge of the clearing where a spore dragon lay seemingly unharmed. Miasma would have been her guess. She poured forth her power.

No one was strong enough to force the spirit of a dragon to do anything, though Claire learned long ago that a willing spirit took only a whisper of her power. This took substantially more, but she was more than able to open the door for Deadfall's ghost to wear the flesh of a dragon once more.

The wyrm moved, hurried but clumsy as the specter controlled the unfamiliar form. Deadfall kept it simple. She stumbled over to the spore dragon clamped down on the death drake, then leaned over to the top of the wyrm's head and bit down.

It takes a good deal of strength to break a bone, a good deal more to crush a skull. Claire watched in amazement as the zombie crunched through the head of Harvest's attacker in one smooth bite.

The sound made the queen sick to her stomach, but the grip around the ebony drake went slack. With no more resistance, her other zombies pulled the coils loose. After a frightening couple of minutes, Harvest began to stir.

Another voice came to Claire through the language of dragons.

"Harvest? *Arrrg*! Are you there? My wing is broken."

The death drake would need time, so Claire moved to the spot where Brook had gone down. For a drake to have a broken wing this far into enemy territory would usually be a death sentence. Thankfully, Claire was pretty good at fixing bone.

Thinking of the crunch of the wyrm's skull, she corrected that assertion.

She was good at fixing *some* bones.

***

The Demon Prince of Autumn earned the title by being a bit of a handful when he got angry. He'd taken up meditation with his Joobel daily after they ate lunch to help him control some of his more destructive inclinations. He took pride in his new self-control and made sure to let his sister decide what punishments to hand out and when to just forgive.

Jack knew it was better that way. Yet his sister wasn't here to make decisions. His Joobel wasn't here to calm him. Someone had taken them from him. That someone was at the top of this tower.

His first thought was to just blow up the whole thing. Whatever fell out of the top part could be dealt with when gravity brought them down. Still, he needed information if he was going to find the two women he loved most in this world.

The elf stood beside him, a tall thin man with power over salad and an arm that could serve as a fire log. Jack didn't dislike the guy, but elves were on a bad list in his mind. He wasn't warming up to this one. The prince asked the question for the third time.

"You're sure this is the best way up?"

Naoki rolled his eyes. He pulled a pouch from his belt and sorted through some seeds, then pushed a wooden finger into the soil. He spoke with the voice of one who was growing tired of the same conversation.

"No. The best way to the top is the stairs inside the tower. I said this was the *fastest* way up."

The elf dropped three bright green beans into the hole and pushed the dirt over them. He looked to his volatile companion.

"You ready?"

Jack had to admit he had no plan before the pair of elves had found him running through town yelling and starting fires. This man had led him to the king and hopefully to answers. He should be grateful, or at least polite, but his rage smoldered inside him as he grew closer to the one who hurt his family.

He looked down as the elf pushed power into the beans. Three stalks of stout vine pushed up through the soil and widened as they climbed, twirling around each other to form a thicker stem. Smaller vines were already branching off and attaching to the side of the white marble tower.

As he watched the stalk move up, he felt so close to answers. The emotion began to overwhelm him. The tears of liquid fire ran down his cheeks, igniting to burn up as they reached his jawline. In seconds his whole head was consumed by bright orange flame.

His guard tunic began to smolder as bright yellow lit his eyes, and he turned to grab onto the climbing vine. His voice held the violence of pitiless flame as he answered Naoki's question.

"Yup."

The vine began to gain speed as it grew up from the soil, Naoki's hand pouring in power as they climbed. Jack knew it really was faster than running up the winding stairs, but he was impatient. He reached over and grabbed the wooden hand that was feeding power into the growing stalk.

He surged raw energy, shifting it to renewal as it left him, and pouring it into the heartwood limb. The vine lurched and began shooting up at almost triple the pace. The elf's eyes grew wide as he realized what was happening. Why Yoshiko was so afraid of this man.

For almost a full minute, they climbed. Guards spotted them and began yelling warnings and shooting various spells and projectiles.

The spells were absorbed and went to fuel Jack's own power; the projectiles were but ash in the wind long before they reached him. He wasn't even concerned. The secret of his true spirit was a low priority at the moment. Naoki slowed them and turned.

"The king is moving. Heading to the main garden. The plants there recognize him."

Jack stopped the flow of power. His rage hadn't cooled.

"Fastest way there?"

Naoki considered, then looked in the direction of the dome.

"The fastest way is to get to a window and take the sky bridge to the upper levels of the gard—"

There was a shudder and loud crash as the prince slammed his palm to the side of the wall. The explosion launched a large chunk of white marble past some rather shocked guards. Jack stepped off the vine and onto a landing that appeared to be a staging area for the men.

The sight of the flaming visage seemed to foster a good deal of hesitation among them. One guard fainted outright. The prince walked toward the doorway and no one made a sound. The elf followed along behind him, growing more and more dubious of his ally.

As the pair moved away, the lead guard looked around.

"That never happened. No one saw anything."

The men all nodded in agreement.

Naoki was running to keep up with Jack, his words labored by heavy breathing.

"The sky bridge... is right up here... then one level down."

Jack stepped off of the balcony and a stout pole of ice formed at his right hand. He slid down and landed lightly. Then he started off in a dead run over the polished white marble of the sky bridge. The elf used the nearby brush to lower himself down and followed.

The light of day was just beginning to dim as the sun flowed down its daily path, allowing faint shadows to form as they ran. The elf wondered if it was the stress of the events or his imagination, but he swore that the shadows under the prince were darker somehow.

They moved on until they reached the outer edge of the domed central garden. Panes of crystal were arranged to allow the life-giving warmth of the sun inside. Jack hardly slowed as he lifted a hand to melt the thick transparent barrier and moved inside to the higher balcony.

He froze as he reached the rail. A large circle of people stood around the king, his power pervading the air and binding each to his will. Jack pushed his own power to protect the elf behind him and began assessing his opponents.

The queen, Sayuri, if he remembered correctly, stood to the monarch's left next to the princess. His ally caught up. Naoki looked down and his eyes went wide.

"Yoshiko!" The elf turned to Jack. "We have to save her!"

Nodding slowly, the prince continued to gauge the power of those present. One fire spirit, Kindle most likely. Three of earth, very strong but none specialized. A renewal user that was overflowing with power, some sort of caster. One water, two air, and one... Enchantment. The other princess was here. No sign of the Wolf Prince.

The group gathered was a force that would give pause to an army. He only felt disappointed that he wouldn't get to face the man who tried to hurt Joobel. Perhaps he would still get the chance.

His calculations finished, all that was left to do was end this. He put one hand on the rail to the balcony and easily vaulted over the side. Just as he landed, the stone beneath him began to vibrate. He leaped to one side as sharp points of rock emerged from where he stood.

Instead of attacking the people around the king, he reached out his power. He ripped the energy of the king's influence from the two closest casters. The air spirit user dropped to her knees and one of the earth casters looked as if he'd been punched hard in the face. He heard Naoki yelling from one side.

"Yoshiko! Fight him; you're no one's puppet!"

Bright flames shot at the elf as he pulled up a wall of bright green, thick blades of grass. Naoki held an impressive amount of power, but he wouldn't hold out long against so many. Jack took advantage of the distraction to leap and roll next to the renewal user under the king's influence.

The prince was correct in assuming that one held a good store of energy. Even though she tried to block him with a thick shield of twining vines, he shot a flaming hand through in a burst of fire and ash, grabbing her arm. She *had* a great deal of energy. Now it was his.

As the woman shrank to the floor, he heard the attack coming hard from behind him. A barrage of razor-sharp thorns shot at his head and he planted a wedge of ice into the floor to divert the attack up. No ordinary caster had created the weave, but the queen of this land. It chipped at the ice until it crumbled.

The thorns kept coming, forcing him to jump to one side. Blades of water and shards of rock came at his new location and his head began to swim as he felt the scratch on his arm. The thorns were poisoned.

That would have been the end had he not been so angry about being drugged once before in the red stone mines of western Autumn. He was burning it from his veins even before it could slow him down. That and the bracelet on his wrist were enough.

The magic in the poison reabsorbed into his own stores of energy. He pushed heat toward the water and deflected the rock with a buckler of thick ice, the impacts driving him back several paces.

Across the room, Naoki was holding his own against Yoshiko, but he wouldn't hurt her. It was a handicap she didn't seem to share. In time, the princess would kill her friend. His anger flared and the fire of his visage grew hotter.

His protection was fading from the two he had freed from the compulsion, each starting to fall back under the spell of control. The Alder King's words came to him as Jack moved and dodged the attacks of so many powerful casters.

"You cannot defeat us all, young prince. For everyone you set free, I can command another!"

Jack fought on, feeling the constant effort drain his stores. The stolen power of the renewal woman was nearly gone. She was already beginning to recover as the land fed her energy. He was a fool to walk in here like he was invincible, like he couldn't lose.

He might be a true warrior, but he would have died in the ice cave if not for Raine pulling him out and his sister's aid. In truth, he'd been beaten many times. If those fights were not fair, then they were a mirror of life.

His father was taken from him before he could form memories, his mother stolen from him from her very bed. His kingdom was under constant threat. Now he might have lost his sister, his cousin, and his true love. Who knew how many of his friends already died outside?

He should have brought help; some were willing. Then he remembered the words Torg said to him years ago when he lost to a guard twice his size.

'In life, be a good man. Have honor and be just.
In battle, be a bastard. Cheat and win.'

The place was a garden. There was energy and life all around him. There was fuel.

Jack thought of the rose, his creation that used his hard-earned ability to manipulate heat into spirit energy. He had power here, even so far from the realm of his home. He just needed to cheat.

The prince dodged hard to his left and rolled into the brush. The trees were tall and dense; the plants were perfect and green. So full of life. So full of water. The moisture that would make it hard to burn was water he could control.

Ripping his hand forward, he began to pull the moisture, not from the air but from all the plants around him. Naoki cried out as the flora of the garden was killed by dehydration, the flow of its water sloshing around on the floor. Jack wasn't finished.

A sphere of heat left his hand and exploded just above him. Not a concentrated blast, but a swirling arc of sparks flew all through the gardens. Everywhere they landed, they found the desiccated leaves and dry twigs he'd created.

They burned. The fire started in a hundred different spots and the garden quickly became a furnace.

The Demon Prince fed on the heat, feasted on the fire. He'd grown hungry. The visage grew bright as he quickly overflowed with energy, taking the warmth and making it his own. He moved to the nearest caster.

The man launched large chunks of stone and marble toward the prince. Jack batted them away with seemingly no effort. As the prince's hand touched the man's shoulder, there was a slight hiss as skin burned and energy was stolen.

He didn't go to each caster, only to the inside of the circle. He was battered with shot after shot of varied types of attack. No one could slow, much less stop, the enraged prince.

Jack stepped up to the Alder King as the man started to run. The tall man immediately fell forward as his feet were locked to the ground by thick bands of ice. The water from the plants moved. A dome of the same thick ice formed over the spot where the king lay as the prince kneeled over him.

Jack laid a hand on the king's arm and said with a half-smile of yellow light that was only faintly visible through the orange flames of his face, "We're going to talk."

As the dome sealed around the pair, the power influencing those serving the Alder King faded to nothing. All were cleansed of the compulsions that dominated their lives for so long.

To some, freedom wasn't a blessing.

***

It was like running through thick fog and leaving the cloud for the bright light of day. Yoshiko felt as if she could think clearly and uninfluenced for the first time in years. Her attempt to retrieve her mother had cost her. Only recently had she realized that the closer the king was, the more powerful his control.

Now it was gone entirely. She glanced around the room and watched in horror as the central garden, the place she so loved, was consumed by hungry flames. Thick smoke filled the upper part of the dome and the trees and bushes, once so full of life and beauty, were engulfed in an inferno.

Naoki was screaming. He tried to use his power to put out the fire, but it ate the growth he fostered in the plants faster than he could raise it.

All around her, people were reacting to their new mental freedom in several different ways. Her mother was curled into a ball, sobbing and muttering words no one could hear. Some of the lords of Amaya were yelling angry words about justice and payment in blood.

There was one reaction she didn't expect, from a person she'd hated for years. Now all she could feel was pity. Harumi Legerdemain was sitting on the floor, rocking back and forth as she shed thick tears. Yoshiko could hear the woman's words and they broke her heart.

"Why, Daddy? Why did you make me hurt them?"

Yoshiko knelt down and wrapped her arms around her stepsister; the woman seemed real for the first time she could remember.

Guards and casters were rushing in, fighting the blaze, though she could see there would be nothing left. All the animals escaped the fire through the halls and the birds through the hole in the dome. Her home and world were broken.

Through the bustle of movement around her, she felt another emotion. Yoshiko released Harumi, whispering a promise she would return. Then moving to the edge of the soil, she pushed some aside, digging a shallow hole.

She reached her hand inside and felt a wave of power enter her body; the emotions of hope and relief filled her. Honey whispered a new word to her in her mind.

'*Kirikaeru*.' This word she also knew. Honey asked her to 'Renew.'

Yoshiko was confused and afraid. She was devastated that her garden was no more. She looked to her mother. The woman she looked up to and the rightful ruler of this kingdom wasn't going to be able to handle things. Queen Sayuri looked broken.

As in most situations, people want to follow someone who seems to know what is going on. She knew that Spring had broken Hospitality and that anything they could do to make amends would help mitigate the consequences. It was time to make things right.

She wiped away the tears and grabbed the nearest guard. Her words were spoken in a clear and commanding voice.

"Get the generals and heads of state. Cease all aggression toward our guests of the other kingdoms. Until the queen can take control, I'm the authority in this land."

The man seemed confused and looked to Queen Sayuri. He saw her incoherent state and turned to the other princess. Harumi could also have a claim to power, but she was little better than Sayuri. The man turned back to Yoshiko. He gave a curt nod and then moved to obey.

The princess knew it wasn't going to be so easy, but it was a start. She rushed to Harumi and then to her mother, trying to help them stand to move to a safer location. She wasn't strong enough to carry the queen.

Her mother had gone quiet, still and unresponsive. Naoki appeared beside her, covered in soot, and looking furious. He picked up the small woman like an infant and helped the princess move Harumi.

It was going to be a long night.

***

Jack had his answers. He wasn't happy with them, and he wanted to turn the man before him to ash. This pitiful wretch had all but sold his Joobel for the sake of an alliance with Summer.

The fool had seen the gnome taken through some sort of portal called a 'fairy ring' to a mundane realm. He didn't know what all those words meant. None of them made him want to spare the man before him.

Killing him would be easy, as simple as breathing. Yet it would be a quick death, mostly painless as Jack had no taste for torture. In this case, there should be some suffering.

Jack considered what this man would hate more than anything. The word humiliation came to mind. The former king's disdain for those who lacked power had shown in every action the man had taken. Yes, that would do nicely.

The Demon Prince put a hand on the king's chest, searching for something. There it was, the spirit of Compulsion. It was intense, the power to make nearly anyone do what you wished. To take away free will and force your whims on those around you.

Jack tore the spirit from the Alder King's core. The man gasped, unable to survive without a bonded spirit. He had a few unpleasant moments of life without it. The prince went to work.

The weave of a spirit was intricate and delicate. A basic spirit could be quite strong. Gray was an excellent example of that. Yet, the ability that came with some spirits allowed some fantastic feats. Bayu was of air and still a bit weaker than Gray, but he could pull the power of storms down onto his foes.

Jack had learned the difference, that part of the spirit that allowed such things. He found the weave that made this basic renewal a spirit of Compulsion. He tore it out.

He proceeded the pull the thing apart like loose threads from a tunic until the remaining power was barely functional. It would still allow Zankoku to live, but he would command only himself. He would have no magic to speak of. The wretch would cast nothing. This former king would demand nothing.

By his own standards, Zankoku would *be* nothing. Jack pushed the weakened spirit back into the man. The elf gasped and struggled until his breathing once more became steady and even.

As the wretch thrashed, his sleeve slid down his arm. The branded writing was strange, a series of words seared into the skin. It was recent and the flesh was raw and swollen around the writing. Jack leaned down to read.

'*They who offer Hospitality and give deceit shall be undone.*'

The prince gave a grim smile and with a tiny blade of fire added a line.

'*Never cross a Demon.*'

Then the prince stood with a satisfied nod. Jack waved a hand and the ice dome melted away. He stepped out into the ruins of the once beautiful gardens. Several people were rushing around but no one bothered to detain him.

It was time to get his hound.

**

Claire arrived back on the hill held by the combined forces of Autumn and Winter just as the sun was starting to drop below the horizon. She had Harvest reach out and was pleased to learn that her people had fought back admirably.

Though there were losses, they were kept to a minimum. The devastation of the lightning strikes and tactics employed by none other than her dear Gray kept enemy losses down as well. She had a good idea of what to expect when Harvest landed near the crest of the hill.

Brook landed as well and Gorn climbed off her back. He was soaked in blood and his eyes glowed that eerie white. He was the only zombie Claire kept from the encounter at the mine.

Raine met them as they arrived, already aware of the state of her friend and guard. The Winter Queen ignored the blood and the fearful eyes as she hugged the yeti. Her words held only love.

"You've done so much for me; I'll never forget you."

Then Gorn pushed her white hair back behind one ear, brushed her cheek with his large hand, and nodded. His mouth croaked out a single word as he put his fist over his heart.

"Love."

Then he slumped as the specter left him. His body was safe to allow his family a chance to mourn his loss. Gorn was a willing spirit and could choose when to move on.

Claire nodded to her cousin, who gave her a sad smile. She started to speak when a tall, dark man hit her from the side. She was shocked to be attacked in the safety of her own people, but quickly realized that it wasn't an attack so much as a greeting.

"I thought you were dead! I'm so glad you're safe!"

Gray looked like he was about to fall over. His face was covered in dust and blood, his eyes bloodshot. He trembled with the effort of standing up. She missed him so very much, hugging him back and giving the man a brief kiss.

Claire looked around as she began to hear cheering. All around her, the people of both kingdoms celebrated the return of the beloved queen. She held up her hands and spoke through her dragon's mind so all might hear.

"I thank you all! Your bravery has allowed us to hold where we should have fallen. As we stand here on foreign soil, I ask that you open your hearts to peace. You have seen how people here suffer. Do not blame the kingdom for the actions of a few. We *will* see justice for those responsible! There will be mercy for the rest."

The crowd grew silent as she spoke. Once again, they were torn between loving who she was and disagreeing with what that made her do. Claire gave a sad smile as she looked out at those faces.

"My brother is missing and my sister has been taken. We have fought hard. We must decide how to proceed. I ask that you allow me to meet with my council and we will plan our next move."

She started toward a stone shelter near the hilltop. Yet there rose a chorus of murmurs from the people holding the hill. The enemy soldiers had moved back.

One lone spore dragon approached from the city. It was massive, perhaps the most colossal dragon in this world. At least if you didn't know about Depth.

It didn't roar or square off for combat, only moved steadily to the base of the hill. A small elven woman rode on Kaiju, his bulk sinking into the soil slightly as he slowed. She stepped down as the wyrm halted.

Raine stepped to Claire's side, her voice a soft whisper.

"It's the elf princess, Yoshiko."

Claire nodded and held a hand up, signaling all to hold. She moved down the hill, Raine by her side. Cruor appeared and stepped into place behind his queen while Gray stumbled along beside Claire. Harvest took to the sky and made a slow circle overhead while Bloom and Brook stood to watch at the top of the hill.

All grew deathly silent. The Princess of Spring sat down on a toadstool that sprang up from the soil, several others popping up in a circle. The voice of Kaiju rang out for all.

"I will step back, but first I must speak with my master." He looked up at Bloom. "The old laws hold true; you hold Dominion over me and I over the others here. No one will trouble you further. Let our people be at peace."

Bloom looked down with anger in her eyes. She would concede nothing, the drake only wanting her gnome returned. His words didn't make that happen.

Claire moved down to take a seat on the cap of a growing mushroom. The others followed her lead. Yoshiko spoke first.

"The king has been stripped of power; I have taken control for now. My mother isn't well, and I don't know how we will decide things in the long term. I was never named Spring Maiden. Too many wished it to be my... sister."

Claire tapped her finger to her lips as she absorbed those words. Her eyes narrowed as she made the connection.

"Your sister? Do you mean the king's daughter?"

Yoshiko nodded slowly, unsure of how to proceed. Finally, she sighed.

"Harumi was a victim... I think. Her mind was taken over as much as the rest of ours. She remembers arguing with him. Her brother was happy with the way things were, but Harumi fought her father's control and eventually was compelled like the rest. I have her under protection right now."

Claire shook her head, then moved on to her real concerns.

"My brother, my adopted sister, an Autumn guard and advisor of Winter are all still missing. What knowledge do you have of them?"

The elf nodded. "Your brother is heading to the dragon caverns and I assume you can find him there."

Claire's eyes narrowed. "You are returning him?"

Yoshiko barked out a frantic laugh, her eyes near tears.

"We aren't doing anything with him. No one dares order him at all. We have given him what he asked for, answered his questions, and let him do as he pleased. It's not my place to say, but there is darkness in that man."

Claire felt her anger bubble up, but she swallowed it. This girl was doing her best and in truth, she knew what her brother was capable of.

"What of Joobel? No one has seen her since this all began. Where is my sister?"

"That's what the prince is asking as well. I have learned she was taken through a fairy ring. I don't know where she went from there. We have reason to believe that Summer wanted her, and it's possible she's being taken to the Arborium."

Claire felt her grief and worry starting to take her composure. Raine seemed to understand and took over for a time, her words clear and commanding.

"Hurley was a victim of the other princess. He was last seen in the royal box. I'd like to know of both him and the troll who was also guarding us."

"Your advisor is safe. I found him being questioned and made sure he received the attention of the best healers available. He's alive and will be returned, though I'm afraid he lost the hand. The troll... we found in the king's apartments." The girl sighed. "He was slain. His body will, of course, be returned to you."

The elf princess began to shed thick tears, the droplets running down her face. It was clear that she felt responsible for what was done. Claire let go of some of her anger. She asked her people to learn to forgive and must lead by example. She stood and retook control of the conversation.

"Yoshiko, whether you become queen or someone else I care not. You will be our contact with this kingdom. You will declare a full surrender to Winter. A treaty will be drawn up that will meet the following demands."

She held up her hands and began ticking off a finger with each condition. The first finger went up.

"Harumi will be turned over to me. She will serve Autumn until she has paid for her involvement."

Yoshiko started to protest but went silent as eyes the color of falling maple leaves flared an otherworldly white. Claire continued.

"She isn't safe here. If Harumi is to avoid paying for her father's sins, she needs a fresh start. I already have a task in mind for her."

Claire took a deep breath, releasing it slowly. Another finger went up.

"Second, you will agree to have all your water sources set up to be brought in from Winter. I will explain more at a later time."

Claire hardened her gaze at the elf. A third finger went up.

"Third, you, and I do mean *you*, Yoshiko, will meet with the Winter Queen and me twice a week to discuss long term plans for interactions between our kingdoms."

A fourth finger went up.

"Fourth, you will sign a treaty, bound to both Autumn and Winter, to assist us should we be attacked. I expect that one will come into effect quickly."

A fifth finger went up just as the Banshee's eyes flashed a pale white.

"Last, and let me be *perfectly* clear, no slaves will be allowed to be owned in or transported through your borders. If you have people you cannot care for, you may send them to me. Otherwise, no one should be hungry or mistreated. Do you have questions?"

Yoshiko sat with her mouth wide open. She was overwhelmed, shocked, and afraid of this woman. Honey said she would be an ally. Is this what the mushroom meant? The Queen of Winter leaned forward and spoke low to the elf.

"Close your mouth, dear. You're not the first to find Autumn's bargains a bit hard to swallow. In time you'll be happy you signed on."

Raine looked thoughtful for a moment and then glanced at Cruor before turning back to the elf.

"Though if you say yes... get an outstanding bodyguard."

Yoshiko stood, her full height still rather unimpressive. She wiped her eyes and spoke, her voice mostly steady.

"I have ordered all aggression ceased, though my authority is far from absolute. We will do all we can to set this right. The old laws were broken. I hate to know my people will suffer for the actions of one man. I accept your terms, though understand my word may not be enough to follow through."

She was silent a moment and then lost her composure. Sobs shook the young elf's shoulders as she struggled to continue.

"Thank you for giving us a chance to make this right.... I want our kingdom to be better. Thank you for the chance to do so."

The Autumn Queen stepped forward and hugged the girl. The elf was so very young, perhaps the same age she'd been when her world fell apart and landed on her shoulders. Claire hadn't been alone and would see to it Yoshiko wasn't either.

They had done all they could in Spring. It was time to go home. She was just getting ready to give the order to pack up and head out when a strange, yet oddly familiar, battle cry came from behind her.

"Baaaaaaaaaaaaaaaaaaaa!"

A sheep was running at her full force, bleating its heart out. Claire looked at the thing in amazement. She was about to laugh at the sight when a large green drake swooped in, caught the animal up in her jaws, chewed twice, and swallowed the whole of it. Bloom landed near the top of the hill and resumed healing the wounded.

Claire cautiously pushed her words out to the dragon.

"Um... Bloom. Was that sheep wearing a tunic?"

"Yes. It was odd attire for food. I've been healing nonstop and I'm growing a clutch of eggs. We haven't eaten yet today.... Did I do something wrong?"

Claire went a bit pale. Now both of her dragons had eaten a human. She thought about it for a moment, then decided some secrets should be kept.

"Not at all. A mother has to eat."

***

Dragons always had the best stuff to chew on. The happy hound had grown to a size big enough to truly enjoy the bone of some enormous beast. One of the spore wyrms had left it for her.

Maeve was bored and lonely after the dragons flew away in a hurry several hours ago. Claire had given her the images to explain her job was to protect the green dragon who was going to have pups. Maeve liked the green dragon and was happy to guard her. Then the green dragon flew away with the other flying dragons and left her here alone.

The long wiggly dragons wouldn't play with her after she had to squish one of them. So the not so little hound found a stash of rather lovely things to chew on. She was happily tearing them apart when she smelled her favorite person in the whole world. He smelled like smoke and blood.

Her Boy moved to sit beside her in her new spot that used to belong to the wiggle dragons. Her head tilted hard to one side. Something was wrong with Her Boy. He seemed so sad. Like someone had taken all the treats in the world and given them to a squirrel.

Maeve let go of a small hill's worth of dirt and rock as she became her standard size of about half the mass of the boy she loved. Her Boy slumped to the ground and leaned against the giant bone she might, or might not, have stolen. Then Her Boy did something Maeve had never seen before.

Her Boy started crying. Not fire; his tears were wet and ran down his face in long trails to drip down. Maeve whimpered and whined as she sniffed for injury, for some wound that would make him sad.

There was none. She cried and paced around him, her concern leaving her confused. Finally, she circled twice and sat on his lap, leaning back to let him know he wasn't alone.

He had Maeve.

CHAPTER 17

The blasted Demon burned them all! Naoki felt the shudder through his body even at the thought. The screams of all those trees: the plants had cried out for help and he could do nothing to stop the slaughter. The Green Man had failed his oath and even now felt empty inside.

The city of Amaya grew dim at his back, the sun setting in front of him as he moved swiftly into the forests. He'd seen what the city was, who the people were. The trees were better; they did no harm and were more worthy of his service.

Sakura's voice came to him. It wasn't the first time she tried to stop him.

"I hear their voices; you need to go back."

He gritted his teeth and ran on. Tears of grief and rage mixed and flowed freely down his face. The wind was chill against the wet flesh of his cheek. He felt the hatred in his heart and he stoked that fire. After several minutes she tried again.

"We serve the realm above all else. Would you ignore her call?"

Naoki felt the bark of laughter leave his lips. The realm watched it all happen. The realm allowed the very atrocities that had occurred. The screams of the burning plants came to him again. He slid to a stop, hands over his pointed ears. The sound still echoed in his mind.

Sakura appeared before him. Her face was wooden and expressionless, yet her emotions were his to feel. She loved him and his pain was hers. The spirit manifested, something she rarely bothered to do. It took a great deal of energy and left her vulnerable. Yet she wrapped her arms around him and pulled him in close.

There was no verbal jab, no quip about how he would prevail. Just a long embrace that told him she would stand by him always. The elf sobbed as he pushed back the agony of those burned to dust.

She spoke slowly, much as she had when they were first bonded.

"For so long we have served the forests. My sisters are not citizens of the realm, we are part of it. The kingdom needs a ruler and for the first time in so long there is a chance at one who is worthy."

Naoki shuddered, the sobs wracking his body. He had so much power and yet he failed. The Demon Prince moved like hungry flame and consumed so many right in front of him. What was worse, the elf still couldn't think of a solution that would have avoided the loss.

He wiped his cheek and pushed away, meeting her wooden eyes.

"The queen lives; I have no influence over her."

Sakura shook her head. "We both know of whom I speak."

Naoki sighed. "Yoshiko is a good person, but I don't have those feelings for her. It's better I allow a clean break."

Sakura disappeared. With her went his connection to the plants around him. His arm was stiff and unresponsive. He couldn't so much as wiggle his wooden fingers.

A surge of fear and panic went through him. Years had passed since he felt the silence, since he had to face his loneliness. Several minutes went by and he felt empty and weak. He fell to the grass, his thoughts his alone.

"It's easy to forget childhood fears. Distant emotions can seem less than they are. We are one, Midori O toko, but you should remember what you were before we weren't."

The elf looked up to see her standing next to him. Not her avatar, but the image only he could see. The heartwood arm seemed to warm at the point where it connected to his shoulder. The power seeped back into him and he gasped at the feeling. He was whole again.

Naoki nodded. "Is it like that for her all the time?"

Sakura stared blankly for long seconds, the connection still not complete. Then her head tilted in a jerk and she answered.

"It is like that for most. You sought help protecting my sisters by entering the Contest. You found that help in the street long before you fought. That girl is hope. Left alone she will not survive. Either her body will be slain, or her mind. Change always has a cost."

He reached his hand down to feel the soil. The voices of the plants around him were still vague in his mind, the language of Spring's flora still alien. He could feel the plants and the realm they relied on urging him back. Back to their chosen queen.

Naoki looked up to Sakura, her leafy hair taking on strange shades as the setting sun poured dim orange light upon her. He wondered if he only imagined that. He shook his head and sighed.

"No more jokes about brides or winning princesses?"

Her wooden face never moved, but he could feel her debating the terms. Finally, she nodded.

"I promise to cut way back. Though I wouldn't mind seeing Green Children someday."

His eyes widened and he growled. "That's what I'm talking about!"

Sakura tilted her head again, then shrugged. "I agree. Sometimes a friend is all that is needed."

Naoki turned, his back now against the setting sun. The city stood in the distance before him. He had debts to pay. Not the least of which would be to the Demon. Still, Sakura was right. If left alone, Yoshiko would make enemies she couldn't hope to fend off.

He stretched his legs once more, all the while pulling power to fuel his sprint. Before he took off, he turned to the dryad.

"You're a good friend. Thank you."

Sakura tilted her head. "I'm flattered, but I don't have those sorts of feelings for you."

Naoki groaned as he ran toward the capital. He knew that the tree spirit was incapable of smiling. If he looked, her face would be ever still.

He *felt* Sakura's grin just the same.

***

The Queen of Autumn arrived back at the Blood Keep late into the night. She was still shaking from her own brush with death as she walked with her arm around her brother. For so long Jack seemed invincible; even his close call with the frost drake only left him more determined.

Now he was lying quietly on a couch just outside Joobel's room. He hadn't spoken a word since she'd picked him up outside Amaya, finally finding him with Maeve at the dragon caves. Claire felt as if she hadn't slept in days, the exhaustion taking over. As much as she wanted to hold Gray, she wouldn't wake him. He'd barely made it back before collapsing.

Claire moved into her bedroom, getting undressed. A hot bath would be wonderful, but she cleaned herself up in the basin. Sleep would come first. The nightgown was brushed linen, quilted and thick. She liked the warmth it brought her. The bone brush pulled through her brown hair with more than a little resistance; she gave up after several minutes. The bed was calling her.

She turned and dropped the comb at the sound of a spectral voice.

"Hello, cousin."

Her stomach dropped as she took in the shape and form of Myrin. Not her original appearance, but the one Claire crafted with her own power. Her cousin stood tall and proud, ghostly whip on her hip, bracelets, and bracer still in place. She held no sadness, but Claire held more than enough for them both. The queen sank slowly to the floor.

"Myrin... I... I'm so sorry."

The ghost just shook her head. Even in this spectral form, the long strands of her now glowing grey hair swung with the motion. The ghost spoke in a calm and even tone.

"I failed my task. Four dragons and close to a dozen casters are moving inside Autumn even now. I did slow them; less than a quarter of the original march still moves on your lands."

Claire knew she should care. She needed to act quickly if this threat was to be stopped. But for a long moment she couldn't move.

Myrin died on *her* order. Died to protect *her* kingdom. This was *her* fault. The words were barely a whisper. Even a hint of her power allowed the ghost to hear.

"I wish I could undo this.... I want you back here with us."

Myrin slowly shook her head. Then a slow smile crept across her features.

"I'm still here. I don't want your apology, cousin."

Claire wiped the moisture from her cheeks. She was still so tired, but needed to give this woman the peace she deserved.

"Then what can I give you? You gave your life for us; what would you ask of me?"

The ghost flared for an instant, drawing on her own power. Claire knew it was careless to radiate it so, but at the moment she didn't care. Myrin leaned down, her spectral eyes narrowing.

"I want you to kill the ones I missed."

***

Yoshiko walked down the halls under the Beryl Gardens, her sandals clapping against the white stone floor. Almost two hours spent interrogating the former king revealed concerning news.

Spring had made some disturbing agreements with the powerful kingdom to the south. Summer's army would be crossing through her kingdom on its way to attack Winter. Thanks to the pompous fool, they would soon be at war.

The soldiers alongside her remained silent. They were the only others who knew they were all in big trouble. Tonight was the first time she would meet with the Queens of Autumn and Winter. They would have much more than trade to discuss. Both women frightened her.

Yoshiko never wanted this responsibility. She only wanted to help the people around her. To aid her mushroom and see her mother happy. Everything had fallen apart. The walk back to her rooms left her feeling so very alone.

Yet as she came into her apartments, she noticed a tall figure standing at the rail overlooking Amaya. His long dark hair swayed in the gentle breeze.

She walked to stand beside him. Her voice was soft, almost afraid to scare the young man away.

"I thought you left the city."

Naoki turned to meet her gaze. He'd been crying. "I did."

She tilted her head, trying to understand. "Won't the dryads of Spring miss their protector?"

He sighed and gave a strained smile. "They were quite clear that the best way to help them, is to help you. They seem to think you are the first worthy queen they have seen in some time."

Yoshiko thought herself more a steward than a queen. It didn't lighten the burden in the least. She tried to hide the fear underlying her question.

"Then... you're staying?"

He looked down at her, his face holding a look of compassion. His answer gave her hope.

"I recently remembered what it is to be alone. You're not. Sometimes we all need a friend."

She leaned into him, hugging him close. The weight of it all shared for a brief instant. She remembered the words of the Winter Queen.

"Naoki?"

"Yes, Apple?"

"Not my name...." She chuckled before growing serious. "Have you ever considered a career as a bodyguard?"

He hesitated for a moment, thinking of Sakura's words. He turned and shrugged.

"I don't really care about titles. Being around people is still new to me. I'm here to help you, whatever name you want to give it."

Yoshiko paused; he was the first real friend that she could remember. She didn't understand everything about how this was supposed to work.

Then she moved away from him. She needed people she could trust. Until she could get her mother on the throne, she would keep everything strictly professional.

"I will give you the title of bodyguard and advisor. Together we will help our realm." She paused and then added, "Both the people and the plants."

The city below was still in turmoil. The destruction of the gardens and the fall of the Alder King left a power void. One that wouldn't fill well without her intervention.

Naoki nodded and reached out a hand. A branch reached up to hand him two ripe pieces of red fruit. He held one out and gave her a smirk.

"Apple?"

She wordlessly took the gift and took a bite.

**

Raine entered her sitting room for the first time in two days. Her body was lethargic from too much sleep and her eyes were puffy and bloodshot from hours of weeping.

Winter's Queen had arrived home just before Claire visited her with the news of Myrin's death. No body was found, but her sister's ghost appeared to her cousin to warn of the approaching Summer forces in Autumn.

The first meeting with Yoshiko proved to be more urgent than first thought. Summer's invading armies aimed at Winter were delayed at the southern border of Spring. This allowed Winter to help focus on those who had made it into the western kingdom.

The Queen of Winter asked to lead the attack to stop Autumn's invading army and Claire agreed. Her cousin only requested that Harvest be allowed to go and help defend his realm. Raine led Harvest, Puddle, and six frost drakes into battle, effectively slaughtering the raiders. Summer's advanced forces fell just short of the town of Thera.

Killing the enemy did nothing to stop the utter sadness Raine felt. Her father, mother, and now sister had all moved on, leaving her with a kingdom on her shoulders. That was two days ago and now she had to force herself to get out of bed.

Raine stepped into the room where she entertained, did paperwork, and spent half her waking hours. To her left was the tall doorway where Gorn needed to stoop to pass through.

She looked to the chair in the corner where she and Sroto would snuggle to read books while her mother worked. She slid her fingertips across the table she and Myrin would play games on.

All of them dead. She was left alone. Yet even as she spoke the words in her head, a man paced the room. He spoke with hopeful tenderness.

"The tanks are nearly empty; will you be able to fill them?"

Raine nodded. It was what forced her to get out of bed. She pulled on her warm clothing and headed to the landing where Mist would be waiting.

Filling the tanks was cold and dull. The expenditure of power always left her groggy. The whole outing provided no distraction from her sadness.

When Raine returned she shambled back into her quarters and began to shed the layers of clothing. As she entered, she noticed a steaming foot bath sitting in front of one of her couches and a stack of papers on the low table nearby. Next to the pile was a plate of food.

Red eyes watched her take off her coat. He didn't ask what she wanted, only walked over and picked her up, carrying her across the large room. Moving her gently, he seated her on the couch. He peeled back the boots and set her feet in the water. Cruor slid the plate toward her, picked up a letter, and began to read.

Dear Winter Queen,

We heard that you are the one who gives us our water. We used to get sick all the time. Pa says it is cause of the well. Now we don't get sick no more. We think it is nice you helped us feel better.

Thank you,

Segu Jorlan

His red eyes looked up and held her gaze as he set down the letter and picked up another.

Hi my name is Chesare. I once had to work in the copper mines, but now I am free to do what I want. I heard we will have a school soon like down south. I want to learn to bake bread and make yummy cakes. Thank you for helping me.

Cruor looked up once more as he set the letter aside and began to reach for another. Winter's Queen broke down crying. Her pale hand waved for him to cease the reading. He did, moving to sit next to her and pull her close. He whispered in her ear.

"Thanks for letting me stop; there are hundreds of them."

She looked over to him, waiting for him to finish the joke. He only nodded, holding her gaze.

"I once thought my life would be nothing but blood. I'm a killer; it is the only thing my power is good for. If your cousin is a demon, then I am no less. Only when I met you did I see other paths. Even when I was soaked in gore, wielding the blood of a hundred men, you still embraced me. You have seen who I really am and have not tried to make me a weapon."

She wiped her eyes and tried to push out the words.

"That isn't who you are, only what you can do. I killed Shaw.... Hurley will never wield a sword again."

"Yet Segu isn't sick anymore. Chesare may one day make honey cakes instead of dying young in a mine. The world is full of injustice. Don't confuse the good and the bad."

She sighed and thought for a second. It broke her heart but was only fair.

"You have earned the title of Winter's Champion. I will announce it in the morning."

The words left her mouth and she winced. The man had earned the title months ago. She only held back out of selfishness. It would take him away from her.

He furrowed his brow. She could barely see the change through the strands of dark hair.

Cruor shook his head. "Find someone else."

She pushed her white hair behind one ear. "There's no one who even comes close. You have earned it."

"No, thank you." His words were firm.

Raine started to hope. "Why not?"

Cruor reached to the platter and took an apple from the tray. A tiny red knife appeared and he cut a slice while he chose his words. He popped a piece in his mouth, chewing the pulp with overly sharp teeth.

"The Winter Champion travels the land, fights incursions, and breaks skulls. I would become an enforcer."

She nodded slowly. "True, but you would have no trouble doing so."

He nodded his agreement. "There was a time when it was my only path. Now I see others. I will take no position that takes me from your side. If that means I die old as a lowly guard, then I will die happy."

Sobs began to shake her slender form. The grief of loss and terror. The fear of Joobel's fate and the looming threat of the Black March. She had to ask him; it wasn't in her to wait any longer.

"There's another position you might be interested in. It comes with some authority. You would still hold all your current responsibilities. I'm afraid there would be no increase in pay. I thought that maybe—"

He cut her off before she could finish. "Will you marry me?"

Raine froze. This was supposed to be a moment of romance and glamour. She should be in a lovely dress with her hair done. Not stewing in a tub. She hadn't bathed since she got the news about her sister. She couldn't get her words out and he continued as she sat stammering.

"The offer of consort is tempting. It comes with a pretty girl and all. Yet I like the sound of husband better. It implies that I'm willing and not forced. Consort is really another word for slave, you know. There are laws against that sort of thing here in Winter."

The smile showed his sharp teeth, his hair pushed aside enough for those red orbs to stare her down. Her hands were shaking as she tried again to respond.

"I thought the queen was supposed to choose whom to ask?"

Cruor shrugged. "The guy she was going to ask got impatient. He's also starting to worry.... The queen still hasn't given an answer."

Raine smiled, despite her grief, looking down at the dirty clothes and her mussed white hair. She pushed several strands behind one ear as she looked back up to him.

"Would it be ok if I cleaned up and fixed my hair... before I said yes?"

***

The ancient girl frantically moved through the workshop, making adjustments and trying to get a reading. This one appeared on the western edge of Autumn, only a day's walk from the Forbidden Sea. She moved the dials and saw that her field would hold. A farmer watched as a doorway started to manifest and then quickly sputtered out, fading away and startling his goat.

A small beeping began and Issabol moved to see where the next portal was set to open. She watched the coordinates appear and moved to divert power to the old ruins in the desert just west of the mountain of Dawn. A scorpion skittered away, surprised by the fizzle and pop of a doorway that failed to fully open in the barren waste.

Another tried to open in the cherry blossom forest in the south of Spring. A bright yellow bird flapped away as the energy gathered. Again, she stopped the portal from forming.

Issabol was exhausted; this had been going on for hours. Varam was helping. His time in the workshops aged him. He could do the job as well as she, but the doorways were constant and he'd gone to rest. Bilney brought food and tea in case she was given a moment's respite to actually eat or drink.

Mini and Toma went to the Keep to warn the queen. The gnome Wemwi was refilling the vials and ingredients she needed to move the defensive fields. Issabol's young body was so tired and there seemed to be no end in sight.

Gray had suggested she set up a defensive ward grid and Jack let her scan the one that Maeve swallowed. Anwir might have been an evil man, but he truly was a genius. It had taken months for her and Varam to reverse engineer the thing, and several more weeks to find a way to block the formation of off-world portals.

Now only the portals she or her student built could hold the frequency to remain stable. She needed to manually adjust the field to prevent entry. Someone wanted to come to this world very badly; the attempts were constant.

The exhaustion and emotion of knowing what was coming pushed tears from her child's eyes. Those eyes, enchanted and old, wise beyond time, knew that Fairie was living on borrowed time. The portals were forming faster and seemed to be testing her limits.

The Black March was coming.

Epilogue

It had been three days since they arrived home in the Blood Keep. Three long days of not knowing where to look, what to do, or how to save Joobel.

Jack was willing to be patient when he thought she was hidden in some remote location in a mundane world. But she wasn't there anymore.

Now the bond reconnected him to his love. The blessing that allowed him to feel her, even faint as it was, would lead him to his gnome. His patience had run out.

He ran straight to the throne room to give Claire the news. She wasn't listening. Slamming a fist down on the desk, he growled at his queen.

"I can take us right to Joobel. Even now, I can point directly at her!"

His sister looked up, startled. She was holding court, and her little office just off the throne room allowed those outside to hear everything.

Jack knew this outburst was bad for Claire's position. His support was essential to her power and office. Yet he couldn't understand why she was resisting him on this.

"Brother, please.... I want her back as well. You're asking me to invade.... It would mean war. Thousands would die, many of them our own people. I'm not saying abandon her, only that we try a diplomatic solution before we—"

He felt the heat forming; his anger was at the surface. He yelled at his queen and sister.

"Diplomatic? Are you serious? They tried to kill you and Raine. They have plotted to destroy us more than once! You cannot tell me there's a way to trust Summer! Tell me Myrin died so that—"

His sister gave up on avoiding a scene. The chair crashed to the red stone floor as the slap caught him across the cheek. Jack reached up to feel the stinging flesh of his face. Claire's jaw was clenched and she eyed the door to her office, even in her anger. Her voice was a low growling whisper.

"I know well of the difficulty we face! I want to call an army of the dead and cut a trail of destruction all the way to that horrid tree. I want nothing more than to cut my sister out of the corpse of that wretched place. I can't give in to such things! Innocent people live there and our own people will die in this fight. It's my responsibility to have a plan, to be a steward of our resources. Don't think to tell me my responsibility, little brother!"

Jack stood tall, breathing hard and fighting to hold himself together. He remembered the circle of casters, remembered his limits. He *had* to get Joobel back; he could already feel himself slipping.

His sister would send letters and diplomats. Claire might take weeks to get the gnome, if a solution could be found at all. Joobel could be facing torture. What if they cut her open to see how she came to be?

They could cut off her wings or take her magic. He'd cried more in the past few days than he had in an entire childhood.

The tears had set half the things he owned ablaze.

He took one more long slow breath. The people in the throne room were silent as the Demon Prince had his first public fight with the Banshee of Autumn. Then he seemed to go cold; a layer of calm covered the enraged man. He spoke in loud, clear words, almost too controlled.

"Perhaps you're right, sister. I have no right to risk our people. Please do what *you* can to bring Joobel home safely."

He turned and strode out of the office, people tripping over themselves to give him a clear path through the throne room. He heard the queen's concerned voice just before he turned the corner.

"Jack.... What are you going to do?"

The prince turned, face calm as he let his orange lit gaze meet hers.

"I'm going to do what *I* can."

Then he left. Had he stayed only a few minutes more, he would have been present when Mini and Toma arrived with news from Issabol.

The walk from the throne room to his quarters wasn't long. He grabbed a few things and leaned down, putting his head against the little hound. She wiggled against him.

Jack held up the sign to command her. The sign meant to 'watch over.' Maeve whined as he walked away, leaving his little brown shadow to guard over his home. He left the door to his room open so she could come and go.

The portal to Issabol's was only a couple of doors down. Through it, he came into the portal room the ancient girl kept, the views looking out to strange places. He moved to one he'd passed through before.

Through the doorway was a land of desolation. That world had been ravaged by an enemy of unending hunger. Little remained in that place.

Jack was last there when they extended an invitation to a great sea dragon and an ancient spirit of water. Fluvial wasn't the only spirit that had survived in that place. Bare feet stepped through the doorway and onto the dead black soil of Heluvot.

He ran the distance from the lakeshore to the base of a mountain. Time moved slowly here and he wasted none in his travel.

Here he'd seen his mother die and his sister become something new. He met his hound in this place and stopped an invasion of his home. For a single brief moment, he had spoken to the great spirit of fire. He'd been wary of the creature then. She hadn't spoken to Claire or the others who were with him, only to the boy who so embraced the flames.

Jack was a boy no longer.

It was several minutes of running before the ground under his feet shifted its power to the realm of fire. He drew some of the energy in and it came to him freely. Jack closed his eyes and took a deep breath. He extended a greeting of power, pushing the aspect of flame into the soil.

Another power moved and shifted underfoot until before him stood a woman, her skin a glowing golden brown. She was tall and lean, with a mane of living fire flowing from her head down her back. She wore a skimpy gown of dark-red flames that barely covered her modesty. Her words came in a sultry voice as she crossed her arms and smiled at the prince.

"We meet again... Flame-Born."

END

Dear reader,

The novel you just read is part of a series. I'm already working hard to get more volumes out and I have over a dozen novels and short stories being revised and edited in this world.

I've decided to work independently of major publishers so I'm able to work toward the story I want to tell as opposed to following trends and taking the risk of stopping before the tale is complete.

When you're finished reading this, please loan it to someone you know who enjoys this type of story. Take a few minutes and leave a review on the vendor you bought it from. A good review on Amazon, Barnes & Noble, Kobo, Google Play, or Apple Books will help me build a reader base that will grow my ability to get more books to market.

Also, taking a moment to log on to a book website and leave a review would do wonders for our small publisher. Goodreads, Library Thing, Book Riot, Bookish, Booklist, Fantasy Book Review, LoveReading, Kirkus, and R/books all have a base of readers who might otherwise never hear about our work.

Finally, visit our publisher website that has previews of current and future books as well as full-color maps. We are working on fan art, character summaries, and accept reader suggestions for future works.

www.decharlathan.com

Thank you again for purchasing this book. Don't miss the other side of this story with *Transfer Student*. The main story continues in *Summer's War*. Available spring of 2022.

Jeremy Graves